Cold
Burn

Also by the author
At Risk
Dead Man's Touch

Cold Burn

Kit Ehrman

Poisoned Pen Press

Copyright © 2005 by Kit Ehrman

First Edition 2005

10 9 8 7 6 5 4 3 2 1

Library of Congress Catalog Card Number: 2004114067

ISBN: 1-59058-143-1

Poisoned Pen Press
6962 E. First Ave., Ste. 103
Scottsdale, AZ 85251
www.poisonedpenpress.com
info@poisonedpenpress.com

Printed in the United States of America

This book is lovingly dedicated to William A. Graber, Jr.

Acknowledgments

I am extremely thankful for my first readers: my mother Kathy Graber, Susan Francoeur, and especially Phil Ehrman. Their impressions, feedback, and suggestions were invaluable in the development of this story. For their painstaking editorial input, I'd like to thank Connie Kiviniemi-Baylor and Beverle Graves Myers, a fellow Poisoned Pen Press "Posse" member and author of the Baroque Mystery Series featuring Tito Amato. For patiently answering my off-the-wall questions regarding equine reproduction, much thanks to Richard Linhart, DVM, Dipl ACT. I'd also like to thank Lt. Richard McLaughlin, Commander, Patrol Services Division, of the Laurel Police Department, for kindly answering my procedural questions. Any and all mistakes are mine. And I'd especially like to thank Clare Bauman for her endless enthusiasm and faith. Thanks, Clare! And to Peggy McMillian for putting up with Steve tagging along on our family vacations! As always, I am grateful to all the hardworking folks at Poisoned Pen Press, especially Barbara Peters and Robert Rosenwald, for their continued support. And finally, this book would not exist without my family, who good-naturedly put up with the writing process, especially my two wonderful sons, Phil and Ray.

*The only thing necessary for the triumph of evil
is for good men to do nothing.*
—Edmund Burke

Chapter 1

At four-thirty on a bitter February morning, the arsonist struck for the third time.

I'd heard about him from the guys who worked the day shift. So far, he'd entertained himself by torching vacant buildings, and as I stood in the doorway at the end of the barn aisle, listening to the mares moving in their stalls behind me, I hoped like hell he'd stick with his game plan.

I slid the heavy door farther along its tracks. An eerie glow marred the horizon as if a monstrous red moon had tilted on its axis and risen behind a screen of cloud and smoke. Without a reference point, distance was impossible to judge. Six miles away, the Rappahannock River snaked through the foothills of Virginia's Blue Ridge Mountains, but the blaze looked much closer, and that worried me.

I had just finished feeding the mares in barns one and two and still had four more barns to work my way through before I was supposed to check seven and eight. They were located on the newest section of the farm, directly to the northwest. Directly in line with the fire.

I decided to ditch the schedule and head over earlier than usual.

When I turned to close the door, the bay mare in the stall to my left angled herself in the corner by her feed tub so she could peer through the bars on the front of her stall. She stared at me with such unnerving intensity, I could have sworn she knew more about what was going on—and what was yet to happen—than I did. But I was letting my imagination run away with me. If anything, her superior senses had provided her with far more information about the fire than I could ever hope to understand. I inched the door down the track, blocking out her image as deliberately as if I'd closed my eyes to her.

I bounced the farm truck down the lane, hung a right onto Bear Wallow Road, and sped past my boss' equine clinic and the fieldstone mansion that gave Stone Manor Farm its name. I made another right onto Cannonball Gate Road, and as I straightened out of the turn, the tension that gripped my shoulders and tightened my hands on the steering wheel eased when I saw that the fire didn't involve the farm. I let up on the gas.

The structure was fully engulfed. Flames shot fifty feet in the air while the strobes on a cluster of emergency vehicles lit up the fallow fields in alternating bursts of red and white. I let the Ford drop down to an idle and could smell the smoke, then, acrid and foul. Like wood smoke with something rancid mixed in.

Up ahead, two pumper trucks had pulled off the road and were parked on the lawn between a farmhouse and the burning building, a huge bank barn that most likely had been constructed in the late eighteen-hundreds with massive hewn timbers and wooden pegs. The column of water, directed toward what was left of the barn, disintegrated into a roiling orange cloud of steam that rose into the night sky. Even with the cab's windows rolled up tight, I heard the roar of the fire and the sound of splintering wood above the rumble of diesel engines and pumps.

As the farm truck drew level with the barn, light from the flames flickered across the windshield and reflected off a river of water that had pooled on the frozen ground. An ancient oak towered over the scene and dwarfed the men beneath its gnarled limbs as they wrestled with hose lines. Where the branches stretched close to the barn, water vapor curled off the wet bark before being snatched by the wind.

I glanced at the farmhouse as I picked up speed. An elderly couple stood huddled on the lawn with their coats drawn tight against the wind. The woman's nightgown fluttered around her legs, and her face looked gaunt in the stark light. They probably stored tons of hay in that barn and a tractor or two and all kinds of farm equipment, all of it expensive. And just like that, it was gone.

A quarter mile down the road, blue strobe lights swept across the barren fields behind a line of road flares. What now? As I drew closer, my headlights bounced off the reflective stripes on the side of a police car. The driver had set up a roadblock at the intersection of Cannonball Gate and Pond Lane.

I eased to a stop. A sheriff's deputy shone a flashlight through the windshield as he approached, and when I powered down the window, he scanned the cab's interior with a practiced flick of his light.

"Your license, registration, and proof of insurance."

I pulled my wallet out of my back pocket, then rummaged in the glove compartment until I found the necessary papers. "What's this about, officer?"

He focused his light on my license. "Columbia, Maryland?" he said. "What brings you to Fauquier County this early in the morning, Mr. Cline?"

"I'm working the foal watch at Stone Manor Farm." I squinted when his light centered on my face.

"Foal watch, huh? I know everybody at Stone Manor, but I don't know you."

"This is my second morning on the job," I said. Morning? Hell, four-thirty felt like the middle of the night, especially in winter, when the sun didn't inch above the horizon until well after seven.

"Who's your boss?"

He'd already swept his light over the Stone Manor logo plastered across the pickup's door, so I figured he was making sure I was legit. "Doctor Deirdre Nash."

"Where you staying at?"

"A friend's apartment, for now. Until I find something permanent."

He went back to his cruiser, and I imagined he was running my information. When he returned, he reminded me to update my license, then waved me on my way.

I didn't tell him that I wouldn't bother, that my job at Stone Manor was temporary, or that I'd only be staying in Bruce Claremont's apartment for as long as it took to find out what had happened to him.

He'd supposedly quit his job on the breeding farm two weeks earlier, and no one had seen or heard from him since. When his sister, Corey, had asked me to try and find him, we'd decided that the most straightforward approach would be for me to take his place, both at work and at home. I'd lucked out when management had actually assigned me his old job. Although, when I thought about it, applicants probably weren't lined up around the block for a job that entailed working nights, outside, in the dead of winter.

In a sense, I owed Corey. She'd helped me in the past, when some horses had been stolen from Foxdale Farm, where I've worked as barn manager for the past two and a half years.

Convincing my girlfriend, Rachel, that this brief foray into the thoroughbred breeding industry was a good idea had been, at best, dicey. I'd requested a temporary leave of absence from Foxdale; although, the way things were going, I considered making the break permanent. Marty, my best friend and reluctant second-in-command, had become so proficient handling my job when I'd been on sick leave for three months, my working there felt redundant. I'd promised myself that I'd look for another job when the day came that I wasn't learning anything new, and I'd moved past that point months ago.

I pulled off Cannonball onto the gravel lane that served barns seven and eight, turned again, onto barn seven's drive, and angled the truck so that the headlights lit up the entry doors in front. Barns seven and eight were new, so new that the electric service hadn't been connected. But they were already filled to capacity.

I grabbed the Mag flashlight off the seat and climbed out. The barns were built on a natural rise that provided an excellent view of the fire. As I stood there, another emergency vehicle approached from the east, probably a rig from one of the stations in Warrenton, and it was a good thing, too. So far, the fire was winning.

The frozen grass crunched under my boots as I walked toward the barn. When I slid the door open, a car engine cranked to life. I paused. The sound was muffled by the bulk of the building, so I figured the vehicle was in the lot out back. As far as I knew, I was the only one working this shift. Maddie, the woman who was training me, might have hung around for some reason, but as that thought crossed my mind, the engine's pitch increased to a whine, and the CV joint squealed as the vehicle spun around the lot. No way would Maddie drive like that.

I cut across the front lawn and sprinted toward the back of the barn.

A small pickup careened around the far corner and barreled down the lane with its lights off. The tires churned through the loose gravel as the driver punched the accelerator.

I skidded to a stop, and when I swung the flashlight toward the truck's front license plate, he veered off course and gunned the pickup straight for me.

I felt like I'd been dropped into another dimension. Each fraction of a second ticking off like a motion picture film advancing one frame at a time. I could no longer hear the engine's whine or the stones popping under the tires. The world had narrowed down to the short distance between the truck's grillwork and the patch of grass I stood frozen to. Five thousand pounds of bone-crushing steel headed straight for me.

For one terrifying second, I couldn't move. Then I dove toward the barn in the exact instant when the driver hauled on the steering wheel and pulled the pickup's nose toward the lane. But he'd waited too long. The back bumper fishtailed around, and the quarter panel bumped my side before I hit the ground.

I bounced off the barn and rolled toward the truck. The rear tire grazed my boot as the pickup continued its slide toward the barn. I looked past my feet as the bumper caught the barn and screeched down the metal siding, gouging out a fifteen-foot-long crease before the driver got the truck under control.

He revved the engine, and as the pickup sped toward the exit, the unmistakable sound of a heavy impact pierced the darkness. He'd clipped the farm truck.

I listened to him peel out of the drive and speed toward Cannonball; then I rolled back onto my stomach and rested my forehead on the back of my hand. My pulse pounded in my wrist like a piston, and despite the frozen ground I was lying on, my skin was damp with sweat. I lifted my head and squinted at the flashlight. It had landed unbroken by the barn's foundation, and where the light stretched across the ground, the frost-coated grass glittered like tinsel. I stretched out my arm and picked up the Mag before rolling onto my side. I assessed the damage, flexed my arms and legs one by one, then cautiously got to my feet. I hadn't broken any bones or torn any ligaments, but my right leg and hip hurt like hell.

I pulled the farm's cell phone out of my coat pocket and called the cops. I told the dispatcher what had happened and said that, in all probability, the driver had headed north on Cannonball Gate Road, away from the roadblock.

"Do you need an ambulance, sir?"

"No."

She told me to wait for one of the deputies, and after I disconnected, I walked back to the front of the building and shone my light on the truck. The impact had crushed the passenger-side taillight and wrenched the back bumper off the frame. It lay twisted and mangled some twenty-five feet farther down the lane. As I stood in the quiet dark, with the cold breeze sharp against my face and the heavy bank of smoke drifting low across the horizon, I imagined what the impact would have done to flesh, and I shivered.

The mares stalled near the entrance skittered around when I stepped into the barn. They were hyped, but there was nothing I could do about it. I checked the wall for structural damage and saw that the impact hadn't affected the interior. When I was satisfied, I pointed the light into the rafters. Most horses don't care for flashlights. They don't like the way the light shines in their eyes or how the long shadows spread across the backs of their stalls.

"It's okay, girls," I said.

I continued to talk to them as I walked down the aisle. Nonsensical stuff, but soothing all the same, and strangely enough, the tension in my own muscles began to ease. When I reached the center of the barn, the unmistakable hollow sound of a bunch of horses galloping over the frozen pocked ground echoed under the eaves.

Barns seven and eight were laid out differently than the barns I've worked in most. They were half barn, half run-in shed. To my right, a row of ten stalls stretched toward the back of the barn, but on my left, a barricade ran alongside the central aisle, and beyond the barricade, the space opened into what was essentially a huge three-sided shed. Feed troughs and hayracks lined the interior walls, and the far end consisted solely of evenly spaced columns that supported the roof overhang. The pregnant mares that weren't due for months were turned out twenty-four-seven, and the shelter gave them an opportunity to get out of the weather.

The rumble grew louder as the herd swirled into the shed like liquid smoke. Their hooves sliced through the straw bedding and kicked up clods of dirt as they spun around and headed back outside, their forms dissolving to nothingness as they disappeared into the night.

A mare behind me whinnied.

The pasture fence butted up against the farm on Cannonball Gate, and I suspected that the horses had been at the far end of the field, and the activity around the fire, and the fire itself, had spooked them.

I continued down the aisle, cut through the storage area at the end of the barn, and slid the back door open. The lot was vacant, and I wondered what the asshole had been doing. I glanced at my watch. Four-fifty. I had standing orders to wake my boss if one of the mares got into trouble, but I decided that telling her about the hit-and-run could wait until she came in at seven. Instead, I called the woman who'd been training me.

Maddie picked up on the second ring.

"This is Steve," I said. "Did I wake you?"

"Nope. Just finished a bowl of Corn Flakes. Is the Cozzene mare going into labor?"

"No." I looked toward the fire. If anything, it had intensified. I could hear an occasional shout that carried on the night air. "There's been another fire, though. A bank barn on Cannonball—"

"Oh, thank God. For a minute, I thought you were going to say one of our barns was hit."

I told her how I'd driven to barn seven earlier than usual, on account of the fire; then I told her about the *incident*. "I'll be stuck here until I give the cops a statement, but I haven't fed three through six yet, and I thought someone should make rounds since I can't."

Maddie sighed. "Is the hay out?"

"Yeah," I said. "I spaced the bales in the aisles as soon as you left."

"I'll be over."

Frustration tinged her voice, and when she hung up without saying anything else, I wasn't surprised. Between the two of us, we handled the night watch seven days a week. As far as I was concerned, I had the easier shift by far. Once I became acclimated to the early hours, doing this job would be a piece of cake. Finding Bruce Claremont, I expected, would be something else altogether.

I stepped back into the storage area, flicked the light around, and looked for anything out of place. Whatever the guy was doing, he hadn't messed with the barn.

The sound of an approaching car filtered through the walls. I'd left the Ford running, and as I stepped outside, a patrol car's headlights pierced the cloud of exhaust that billowed into the air and drifted toward the east. The driver had swung the vehicle onto the grass to avoid the bumper, and as he idled the Crown Vic to a stop, the lightbar's blue strobes illuminated the farm truck's grit-streaked windows. The door creaked open, and the deputy stood and stretched his spine. He pointed his flashlight at the pickup. The cone of light swept down the back fender, then lingered over the crumpled taillight. When he stepped around the doorframe, I realized he was the same guy who'd stopped me at the roadblock.

Sergeant Bodell introduced himself as he zipped up his leather jacket against the cold breeze. It curled around the corner of the barn and lifted strands of his gray hair away from his scalp. He smoothed his palm over his head, then reached back into the cruiser and grabbed a hat off the console.

"Did you find the driver?" I said.

"No." He jerked his head, indicating that we should go in the barn.

I followed Bodell into the aisle. When he pivoted around and shone his light along the doorframe, I said, "The electric's not hooked up yet."

He humphed under his breath. "Did you catch a plate number?"

"No, sir."

"Got any idea what kind of truck it was? The make? The color? Anything like that?"

"Maybe a Toyota or compact Ford. Dark color. Other than that, I have no idea."

I told him how the driver had tried to run me over, and he grudgingly went back outside. He hunkered down and peered at the newly etched channel gouged into the siding.

"Are you going to take paint scrapings?"

Sergeant Bodell paused, then turned his head slowly and looked at me. He braced a hand on the barn, and his knees creaked when he hoisted himself into an upright position. He lifted his flashlight and swung it around until the beam centered on my chest. "Don't tell me. Lemme guess. You're a *N.Y.P.D. Blues* fanatic." The corner of his mouth twitched. "Or maybe you've watched one too many episodes of *CSI*. You know, that show's a load of crap."

I smiled.

He inhaled deeply, then puffed his cheeks as he expelled a breath. "Yeah…Steve, is it?"

I nodded.

"It'll take me about an hour to process the scene. Then you can take the truck." He looked over his flashlight at me. "And yeah, I'll take some paint scrapings and see if I can't find some glass fragments."

Bodell was a big man. Three inches taller than my five-eleven, with broad shoulders and a bulkiness that settled around his gut like a partially inflated inner tube.

"So, you sure he wasn't just turning around back here? You think he was parked?"

"Yeah. I heard the engine start up."

He pointed across the gravel lane at barn eight. "Been over there yet?"

"No, sir. I'm going there next."

"I'll go with you when you do, but let's finish up here." Bodell opted for cutting through the barn to get to the back lot. Once we'd crossed the storage area, he squeezed his bulk between the doors, stepped outside, and paused. "Well, well, well…"

I stood alongside him and followed his gaze. "Well what?"

"Got a great view of the fire, don't we?"

"So?"

"So, I bet whoever set it came over here and watched his handi-work."

"Maybe." I followed him as he strolled toward the middle of the lot and swept his light in broad tracks across the gravel.

Bodell shook his head. "Dr. Nash. She'll be all over her electrician, now. You wait and see."

"I suppose."

He snorted. "You don't know your boss real well, do you, son?" When I didn't respond, he looked at me. "What was the first thing she asked when you applied for a job?" Before I could answer, he said, "I'll bet it wasn't if you'd ever foaled out, or even if you'd worked with horses before, am I right?"

I nodded.

"Right. Dr. Nash asked if you smoked, didn't she?"

"Yeah. She did."

"Everybody's got something they fear more than anything in the world." Bodell pivoted on his heel and gazed across the pasture, narrowed his eyes, and studied the fire. "And that there's what Dr. Nash fears most. Fire. Personally, drowning's got my vote as the worst way to check out."

What I feared most tried to work its way into conscious thought, but I closed my mind to it and turned slowly around. The barn stood behind us, dark and silent against a black sky. A barn full of highly combustible hay and ten living, breathing, pregnant mares, each trapped in a fourteen-by-fourteen stall. The idea of someone torching one of our barns made the blood run cold in my veins.

He wouldn't, would he?

I cleared my throat. "Besides the obvious, why's Dr. Nash so obsessed?"

"Shit, most everybody 'round here knows why." He flicked me a look. "You call her yet? Let her know what happened?"

"No. I thought it could wait until she comes in at seven."

"Good, man. She don't need to get all worked up any sooner then she has to." Bodell took off his hat, smoothed his thinning gray hair flat against his scalp, then tightened the brim down on his head. "Deirdre was still living with her parents. Same house she lives in now, matter of fact. They had a barn full of field hunters and broodmares right about where barn one stands now."

My gut tightened as I anticipated where he was going with his story.

"One muggy autumn night, it burned clear to the ground."

I inhaled sharply, and the icy air slid into my chest.

"Two pregnant mares and five riding horses died that night, but that wasn't the half of it. A guy who boarded a couple hunters with her parents burned to death." Bodell shook his head. "Stupid bastard was trying to get them out."

Bodell wrenched his shoulders forward under his heavy leather jacket as if a chill had slid up his spine; then he looked at me. "You ever find yourself in the same position, get the hell out. No horse is worth that."

The breeze kicked up, and leaves swirled across the lot.

"It was horrible. The stench was enough to knock you off your feet. Come on," he said. "Let's get out of this wind."

We walked back into the barn, and I slid the door closed.

"Two mares survived that first night, but they would've been better off dead, believe me." He rubbed his face. "Deirdre's father moved them over to that old bank barn behind the house, and she nursed them twenty-four hours a day. Slept in the damned barn with the bugs and the mice and the damned cold nights, but in the end, they had to have old Doc Morgan come out one last time. Deirdre held them herself when he stuck the needle in, and that takes guts, let me tell you." As we left the storage area and walked into the aisle, he said, "She's one classy lady."

Tough would have been my choice, but who was I to say?

Bodell paused, and the mare next to me shifted around to look at us. Her huge pendulous belly swayed gently as she stepped forward, and her soft round eyes glimmered in the diffuse light. When I gripped one of the vertical bars that formed the upper portion of her stall, the mare stretched her neck and snuffled. As her hot moist breath eddied across my fingers, the horrific image of her trapped in a burning barn edged its way into my mind, and it wasn't the first time I regretted having such a vivid imagination.

"You know her pretty well, then," I said.

"We're distant cousins."

I let go of the bar. "How long ago was the fire?"

"Hmm." Bodell rubbed his chin. "It's getting on twenty years, now. The kicker is, the guy who died in the fire," he looked at the mare, then back at me, "was Deirdre's fiancé."

◇◇◇

Twenty-five minutes later, I'd given Bodell a statement and helped him take measurements before we moved the bumper onto the grass verge alongside the lane. We verified that barn eight was undisturbed, then I headed back to the main section of the farm. Additional emergency vehicles clogged Cannonball Gate, even though the fire had been reduced to a heap of smoldering rubble and billowing clouds of smoke that glowed orange beneath a haze-filled sky.

I slowed as I entered the curve that swept around the mansion's lawn. On the first floor, someone had switched on a light toward the back of the house. It cut through the central hallway and pooled against the front door's heavy leaded glass and fractured into a thousand sparkling needles as it bent through the beveled edges. I coasted past the clinic, then turned onto Stone Manor Lane. A lake filled the corner of the field. Its banks rose to eyelevel, and the black water looked cold and empty and bottomless.

Lights blazed from the windows and open doorway of the first barn on the right. Barn six. Maddie had already worked through barns three, four, and five, which was pretty damned fast.

As I turned onto barn six's drive and rounded the four-board fence that enclosed the front paddock, headlights flashed across the windshield as a little sports car flew straight toward the Ford's grillwork. I slammed on the brakes, and the tires slid through the gravel before the pickup rocked to a stop.

The car veered to my left and skidded on the frozen grass before coming to rest alongside the opposite fence. I rammed the gearshift into park and recognized the vehicle as I jumped from the truck. A black Maserati Spyder. My boss' car.

Chapter 2

The heel of her suede boot pivoted on the frozen grass as Dr. Nash stepped out of the car. When she straightened to her full height, the car's exhaust billowed across the airfoil and swirled over the roof. She slammed the door and strode through the mist toward me with her leather duster flapping around her calves.

Dr. Deirdre Nash stopped a pace short of bumping into me. "What the hell's going on?" Her voice sounded hoarse, as if she'd just woken up, yet an element of tension strained her vocal cords and clipped her words.

While I explained that I'd surprised someone at barn seven and described how he'd sideswiped the barn when he tried to run me over, her shoulder-length brown hair whipped across her cheek in the wind. A few strands caught on her eyelashes. As she jabbed at them with her fingernails, I repeated Sergeant Bodell's theory that the arsonist might have been using the back lot as an observation post. Her hand froze.

"Oh, God." She spun around and sprinted for her car, and I don't think she would have moved any faster if the fire were blasting across the fields toward us.

"Sergeant Bodell might have left already," I yelled as she slid onto the bucket seat and slammed the door. She punched the gas, rocketed the Spyder back onto the drive, and slieved the little car around the corner.

"Well, thanks for asking if I'm okay," I said to the air that seemed to shudder in her wake.

Dr. Deirdre Nash reminded me of my mother. Both women were exquisitely elegant, tall and thin, with a natural grace and poise that made you sit up and take notice. Even if they weren't conventionally beautiful, their confidence and carriage made you believe they were. And they were both about as fluffy as a glacier. I pulled the farm truck past Maddie's car and walked into the barn.

She'd already grained the horses and was tossing them their hay. The barn was alive with the sounds of twenty large animals shifting around in their stalls. They pawed their hay or buffeted their feed tubs, searching for a stray piece of corn or sliver of oat. Maddie jarred one of the stall doors against the doorframe and rammed the bolt through the latch. She turned and caught sight of me.

"Hey," she said. "It's about time."

I shrugged. "Sorry."

She brushed wisps of hay off the front of her jeans, then crossed the aisle and stood beside me. "The last six need haying, then you'll be done." She looked out the open door and all but rolled her eyes. "D-o-c-t-o-r Deirdre sure was wired." Maddie had a way of saying the boss' name that made it sound like she was wadding it in her mouth just before she spat it out.

"Wouldn't you be," I said, "if this was yours?"

Maddie shot me a quick glance.

"Did you call her?" I said.

"No, I thought you did. The sirens must have woke her." She slowly zipped up her denim coat, then slipped both hands behind her neck and pulled her thick curly hair from beneath the fleece collar. She had a way of moving that was just a little too deliberate and made me think her actions were for my benefit. An understated come-on.

Maddie was a true redhead with pale skin and freckles and hazel eyes that alternated between brown or green or blue, depending on the light and the color of the clothes she wore.

This morning, they looked brown in the incandescent light that turned her auburn hair to gold where the curls corkscrewed onto her shoulders. She was short, maybe five-three, and a good bit chunkier than Rachel, but she filled out her jeans rather nicely, in a way that emphasized everything that was wonderful about her sex.

"The Cozzene mare's got wax on her teats a quarter inch long." She glanced at me, then went back to staring outside. Beyond the reach of the security lights, the sky had lightened to a pewter gray. "You just might have a foal tomorrow morning, if she don't go before that."

Maddie headed down the aisle and said over her shoulder, "See you tomorrow, Steve." She smoothed a hand over her ass like she was brushing off the seat of her pants; then she turned the corner, and a second later, the car's hinges squawked when she opened the door.

The engine cranked over as I glanced at my watch. As long as none of the mares were in danger of imminent labor, my lunch break started at six-thirty, which gave me exactly twenty minutes to make my rounds. I finished haying, then stepped outside.

A band of red stretched across the eastern horizon beneath fragmented cloud that hung low in the sky, dark purple against aqua. The frost was so thick, it looked like snow. Every blade of grass, each fence board, even the barns, were coated with it. I pivoted around. The pastures spread out in all directions, defined by fence lines that rose and dipped with the terrain and vanished in the swales where a ground-hugging mist had settled during the night.

I checked the mares in barns one through five, and when I was satisfied that breakfast was the only thing they had on their minds, I drove to the clinic. Six vehicles were parked in the lot. My Chevy, two Stone Manor trucks, and the stud manager's Ford sat at the end closest to the road and looked like the rest of the landscape, cold and inert, shrouded beneath a layer of frost. Dr. Nash had nosed her Spyder right up to the office door. It looked like she'd just driven it right off the showroom floor. A dark brown cop car idled next to the Spyder, half on the grass, half on the gravel. Cops. They parked wherever they damned well pleased.

The side of the cruiser was streaked with slashes of gold that flowed over the wheel wells and underlined the words *SHER-IFF Fauquier County*. I wondered if Sergeant Bodell was the driver.

I cut to the left, bypassed the office door, and squeezed through the opening between the large sliding doors that accessed the central aisle. The clinic was larger inside than its profile suggested. The central aisle was fourteen feet wide and continued all the way down to the far end of the building. The office was immediately to my right, followed by a restroom and living quarters, then three fourteen-by-fourteen stalls that housed the stallions. I was certain they'd heard me come in, but they knew they weren't going to be fed. Not yet, and not by me. The stud manager was solely responsible for their care, and his shift didn't begin until seven.

There was an open area to the left of the central aisle where rubber chips covered the ground, and the walls were padded with thick foam rubber mats. Although I hadn't been around long enough to see them do it, they bred the mares there. The actual clinic was located just beyond the open area, and three more stalls completed the left side of the barn.

Both the clinic and office had large Plexiglas windows that faced the central aisle. The clinic was dark, but light edged around the closed Venetian blinds in the office windows. I used the restroom, and as I stepped back into the aisle and flipped through my keys, the office door opened.

"You don't know that!" Dr. Nash paused in the threshold. Her thin fingers tightened around the doorknob as she looked over her shoulder at Sergeant Bodell.

He stood on the mat in front of the receptionist's desk with his hands jammed in his pockets. "Come on, Deirdre. Be reasonable."

"Emmett, I swear to God. If I catch him on my property, I'll kill him myself."

Bodell glanced at me, stepped toward her, and lowered his voice. I turned my back to them, and as I slotted my key in the lock, her voice carried across the aisle.

"Calm down. How can I?"

He said something I couldn't hear.

"A lot of good your extra patrol's done so far," Dr. Nash said as I stepped into the clinic and closed the door.

I'd been out in the cold since two-thirty, and the warm air felt wonderful. I hung my coat on the back of a chair, grabbed my lunch out of the fridge, and dropped the ham and cheese sandwich into the microwave.

The clinic looked like an oversized kitchen with cabinets lining three walls and long stretches of bare countertop, but that's where any similarity to a domestic environment came to an abrupt halt. Instead of cookbooks, binders and veterinary manuals lined the counters. An autoclave sat in the far corner of the room, and the cabinets were stocked with cotton rolls and bandages and boxes of syringes and needles and who knew what else. Vials of acepromazine and Banamine and rows of brown penicillin bottles cluttered the racks in the refrigerator.

When the microwave alarm chimed, I popped the door. As I peeled the plastic off my sandwich, I glanced into the barn aisle through the Plexiglas window. Sergeant Bodell stood behind Dr. Nash as she rapped on the door that accessed the living quarters. The stud manager lived there, if you call inhabiting a fourteen-by-fourteen room living. I knew what that was like, and it was not a lifestyle for the claustrophobic or the ambitious.

When Frank Wissel opened his door and squinted at Dr. Nash, she leaned forward and gestured with her arms. Her raised voice vibrated across the Plexiglas and filtered through the walls. Her words were garbled, but I had no trouble imagining the topic of conversation.

Frank must have said something in response, because the stallions at the far end of the barn whinnied, and a thump reverberated through the wooden planks that lined the exterior wall. As far as they were concerned, the sound of his voice meant that breakfast was on its way.

I wheeled one of the office chairs over to the west-facing window and sat down. The clinic was surrounded by a maze of paddocks, and the fence lines stretched all the way over to the gravel drive that wound past the Nashes' home and ended at an old bank barn. A barn much like the one that had just burned to the ground.

I thought of my boss, sleeping there after the fire that had leveled her parents' barn, worrying over those broodmares, knowing four lives hung in the balance, not two.

I pictured the burns, patches of raw flesh that radiated heat into the chill air and oozed serum that matted the singed hair in foul streaks. I imagined the smell.

Behind me, the industrial-sized heater that hung from the ceiling vibrated to life and pushed a wave of warm air across the room. I blinked, then glanced down at the can of Coke in my hand. I cracked it open and settled back in the chair. I could just make out a fire engine parked on Cannonball Gate, but the rest of the scene was blocked from view by the Nashes' house. A huge column of smoke and ash had risen toward the cloud base and drifted southeast until it was difficult to see where one ended and the other began. As I watched, the sun inched above the horizon, and in the west, the rim of the Blue Ridge Mountains glowed red against a dark sky as if a wildfire had crested the ridge. As the sun inched higher, the golden light cascaded down the slope. It spread across the valley floor, racing to meet the sun, and the colorless landscape and mist that blanketed the ground momentarily turned pink before the day brightened.

When I'd swallowed the last of the sandwich, I balled the wrapper in my hand. As I got to my feet, the door opened. One of the day crew came in. He nodded in my direction, then yawned as he flipped through the timecards slotted in a metal rack on the wall. The woman who'd handled the paperwork when I was hired told me they were supposed to be kept in alphabetical order, but when I'd punched in the next morning, they were jammed into the slots every which way.

I remembered the guy's name as I drained the last of my Coke. Paul…something. Something Italian. He fished out his card, punched it, then shrugged out of his parka.

Paul removed the filter basket from the coffee machine and dumped the grounds in the trash. He slipped the pot off the hot plate and glanced at me before he set it in the sink and turned on the hot water. "What's your name?"

"Steve."

"Maybe Maddie didn't tell you, but the guy who used to work your shift made the coffee every morning. Would be nice if you did, too."

I didn't say anything, and in a second or two, he looked over his shoulder. Although Paul was my height, he outweighed me by a good forty pounds. A solid forty pounds that he hadn't sculpted solely by mucking stalls. Physically, he reminded me of Marty with his dark complexion and thick black hair. I guessed he was a couple of years older than me, maybe twenty-four or five, and I had the distinct impression he used age as a yardstick, a way of sizing someone up or classifying him when, in fact, age meant very little. What mattered most was what you did with your life, and sometimes, if you were unlucky, what mattered most was what was done *to* you.

"What's happening over by Pond Lane?" he said as he reached across the counter to open one of the cabinet doors. Genoa. That was his last name.

"A barn burned down."

His hand froze at shoulder height; then he slowly lowered his arm and turned around. "You're shitting me?"

"Nope."

"Man, that's the third one in three weeks."

"Wasn't the first one set the same night the guy who worked my shift quit?"

"You mean Bruce?"

I nodded.

"Sometime around then, but I'm pretty sure he was already gone. Why?"

"You think he's setting them?"

"Why the hell would you say that?"

I shrugged. "Timing. Maybe he got fired and is pissed."

"Nah. Not Claremont. Anyway, he quit."

"Well, seeing as I'm gonna be doing his job, you know why he left?"

"All I know is, he showed up like usual…" Paul leaned back on his heels and looked at the ceiling. "Must've been a Saturday, his long day, 'cause I picked Maddie up around midnight, and he was just punching in. Anyway, he started his shift like he always did, but by the next morning, the little weasel had gone and quit. Course, at the time, we didn't know that. Everybody thought he'd gone home sick like he'd done Friday morning."

"Sick. How?"

"Awh, nothing, man. Just a lousy cold. Then, when Maddie come in Sunday, just after midnight, Frank was working in Bruce's place. When he told her he'd quit, she was madder than a cat with its tail caught in a hay tedder. It was her long day, see? And she thought for sure she'd have to work both shifts the next night, too, even though Nash said Ronnie was gonna work Bruce's shift."

"Why'd she think that if management told her otherwise?"

He turned back to the sink and shut off the hot water. Steam coated the window so that it was no longer possible to see through the glass. "What the bosses say they're gonna do and what comes down ain't always the same thing. You'll figure that out for yourself, soon enough. Anyway, the season had already started off with every fucking thing that could go wrong doing just that. A week before Bruce quit, a shipment come up from Florida—"

"A shipment?"

Paul looked at me like I was crazy. "A load of mares, man. Ain't nothin' else coming in here in the middle of the night. Anyway, one of the mares walked off the trailer sick as a dog, and Dr. Nash had to put her down. Then, if that wasn't bad enough, two mares dropped their foals on Maddie's long day, right after Bruce split." Paul filled the pot with cold water, emptied it into the machine, and slid it back onto the hot plate. "The first two of the season, and they're born the same night. You know what the odds are of that happening?"

"Not especially," I said, and Paul shot me a look.

He wedged a filter into the Mr. Coffee and peeled the lid off a can of Folgers. "Well, it don't happen much. Not this early in the season. The mares always start off slow. Now, come April, that's a whole different story. By then, you and Maddie'll be foaling two or three a night. Anyway, Bruce is a no show, and we've got two new babies on the ground that we gotta make sure are nursing good. Well, you can't have just anybody looking after them at night." Paul dumped some coffee into the filter, closed the lid, and hit the switch. "Seems like with horses, if something bad's gonna happen, it happens at night, but I guess Ronnie did okay."

Paul stretched his arms behind his back and braced his hands on the edge of the countertop. "Anyway, I knew Bruce was a loser, first time I laid eyes on him."

"Why's that?" I said.

"Except for the girls, working here didn't hold his interest much. The guy had bigger plans."

"Like what?"

"I wouldn't know. You could just tell."

We both glanced at the Mr. Coffee as the first drops of hot water spurted and gurgled into the filter.

"Personally, I'm glad he's gone. The guy thought he was hot shit. He stayed away from Maddie, though—" Paul looked me straight in the eye— "once I made it clear what would happen if he didn't."

I held his gaze, and in that instant, the door flew open, and some of guys on the day shift barged into the room, followed by a blast of chilly air that swirled across the floor. When their excited voices faded away to nothing, Paul frowned, then reluctantly looked away. I crossed my arms over my chest and shifted. Without thinking, I leaned against the counter, and a twinge of pain cut into my hip where the pickup had slammed into muscle. I shifted my weight squarely onto my feet and straightened my spine.

The crew had been talking about the fire, and after a moment of awkward silence, when they punched their timecards and slid a few curious glances our way, they started up again.

Ronnie Townes dumped his parka on the counter and pushed a mass of frizzy dreadlocks off his forehead. "Who you think done it?"

"How the hell should I know?" one of the older men replied.

"Man. I'm glad I ain't working nights no more."

Ronnie had rough, dry skin and a scrawny neck creased with horizontal lines that looked dirty. He'd dyed his hair sometime in the distant past, and the ends had faded to the color of baling twine.

One of the crew, a sleazy-looking guy whose brown hair hung in greasy strands down his forehead, draped his arm across Ronnie's shoulders and pulled him off balance. "What, Ronnie?" he mocked as he ruffled the kid's dreadlocks. "You afraid the big bad firebug's gonna get you?"

"Knock it off, Tiller." Frank Wissel, the stud manager, stepped into the room, followed by three crewmembers.

Wissel punched his timecard, then moved to the center of the room. After years spent working outdoors, his age was difficult to judge. He was light on his feet and reasonably fit, and I had a feeling he was younger than his weathered skin and gray hair suggested. "Anything to report, Cline?"

"You know about what happened at barn seven?" I said.

He nodded.

"That's it, then."

"Okay." As Wissel told us about the fire, it appeared that everyone had either driven past the scene or had heard about it secondhand. When the stud manager mentioned the hit-and-run, I scanned the faces of the men and women as they lounged in office chairs or leaned against the counters or sat cross-legged on the floor and noted that they all seemed genuinely surprised.

As Wissel went over the day's schedule, my gaze once again drifted around the room. We were a sorry looking bunch, wearing tattered jeans or stained overalls, mud-caked boots and worn coats. Ronnie's parka had duct tape at the elbows, and his zipper was busted. Tiller's watch cap was so stretched out of shape, it hung down the back of his head like an empty feedbag.

Wissel eventually separated us into groups of four, and as he assigned the barns we were to muck out, Paul Genoa folded his arms across his chest and stared at me. I'd lucked out. We wouldn't be working together for the rest of the morning.

"Okay, that's it," Wissel said.

Chairs creaked and fabric rustled as everyone pushed off the walls or stood. Half of them scooped gloves and hats and travel mugs steaming with coffee off the countertops; then we drifted toward the parking lot.

Chapter 3

Both Ronnie Townes, the guy with the frazzled dreadlocks, and Tiller, the man who'd been horsing around with him, were assigned to my crew along with a skinny blond kid whose name I did not know.

Tiller slowed as we neared the farm trucks. When he turned toward me, the sunlight glinted off his wraparound sunglasses. He stretched out his hand. "I'll drive."

I paused. Since I had just spent the last four hours driving the Ford from barn to barn, and still had possession of the keys, the privilege of chauffeuring our little group around the farm was mine until I punched out at noon. According to Maddie, it was one of the shift's few perks. As far as I was concerned, if Stone Manor had been my permanent job, working the early shift was a perk in and of itself. Rising early and working six days a week were long ingrained habits, but getting off at noon was a proposition I looked forward to for as long as the job lasted.

What I didn't look forward to was dealing with jerks like Paul Genoa and, now, Tiller.

Ronnie and the blond kid had stopped walking. They shuffled around so they could see my reaction. Ronnie huddled in his parka and shifted his weight as his gaze swiveled between us.

Tiller took my hesitation as a sign of indecision, and a slow smile spread across his face.

I had dealt with enough bullies to last me a lifetime and had no patience for his game. I looked past him, jerked my head toward the truck, and said to Ronnie and the blond kid, "Get in the cab." I paused, then switched my gaze to Tiller. "You, ride in the bed."

"What the fuck?" Tiller leaned toward me, his weight on the balls of his feet, his arms locked at his sides. "You can't do that."

Barn one wasn't all that far away, but early in the morning, with a hard wind blasting across the fields, a short ride in the open bed of a pickup was still preferable to a longer walk under a weak sun.

I kept my voice calm. "Ride in the back or walk. I don't care which."

"Awh, man. This is bullshit. You had the truck all night. Now it's my turn." He held out his hand. "Give me the damn keys."

I ignored him, and as I pivoted on my heel, Tiller latched onto my shoulder. I spun around, brought my arm up in a quick block, and broke his grip. "Touch me again," I said, "I'll put you on the ground."

Tiller froze.

I don't know what he saw in my eyes, but he eased his weight back until he was standing flatfooted. The cold breeze whipped his greasy bangs over the edge of his watch cap, but I suspected the color flushing his cheeks had little to do with the weather.

I turned away from him.

Ronnie and the blond kid glanced at Tiller, then hustled over to the truck and scrambled onto the seat. Ronnie clicked the door shut as I slid behind the wheel. The wind had drained every trace of heat from the cab. I started her up, checked the rearview mirror, and backed out of the slot. When I paused alongside Tiller, he sullenly stepped into the bed and sat on the wheel well on the passenger's side. I could feel his gaze boring through the glass as I slipped the transmission into drive and pulled onto Bear Wallow.

As I swung the Ford onto Stone Manor Lane, the private road that served barns one through six, both of the guys up front glanced sideways at me, then snapped their heads back around when I straightened the wheel.

"What's your name?" I said to the blond kid, and both of them blurted their names in unison. I grinned. Ben, who was stuck in the middle, looked like he wished *he* were in the bed with Tiller. I cleared my throat. "Steve Cline."

They mumbled "hello."

Ronnie looked forward through the windshield and smiled. "Took Bruce a month to figure Tiller was jerking him around."

"Bruce?" I said.

"Yeah. Guy who had your job."

"Did he quit because of Tiller?"

"Nah," Ronnie said. "Ain't nobody know why he quit. He just don't show up one day is all."

I eased the pickup onto barn one's drive. "Just like that?"

Ben shook his head. "Job like this, it happens all the time."

"Yeah," Ronnie said. "The pay sucks."

"So do the hours," Ben said, and they both nodded.

"Working nights sucks, man," Ronnie said. "Give me the creeps, especially over at seven and eight, with the electric not hooked up."

"Gonna be now," Ben said, and Ronnie nodded.

"I hated those barns. The horses turned out over there at night, you can hear them moving around, but you can't see them 'til suddenly, bam! They're in your face. Moving in and out of the shed like friggin' ghosts. Man, I tell you, gave me the creeps. I checked them barns and got the hell outta there."

I pulled the Ford off the drive and parked in front of the big aisle doors. Tiller must have jumped out of the bed before the wheels rolled to a stop, because he skirted the front fender and disappeared into the barn before I'd switched off the engine.

Ronnie jerked up on the door handle. "And now we got a torch to worry about. I am s-o-o glad I'm not on nights no more.

First night I came in, there was a barn fire just south of here. Started on Maddie's shift though."

When I climbed out of the cab and stretched, a muscle in my thigh burned. "Ronnie, how many nights did you end up working?"

"Eight, and I hope to God I never gotta do it again," he said as he wrapped his coat flaps around his chest. "So don't go quitting on me, man."

I smiled. "Guess you were caught off guard when Dr. Nash asked you to work that shift, huh?"

"Weren't her who asked. Mr. Nash called me Sunday morning, my friggin' day off. Wakes me up to ask if I can come in Monday at two-thirty in the fucking morning."

Ben strolled into the barn, and Ronnie followed, saying over his shoulder. "Ain't natural, being up all night."

"Not unless you're a vampire," Ben added. "Or a werewolf."

I smiled at his comment. It reminded me of a guy I'd worked with at the track. He'd held a similar opinion of night work and the people who chose it.

The air inside the barn felt warm, relatively speaking, and was filled with the long familiar odors of horse, hay, and straw. And noise. The horses weren't as anxious as they would have been if we were there to feed them, but they were restless. Restless and alert to any action on our part that signaled we were ready to turn them out. They reminded me of school kids waiting for the clatter of the dismissal bell at the end of the day. And they didn't care how cold it was, either.

Metal screeched against metal as Tiller opened the back doors.

All of the foaling barns on the main part of the farm housed twenty mares, and out of the twenty in barn one, two had foals on the ground. The rest were due to foal within the next twenty-four hours to two weeks. Or longer. Horses were difficult to judge, and they were sneaky. Eighty percent of them foaled at night, and according to Maddie, they preferred foaling without human intervention.

After Tiller backed the tractor and muck wagon outside, each of us grabbed a lead rope. We started at the far end of the barn and silently worked our way down the length of the aisle, leading each mare to the back gate and turning her loose in one of the large fields. The horses were anxious but well behaved, and as I led a pretty bay mare across the back lot, I reflected that the start of the morning's chores mirrored so many other days in the past. The same routine, the same smells, the same rhythm played out on horse farms across the country, dictated by the needs of the animals themselves. The same everything except a lingering feeling of unease that had settled in the pit of my stomach ever since I'd seen the fire's glow reflect off the cloud base.

When the pregnant mares had been turned out, we split into teams. I followed Ben into a stall, and he clipped his lead onto the mare's halter. She was a big dapple gray, about sixteen-two, with an underdeveloped neck and a head that would have been ugly if not for her huge expressive eyes.

Her colt strutted over to me and nudged my chest with his nose.

I clipped my lead on his halter, and he tilted his head and tried to grab the cotton rope between his teeth. "How old's this guy?"

"About two weeks," Ben said. "Be careful when we get outside. Ornery as he is, ain't no question he's a stud colt."

I moved into position alongside the colt's left shoulder, and he tried to swivel around to face me but ran out of room when his right haunch bumped into the heavy oak planks that formed the partition between stalls.

Ben led the mare through the doorway, and Junior bounded forward. I made him wait until I'd stepped into the aisle before I let him proceed. He pranced into the aisle and whinnied to his dam with a high-pitched immature voice. His steps were light on the asphalt, his stride as long as mine as he tried to muscle his way past me.

We walked outside, into the pale sunlight, and after we'd gone two paces, his front end came off the ground. I fed the lead through my hand and walked alongside him. When he came back down, I snatched the lead and told him to quit. He responded by rooting against his halter. He snaked his head from side to side and loped forward. His steps sounded hollow on the frozen ground as we followed Ben and the mare into one of the private paddocks. I turned him to face the gate, and when I set him loose, he skittered around and took off after his dam.

"That colt's gonna be a bitch to break," Ben said as he slipped off his gloves and latched the gate. "Been a handful since he was born."

"He's confident," I said.

"Yeah." Ben jammed his hands under his armpits. "Ain't afraid of nothing."

Too young to know better, I thought as I followed Ben into the barn.

We spent the rest of the morning mucking stalls, and at noon, when everyone broke for lunch, I punched out and drove into Warrenton to meet Corey, Bruce's sister. Except for Dr. Nash's chilly appearance first thing that morning, I didn't see her again. Ordinarily, I wouldn't have expected to since I'd been assigned to the stall-cleaning detail. But I'd half expected her to question me about the incident after she'd settled down.

I ate a leisurely lunch at McDonald's, then backtracked down Broadview. Up ahead, the traffic light turned yellow, then red. As I coasted to a stop, I relaxed into the bench seat and sighed. Farther down the block, sunlight flashed off street signs as they were buffeted by the wind. 17N on one, N 29 Business on the other. Then 211E. My grip tightened on the steering wheel.

I glanced around reflexively. Noted the van pulling up alongside me, the elderly woman stepping off the curb in the crosswalk, her bony hand clutching a scarf at her throat.

A quaint, quiet, middle-America town, and here I was, isolated in my pickup, feeling a sudden rush of panic squeezing my chest. I had known someone, once. Someone who'd disappeared off the face of the earth after the universal joint on his sedan fractured, and the drive shaft had gouged into the asphalt on 211 just west of town.

Hours before, he'd tried to kill me and had come within a knife's breadth of succeeding.

The driver in the pickup behind me tapped his horn. I glanced at the light, then accelerated through the intersection. But that was the past. He'd dropped out of sight because the law was after him. Bruce Claremont's disappearance felt much more ominous.

I spent an hour exploring the town and getting my bearings before cruising past Fauquier High School. Rock Glen Apartments, Bruce's home for the past eight months, sat on a rise directly opposite the school. I turned into the lot and parked in front of unit six-forty-one.

I jacked up the heat, cranked the blowers on full blast, and settled against the backrest. Corey had arranged to take off early so she could let me into her brother's apartment, but I didn't expect her for another hour. She'd wanted to give me a key when I'd accepted the job, but the idea of going in without her hadn't felt right.

Rock Glen Apartments had probably been nice twenty-five years ago, but time and neglect had taken its toll. Beneath the balcony railings and rain gutters, rust and mineral deposits streaked the brick walls, and the foundation shrubs obliterated the first floor windows.

I wondered why Corey had contacted me on her own after the police investigation had gone nowhere. What about her parents? Weren't they worried about Bruce?

When I shut off the engine, the heater in the old Chevy had only made a marginal dent in the cold. I slipped my feet over the transmission hump, stretched my legs, and scrunched down in the seat.

I must have dozed off. When I next opened my eyes, the sunlight slanted into the cab through the grimy back window and glinted off the rearview mirror. Close by, grit crunched under tires as a vehicle pulled up alongside the Chevy's passenger door. I sat up, and the change in position dispersed the body heat that had accumulated in my clothing and sent chills across my skin. I shivered.

Corey waved and flashed a tentative smile in my direction before she hunched forward over her steering wheel and switched off the ignition. She strode around the pickup's nose, hopped off the curb, and paused at the open door as I levered myself off the seat and slowly straightened to my full height.

"Oh, my God. You're frozen."

"Hmm." I reached back into the cab and yanked my duffel bag off the seat.

"How long have you been here?"

"Not as long as it looks, apparently."

She crossed her arms over her chest and rubbed her gloved hands up and down her biceps. The temperature felt like it had dropped into the teens, and the wind was still blowing.

"Let's get you inside." She pivoted around and bounded up the steps like the athlete she was.

I followed more slowly and half expected to find her jogging in place as she waited for me on the landing between the first and second floor. A smile flitted across her face before she headed up the next set of stairs with her sneakers squeaking on the concrete. She appeared weightless as her thigh muscles pumped under her woolly black tights.

Corey stopped on the second floor landing and fumbled through her keys in front of a maroon door with *2D* centered above the peephole. The steps continued up to the third floor and provided a cover over our heads. Otherwise, the stairwell was open to the weather, and the wind picked up a hell of a lot of momentum as it careened across the high school's grounds. It blasted into the alcove, and a cluster of dead leaves skittered across the landing and swirled into a mini cyclone in the corner.

The key turned in the lock; then Corey pushed the door inward and switched on the lights.

The foyer was defined by a four-by-four section of linoleum beneath our feet and a coat rack stuck in the corner with a Ravens windbreaker and two hooded sweatshirts draped over the brass hardware. Since we were in Redskins country, I wondered if Bruce ever caught any flack over that windbreaker.

I set my duffel bag on the floor and took off my coat as Corey strode briskly toward the back of the apartment. She returned a second or two later with her arms folded over her chest as if she were still trying to get warm. "He hasn't been here."

She gripped her lower lip between her teeth, then crossed the living room and drew back the curtains. The late afternoon sunlight stretched halfway across the room and puddled on the carpet in a pattern defined by the balcony railing. The room was sparsely furnished. A computer sat on a narrow stand in the corner to the right of the glass doors, and a functional sofa hugged the far wall, but a worn recliner close to the door looked to be Bruce's favorite spot in the room. It faced off with the entertainment center, and by the looks of it, he'd sunk the majority of his disposable cash into a big screen TV and impressive stereo system. A bulky homemade afghan had been folded and placed neatly on the sofa's backrest. A smaller one hung off the recliner. I wondered who had knitted them as I watched Corey walk into the dining room, essentially a nook cropped out of the main living space.

She dropped her gloves on the table, unwound a woolly scarf from her neck, and laid it across the back of one of the chairs. Strands of her short blond hair floated upward, charged with static electricity. Her purple shirt matched one of the colors in the complicated weave of her heavy fleece vest, and despite its bulk, her profile was straight and slender.

I walked over to her. "You okay?"

"He's never just disappeared like this before."

I wanted to reassure her, to tell her I'd find him, that everything would be all right. Instead, I said, "Mind if I look around?"

"No. Go ahead."

"Could you find a calendar and something to write on?"

She nodded, then headed into the kitchen. I glanced in as I walked past. The dining room's layout was generous compared to the kitchen's three-foot-wide aisle that was lined on both sides with cabinets and cheap appliances. I used the bathroom and noted Bruce's toothbrush wedged in the ceramic holder on the wall. Just like Corey had said. Nothing about the apartment indicated that he'd been planning a trip. I continued down a short hallway, past a closed door on my left. I paused, stepped back, and opened the door.

Bruce had crammed mismatched towels and bed sheets on the shelves along with a small Tupperware container stuffed with cold remedies and ibuprofen and orange plastic bottles of prescription medicine. I sorted through them. Prevacid, amoxicillin, Zithromax. Most were nearly empty. Apparently, the risk of perpetuating drug-resistant strains of bacteria was not one of his pressing concerns. I slid the container back onto the shelf and closed the door.

Except for the alarm clock's digital readout, Bruce's bedroom was pitch black. I switched on the overhead light and walked around the bed. When I tried to pull back the curtains, I realized Bruce had tacked them to the window frame, and he'd wedged bath towels behind the curtain rods. Simple but effective light control.

A queen-sized bed and dresser took up most of the floor space. Closets lined the back wall. I opened one of the bi-folds, and a basketball rolled off the shelf and bounced across the floor. It came to rest at the foot of the bed. I tossed it back on the shelf, folded the door into place before something else toppled out, and decided that a thorough search would have to wait. I paused when I noticed a key ring on his dresser. I fingered the keys, then snatched them up.

Corey had organized a calendar, writing pad, and pen on the table like a place setting. She was sitting in an adjacent chair, flipping through a phone book. She'd crossed her legs and bounced them with nervous energy.

She looked up when she heard me step into the room. "Do you like pizza? Or maybe a sub? I thought we should probably have something delivered instead of going out," she gestured to the calendar, "so we can get to work."

"Sure. Pizza sounds good. Anything but anchovies."

"When do you plan on going to bed?" She covered her mouth with her hand and looked up at me. "I didn't mean that the way it sounded. What I mean is, how long do we have to work? You have to get up early, right?"

I smiled as I took a seat. Wishful thinking had me wondering if her comment had been a Freudian slip. "Because I'm training, I need to be there at two-thirty."

She nodded. "That's what I thought. Bruce had to do that, too."

"So, that gives us a couple hours. More if necessary." I laid the keys on the table. "Are these Bruce's?"

Corey's breath seemed to catch in her throat before she breathed out a throaty "Yes."

"His only set?"

"I don't know. Probably. That's why I'm positive something's happened." She lifted her slender arm, palm up, and gestured toward the door. The overhead light blanched her wrist, and the tendons beneath her skin bulged as she tightened her grip around a tissue. "Unless he has a spare, he can't even get into his apartment without going to the landlord."

"And his car?"

"It's in the lot."

"I don't get it. What did the police say when you told them both his keys and car are here?"

She shrugged. "Nothing. Just that he could have gone off with someone, taken a spare to the apartment and left the rest because he wasn't driving. It didn't seem to faze them one little bit." Corey sank back in her seat and wedged her hands between her thighs as if she were drawing into herself like a scared little kid.

I fingered the calendar. I had a million questions. What was Bruce like? Who were his friends? Did he have a steady girlfriend? What did he do in his spare time? But it seemed prudent to go slow. Even necessary. She'd returned to her brother's apartment, hoping against hope to find him.

When she got up and went into the kitchen to use the phone, I took out my own set of keys and matched up the clinic key I'd been given the day I started at Stone Manor with one on Bruce's key ring. They were identical. So, if he quit, why hadn't he turned it in?

I pocketed my keys, flipped the calendar open to February, and circled the twelfth, my first day on the job. From there, I counted back eight days, then one more to account for Ronnie's scheduled day off. If his memory was accurate, and I suspected it was, Bruce's last day on the job must have been February second, a Sunday. But that wasn't right. Maddie's long days were Sundays, when she worked both shifts.

Bruce's schedule, now my schedule, was easy to lose track of, so I scribbled it out on a sheet of paper.

> Sunday – off
> Monday – 3:00 a.m. to noon
> Tuesday – 3:00 a.m. to noon
> Wednesday – 3:00 a.m. to noon
> Thursday – 3:00 a.m. to noon
> Friday – 3:00 a.m. to noon
> Saturday – midnight to 7:00 a.m.,
>   then 6:00 p.m. to midnight

I scanned the sheet. For the time being, I had to report in a half-hour early for training; otherwise, Bruce's and my schedule were one and the same. I looked back at the calendar. Bruce's last day had to have been Saturday, February the first, and that sounded likely. Paul had described how he'd picked Maddie up at midnight, and the only time she got off at midnight was at the beginning of each Saturday, her day off and Bruce's long day. Paul had seen him punching in, but he'd quit by morning. I moved my hand to circle the date and paused. Below the pen's tip, someone had scribbled with a heavy black marker in a sloppy hand *Corey B-day.*

She must have seen something in my face because she gripped my wrist with her long slender fingers and moved my hand aside.

She read her brother's words.

Her fingers already felt cool against my skin, but now, the last bit of warmth seemed to drain out of them. Without taking her gaze off the ragged print, she released her grip and sat down. "Twenty minutes."

"What?"

"The pizza. It'll be here in twenty minutes." She looked up at me, then, and a single tear caught in her long pale lashes before slipping onto her cheek. She brushed it away with a trembling hand.

"I'm sorry, Corey."

"This job was the first time he'd ever worked nights, and he was worried that he wouldn't like it, but he did. He was looking forward to delivering his first foal." Corey sniffed and wiped her nose with the back of her hand. "Because of his hours, we had to schedule family get-togethers on Sundays. When he missed my party, I knew something was wrong."

I glanced down at the calendar and noticed that he'd scrawled *7:00 p.m.* in Sunday's box. "What do your parents think?"

She shrugged impatiently. "Dad's not worried. He says there's nothing unusual about a guy his age going off and not telling anyone what he's doing or where he's at."

"Bruce is what, twenty-six?"

"Twenty-five. A year older than me."

I'd never tried to guess Corey's age before but realized I'd automatically assumed she was around my age, or younger, when in fact, she was two years older.

She unsnapped the bulky fleece vest she wore and let it slump onto the back of her chair; then she leaned forward and pulled a thin wallet from a back pocket. She fished out a photograph and handed it over.

Bruce stared intently into the camera's lens with serious green eyes, but if you looked closely, you could see the faintest of smiles tugging the corner of his mouth, as if he were trying not to smile. But as I studied the photograph, I wondered if, instead, he was forcing a smile. There was something about his eyes, a hint of weariness or disappointment that made me think the latter. The picture was taken outdoors, on a sunny autumn day. The kind of day when the air feels cool, but the sun seeps into your clothes and warms your skin. Bruce was standing alongside a goalpost, holding a football in his right hand, and he was wearing the same Ravens windbreaker that hung on the coat rack in the living room. Everything about him, from his neatly pressed slacks to his short brown hair and clean-shaven face, spoke of an all-American guy who was going places. Everything except that hint of discontent beneath his penetrating gaze.

When I held out the photograph, Corey flapped her hand. "Keep it for now."

"Okay." I cleared my throat. "When did you talk to him last?"

"January twenty-sixth. I checked my phone records to be sure." She stood up. "That reminds me. I didn't get the mail."

"No, wait. I'll get it. I need to figure out his keys, anyway."

A frown creased her forehead as she watched me grip the table and lever myself out of the chair. She arched an eyebrow and cocked her head. "I don't believe it. This job's making you sore?"

"Not likely." I lifted Bruce's keys off the table and told her how some guy in a pickup had tried to run me over. Then I told her about the fires.

"Oh, God, Steve. How bad are you hurt?"

I shrugged. "Just stiff."

"Was he really aiming for you? Maybe he didn't see you."

"Oh, he saw me, all right."

"Oh, my God."

"It's all right, Corey."

"That's so spooky. Do you really think he was the arsonist?"

"The cops consider it possible." I rubbed the back of my neck. "Of all the barns at Stone Manor, barn seven's closest to the barn that burned down, and we only check that section of the farm twice a night. I wouldn't have driven over there in the first place, except for the fire."

I picked up the pen and printed FIRE in February thirteen's block, today's date; then I looked at the beginning of the month. Saturday the first, Bruce's last day at Stone Manor. Then Maddie worked all day Sunday, which meant Ronnie's first day on foal watch was Monday, February the third. As a reminder to myself, I printed Ronnie's name in that block, followed by FIRE. There'd been a second fire between the two, but I didn't know when. A quick trip to the library would fill in the blanks.

"Everyone on the farm would know the schedule, wouldn't they?" Corey said.

"Not necessarily," I said, thinking the only people likely to know the routine were management and any of the staff who'd worked the foal watch.

"You're not thinking the fires have anything to do with Bruce leaving, are you?"

I looked up and laid the pen on the table. The central heating kicked on with a vibration that sounded through the walls. "What do you think?"

She shook her head. "Maybe he found out who was setting them."

"Maybe, but the first fire wasn't set until after he quit."

I thought about Dr. Nash's fear of fire. Although I doubted many of the crew knew the story behind it, it appeared that most everyone knew her feelings on the subject. If I'd wanted to torment her, and I was diabolical enough for it, fire would be my first choice. Even if I couldn't manage to torch one of her buildings, one in the vicinity would carry enough impact to rattle her. Or send a message. What if Bruce hadn't quit, like everyone said, but had been fired, instead?

"What if he got fired," I said, "and held a grudge—"

"No." Corey shook her head. "He would never do that."

I glanced at the entertainment center. At the recliner and remote control readily at hand. "I agree. It doesn't explain his not coming home."

I had her show me which key fit his mailbox and which opened the apartment door; then I hustled down the steps. A Papa John's delivery guy pulled up while I was yanking Bruce's mail out of the box. He ran around the hood of his car, took the steps to the landing two at a time, and seemed relieved at the speed of the transaction. I was still fumbling between keeping the mail from being blown off the pizza box, jamming my wallet in my back pocket, and wiggling the key out of the lock when he peeled out of the lot.

When I returned, Corey was standing in the middle of the living room, looking disoriented, like she couldn't exactly remember where she was. She brushed the bangs off her forehead, and they flopped back down to her eyebrows. "Oh, I was going to pay for that." Her voice cracked. "How much—"

"Don't worry about it." I set the box on the table, went into the kitchen, and opened the refrigerator. "What do you want to drink? Coke, beer, 7-Up?"

She stepped around the corner. "Beer?"

"Uh-huh. Miller Lite."

She frowned. "I'll have a Coke."

I placed the sodas on the table, and she peeled apart two slices of pepperoni pizza and dropped them on paper plates. She licked some sauce off her fingers as she sat down and tucked one leg beneath her in a maneuver that would have put me in traction.

She stretched over the pizza box, picked up Bruce's mail, and sorted the pieces like she was dealing a deck of cards. Junk mail in one pile, bills in the other, roughly in even measure, and nothing personal as far as I could see. One was stamped with FINAL NOTICE in red ink.

"Open his mail if you see something that could be a clue, okay?"

"All right," I said and wondered what law I'd be breaking doing it. "When did you go to the police?"

"My parents and I drove down last weekend, on the eighth." She slumped back in her chair and folded her hands in her lap.

"I called him the Sunday before, when he didn't show for the party. Then I tried again, Monday and Tuesday. When I didn't get him on Thursday, I called Stone Manor, and they told me he'd quit."

I jotted down COPS on the eighth and said, "Who'd you talk to at the farm?"

"The secretary, and after a good deal of hysterics on my part, she put me through to the woman who runs the place."

"Dr. Nash?"

Corey nodded.

"What did she say?"

"Just that he'd quit. She didn't talk to him when he left. Her husband did. I took off from work Friday and went out there. Talked to him and some of the employees. Saturday and Sunday, I talked to Bruce's neighbors and went back to the police station again, and the farm, and got absolutely nowhere. If I'd had any idea he was going to stay missing, I wouldn't have waited so long."

"He's done this before?"

"Not exactly. He's forgetful though, and not terribly responsible. It's not the first time he's missed a family get-together."

By Sunday evening, she'd been frustrated enough with her lack of progress to ask me for help. I finished my pizza, and as I leaned forward and hooked another slice out of the box, I noticed that she'd only taken one bite of hers. "What else did the police do?"

"Nothing." She flapped her hand, glanced at the ceiling, and blinked back tears. "Well, I mean, they took a report and everything, but because of his age, and the fact that there weren't any signs of foul play, that's all they would do. In thirty days, if we still haven't heard from him, they'll put together a longer report and enter it into some kind of national database." She bit down on her lower lip. "The detective we talked to, he didn't come out and say it, but I got the impression that the information would be used for identification purposes," she swallowed, "if they found a body."

I glanced at Corey. She was keeping it together, so far. I ticked off thirty days from the eighth and wrote NCIC on Monday, March the tenth. For her sake, I hoped we'd have an answer by then. As I lifted my head, a tear slipped through her lashes and trickled down the side of her nose.

"I'm sorry," she said. "I thought I'd do better than this."

"You have nothing to apologize for."

She folded her arms under her breasts, and her face crumpled as she bowed her head. "I'm just so scared."

I lowered my gaze to the calendar. A current of warm air flowed from the vent above our heads, and the plop of water from a leaky faucet echoed in the kitchen like a metronome. The sound seemed to grow, pressing against the air around us, pressing against my skull. Something clattered to the floor above our heads, and a woman shouted.

After a moment, Corey lifted her head, snatched a napkin off the table, and blew her nose. "You must wish you'd never agreed to do this." She looked me in the eye and took my hand in hers. "But please. Stay with it, for a little while, at least."

I cleared my throat. "I'm not going anywhere."

"It's so much to ask. I know that."

"It's okay, Corey," I said and thought of my own selfish reasons for agreeing to her request. My desire to get away from a job I'd outgrown, to try something new. Some people would consider that kind of flexibility an asset. Others, a character flaw.

Corey went home soon afterward. I threw the leftover pizza in the fridge, took a shower, and lay on Bruce's bed. I wondered if he was trying something new, and as I drifted off to sleep, I hoped that was all he was doing.

Chapter 4

As soon as I turned on the lights in barn six Friday morning, I knew something was up. My rounds took me to each foaling barn on an hourly rotation, and between visits, the horses had a chance to recover from the previous intrusion to their night. I often found them flat out in the straw or on their feet, dozing, and they'd invariably swivel their heads around and squint at me, annoyed. But this time, the mares were clear-eyed and alert. One or two by the door didn't even look my way but craned their necks and peered between the bars on their stall fronts. Something deeper in the barn held their attention.

The Cozzene mare.

I hurried down the aisle, then slowed as I approached the sixth stall on the left. The bay mare was on her feet, not flat out, straining to deliver her foal. But as I exhaled a lungful of air, I saw that she had entered the first stage of labor. Or at least I thought she had.

Patches of sweat darkened her bay coat to black, and water vapor rose from her flanks and the underside of her neck as she circled the stall. Her attention was directed inward, focused on her pain. I simply had to determine if that pain resulted from colic or labor. Both required a phone call, but to different people. Dr. Nash for colic. Maddie for foaling out. I glanced at my watch and saw that it was already five-forty-five. Maddie had gone home at three and had probably been asleep for an hour and a half.

The mare lowered her head and pawed the bedding, and as she shifted her hindquarters to the side, a thin stream of milk squirted from her udder.

I pulled out the phone and punched in Maddie's number.

"The Cozzene mare's foaling," I said when she picked up.

"Uh."

"Maddie?"

"What's she doing? Has her water broke?"

I slipped into the stall. When I touched the mare's hindquarters, she jerked her tail higher. "I don't think so." I described her behavior.

"I'll be right over."

"Want me to get some hot water and wash her down?"

"No. Stay there. I'll stop at the clinic on my way over."

The line went dead. I flipped the phone closed, hurried to the storage area at the end of the barn, and returned with a foaling kit. The mare across the aisle glanced at me, then went back to staring at the Cozzene mare. I wondered how she knew. What did her senses tell her? Could she smell the dam's milk? Or pheromones? Or was there some other form of communication going on that humans could only guess at? I didn't understand how anyone could miss one of the births. All you had to do was pay attention to the horses, and they'd tell you everything you needed to know.

I cracked the door to the stall, dragged a hay bale over to the opening, and sat down. Staying out of her direct line of sight seemed less intrusive. Yet, I was certain, on some level, the mare knew exactly where I was and that I was watching her. I lifted an index card and pencil out of the foal kit and wrote the date and time on the first line. Then I waited.

The barn was unusually quiet, and it dawned on me that the mares were being purposefully still so they could better hear what was going on. I leaned forward and propped my elbows on my knees. The mare's right hind leg, from stifle to hock, was visible through the crack, and as she stepped forward, I saw that a strip of hair on the inside of her opposite leg appeared sticky with liquid that I assumed was milk.

I looked down at the foaling kit. It was stocked with bottles of disinfectant and iodine, boxes of enemas, Vetrap bandages and thick rolls of cotton, a bundle of towels and a Ziploc bag stuffed with equipment used for bottle-feeding, and lastly, a twitch and a wicked-looking pair of scissors. As I scanned the contents, I ran through everything I'd learned in the past two nights and sighed. Here I was, preparing to foal out my first mare, a job that should have been Bruce's.

As dawn inched closer to the horizon, I sat there and wondered for the hundredth time where he was and what he was doing.

The mare's knees buckled, and she groaned as she lowered her bulk to the floor. I pushed off the hay bale. Pain tore through a muscle in my thigh, and though I couldn't remember my knee taking a direct hit when the truck had sideswiped me, it had been throbbing ever since I'd climbed out of bed at two o'clock. I checked the mare's position. She rested on her left side with her spine closest to the stall front and her hooves pointing toward the exterior wall. After working with racehorses over the summer, the massive swell of her belly, as she lay prone in the straw, amazed me. She flicked her tail, and the long black hairs swished against the oak boards that formed the stall wall, then tangled in the golden straw. I glanced at my watch.

The rumble of an approaching vehicle sounded against the front of the barn, followed by the squeak of brakes. A car door slammed and Maddie stepped into the doorway, carrying a steaming bucket of water in each hand. Behind her, the sky had lightened to a translucent blue.

She clomped down the aisle, wearing bulky work boots that she hadn't bothered to lace. She clattered the buckets onto the asphalt and peered into the stall. "Has her water broke yet?"

"Not unless it happened before I found her." I shifted so Maddie could get a better look. "Is she too close to the wall?"

"It's tight, but she'll probably get up and down a couple times before she's done. Anyway, if we have time, I need to show you how to do up her tail and wash her."

I nodded.

"You know how to braid hair?" When I didn't answer, she tore her gaze away from the mare, and her lips twitched when she noted my expression. "Guess not."

As she bent over and grabbed a cotton roll out of the kit, her long curls slipped forward over her shoulders. Her red hair had frizzed and was impossibly tousled from her pillow. Maddie tore six handfuls of cotton from the roll and dropped them into one of the buckets before squirting a glob of strong-smelling disinfectant into the water.

"First," Maddie said, "we do up her tail to keep it out of the way and to keep it from getting soaked in amniotic fluid and blood, then I'll show you how to wash her down." Maddie fished a pink Vetrap bandage out of the foal kit and broke it out of its package.

As she struggled to peel apart the end of the self-adhesive bandage, I said, "I prefer blue, myself."

She grinned, then stuck the free end in her mouth, unzipped her coat, and tossed it onto the hay bale. Her breasts jiggled as she rolled up the sleeves of a maroon pajama top with a flowery print and lace collar that touched her throat. Something my grandmother might have worn, but there was nothing grandmotherly in the way her nipples hardened in the cold air and pressed against the fabric. When she reached up and twisted her hair into a knot at the back of her neck, soft folds of cloth caught under her full breasts. The fabric separated between the third and fourth buttons, exposing a pink oval of flesh. And in each movement, in every little twist of her hand or flick of her wrist, her gaze never left mine.

I turned away and saw that the mare had lumbered to her feet.

Maddie slid the stall door open and stepped inside. She mumbled around the Vetrap dangling out of her mouth. "Okay.

Since you can't braid, just divide her tail into two sections and twist them around each other, then double them up like this."

I watched Maddie fold the mare's long black tail up around the tailbone. She twisted the hair this way and that, then expertly wrapped the resultant shaft in the pink bandage.

"What if I don't get their tails done up?" I said.

She shrugged. "No biggie. Even I don't get to it every time."

Maddie stepped into the aisle and stood over the stainless steel bucket containing the mass of saturated cotton. She squirted some antiseptic into her palm, scrubbed her hands, then bent from the waist and dunked them in the hot water. The vapor rose toward her face and coated her curls with a fine mist that glittered under the lights.

My gaze drifted to the cut of her jeans. The seam between her legs pressed high and tight into her flesh, and her shirttail had ridden up, exposing the small of her back. Goosebumps covered her pale skin. I turned away and focused on the mare. I was certain Maddie had chosen her clothes with care or, at the very least, recognized the impact they would have, and I wondered if she had any idea how dangerous her game could be.

I thought of another young woman, and the sadness that had lodged in my chest and weighted my limbs since her death churned through my blood and expanded in my skull until my head throbbed with it.

Maddie hefted the bucket and carried it into the stall. "Come on, Steve. This next part *is* important."

I jerked out of my thoughts and joined her. She showed me how to wash the mare under her tail; then she reached beneath the mare's wide belly and washed her udder. The sudsy water ran down Maddie's arms and streamed from her elbows and dampened the denim over her thigh. With each jab of her arm or swipe of her hand, her breasts bounced beneath the flowery pajamas, and I wondered how in the hell she expected me to remember anything. When she finished, we stepped into the aisle.

I sat on the hay bale. While Maddie dried her arms, I lifted the pair of stainless steel scissors out of the foal kit. "What are these for?"

Maddie dropped the towel onto the hay bale and took the scissors out of my hand. "You know what a Caslick's procedure is?"

"Sure. Lots of fillies at the track are sutured to cut down on uterine infections."

"Right. Same thing here. After a mare's bred and determined to be in foal, they stitch up the vulva, except for an inch or two at the bottom. It cuts down on contamination. Well, they're pretty good about remembering to take the stitches out before the mare foals, but sometimes one slips past them, and when that happens, you have to open her up with these." Maddie turned the scissors in her hands, and the overhead lights glinted off the steel.

I made a face.

"If you don't, she'll tear." Maddie lowered the scissors and noted my expression. "Don't worry, Steve. It probably won't happen, but if it does, it's not a big deal. You just cut upwards until you meet resistance."

"What about the mare? How's she going to stand that?"

"Wait until she's really straining, and she won't even feel it."

"Easy for you to say." I smoothed my hands down my thighs. "Don't be surprised if you get a phone call."

The corners of her mouth twitched as she gazed down at me. Her lips were full and moist, and her hazel eyes sparkled beneath thick red lashes.

The mare groaned as she sank to the floor once again, and the sound of spurting water emanated from the stall. The same sound water makes while disgorging an ice jam from a partially frozen hose. I stood and looked between the bars. Her water had broken, which meant she'd entered stage two. For some reason, I'd thought the process would take much longer. Okay, so maybe they could sneak past us and foal unobserved. I wrote down the time.

"Here we go," Maddie said as she picked up her denim coat.

I watched her slip it on with a twinge of regret.

"Better take yours off, Steve. Your turn to get dirty."

We crowded together in the open doorway, and Maddie whispered as she described what was happening, though I doubted the mare would have noticed if she'd shouted at the top of her lungs. Water vapor rolled off the mare's chest and flanks, and her lips were drawn back from yellowed teeth as she dealt with the pain. Her hind legs were stiff and rigid and jerked above the churned up straw as she bore down. Horses were such amazing, elegant creatures, yet I'd never seen one prone without being struck by their inherent vulnerability. They seemed deflated, somehow, and the dichotomy was unsettling.

A milky white sac swelled from under the mare's tail. After a few long minutes, when it ballooned to the size of a melon, a tiny hoof slid into view. I stepped around Maddie and moved farther down the aisle so I could get a better look. "Shouldn't there be two hooves?"

Maddie shook her head. "One precedes the other by about six inches, followed by the muzzle. That way, the foal's shoulders aren't lined up, so there's less mass for her to push through the birth canal at one time."

When the head had been delivered, Maddie told me to break the sac and peel it away from the foal's nostrils. I squatted at the mare's hindquarters and touched the gelatinous membrane with my fingertips. It was slippery as hell and surprisingly tough. I tore it after the third try, and a cloudy yellow liquid flowed into the straw. An unpleasant and wholly unidentifiable smell clogged the back of my throat.

"You'll get used to it," Maddie said as if she'd read my mind.

In the next ten minutes, the damp little creature had been delivered into the world.

We left them alone and sat side by side on the hay bale.

"I'll never get over the wonder of it," Maddie whispered, then nudged my arm. "So, what did you think?"

"It was more violent than I expected."

Maddie nodded. "That was my thought, too, first time I saw one born." She leaned forward and propped her elbows on her knees. "But think about it, Steve. They're awfully big. The foal weighs what? A hundred pounds? And they're leggy as hell. They're taller than that dog breed that's so huge."

"Irish Wolfhounds?"

"Yeah, I think that's it."

We sat there without speaking as an occasional vehicle drove past on Bear Wallow. I shifted to look over my shoulder, and my bruised thigh pressed against Maddie's. The mare in the stall behind us stood at attention, watching us watch the mare.

"It seems like the horses know what's going on," I whispered as I turned back around and broke the contact between our legs.

"Oh, they do."

"But how?"

Maddie shrugged. "Smells we aren't even aware of. Pheromones or fluid that's leaked from the birth canal. Plus, any of the mares who've foaled before know what they're here for." She leaned to her left so she could peer into the stall, and her shoulder touched mine. "The foal's kicked free of the umbilical cord."

Maddie spent the next fifteen minutes running me through a postpartum routine that incorporated an extensive list of procedures I'd never given thought to much less done, from dipping the foal's navel in iodine to clamping a metal tag in the foal's short black tail hairs.

"What's that for?"

"You'd never think it, but sometimes the mares and foals get mixed up." Maddie grasped the colt's forelegs and dragged him across the stall until he was beneath the mare's nose.

A deep whinny rumbled in her throat, and the foal responded with a high-pitched, clearly immature voice. Nearly half the mares in the barn whinnied in response. I spun around.

The mare across the aisle arched her neck and pricked her ears toward us. Even though the newborn and his dam were hidden from view as they lay in the straw, her wide gaze locked on the empty space above the wooden planks with an all-consuming passion.

"What's going on, Maddie?"

"This is the first foal barn six has had this season, and every single year that I've worked here, it's been the same. In each barn, the matron mares, the ones who've already had a foal or two, get excited when the first one arrives. You see, they know why they're here. They're waiting for their foals."

"You're kidding, right?"

"Uh-uh." Maddie slipped out of the stall, and I slid the door closed but left it unlatched. She jerked her head. "That Storm Bird mare down the aisle—"

"The chestnut with the wide blaze?"

"Yeah. She had a speck of wax on her teats when I came in at six. I wouldn't be surprised if she foals in the next day or two."

I looked down at Maddie. She'd grasped one of the bars that formed the upper portion of the stall front and hooked one boot behind the other. "Because of this?" I said, gesturing to the new foal lying in the straw.

Maddie nodded, then shifted her weight and pressed her forehead against the bars so she could peer down at the foal. "That happens all the time, too. It's like they can control it."

Footsteps scrunched on the asphalt to my left.

Paul Genoa's gait slowed as he caught sight of Maddie standing behind me, and I sensed more than saw her bunch her coat flaps together. But it was too late. Paul had seen her get-up and understood its significance all too clearly. He stopped.

"You slut," he said under his breath.

"Fuck you. I get woken up in the middle of the night, I'm not gonna go to a lot of trouble getting dressed, all right? Plus, this is Steve's first foal, and she was going quick, wasn't she, Steve?"

"Yeah, quick."

Paul stepped closer, and I felt my weight automatically shift to the balls of my feet. "Like you, huh, Maddie?"

"Oh, fuck you." She zipped up her coat and yanked her hair from beneath the collar. "You don't have a say in how I run my life." Maddie bent over and pulled two Fleet enema boxes out of the foal kit. She turned to me. "Steve, the water's gone cold. Go over to the clinic and get some more so I can show you how to give the foal his enemas."

I looked back at Paul. His gaze shifted from Maddie to me; then he shook his head and crossed to the far side of the aisle. He leaned against the stall front, hooked his thumbs in his pockets, and crossed his ankles.

"Go on, Steve. I want to get home," Maddie said.

I reached past her, latched the stall door, and picked up both buckets.

"You only need to bring one back," she said.

"All right." I glanced at them before heading to the truck.

Chapter 5

The clinic parking lot was crowded with the day crew's personal vehicles. Several windshields had received only a cursory swipe or two with an ice scraper, and I wondered how the drivers had made it to work without running off the road. I nosed the Stone Manor truck right up to the aisle doors and left it running. The Spyder was back in its slot by the office. Another sports car sat beside it. I considered the pedigree charts I'd seen on the name plaques tacked to each stall door, bloodlines even I recognized, and decided that Virginia's thoroughbred industry was alive and kicking. As I lifted the buckets out of the truck's bed, I scanned the lot. An old Chrysler with plastic where the back window should have been, a pickup pockmarked with rust splotches, a panel station wagon. Hell, they'd quit making them years before I was born. As usual, the lucre didn't trickle down to the help.

I detoured around my boss' Spyder so I could get a better look at the new car, a silver Dodge Viper. The sharp edge of the barn roof above my head reflected off the tinted windshield, and the sleek finish and curve of the hood absorbed the weak sunlight and looked like liquid mercury. Between the two vehicles, their combined sticker prices added up to more than I could hope to make in a decade. Make that two decades. As I turned toward the doorway, I pictured the car I'd given up when I'd left my parents' house, an MX-5 Miata, and the irony of my life settled on my shoulders like a grin. I'd lived in both worlds but felt at home in neither.

I squeezed between the open doors and almost bumped into a little girl as she skipped across the aisle in a pair of black patent leather shoes and white tights. A purple nylon parka reached the hem of her skirt, and she was holding a half-eaten chocolate éclair in her right hand. Her eyes widened, and her pink lips formed a silent "O" as she took in the stainless steel buckets in my hand. A smudge of icing marred her upper lip.

She tilted her head and looked up at me with impossibly big brown eyes. "You had a foal last night? Which barn?"

"Six."

She pursed her lips. "You're new. What's your name?"

"Steve."

She twirled around and raced down the aisle. Her dress shoes smacked the asphalt, and the sound vibrated across the Plexiglas. A tall blond man who'd been standing at the office door, engaged in conversation with Dr. Nash, turned his head and watched her run toward them.

"Mom! Mom! Barn six had a foal last night. Can I go see? Please?"

Dr. Nash pursed her lips exactly as her daughter had done; then she glanced at me and frowned.

The little girl bounced on her toes. "Please, Mom?"

A pink translucent backpack hung from her shoulders, and the notebooks and pencil case inside rattled against the stiff plastic, and a clutch of beaded animals jangled from the zipper pull. I caught up with them as the blond man shifted his amused gaze between mother and daughter. A white paper bag dangled from his hand, and I suspected the contents were the source of the delicious aroma of fresh-brewed coffee and pastries that hung in the air around them.

When Dr. Nash lifted her head and locked her gaze with mine, her expression had softened to something bordering on benign, except for an unspoken warning that shone in her gray eyes like white light reflecting off a knife's blade. Or, more appropriately, a scalpel. Her look seemed to imply what she would do with that scalpel if any misfortune befell her daughter.

"Is Maddie still there?" she asked casually.

"Yes, ma'am."

She sighed, then squatted so that her face was level with her daughter's. "All right." She wiped off the chocolate with the pad of her thumb, then kissed the little girl's cheek. "You have a good day, okay?"

"Okay, Mom."

"I love you."

"I love you, too."

Dr. Nash stood and automatically pressed her hands down the front of her hips, smoothing out nonexistent wrinkles. She'd ditched yesterday's leather duster and spike-heeled boots for a crisp navy coverall and tan Wolverines, yet I couldn't look at her without being conscious of an overpowering air of sophistication that hung around her like a shield.

"Please take Jenny over to see the foal, then have her back here by seven-thirty. She catches the bus at the entrance to the lot."

"Yes, ma'am," I said, and Dr. Nash thanked me as I turned toward the clinic door.

"Jenny. Wait for Steve in the office."

"Awh, Mom." Jenny watched me cross the aisle with a frown puckering the smooth skin between her brows.

As soon as I stepped through the doorway, I understood Dr. Nash's reasoning. As with any low-paying job, the crew consisted of men and women with varied and not necessarily desirable backgrounds. A few of the men, in particular, were a little rough around the edges. Sure, some of the employees worked the job because, like me, they loved working with horses, despite the low pay. Some because it was the only job they could get. And a few, because they'd simply fallen into it.

Michael Tiller had his backside propped against the counter-top in front of the sink as he blew across a Styrofoam cup. Two days' worth of stubble darkened his jaw, and his hair looked as greasy as ever. He wore a pair of wraparound sunglasses. Even though I couldn't see his eyes, the sudden rigidity in his muscles told me my presence hadn't gone unnoticed. His head moved fractionally as he tracked my progress across the room.

"Hey, man." Ronnie placed his hand on my shoulder as I moved alongside him. "We got a foal last night?"

I nodded but kept my gaze on Tiller.

"Which barn?"

"Six."

"Ah. The Cozzene mare?"

"Uh-huh."

"We was taking bets and…" Ronnie's voice dropped off, and his gaze left the side of my face as he caught sight of Tiller, "…look like I won."

"Good, Ronnie."

"This your first?"

I nodded.

"Yeah, uh, well, congratulations."

"Thanks." I stepped in front of Tiller. "Excuse me."

"Huh?" He glanced over his shoulder like he hadn't realized he was in the way. "Oh. You need the sink?" Tiller pushed off the edge of the counter, and as he straightened, he knocked his coffee cup against my arm. The hot liquid seeped into my sweatshirt and spread across my skin, soaking into my long underwear like kerosene through a wick.

"Oh, man. I'm sorry." Tiller set the cup down and snatched a roll of paper towels off the counter. "Geez." An oily grin slid across his mouth as he yanked a couple of towels off the roll. "I'm such a klutz."

When he reached out to blot my shirt, I grabbed his wrist. "Don't."

Tiller glanced toward the door, then held up his hands and backed off. "Hey, come on, man. I didn't mean it." His voice rose in a melodramatic whine, and I realized he was trying to set me up. "Really, I didn't. It was just an accident."

"Problem?" The stud manager stepped to my side.

"No, sir."

Frank Wissel stared at me for a second or two, looked at Tiller, then back at me. He put his hands on his hips, and as he lowered his head and sighed, he noticed the buckets. "Who foaled?"

I turned away from Tiller. "The Cozzene mare, sir."

"You finish up yet?"

"No, sir."

"All right. Hook up with the crew in barn five when you're done."

"Yes, sir."

Wissel fastened his gaze on Tiller, and although the younger man didn't move, his bravado drained away like the sea at low tide. "You have anything to say, Tiller?"

Tiller flicked his gaze my way, then shook his head.

"Well move outta the way, then."

Wissel's crooked teeth, weathered skin, and calloused hands spoke of decades of hard labor and poor pay. Both could presume a lack of intelligence if you hadn't taken the time to look him in the eye.

Tiller stepped aside, and as the stud manager moved off, I set one of the buckets in the sink. When I cranked open the faucet, Tiller reached around, dropped the paper towels into the stream of water, and whispered, "Asshole." His stale breath hit the side of my face and smelled of cigarettes.

The light that angled through the window muscled its way behind his lenses and allowed me to see the contempt simmering in his eyes. "I wonder what Dr. Nash would think if she knew you smoked?" I said.

"Kiss my ass."

He joined the rest of the crew as Wissel handed out assignments. Steam rose from the sink and coated the lower edge of the window. The warmth felt wonderful on my face but had nothing to do with the heat spreading across the back of my neck or the pulse hammering in my ears. Tiller undoubtedly fell into the second group of crewmembers, the ones who couldn't get another job, partly because he was stupid and partly because he couldn't play well with others.

I shut off the water and lifted the bucket out of the sink. As I reached the door, it swung inward on its hinges. Paul hesitated in the doorway before brushing past me.

As soon as I stepped into the aisle, Jenny emerged from the office and joined me.

"How long since the foal was born?"

I glanced at my watch. "Hmm. About thirty minutes."

"Good. It hasn't stood up, then."

"No, I don't think so."

She peered up at me and frowned as we stepped into the sunlight. "Well, of course it hasn't. They never stand this soon," she said, and her tone clearly implied that I didn't know much. And as far as foaling was concerned, she wasn't far off. "What sex is it?"

I set the bucket in the bed and opened the Ford's passenger door. "A colt."

Jenny cocked her head and considered my answer with a healthy dose of skepticism before she stretched on tiptoe and brushed the roof handle with her fingertips. She gave it another go and this time latched onto the handle with both hands. She planted her left shoe on the running board and grunted as she pulled with all her might, but her foot slid out from under her. She lost her grip and dropped to the ground. The notebooks and pencil case rattled in her backpack, and the beaded animals jingled. She tried again with the right patent leather wedged on the running board while I stood awkwardly behind her with my hands bracing the air, ready to catch her if she fell but not comfortable enough to give her a boost. Not with the image of a well-honed scalpel hovering in the back of my mind. Jenny clambered onto the vinyl seat, and I breathed a sigh of relief.

When I slid behind the wheel, she'd already latched the seat belt across her waist. I shifted into reverse, and as I twisted around and rested my arm on the backrest, movement in the office window caught my eye. Dr. Nash stood behind the frost-edged glass, watching. I backed away from the building and swung the pickup into an empty space. She was still standing there when I jammed the gearshift into drive and turned toward the road.

Jenny bumped her calves on the front edge of her seat, and her feet dangled in space. "What color's the foal? Does it have any white?"

"A star, thin stripe, and a snip," I said. "As for the color, I'm not sure."

"Yeah. It's hard to tell when they're still wet. And lots of them change color when they shed out, you know? Especially if they're going to be gray."

I pulled into the curve around the lake's high bank, then turned into barn six's drive.

"Mom and Dad don't like grays, but it's my favorite color. They think they're too much work to keep clean."

"Hmm."

"You're not listening."

I glanced down at her as I pulled alongside Maddie's car. She studied me with those serious brown eyes of hers, and the effort creased the smooth skin between her eyebrows. They were as pale as her lashes and matched the color of her hair, a blend of red and blond that no doubt had a fancy name. "Yes, I am."

She shook her head. "No, you're not. When adults say 'hmm,' they're pretending that they're listening when they really aren't. They're thinking about work or bills or what they're going to make for dinner."

"Really?"

"Yep." She released her seat belt and wrestled with the door latch.

"Here, I'll get that." I walked around the hood, but she'd already slid to the ground. She pressed both hands on the door and shoved until it clicked shut. She'd splayed her fingers on the pickup's salt-spattered finish, and each tiny pink fingernail had pressed into the gritty film that coated the truck. When she dropped her arms and left behind smudges in the grime, I sighed.

"What?" Jenny said.

"Nothing."

"And when adults say 'nothing,' what they really mean is that they don't feel like telling you what they're thinking, or they think you won't understand if they did."

I frowned at her as she turned and strode toward the barn with her reddish blond curls bouncing in the sunlight. How old was this kid, anyway?

I grabbed the bucket of hot water and caught up with her in the doorway. Maddie was sitting on the hay bale with her legs stretched out in front of her and one ankle hooked over the other. Her shoulders and head rested against the stall front, and for a second, I thought she'd dozed off, but she turned her head when she heard Jenny's voice.

"Did you see the fire the other night?" Jenny asked me.

"Uh-huh. Did you?"

"Yep. The sirens woke me up. This is the third one, you know?"

"So I've heard."

"They make me nervous, especially now that my ponies are in barn ten instead of the bank barn."

"Barn ten?"

"Yeah, one of the training barns. I wish you guys checked those barns at night like you used to check the bank barn."

"We never checked the bank barn," Maddie said as she sat up and reached for the foal kit.

"Bruce did." Jenny grabbed the stall latch with both hands.

I looked at Maddie, raised my eyebrows, and gestured toward the little girl. "Can she go in there?"

Maddie rolled her eyes. "Sure. Mom lets her do whatever she wants." She tore open one of the Fleet boxes, and as she dropped the enema bottle into the hot water, she caught my eye and mouthed, "Spoiled brat."

Jenny worked the latch, and when she squeezed through the gap, I pushed the door farther along its track so I'd be in position to react if something went wrong. The mare simply looked at the little girl as if Jenny's presence in her stall was an everyday occurrence. She lowered her head and nosed a flake of hay. Since I'd left, she'd risen to her feet, and I was struck by the swell of her belly. Its profile hadn't changed as I'd expected. Straw clung to wide patches of sweat-soaked hair that spoiled her sleek winter coat, and the semi-translucent mass of afterbirth still hung between her legs.

"What am I supposed to do about the afterbirth?" I asked Maddie.

Jenny stepped cautiously toward the foal and said, "You have to get baling twine and tie it up so she doesn't step on it." I glanced over my shoulder and caught Maddie looking toward the rafters, shaking her head. "Then, when it comes all the way out, Mom has to check it to make sure the mare's healthy, so you need to get it out of the stall right away." Jenny crouched down, stretched out her arm, and placed one small hand on the foal's rump. He jerked his head at the strange stimulus. "Sometimes the mares eat it." She looked over her shoulder at me. "Did you know that?"

I shook my head.

Jenny crinkled her nose. "It's disgusting."

Maddie's voice drifted in from the aisle. "Maybe Jenny oughta be training you, Steve."

Jenny scowled at the empty doorway, then turned back to the foal.

Despite Maddie's comment, she hustled through the rest of the procedures. "After you drop little Miss Jenny off, muck out the stall a section at a time, and bed it down as you go."

"Is there a wheelbarrow I should use?" I asked since the tractors and wagons were in barns one and five.

"No. Just pile the old bedding in the aisle. The day crew will clean it up. Hey," Maddie said through a yawn, "what was the number on the tail tag?"

"Three two seven."

She scribbled on the index card and slipped it behind the stall's ID plaque. "Well, Steve. Congratulations. You're catching on quick. I don't see any reason for you to come in for training anymore."

"Thanks."

"I'm going home. Don't forget, though. I'm off tomorrow, so you need to be here at midnight."

"Right."

"If the colt doesn't nurse in an hour, get Dawn in barn five to give you a hand since our expert here will be in kindergarten by then."

"Huh." Jenny's voice drifted from the stall. "Third grade, you mean."

Maddie sighed as she smoothed the bangs off her forehead. She stepped closer and lowered her voice. "Next time, do yourself a favor and don't bring the kid."

I watched her walk down the aisle. Her bootlaces flicked languidly through the air and snapped the asphalt with a soft clicking noise that sounded like mice scurrying over concrete. It seemed that Maddie's energy had plummeted as quickly as the day had brightened. Maybe *she* was a vampire. I grinned as I checked the time. "Jenny, we gotta go."

"Already?" A little whine. She stepped out of the stall.

"'Fraid so." I slipped on my coat and latched the door behind her.

As we headed for the truck, she said, "Do you think they'll catch whoever's setting the fires?"

"I hope so."

"Me, too." She waited while I opened the passenger door; then she tilted her head back and peered into my face. "Could you check my ponies at night? They're in barn ten."

This time, I put my hands around her waist and hoisted her onto the seat. "Barn ten's not on my route, Jenny, but I'll ask your mom."

"Ask Dad, instead. He's in charge of the training operation."

"I guess I'll have to ask both of them, then, won't I?"

"I suppose."

As I spun the truck around and headed for the clinic, I felt her staring at me. "What?"

"Do you like Maddie?"

"Uh, she's okay."

"I don't. I think she's mean."

I glanced at her. "Any reason in particular?"

"Uh-uh."

"What about Bruce? Did you like him?"

Jenny nodded. "He was real nice. He never talked down to me, like some people."

"Maddie, for instance?"

"Yeah, Maddie." She flexed her feet and pointed her toes toward the cab's ceiling. "Mom likes her, though. Mom says she knows her job real well. She must like you, too."

"Who? Your mom?" I said, thinking I'd misunderstood.

Jenny nodded, and the butterfly barrette that pinned back a section of her fine curls slid down a notch. "If she didn't, she wouldn't have let me go with you."

I thought about that for a moment. "Did she let you go with Bruce?"

"No. He didn't have any foals."

I nodded. "Do you know why Bruce left?"

"He just quit, is all I know. Dad was real mad, though."

"Do you know why?"

"Uh-uh. Except he said it was 'rotten bad luck.'"

I nosed the Ford up to the clinic doors. "'Bad luck,' huh?"

"Yep. Dad's always complaining about the crew. He says it's impossible to find good help these days, people who aren't afraid of a little hard work. Lots of them get bored and quit. Or he has to fire them. When I have a farm like this, I'll pay the good ones thousands of dollars, and then they'll stay."

"Was he talking to you when he said it was 'rotten bad luck'?"

"Not me." Jenny frowned. "Maddie, I think. Or Mr. Shane."

"Who's he?"

"You already met him. He brought the éclairs. He always brings something, but they're my favorite." She swiveled around on the seat and pointed to the Viper. "And he has the coolest car."

Since the crew had dispersed, I had Jenny wash her hands in the clinic. After she caught her bus, I rinsed and dried the stainless steel buckets. When I opened the cabinet door and crouched down to stow them under the sink, a stack of hand towels tipped over and fell to the floor. I rearranged them and pushed a long cylinder-shaped object to the side as I slipped the towels farther back into the cabinet. I frowned, then picked up the cylinder and turned it in my hands. A leather sleeve covered the central portion of the cylinder and included two leather grips. One end of the cylinder was made of hard plastic, and the other end was fitted with a large dome-shaped rubber cap. It measured about sixteen inches from end to end and reminded me of an oversized thermos. I looked up when the door opened.

Frank Wissel, the stud manager, crossed the room with a clipboard tucked under his arm. He glanced in my direction and paused. "What are you doing, Cline?"

"Cleaning up, sir." I held up the cylinder. "What's this?"

"Put it back and go check on that foal. Has he nursed yet?"

"No, sir."

"Well, go see that he does, and if you need help, ask one of the girls in five to give you a hand. Did Maddie tell you we like to see them nurse within the first two hours? Three at the latest?"

"Yes, sir. She did."

He nodded. "Get busy, then."

I put the buckets away and headed for the truck. When I stepped outside, Mr. Shane, the blond guy who'd brought the pastries and coffee, was standing on the sidewalk in front of his silver Viper, talking to Elaine Daniels, Stone Manor's receptionist. She worked in the office, the outer office, really, as Dr. Nash had the back room to herself. Tuesday morning, Elaine had given me an application to fill out. Only three days ago. Apparently, they'd been desperate to find a replacement for Bruce or, more likely, to get Ronnie off nightshift. As far as I knew, they hadn't bothered checking my references, either. I nodded to them as I walked around the pickup's hood.

"Hey, hold up." I paused, and the blond guy jerked his head for me to join them. "Shane Hadley." He held out his hand, and I shook it.

"Steve Cline." I glanced at Elaine and caught her gazing at Hadley. She must have grabbed her purse and slung her coat over her arm, anticipating a quick walk into the barn before she'd bumped into him. A gust of wind pressed her wool skirt hard against her thigh and lifted the flap of her tweed jacket, but judging from her expression, she wasn't feeling the cold.

Hadley reached into his pocket and withdrew a pack of Marlboro 100's and a gold lighter. "Elaine tells me you foal out along with Ms. O'Connell," he said, referring to Maddie.

"That's right."

As he tapped a cigarette out of the pack, the morning sunlight glinted off the cellophane and the edge of a ring on his right hand. He lit up and inhaled deeply before letting the smoke trickle from his nostrils. Hadley snapped the lighter closed and slipped it back in his pocket. His khaki jacket and pressed jeans were immaculate, and I imagined the most use he'd ever gotten out of his expensive leather work boots was depressing the Viper's clutch. They sure as hell hadn't seen the inside of a stall.

"I have a mare in barn two, Steve. Sumthingelse out of Summing. She isn't due to foal until the first week in March, but she's lost her last four foals because of detached placentas. I talked to Deirdre…Dr. Nash about it, and she'll want you or Ms. O'Connell to call her when the mare goes into labor."

I nodded.

Hadley slipped his wallet out of his back pocket, withdrew two business cards, and handed them to me. "I'd like to be notified, as well. Would you mind giving a card to Ms. O'Connell for me?"

"Sure. No problem."

He squinted at me through the smoke. "How long have you foaled out?"

"This morning's delivery was my first."

He'd been pulling on his cigarette, and the smoke seemed to catch in his throat. He swallowed. "Well, then, I expect you'll be getting some special instructions before long. As I recall, they kept an oxygen tank and emergency drugs in the barn when they thought she was getting close. Not that you'd be using them. They were there for Dr. Nash, I believe." He glanced at Elaine. "My point is, Steve, I'd just like you to pay a little extra attention to her for me. She's in foal to Elusive Quality this year, and I'll be damned if I'm going to lose that foal."

"I'll keep my eyes open," I said. "But you won't be relying strictly on my abilities, sir. Ms. O'Connell works the earlier shift and seems adept at predicting how close the mares are to foaling. I'm sure she'll give me a heads-up if she suspects anything. And Dr. Nash, of course."

Hadley grinned suddenly and clapped his hand on my shoulder. "You're in the wrong line of work. Management or sales. You'd be good at either. So, what are you wasting your time here for?"

"I'm doing what I like...while I have the chance."

Hadley had two dimples in his right cheek and the whitest, straightest teeth I've ever seen, and when he smiled, the network of lines that radiated outward from the corners of his eyes deepened. His smile faded as he contemplated my answer, and I was struck by the transformation.

He nodded. "Smart."

"If you don't mind, sir, I have to check on that foal."

"Of course."

I nodded to Elaine, then headed back to barn six and my first ever attempt at getting a newborn to nurse.

Chapter 6

I collected Bruce's mail and let myself into his apartment. After spending the better part of the last ten hours outside, it felt good to be out of the cold. As I draped my jacket on the coat rack, I noticed the blood that had dried under my fingernails and worked into the creases where my skin was chapped. The sleeves of my sweatshirt were streaked with blood and amniotic fluid and urine and smelled wholly unpleasant. I stripped, used Bruce's shower, and after I toweled off, I felt like crawling into bed.

Although I hadn't slept well the night before, after Corey had gone home, I had a feeling I wouldn't have any difficulty now. It was lunchtime on a Friday afternoon, and the apartment complex was as quiet as a ghost town. On Wednesday, my first day on the job, I'd commuted the seventy-eight miles between Columbia and Warrenton, then driven back Thursday morning, and the hours were catching up with me. But I had work to do. A thorough search of the apartment, for one thing.

I pulled on a T-shirt and jeans that smelled of laundry soap instead of a horse's bodily fluids and snatched the bedroom phone off the nightstand. With luck, I'd catch Rachel at her desk.

"Hey, it's me," I said when she answered.

"Hey, you." A smile sounded in her voice. "Where are you calling from?"

"Bruce's apartment."

"You're off work already?"

"Yep." I flopped back on the bed. "I get off at noon."

"Lucky you. What's it like?"

"The job or his apartment?"

"Both."

"I delivered a foal this morning."

"You're kidding me? I can't believe it."

"Yeah, well. It was bound to happen one of these days."

"I am so envious. A colt or filly?"

"A colt."

"You're only on the job for three nights, and you have a foal? Man. I helped a friend of mine with foal watch on her mare for two and a half weeks, and you know what?"

"What?"

"We both missed it."

I chuckled. "Well, that's to be expected with amateurs."

"Excuse me?" Rachel's voice squeaked. "You'll pay for that, boy."

"I bet I will. Anyway, I have a feeling I'll be delivering a couple more before I'm through. They've got a ton of horses here. A hundred and twenty are housed in the primary barns."

"Meaning?"

"Meaning their due dates are anywhere from a day to four weeks out."

"Wow."

"Yeah. I expect I'll be busy." I described the birth and how odd it had felt to be right with the mare while she was down in the straw. "It puts it in perspective, how much pain she was in."

"Hmm." Rachel was quiet for a moment, and I wondered what she was thinking. "What are the people like?"

"Your typical farm crew. Just like at Foxdale. Hey, can you come down this weekend?"

"I've got that clinic, remember?"

"At Hidden Hollow?"

"Yeah, and I won't be back 'til late Sunday because my last ride's at four-thirty."

"What about Monday? I can drive up, and we can go to—"

"I have my Applications class, remember?"

"Oh, yeah." Rachel had started a night course at UMBC, and I hadn't gotten used to her schedule. "How about Tuesday? We can go to the lake."

"That would be nice." Papers rustled, and the talking that I'd heard in the background grew louder. "Look," Rachel said, "I gotta go. Meet me at Foxdale?"

"What time?"

"Is six-thirty okay?"

"Great." I hesitated. "I miss you."

"You, too," she said, then disconnected.

Rachel hated taking personal calls at work. As I grabbed the leftover pizza and a Miller Lite out of the fridge, I convinced myself that that was the only reason her response had been less than I'd hoped for.

I parked my lunch on the coffee table in the living room and checked the selection in Bruce's CD player—Staind, Puddle of Mud, Three Doors Down. I hit PLAY, cranked the volume way up, then thought better of it. At home, my only neighbors within shouting distance were the horses downstairs, and they never complained. As I lowered the volume, I noticed a wooden crate wedged between the recliner and television. I dragged it out and sat on the sofa. While I ate, I flipped through a seemingly endless variety of car magazines, several outdated issues of *TV Guide*, a few copies of *Men's Health*, and a skin magazine or two. I resisted the urge to study them in detail and, instead, turned my attention to a notepad lodged between a *Popular Mechanics* and *Car and Driver* magazine.

The top page was blank. I fanned through the rest of the pages and found nothing, but when I held the pad at eyelevel, the afternoon sunlight that slanted through the sliding doors highlighted scratches in the top sheet. With growing anticipation, I grabbed a pencil off the kitchen counter, flattened the lead on the first line, and feathered the graphite over the indentations.

Bruce had listed information down the left margin: *wax, raised tail, cramping, water breaks (write time on index card)*. I finished drawing out the rest of the words without any hope of moving closer to the truth of his disappearance. I tossed the pencil on the counter. Bruce had simply taken notes on the foaling-out procedure. Probably when Maddie had trained him.

"Goddamn it, Bruce. Where the hell are you?" I tilted my head back and closed my eyes. You should have been the one with your hands clamped around that colt's slippery cannon bones this morning. Helping him find his mother's teats. Coming home tired, with your clothes stinking of urine and blood.

You should have been the one to see him take his first breath in this world.

I spent the next two hours searching Bruce's living room. I opened every CD and DVD; then I rifled through his videos. My pace slowed to a crawl when I reached an impressive stack of triple X-rated flicks. I sat cross-legged on the floor and flipped through them. At least I didn't have to worry that Bruce had been a victim of gay-bashing. His running afoul of a jealous husband seemed much more likely. I pictured Maddie's breasts straining her flannel top. Or a jealous boyfriend.

I looked under the furniture cushions and flipped through every magazine and book before turning my attention to his computer. I started by opening the My Documents folder and thought it a bad sign when I found it empty. What was worse, he didn't appear to have e-mail. A more extensive search pointed to Bruce's primary reason for owning a computer in the first place. The Program folders were crammed with an outstanding array of recently released games, and that impression was supported by the assorted joysticks, steering wheel, and controllers dumped in a plastic container on the floor. Maybe Corey would find something useful. I switched off the computer, and as I scanned the room, my gaze fell upon Bruce's Ravens windbreaker. I went through the pockets. Change, a few crumpled bills, gum wrappers, a matchbook. I flipped it over. Sullivan's Bar & Grill was embossed in gold script on a white background. I slipped it into my jeans pocket.

I retrieved the pizza box and beer can and opened the door under the kitchen sink. The trashcan wasn't full, exactly, but it stank. I grabbed another garbage bag out of the linen closet and used a fork to sift through Bruce's trash as I transferred it into the plastic bag. I'd hoped for a significant piece of mail or a discarded love letter. Hell, even a receipt would have been nice, but unless a clue was hidden among the coffee grounds, eggshells, and beer cans, I needn't have bothered. I emptied the trashcan in the bathroom, then decided to go through the fridge before I took the bag out to the Dumpster.

Bruce's and my eating habits held much in common, running along the lines of pizza, soda, beer. More pizza. The date on the egg carton was a week old, but I figured they'd be okay for a day or two longer. I did throw away a Tupperware container full of spaghetti because I had a sneaky suspicion that the colorful blotches visible through the lid weren't chunks of green pepper. I poured the milk into the sink, tossed a bag of lunchmeat but kept the sliced cheese. As for the Chinese takeout cartons crammed toward the back of the top shelf, I dropped them unopened into the trash before grabbing Bruce's picture off the dining room table. I slipped his Ravens windbreaker over my sweatshirt and headed for Sullivan's Bar & Grill.

Although it wasn't quite five in the afternoon, half of the booths were occupied, and a haze of cigarette smoke hung near the ceiling like a cloudbank. Like most establishments in the historic part of town, the room was long and narrow. Toward the rear, an antique horseshoe-shaped bar jutted from the back wall. Rope lighting outlined the bar's contours as well as the overhead track that displayed the stemware. The tiny white lights strung along the upper level reflected off the polished floor. As I crossed the room, my sneakers squeaked on the wide wooden planks. I slid onto a stool and propped my feet on a brass railing that rimmed the lower edge of the bar. A matching railing encircled the countertop itself. It must have been hell to clean, but like everything else in the room, it glistened under the lights. The barkeep, a heavy, balding man with sideburns the color and texture of steel wool, walked toward me, smoothing a white cotton cloth along the walnut countertop.

He shifted a toothpick from one side of his mouth to the other. "What'll it be?"

"You got a menu?"

He nodded, leaned to the side, and produced a menu from under the counter with a flourish. He placed it squarely in front of me.

I scanned the entrée selection. "What's good?"

"Everything's good, but we're known for our fried chicken strips. Lightly breaded, spicy, tender."

"Sounds good."

"It do, don't it?" He replaced the menu and absentmindedly swiped the cloth over the polished wood. "Want fries with that?"

"Sure. What've you got on tap?"

"Heineken, Miller, Pabst."

"I'll take a Heineken, then."

He nodded, and his gaze briefly settled on the Ravens' logo before he ambled toward the kitchen door at the far end of the bar. His gait had an odd, rolling quality to it, as if one leg were shorter than the other, but the effect could have been the result of his habit of keeping that bar towel planted on the countertop. I swiveled back around on my stool. Two women in a booth across the room quickly turned their heads, and I realized they'd been watching us.

A minute later, the barkeep returned, centered a cocktail napkin in front of me, and placed the Heineken in the exact center of the square. I watched him cross to the other side of the bar, wondering if his compulsions ever intimidated the customers. I swallowed a mouthful of beer, wiped the froth off my upper lip with the back of my hand, and relaxed onto the stool with a sigh. The room was filling up, mostly with professional types, but four guys in a corner booth were laborers of some sort. Based on their mud-caked boots and grimy jeans, I assumed they worked construction or on a farm.

The service was efficient, and after a waitress brought my food and handed me a set of silverware rolled in a napkin, the barkeep returned. "Want a refill?"

"Sure."

He smoothed his towel across the wood, and as I watched him head toward the taps, I wondered if he didn't repeat that move over and over in his sleep.

When he came back and peeled a fresh cocktail napkin off a pile stacked next to a half-full bowl of pretzel sticks, I said, "Hey, a buddy of mine comes in here, and I wonder if you've seen him lately?"

He narrowed his eyes as if he'd just tasted something sour, and I sensed more than saw the muscles along his spine tense. He focused on placing the new drink next to the old before he swiped the towel across his edge of the bar. He'd probably been lied to more times than he cared to remember and naturally distrusted people fishing for information.

"We both went to College Park," I said, and when his gaze flicked back to the Ravens' logo, he seemed to relax. "His name's Bruce. Preppy-looking guy. Short brown hair. Built like a football player. You know who I mean?"

"Works on a horse farm?"

"Yeah, that's him."

"Some of the guys who work at Stone Manor come in from time to time, but I ain't seen him for a couple weeks."

I needed to keep him talking, and the best way to do that was to pretend I knew more than I did. "Really? A couple weeks?" I frowned. "Didn't he come in here Monday night with a skinny black kid, got his hair done up in blond dreadlocks?"

"Nope. Ain't nobody like that come in here. Last time I saw your buddy, he was with a big blond man, got a ponytail halfway down his back."

"You know his name?" The women across the room, one blond one brunette, watched openly now.

"Nope. Haven't seen him before or since. Bruce and him sat in that corner booth back there," he pointed over my right shoulder, "couple hours at least, all through my busy time. We were packed that night, so it must've been a Friday or Saturday. Then, after your buddy left, some other guys came in and joined Ponytail. Didn't leave 'til closing time."

"You know those guys?"

"Never seen them before or since, either. Why you looking for him, anyway?"

"He owes me money." I looked up from my drink and grinned. "We're friends and all, but money's money."

He snorted. "Sounds like him."

I picked up the fresh beer and took a swallow as he drifted off to serve another customer. *A couple weeks.* Bruce had quit his job and disappeared off the face of the earth two weeks ago.

On the drive back to the apartment, I contemplated what little the barkeep had given me. Bruce had been there on a Friday or Saturday night. If he'd been there Saturday, he'd come in the day he quit. Saturdays had been his long days. And now, they were mine. I glanced at the clock on the dash. I needed to switch off with Maddie at midnight, work until the day crew came in at seven, then be back in time for rounds at six. But what I really needed was a lead on Ponytail.

◇◇◇

When the alarm blasted me out of a dead sleep, I bolted upright and slammed my palm on the snooze button. In waking, I was intensely aware of the unfamiliar smell of the dark room, of the feel of bed sheets that weren't mine, of the heavy comforter that had slid down to my waist. The memory of where I was, and why I was getting up at eleven-thirty in the middle of the goddamn night, kicked in like a toggle switch being flipped. I groaned and flopped back on the mattress.

Four hours' sleep before my long day.

I didn't bother with a shower. If I was going to get drenched in amniotic fluid and horse urine, what was the point? When I got to Stone Manor just before midnight, every single barn was lit up. A flutter of anxiety churned through my stomach before I realized that the lights were most likely controlled by timers. Greg, my landlord, did the same thing. Extending the perceived daylight hours brought the mares into estrus earlier than nature intended, and in the thoroughbred industry, the earlier in the calendar year a foal is delivered into this world the better. Each month of growth and development he gained over his contemporaries would work to his advantage. He'd be just a little stronger, just a bit more coordinated, and with luck, faster than his stablemates. I punched my timecard, picked up the keys to one of the farm trucks, and went in search of Maddie.

A plume of exhaust drifted from a Stone Manor truck that idled by the doors to barn six. I pulled into the drive and spotted Paul Genoa's car parked on the grass. I left the engine running and approached the doorway, mildly annoyed.

My annoyance shifted to concern when Maddie's shrill voice cut through the still air. "I am not!"

I strode into the barn.

"And even if I was," she yelled, "it's none of your damn business."

They were midway down the aisle, and Paul had his left hand clamped around Maddie's elbow. "Come on, honey. Don't do this to me. You're my—"

"Don't you get it?" Maddie shrieked and yanked her arm free. "I'm not your anything."

Paul latched onto her arms, and she pulled back.

"Let her go, Paul," I said, and their heads whipped around at the sound of my voice. I walked calmly toward them.

Maddie wiggled out of his grasp and stepped sideways toward me while keeping her focus on Paul.

He raised his hand and pointed a shaky finger at her face. "You'll be sorry, girl. No one will ever love you the way I do."

"Let's hope not."

Paul clenched his fists and stepped toward her. I quickly moved between them, and it was as if the three of us were engaged in a grotesque dance, with Paul moving to my left and

Maddie ducking behind my back, while I tried to keep them separated without touching either one of them. I had a feeling that physical contact on my part would tip him over the edge. He glared at Maddie over my shoulder.

"You're a bitch, Maddie." Spittle shot from his mouth along with a healthy dose of alcoholic fumes. "You know that? A stinking little bitch." His voice cracked. "I give you everything you could possibly want, and this is what I get in return."

Paul cranked his gaze around to my face as if his movements were controlled by a faulty gear. "You stay away from her, Cline. You hear me?"

"Yeah, Paul. I hear you." I exhaled through my nose.

He looked back at Maddie, and his face crumpled. "Please… come home with me. I love you, Maddie. You know that."

I had the distinct impression he'd be weeping if he hung around much longer.

Maddie sighed. "Go home, Paul."

He leveled his gaze on me, like it was my fault he was being asked to leave. It took him a second or two of concentrated effort, but he eventually turned and walked toward the exit. We listened to his car start up, crunch through the gravel, and bump down the drive toward the main road.

Maddie rubbed her arm.

"Did he hurt you?"

She bit her lip, and when she shook her head, I realized her curls had worked free from the clip she'd used to gather them off her neck. It dangled halfway down the back of her head. I stepped closer, and when I reached around her, she became very still. I fumbled with the spring, feeling her warm breath on my throat. A stream of images ran through my mind. Her nipples pressing against those pajamas, the soapsuds dripping off her elbow, the seam of her jeans digging into her flesh.

I rotated the clip, and the last of her silky curls slipped from between the teeth. I held it out to her. "Here you go." My voice felt clogged.

Her warm fingers covered mine as she pressed them around the plastic. Without lifting her head, Maddie slowly raised her eyes and looked at me through her lashes. Her lips were parted, and on the edge of my field of vision, I could see her coat move as her breasts rose and fell with each breath she took.

She licked her lips.

I stepped back a pace. "Uh…" I cleared my throat, "do you know who Mr. Hadley is?"

"What?"

I shifted my weight from one foot to the other. "Mr. Hadley. He owns Sumthingelse in barn two."

Maddie crossed her arms under her breasts and frowned at me like I'd gone mad. The look in her eyes had left little doubt that a passionate romp in the haymow wasn't entirely out of the question, and I imagined she would have been damned good at it.

"Yeah, I know him. So what?"

I slipped my wallet out of my back pocket and handed Hadley's business card to her while I relayed his concerns.

"That mare isn't due for three weeks."

"He said two."

She rolled her eyes and flicked the air with his card. "Two, three. Doesn't make any difference because she isn't showing any signs that she's getting close. When her tail head and vulva begin to soften, then you can start worrying." She smoothed her hand down her ass as she slid Hadley's card into a back pocket. "Come on. Drive me over there, and we'll look at her together."

Maddie spun around. I glanced at the Cozzene foal, then followed her down the aisle. For the most part, I managed to keep my gaze off her ass, until she yanked open the passenger door to the truck I'd been driving and climbed inside.

I got the Ford turned around, and as we neared Stone Manor Lane, a car passed the mouth of the drive.

"Paul," Maddie whispered.

"You sure?"

"Yes."

I eased up on the gas, and we watched him pull onto Bear Wallow. "What's he doing?"

She exhaled sharply. "He's always like this. That's why I dumped him."

"You broke up with him tonight?"

She shook her head in the dark. "No. New Year's Eve, as a matter of fact. Thought I ought to start the year off right."

"Maddie. It's the middle of February. The way he talks, you'd think the two of you are still together."

"Yeah," she said. "He's a little slow on the uptake."

Only when we turned onto barn two's drive did it dawn on me that the barns were dark. The timers had switched off. But because of the full moon and a hard frost that covered the earth like a blanket, we could see clear across the fields, all the way to the Blue Ridge Mountains. The boundary between mountain and sky was a clear sharp line that crawled across the horizon. I switched off the headlights as I approached the barn, parked, and turned off the engine.

"I do that, too," Maddie whispered. "It disturbs them less."

She'd turned in her seat to face me, and I imagined what it would be like to stretch over the cold vinyl and kiss her warm mouth. I climbed out and could have sworn she sighed as I clicked the door shut. We checked Sumthingelse, and Maddie was right.

She palpated the mare's hindquarters, lifted her tail, then stepped to the mare's side and peered under her belly. "Look. Her bag's not even big enough. She foals now, she won't have any milk."

"Okay, Maddie. I get it."

Maddie closed the stall door and leaned forward to study the index card wedged behind the plaque, and I didn't even look at her ass. "See. Her due date's March six. That's more like three weeks."

"Okay. Good."

She needed to return the farm truck to the clinic lot for the morning crew, so I drove her back to barn six. On the short drive, she explained what they did when faced with a detached placenta, but I was only half-listening. My attention was on a vehicle moving slowly down Bear Wallow. She noticed it, too.

"Paul?" I said.

"God knows. He's probably timing us, seeing how long we spend in each barn."

Shit.

Maddie handed me the farm's cell phone, and even though it probably wasn't necessary, I followed her back to the clinic when she punched out. I watched after her until her taillights disappeared over a rise as she headed for Warrenton.

Thanks to Maddie's boyfriend troubles, my first round kicked off thirty minutes behind schedule and now included the training barns per written instructions left clipped to my timecard. From now on, I'd be checking barns nine, ten, and eleven once a night. *Once* had been discreetly underlined. Somehow, I suspected one check in a twelve-hour period wasn't going to placate Jenny for long. By one-fifteen, I'd checked every horse on the farm, and none of them had anything on their minds but sleep. However, the mares in barn one were out of luck since their stalls were scheduled for cleaning between rounds.

I spaced straw bales down the aisle, then fired up a flashy new John Deere 5220 that was parked in the storage area. I centered the muck wagon between the first set of stalls and was raking a clump of soiled straw into a pile when I heard the heavy rumbling throb of a diesel engine in the distance. What caught my attention was the fact that it was idling. I walked down the aisle and paused in the doorway. What the hell? A tractor-trailer had pulled up to the old bank barn behind the mansion. A horse van, I presumed, but why had the driver gone there? I double-checked that I'd latched the stall door; then I hopped in the Ford and turned into the Nashes' driveway. It wound past their house and a detached four-car garage and ended in a lot alongside the bank barn. Light blazed from windows on the lower level and streamed through the wide doorway that accessed the bowels of the barn.

The side of the trailer was snugged up against a chute used for offloading livestock. As I climbed out of the cab, a man led a mare through a side door and down the ramp. Her head towered above his, and as her ears swiveled around in alarm, I realized fear of an unfamiliar location wasn't her only concern. She had a foal at her side. But she needn't have worried. Her baby was glued to her as they crossed the lot. His high-pitched whinny echoed under the barn's forebay when his dam was led over the threshold.

I started across the lot, but paused as the driver returned, followed by Dr. Nash and another man I recognized as her husband. I'd seen him in the office, although we'd never met.

"...made good time after we cleared Jacksonville," the driver said before draping the cotton lead over his shoulder. "Then we hit the construction zone just south of Richmond. Ain't no way getting 'round that."

"Did they travel well?"

"Yes, ma'am. Like veterans. All three of them."

My boss and her husband were dressed in jeans and overalls and jackets, and you would have thought it was the middle of the day. Mr. Nash caught sight of me a fraction of a second before the others.

When Dr. Nash turned away from the driver and saw me standing there, she flinched. "Oh, Steve. What are you doing here?"

I thought it obvious but said, "Sorry. I didn't mean to startle you." I gestured to the driver. "I wondered if he'd gone to the wrong barn."

"Oh, no. He's fine. I quarantine horses that come up from Florida strictly as a precaution. After a couple days, when I'm satisfied that they're healthy, we'll move them into a regular barn."

Another man came out of the building and walked past without giving us a second glance.

"I like to keep traffic to a minimum, Steve, so I'd prefer that you come over here only if Victor or I send for you."

"Yes, ma'am."

Victor Nash stepped around his wife and extended his hand. "Steve, good to meet you."

I shook his hand. "You, too, sir."

A mischievous grin spread across his face. He clasped his hands behind his waist and rocked back on his heels. "So. I hear my daughter's got you working for her now."

"Uh…" Wood slammed against metal as the trailer's ramp was dismantled.

"Oh, Victor. Don't give him a hard time. You know how she is."

Mr. Victor, as Ronnie called him, put his arm around his wife's shoulders. "Yeah. Just like her mother." He looked at me and winked.

I stepped back a pace. "Well, I'd better get to work."

As I neared the farm truck, I glanced over my shoulder. Victor was still smiling, but Dr. Nash's face was unreadable as she stood in her husband's shadow.

I returned to barn one, bedded down the stall I'd been mucking out, and when I started my two o'clock round, I paid extra attention to the Storm Bird mare. Maddie anticipated that she'd be the next to go since the Cozzene mare had foaled, but when I flipped on the lights in her barn, she squinted at me the way they do when they've been dozing. Even from the aisle, the thick yellowish plugs of wax that hung from her teats were noticeable. I studied the muscling over the mare's croup and tail head and thought I understood what Maddie was talking about. The area looked sunken. Maybe Maddie would luck out, and the mare would foal tomorrow night. I paused and looked in on the colt I'd delivered. He was flat out in the straw, and as I watched, a front leg twitched as if he were dreaming. What did a foal dream about, anyway? Right now, his world consisted of this fourteen-by-fourteen stall and his mother's wide body swaying over him. I watched his ribcage for a moment, and when I was satisfied that he was comfortably asleep, I headed back.

My two o'clock round also took me to barns seven and eight. I chuckled when I discovered, as predicted by Sergeant Bodell and half the crew, that the electric service had been connected. Victor was right. Jenny wasn't the only female who knew how to get what she wanted.

When I headed back, the moonlight slanted into the cab and backlit a few scattered clouds that clung to the mountain's rim like clumps of cotton candy. I slowed as I entered the curve in front of the mansion. Headlights cut across the road up ahead. At first, I assumed the semi hadn't left as I'd thought, but the vehicle waiting to pull out of the Nashes' drive was a mid-sized car. As I cleared the retaining wall directly in front of the house, an orange flash lit up the car's interior as the driver bent to light a cigarette. He tilted his head back and directed a column of smoke toward the ceiling. I glanced at the road, and when I looked back, the lighter had snuffed out.

I didn't think the driver was Mr. Nash, especially since he was smoking, and I didn't recognize the car, either. So, who in the hell was leaving their house at two in the morning? The house had been dark for hours. It wasn't like they'd been entertaining; yet, the Nashes had been dressed like they'd never gone to bed. Maybe they'd been out and had returned just before the semi's arrival. That would explain everything but their late-night visitor.

As I turned onto Stone Manor, the lake's cold black water drew my gaze like a magnet. The surface was perfectly still, reflecting the sky like a sheet of glass, but a rim of ice was growing outward from the banks, and in no time at all, the water would be sealed beneath it.

Chapter 7

I slept until noon Saturday and was pulling on a pair of jeans when the doorbell rang. I stumbled out of the bedroom, yanked the waistband over my hips, and zipped up. As I stretched my hand toward the doorknob, I considered the possibility that the person on the other side of the door might not be Corey, after all, but Bruce. I shook the sleep out of my head. Of course it was Corey. Bruce wouldn't have a reason to knock.

Just the same, I squeezed one eye shut and squinted through the peephole. Corey stood on the threshold, and her arms were weighted down with a grocery bag.

I opened the door as an icy breeze lifted her bangs, then curled into the apartment and ruffled my T-shirt. Her cheeks were flushed from the cold, or running up the steps, and when she smiled, the skin around her eyes crinkled. Her pale lashes looked transparent, and her eyes were as blue and as clear as an autumn sky.

"Morning," I said.

Her grin broadened. "You mean afternoon."

"Uh…so it is."

"Well? Can I come in?"

"Oh, yeah. Right." I quit gawking at her and backed up. "Here, let me get that." I took the grocery bag from her arms and carried it into the kitchen.

She followed me into the tiny room, and as I set the bag on the counter and peered inside, she flattened her hand on my arm. "I'll do it. Have you eaten yet?"

"Yeah. When I got home this morning."

She paused with a loaf of bread in her hand and turned to look at me. "Well, do you want something now?"

I shook my head. "Oh, but if you're hungry…"

"No. I'll wait." She unpacked a bag of potato chips and lunchmeat and a gallon of milk. "Want some orange juice?"

"Sure." I watched her rinse out two glasses. She wore the same black and purple vest as before, but today, she'd added charcoal-colored riding breeches flecked with horse hair. I suspected the purple knee-highs and white sneakers weren't the fashion statement she'd intended but the result of switching out of her riding boots. The look was common enough in the circles we ran in, and based on the horse activity around Warrenton, it probably wasn't out of the ordinary here, either.

"What's on today's agenda?" she said over her shoulder.

"I'd like to begin by going to the library and reading through the local papers, starting with the last week in January. I want to know everything that's happened around here that was significant enough to make the news. Especially the fires, not that I think Bruce had anything to do with them."

Corey handed me a glass of orange juice and took a swallow of hers.

"It's unlikely we'll find anything that's connected to your brother's disappearance," I said. "And even if we do, we may not recognize it for what it is, but getting a lay of the land feels like a good starting point. Then, when we get back, it'll probably be time for me to go to work, but maybe you could search through his computer this weekend."

"Sure."

"We need to find his phone book, too." I swallowed some orange juice. "His private one, I mean."

She lifted a carton of eggs and package of bacon out of the bag and frowned. "You haven't seen it?"

"Not yet. I've only had time to search the living room and kitchen."

She picked up the grocery bag and began to fold it, but her thoughts were elsewhere. She crimped the bag until it was half closed and paused. "You know…" she said so softly, I had to lean forward to hear her. "On my drive home the other night, I decided, if I'm going to be any help at all, I have to pull myself together." She looked into my eyes.

The refrigerator hummed to life behind me, and the walls of the tiny room seemed to push inward, moving us closer, until we were almost touching.

She tilted her head to the side. "You've been so kind and patient, Steve, and I really appreciate it…"

"But, you have every right to—"

"No." She held up her hand. "I promise. I'll do better."

I shifted my weight and rested against the opposite counter. "Corey, you've been fine."

She bit her lip, and when she shook her head, her short blond bangs flipped across her forehead. "No. I haven't. But, I'm taking my cue from the police," she glanced at the ceiling, "of all people, and I'm going to focus on the fact that we haven't found anything to indicate that he's in trouble or…hurt. He really could be all right."

"Yes, he could."

"And if he is…" a smile touched her lips, "I'm going to ask you to do one last thing for me."

"What's that?"

"Punch him."

◇◇◇

"Tell me, *again*, what we're looking for."

I glanced up from a stack of newspapers. We'd taken over a conference table in the Virginia Room of the Fauquier County Public Library, but in actuality, we had the entire room and most of the library to ourselves. I was working my way through the *Fauquier Times-Democrat* while Corey checked the *Citizen* and several regional papers.

"Anything that doesn't sound…normal."

"Well, gee, Steve. If it's normal, it's not going to be in the paper."

I leaned back and ran my fingers through my hair. "Okay, we don't care that the board of supervisors has some tough budget decisions to make or that they're refurbishing a restaurant on Main Street or that the school board wants a bigger share of the tax pie." I paused and glanced at the article I'd been skimming about a planned renovation/addition to the county jail in Warrenton that was expected to cost more than the officials had predicted. Damn.

Corey leaned forward. "What?"

I tore my gaze away from the paper. "Uh…nothing." I cleared my throat. "I mean, I can't really predict what might be useful later. If you think an event has potential, jot it down or photocopy it."

"Okay." Corey did that thing she does with her legs, crossing them beneath her, while my gaze was drawn back to the jail article. What if Bruce had been arrested and was too embarrassed to tell his family? I didn't know if a standard missing person's report would spur the cops into checking their own backyard, so to speak. I jotted JAIL on my notepad and decided to look into it Monday afternoon.

Most of January held nothing of interest and consisted of articles covering suburban sprawl, a proposed hundred-and-fifty-four acre business park, tobacco revenues lost to online sales, more tax concerns. I flipped to the January thirty-first edition, and an article on the front page caught my attention. Or rather, the color photograph did. It sprawled across four columns and depicted a snowy nighttime scene of a mangled tractor-trailer hanging precariously from a guardrail.

FIRST SIGNIFICANT SNOWFALL
CONTRIBUTES TO I-95 ACCIDENT

A Shreveport, Louisiana man was uninjured when the tractor-trailer he was driving jackknifed on I-95

northbound and mounted the guardrail.
The incident occurred early this morn-
ing, around one o'clock, south of the
Fredericksburg exit.

Maynard Blue, 45, from Shreveport,
Louisiana was hauling a load of Libbey
glassware when the tractor-trailer he
was driving jackknifed and slid across
three lanes of interstate I-95, causing the cab to mount the guardrail in
the median.

According to First Sgt. Raymond
Murphy, of the Virginia State Police,
all three lanes of northbound I-95
were closed at one-fifteen and remained
closed for the next two hours to allow
emergency responders time to remove
the tractor-trailer and clean up
debris on the roadway. A crane from
Reynolds Crane, Inc. out of Fredericksburg, Virginia was brought in to
lift the cab off the guardrail.

First Sgt. Murphy reported that
slick conditions likely contributed
to the accident which is still under
investigation.

Interesting. Even though I didn't see how it related to Bruce,
I set it aside. I flipped through the rest of Friday's edition, then
moved on to Saturday's, the first day of February and Bruce's
last day at Stone Manor. The coverage was equally disappoint-
ing. Not one event or announcement or happening hinted at
a possible connection, and I was beginning to think we were
wasting our time. I looked across the table at Corey. Her paper
had slipped into her lap, and she was chewing on her lower lip
as she read something that had caught her attention.

"Find anything?"

She looked up. "Oh…ahem." She shook her head as she
closed the section. "No. Nothing."

"You looked rather enthralled for 'nothing.'"

A faint blush rose to her cheeks. "Um." She licked her lips. "I, uh...I was reading about the Blue Ridge Hunt Point-to-Point. They have steeplechase and flat races." She slid the paper onto the shorter stack to her right. "Sorry. I got sidetracked."

I grinned.

Corey leaned forward in her chair, and her blue eyes sparkled under the lights. "It's just that it sounds like so much fun. I'll have to give it a try one of these days."

"Oh, boy."

"Oh, boy, what?"

I rested my elbows on the table. "Nothing. I'm sure you'd be good at it. You're light enough. Heck, you'd probably have to carry lead." I pictured Corey barreling across the rough terrain, crouched over her horse's withers with the wind in her face. And I pictured the rest of the field, bunched close, riding hard, the horses' legs swinging over the ground, their hooves slicing into the turf with a thousand pounds of bone-crushing weight behind them.

"Have you found anything?" Corey said.

"No." I settled back in my chair and turned over Sunday's paper.

MAN KILLED IN METH LAB EXPLOSION

A Warrenton man was killed in a meth lab explosion shortly after midnight Sunday. Andrew Johnson, 35, of 1379 Brittney Lane was pronounced dead at the scene. Neighbors called police when they heard an explosion that rattled their windows. When emergency responders arrived, an outbuilding on Johnson's property was fully involved. Police say there was evidence that Johnson had been in the process of extracting ephedrine, one of the ingredients necessary to produce methamphetamine, from a cold medicine. Officers evacuated several neighbors

until the threat of additional explo-
sions was eliminated.

Warrenton Police Detectives Jim
Brandon and Daniel Sweeney discovered various solvents and fixers used
in the production of methamphetamine
in a back bedroom in the residence as
well as a small amount of marijuana
and assorted drug paraphernalia.

I checked the date in the header, Sunday, February second. I glanced at Corey, then studied the photograph of what was left of the outbuilding. Later that same day, her family had gathered to celebrate her birthday. Everyone except Bruce. His absence had been the first indicator that something had gone wrong. The article was unusual enough to warrant a trip to the photocopier. I skimmed the rest of the pages, then placed the section on top of the I-95 article.

Corey looked at the pile sitting off to the side and frowned. "You found something?"

"An accident on I-95 and a meth lab explosion."

"And?"

"Well, they beat county budgets and tax referendums."

"Drugs? Bruce wouldn't have anything to do with that."

"I'm sure you're right, but it happened on the second, so…" I shrugged.

"You're right." She looked back at the paper she'd been leafing through, but I had a feeling she wasn't focusing on the print.

An account of the first arson was printed in Monday's paper.

FIRE DESTROYS ABANDONED BARN

A suspicious fire destroyed an aban-
doned barn on Paddock Way south of
County Road 628 early Monday morning.
At approximately 1:15, John Nobel of
Culpeper noticed flames shooting from
the barn's roof as he drove west on
County Road 628. Nobel used his cell
phone to call 911, but when firefighters

from Company Nineteen out of Warrenton
Training Center arrived seven minutes
later, the roof had already collapsed. Firefighters worked to contain
the blaze and kept it from spreading
to a house on the property. Both the
barn and house have been vacant for
several years.

Company Nineteen Firefighter Wayne
Terry said losses are estimated at
$70,000. The cause is still under
investigation, however, arson is suspected since the barn was vacant and
without electricity.

That section went in the photocopy pile as I reflected that
the fire department had had a busy two days.

Corey looked up again.

"Barn fire." I explained the niggling suspicion I couldn't shake
that the fires were someone's attempt to intimidate my boss. "And
we should keep tabs on anything that impacts the farm, because
anything connected to the farm could be connected to Bruce…"
I noted the doubt behind her eyes and added, "…somehow."

She nodded, then flipped over a section and pulled it into her
lap. I glanced at my watch. It was already ten after three, and I
had to be at work by six. The room was warm and oppressively
quiet, and the lack of sound and stale air bore into my skull and
weighted my eyelids.

I flipped through the next five days and found an article
covering the second fire in Saturday's edition. No wonder the
sheriff's department had set up a roadblock with the fires happening so close together. The second fire had been discovered
just after midnight by a neighbor walking his dog and involved
a bank barn in the 8400 block of Dunnottar Lane. Where in
the hell did they come up with these names, anyway? The third
fire, my fire, happened five days later.

THIRD SUSPICIOUS FIRE IN ELEVEN DAYS
HAS AREA RESIDENTS SPOOKED

A bank barn that has stood for more than one hundred years was destroyed in less than three hours early Thursday morning. The barn, located at 8203 Cannonball Gate Road, belonged to Winifred and Jonathan Keller. No one was injured in the blaze, but losses were substantial due to a large assortment of agricultural equipment and hay stored in the barn. An estimate has not been determined but is expected to top $200,000.

Firefighters were on the scene for approximately twelve hours as mounds of half-burnt hay smoldered and rekindled, sending a huge column of smoke into the air that was visible from Old Town Warrenton. State Fire Marshall Chuck Holmes said the cause is still under investigation, but he was called to the scene almost immediately because of the rash of barn fires plaguing the area.

Units from Warrenton Training Center and Warrenton were dispatched to the scene. Assistance was also provided by the Fauquier County Sheriff's Office.

I scoured the rest of Thursday's edition and thought it interesting that the *incident* at barn seven hadn't made the paper. It wasn't even listed in the Police and Court Notes. I blasted through Friday's edition, then went to photocopy what little I'd set aside. When I came back, Corey had straightened our table and looked as ready to get out of there as I was.

"I'm starved," I said. "Let's get something to eat."

She slipped on her vest, and her gaze fell upon the papers stacked neatly in the center of the table. "We didn't do so good, did we?"

I shrugged. "Time will tell."

We went to Sullivan's Bar and Grill and chose a booth by the front window. The afternoon sunlight streamed over the rooftops across the street and angled through the bar's plate-glass windows where it pooled on the wooden floor. Light glinted off the cars parked along the sidewalk and winked across the glass as traffic moved along Main Street. Its implied promise of warmth was deceptive, at least on the other side of the glass. The temperature hovered in the mid-twenties and would drop fast once the sun set.

A muted TV screen flickered in the back of the room, and a local radio broadcast piped out of speakers in the ceiling, sounding louder than my previous visit since the bar was almost empty. I hung my denim jacket on a coat hook and offered to take Corey's vest, but she shook her head. "I'm still cold."

When I leaned against my backrest, the cushion was warm from the sun. "You might want to sit here." I patted my seat. "It's warm."

Her hand paused in midair as she reached for her napkin.

"I mean, we could switch."

She smiled softly. "Yeah, but the sun's in your eyes."

"Won't be for long."

"True." She picked up her menu and studied me over the top edge. "I had you pegged as a fast-food junkie. Guess I was mistaken."

Although I couldn't see her mouth, I had a sneaky suspicion she was grinning based on the deepening lines that radiated outward from her eyes. "Nah, you got me. I checked out this place the other night because some of Stone Manor's employees come here."

"Bruce?"

I nodded and watched her scan the room.

"Who'd you talk to?" she said.

"The barkeep. He's not here right now. When the waitress takes our order, maybe we should show her his picture. See if she knows anything. And there's one guy in particular I'm interested in. He's a big guy with long blond hair that he wears in a ponytail. Does he sound familiar?"

Corey frowned as she thought it over. "No. The last couple years, I've lost track of his friends, and it's gotten worse since he moved down here. I don't think I've been to his apartment more than twice. When I do see him, we're usually at our parents'."

I thought about my own sister. Except for her husband, I would be hard pressed to name one of her friends. Time apart, almost five years, and distance, three thousand miles, had a way of doing that to a relationship.

Corey started to ask me about Ponytail but stopped when our waitress strolled over to take our orders.

I held Bruce's picture out to her. "Do you know this guy? He comes in here from time to time."

She glanced from me to Corey and snapped her gum as a blush crept into her cheeks. "Who wants to know?"

Corey looked at me, then sat taller in her chair and slipped her hands into her lap. "I'm his sister. He's missing."

"Oh." Our waitress exhaled as if she'd been holding her breath. "For a second, I thought you were gonna say you're his girl. He's missing, huh?" She checked both our expressions, then peered at the two-by-three photo. "We dated for awhile last spring."

"Do you have any idea where he is?"

She shook her head, and her long silver earrings whipped against her neck.

"What about friends? Do you know anyone he hangs with?"

"Uh-uh. We were strictly bedmates," she threw Corey a quick glance, "if you know what I mean. He comes in here with some guys from the farm he works at. That's all I know."

"When did you see him last?"

"Three weeks. Four. It's hard to keep track in this job."

"Do you know if he…dates anyone else who works here?"

"Not that I've heard."

"We're also looking for a big blond guy. Broad shoulders, wears his hair in a ponytail. You ever see him in here?"

She popped her gum and shrugged; then she handed Bruce's picture back to me. "Sorry."

She took our orders, and Corey watched her return to the kitchen. The sunlight slanted through the window behind Corey, highlighting her windblown hair and lighting the side of her face. It caught the edge of her eye so that it appeared lit from within. She lowered her head, and the trick of light was lost to shadow.

"Why are you interested in this guy?"

"The barkeep doesn't know who he is but said he hung out with Bruce shortly before he disappeared. A name would be nice."

I sat through the beginning of the meal, wondering how hard I should press Corey for information. I swallowed some iced tea, placed the glass on the table, and watched her pick at her chicken strips. "Don't you eat?"

She looked up and smiled. "Sometimes." She sat back in her seat and sighed. "I sense you're waiting for something. What is it?"

"I'm not really sure where to start looking for your brother. I have to admit, this afternoon was a bit discouraging, but I guess our best bet is for me to learn as much as I can about the people at Stone Manor."

"What's it like working there?"

I described the job and employee hierarchy, which was fairly basic and typical of most farms. Dr. Nash handed down orders to the stud manager who oversaw the crew, and as usual, there was little incentive for anyone else to assume a leadership role and, therefore, responsibility. As far as I was concerned, the practice smothered initiative and discouraged pride, and I was fairly certain it was driven by economics.

"Because of their attitudes, I'm particularly interested in two guys, Michael Tiller and Paul Genoa. Do you recall Bruce mentioning either one of them?"

Corey shook her head.

"Did he ever talk about problems at work?"

"No." She leaned back in her seat and picked up her Diet Coke. "Work was just that. Work. He isn't..." she paused, searching for the right word, "passionate about horses like I am. That's not to say he doesn't enjoy the job. He does, even though he's never cared much for riding."

"Like you?"

"Oh, God. Yes," she breathed.

"Who'd you ride today? It wasn't Sweetwater," I said, naming her chestnut warmblood.

Her eyebrows disappeared under her bangs. "How'd you know?"

I grinned. "You have gray horse hair on your breeches."

She glanced at her lap, then looked up at me and grinned. "Huh, so I see." She took a sip of her drink. "I breezed a couple horses at Bowie this morning."

My mouth fell open. "When'd you start that?"

"Couple weeks ago. I'm just doing it on the weekends, but I might start working at Washington Park in the morning, before I go to work. It'll keep me in shape."

"Uh-huh. Like you're not?"

She ignored the implied compliment. "So, what about these two guys?"

"Tiller's your typical bully, but he backs down easily enough. The other guy, Genoa, seems a bit unstable."

"How?"

"He's extremely jealous of his girlfriend, and she works at night, right before Bruce's shift."

"What's she like? Would Bruce be attracted to her?" I pictured Maddie's breasts pressing against her pajamas, and Corey must have read something in my expression, because she said, "Hmm, guess so."

I smiled. "Yeah. He'd be interested." I swiped my last French fry through a glob of ketchup and tried not to eye Corey's stack of chicken strips. "In general, what's Bruce like? Does he make friends easily?"

"Yeah. He's always had tons of friends. Male and female." She leaned forward and propped her chin in her hands. "But not close friends, and as far as I know, he's never been in a long-term relationship." She looked up at me through her bangs with the saddest eyes I've ever seen. "And I don't know why. He's funny and friendly and drop-dead gorgeous." She smiled. "At least that's what every girlfriend I've ever had has been sure to tell me. Repeatedly. But he never gets…close. I don't know. It's like he's searching for something he knows he'll never find."

Chapter 8

Sunday morning, the start of my day off, I awoke to the combined sounds of traffic noise and the faint indistinguishable throb of a radio playing in an apartment upstairs. Every muscle in my body was totally relaxed, and I felt as if I'd sunk into the mattress. I closed my eyes, and as I enjoyed the sensation, the aroma of frying bacon and freshly brewed coffee drifted into my nostrils. I slowly turned my head and checked the time.

"Shit." I bolted upright. Corey and I had agreed that she should come over at ten, and it was almost eleven.

When I opened the bedroom door, I heard the scrape of a utensil and the clatter of something metal being placed on a hard surface. And soft humming. I stepped into the kitchen doorway. Corey hadn't heard me, so I propped my shoulder against the wall and watched her fool with something in the sink. She hummed an occasional bar or two but became easily distracted as she concentrated on whatever it was that she was doing. She'd pushed the sleeves of a light blue sweater up to her elbows, exposing long slender muscles that glided smoothly under pale skin. When she bent forward to peer at something in her hand, her silky blond hair shimmered under the fluorescent light.

She glanced over her shoulder and smiled. "Morning. I didn't know what to do when you didn't answer the door. I hope you don't mind that I let myself in."

"Not at all." I stepped to her side. She'd been scrubbing a frying pan, and by the looks of it, domestic chores weren't Bruce's strong suit. I moved to help her, and she blocked my way.

"Uh-uh. You eat. Your plate's in the oven. Be careful, though. It's hot."

I grabbed a potholder and lifted my plate off the oven rack. "Aren't you eating?"

"I already did."

I took my food out to the dining room table, and Corey followed a minute later with a mug of steaming coffee. She sat next to me.

"You don't have to feed me, you know?"

"I like to cook." She reached across the table and snagged a slice of bacon. "I fooled around with the computer again." She exhaled, and her breath lifted the bangs off her forehead. "It's infuriating. It's like he's never grown up."

"Hmm."

"And I got the mail. Nothing but junk mail and bills. One with FINAL NOTICE stamped on it like the last batch. Do you think that's significant?"

I swallowed some orange juice. "I'd say it's a good sign. He's only been missing for two weeks. Maybe his financial situation just got to him, and he decided to take off temporarily. I know what it's like to have bills coming in when you have no idea how you're going to pay them off."

Corey's eyebrows rose into her bangs. "You?"

I nodded. "Medical bills. They're hell."

"Oh, yeah. That's right. The Foxdale thing."

I grinned. "Things."

She leaned forward and rested her chin in her hand. "You've certainly had an interesting life."

I chuckled. "Getting shot isn't all that interesting, believe me."

Corey fiddled with her coffee mug, slipped her fingers around the handle and smoothed her thumb across the top edge as if she were wiping off a smudge. "What's on the agenda today?"

"Finish searching the apartment. We really need to find his phone list." I bit into my sandwich. She'd toasted the bread and added sautéed onions and fried ham to the egg and cheese mix. "This is delicious. Thanks."

I watched her sip her orange juice, thinking it had been a long time since someone had cooked for me. Rachel hated cooking. We either went out, or I cooked. Not that anything I did in the kitchen had advanced beyond keying a number into the microwave. For an act as simple as someone cooking for you, it sure had a nice feel to it.

I slid the Fauquier County ADC map that I'd purchased last night out of its bag and flipped to the index in the back.

"What's that for?"

"I want to plot out the fires."

I reread the article covering the first fire and looked up Paddock Way in the street index, then flipped to page twenty-five. Paddock Way was a short, twisty road located a quarter-mile southeast of Stone Manor Lane, if that far. I scribbled an asterisk on the map, then repeated the process for the second, and when I drew the final asterisk on Cannonball Gate Road, Corey glanced at my face then peered at the map.

"Oh," she said.

Oh was an understatement. I wedged the pen in the book's crease and leaned back in my chair. If I were Dr. Nash, I wouldn't be able to sleep nights. Together, all three fires formed a tight little cluster around the farm.

"What does it mean?" Corey said softly.

"It means they aren't random."

I skimmed the article on the guy who'd blown himself up; then I located his street on the map. His home was on Warrenton's south side, and although it wasn't that far away, it definitely did not fall into the same pattern as the others.

I rotated the sheet of paper and pointed to his photograph. "Do you recognize this guy?"

"But, I told you. Bruce wouldn't be involved in something like that."

"I know. But humor me, okay?"

She studied my face, then looked at the picture. "This looks like a mug shot."

"It probably is." The guy's haggard eyes were sunk into a mass of puffy flesh as he stared vacantly into the camera's lens. Most druggies looked gaunt, but this guy obviously had other problems. Stubble darkened his chin, and strands of short dirty blond hair had fallen into his eyes. His tight thin lips didn't sit well above a double chin.

Corey shook her head and settled back in her chair. "I've never seen him before."

After I did the dishes, we started a search of Bruce's bedroom that ended almost as soon as it began when Corey found his phone list tucked inside an automotive magazine in the nightstand.

We returned to the kitchen table and went through it together.

"Do any of his friends' names sound familiar?" I said as she scanned the list.

She flipped the paper over and crinkled her nose. "This isn't any good. We've got a Brian, a Judy, a Debbie," she tilted her head from side to side as she read off the names, "Louise, A.J., Kent, Maryanne, Cynthia, Donna, Mark, Mike, Connie." She looked up at me and laid the list on the table. "This is pathetic. Doesn't he believe in last names?"

"You tell me. He's your brother."

She gestured toward the paper. "It's like I said before. It's a symptom of how he views his friends. They come and go with no real need on his part to establish a meaningful relationship."

"Well, he certainly isn't worried about exchanging Christmas cards, is he?"

A smile broke across her face. "So, what do we do now?"

"Call them. Tell them he's missing. Ask if they have any idea where he is and find out when they saw him last."

She peered down at the sheet and counted under her breath. "Twenty-four. This is gonna take awhile. Do you want me to do it?"

"Yeah. It'll sound better coming from you."

Corey got busy on the phone, and I went back to the bedroom and searched the bureau. The upper drawers held nothing of interest, but the bottom middle drawer, the infamous junk drawer, held promise. I got on my knees and peered at the jumble of skin magazines, a flashlight, a box of kitchen matches, shoelaces, candles, and a pocketknife. Packets of condoms, a vibrator, and other assorted sex toys crammed the drawer. Apparently, Bruce had a more active imagination in the sex department than I did. I piled the magazines on the bed but was reluctant to touch the rest. I pulled out a yo-yo, two mismatched gloves, three music CDs, and some computer game cheat books.

Corey strolled into the room with her gaze focused on the phone list in her hand. She absentmindedly sat on the edge of the bed as I turned to pick up the stack of magazines. Before I could grab them, they slithered off the comforter and plopped on the carpet by my knees. She glanced at them, then looked in the drawer while I scooped the magazines into a pile and casually set them on the floor alongside the bureau where they wouldn't be so obvious. When I pivoted around, her lips twitched, and despite my best effort, heat flushed my face.

I dumped the stuff back into the drawer and shoved it closed. When I turned around, she'd clamped a hand over her mouth, and her shoulders trembled in little spasms.

I stood up. "What?"

"You should have seen your face."

"Ha, ha."

Her lips twitched. "Sorry, I couldn't help it."

"Okay." I took a deep breath. "What luck are you having with the phone calls?"

"Not much." She cleared her throat, then ticked off the names she'd called so far. "Brian got a job working at a winery three months ago and hasn't seen or heard from my brother since." She flipped the sheet of paper toward her chest and grinned. "He did ask me out, though." She looked back at her notes. "Judy told me to drop dead. Debbie dates Bruce on and off and never knows when she'll hear from him." She paused. "I guess 'dates' is a relative thing. Louise hasn't heard from Bruce since Halloween. A.J.'s phone's been disconnected. Kent and Bruce go to a Caps game from time to time but haven't so far this season. Maryanne hung up on me."

She sighed and lowered the list to her lap. "You might want to try your luck with her and Judy. Maybe they'll be more responsive with a guy on the other end of the line."

We worked on the phone list for a couple more hours. I struck out as thoroughly as she had, and in the end, we'd learned nothing of value. By three o'clock, Corey needed to go home.

"You don't mind, do you?" she said as she slipped on her vest.

"Of course not."

She looped her scarf around her throat and pulled on a pair of gloves. "I need to ride Sweetie before it gets too dark," she said, referring to Sweetwater by his barn name.

I smothered a grin as I bent over and snagged Corey's duffle off the floor. When I straightened, she nudged my arm. "Don't make fun of my horse."

"Sweetie," I repeated, and she rolled her eyes and headed for the door.

When we reached the parking lot, she pointed out Bruce's car, a red Pontiac Firebird. "He bought it used a year ago and has had nothing but trouble with it."

We both leaned over and peered through the tinted windows. I ran back inside, grabbed Bruce's keys, and opened her up. Bruce's apartment was relatively neat, but the Firebird was spotless. I looked under the seats and in the console and above the sun visor; then I popped the trunk. Except for a little cone of white powder that looked like it had oozed out of a package of flour, the carpet was cleaner than the apartment's.

Corey thoughtfully watched me press the trunk lid closed, and the earlier playfulness had drained out of her eyes. "Where is he?"

We stood there silently, saying nothing because there was nothing to say.

After she turned right onto Waterloo, I was still standing by Bruce's car when an elderly gentleman stepped off the sidewalk by the street and crossed the lot toward me. A poodle bounced around on the end of its leash, straining the old man's tenuous hold. They'd walked past earlier, when I was searching behind the driver's seat, and the dog had pressed its nose against my pant leg.

"Evening," he said as they drew closer.

I nodded.

When his dog planted its paws on my thigh, the old guy jerked on the leash. "No! Get down, Fluffy."

"That's okay," I said. "He's just checking me out, aren't you, boy?" His cold wet nose searched my hands; then he peered up at me with wide brown eyes half-hidden behind wiry corkscrew curls. I was pretty sure he had visions of pork chops or dog biscuits or rump of roast rattling around in his brain, and not much else.

Fluffy's owner gestured toward the Firebird. "You thinking of buying it?"

"Uh, no. I'm looking for the owner, though."

"Ain't seen him around for a while. Not in the past couple weeks, anyway." The old guy braced his hand on the Firebird's roof to keep his balance. "About the time somebody dropped off his car."

A shot of adrenaline kicked into my bloodstream. "Someone else left his car here?"

The old guy nodded. "Don't think it's moved from this spot since. But then, it was always breaking down. Had a faulty starter or ignition or something. I'd see him, sometimes, pushing this lemon down the road, trying to get the starter repositioned so it would crank over. There oughta be a law, selling cars as new as this that—"

"When, exactly," I interrupted, "did you see someone other than Bruce leave his car here?"

"That's his name?"

"Yes." I gritted my teeth.

"It was late at night. Maybe even as late as one-thirty or two. Fluffy was having the runs cause he'd got into the trash. Like I've told Mildred a hundred times, you can't—"

I cut him off. "Do you remember what day it was?"

"Huh?"

"The day someone dropped off his car."

"Nah." Fluffy wound his leash around my legs, and the old man handed me his end so I could disentangle myself. "When you're as old as I am, retired and all, one day's like the next."

I ended up holding Fluffy's leash, so I shortened on the little hairball so he'd stay put. "Well, was it quiet like a work night, or was the lot emptier than usual because some of your neighbors were still out?"

"Oh, I get it." He considered my question while his dog strained at the end of the leash. "Now that you put it that way, I'd say it was a weekend."

"Is there anything about that day that might help you pin it down?" I gestured toward the high school. "Like an event next door, or a TV program that you watched that evening?"

He shook his head. "Not that I remember."

"Did another car follow Bruce's into the lot?"

"Could of, but I wasn't looking for it, so who knows?"

"What did the driver look like?"

The old guy shrugged. "I only glanced at him when he climbed out. He flicked a cigarette into the gutter. Then he bent over to check that he'd locked the door. He looked Hispanic, but he was taller than most of them get. All legs and arms. Straight black hair slicked back like a greaser."

The first person I thought of was Paul, but we were the same height.

"Was he taller than me?"

"Yeah. By a couple inches, I'd say."

Fluffy yapped, and I realized the dog was shivering. I handed over the leash. "And you think it was about two weeks ago?"

He nodded. "Sounds 'bout right."

"Thanks for your help. I'm in unit six-forty-one, apartment 2D. If you think of anything else, I'd appreciate it if you'd get in touch with me."

"Sure."

I moved aside, and Fluffy's owner set his arm against the pull on the leash as the little dog steamrolled toward the steps like he was dragging a sled across the frozen tundra.

◇◇◇

I turned onto 211 and headed northwest on Bear Wallow at two-fifty Monday morning, after I'd downed a super-sized coffee from 7-Eleven with the hope that the caffeine would pry my eyelids open. I'd gone to bed early enough, but a growing sense of apprehension had kept me staring at the ceiling until well after ten. Someone other than Bruce dropping off his car could have been innocent, I supposed, but the fact that no one had seen him since did not sit well with me.

Most nights, figuring out which barn Maddie was working in was a simple matter of driving to the only building that was lit, but tonight, the clinic and all the barns had lights burning. Every single one of them, but the light was dimmer than when they were controlled by timers. Even the bank barn had a light blazing in the forebay. As I cruised past Stone Manor Lane and turned into the clinic parking lot, I realized that the only lights switched on were the aisle lights. The stall lights were dark. I pulled alongside a Stone Manor truck that had been left by the clinic entrance. It looked like Maddie was ready to punch out. I stepped into the aisle as one of the stallions moved around in his stall.

When I opened the clinic door, Maddie was perched on a chair, sipping a Diet Pepsi. She lowered the can from her lips. "Geez, Steve. You're supposed to come back to work from your day off looking rested, not like you went ten rounds with your girlfriend and lost."

I fished for my timecard, wondering if she meant ten rounds in bed. "Busy weekend," I mumbled.

"I bet. Punch me out while you're at it."

I punched my card, slipped it into the rack, and found Maddie's card right on top. "Anything going on?"

"No. And I can't believe it. The Storm Bird mare still hasn't gone."

As usual, the clinic was warm, and I noted that Maddie had shed her flannel shirt. The white T-shirt she wore beneath it looked like a guy's cheap undershirt, and I wondered if it had belonged to Paul. The fabric was thin, and the outline of her lacy bra was clearly visible. I swallowed. "Think she'll go on my shift?"

"No telling. She's quiet, though." Maddie stood and arched her back as she stretched, and her breasts swelled over the bra's lacy edge.

I tried to look away, but my gaze centered on her chest. She lowered her arms and caught me looking. Like there was any doubt? I opened the fridge, leaned over like I needed to find room for my lunch, and let the cold air blast my face. "Why are all the lights on?" I asked.

Maddie moved around behind me, and the cold air lost some of its oomph.

"What did you say?"

I straightened and dumped my lunch on the top rack. "Why are the lights on?"

"Doctor Deirdre's paranoid. That's why."

I turned around. "The fires?"

"You got it." She handed me the farm's cell phone.

"Maddie," I closed the refrigerator door, "don't they bother *you*?"

"Don't get all pissed. Whoever's doing it is only torching empty buildings, or haven't you noticed?"

"Yeah, I noticed. What if he changes his M.O.?"

"If he has any sense, he'll go somewhere else. Besides the lights, the police have picked up their patrols. I must have seen them four times tonight. That's more than the entire season last year. So, don't get all bent out of shape."

When I didn't react, she slipped on her coat and dropped her soda can in the trash.

Maddie lifted her flannel shirt off the back of the chair. "A van came down from New York earlier this evening with four horses. For some reason, Frank thought they were only bringing three, so I didn't have enough empty stalls. Since it's not snowing, I put one of the mares in a paddock behind barn seven and gave her some hay. She should be fine 'til morning, but make sure you check on her, okay?"

I nodded and glanced at my watch as I moved toward the door. "A van came in Saturday, too, and unloaded at the bank barn."

"From Florida, then."

"Yeah."

"The drivers try to get here before midnight, so you're lucky. Probably the only time you'll ever have to deal with them will be on your long days. I hate fooling with them. Those guys never know where they're going, and you have to stop what you're doing and track them down and show them what to do. It's a real pain in the rear end, and sometimes Frank forgets to tell us, and let me tell you, that's real fun when you don't know where to put them. Bruce only had one trailer come in on him, but I'm sure it threw him for a loop."

"Why's that?"

"He wasn't expecting it because I forgot to tell him. And what was worse, the snow must've made them late, because they didn't get here until four-thirty, right when he was trying to feed." She zipped up her coat. "Well, I'm outta here."

I opened the door for her. "Where'd that van come from?"

"Florida, cause they unloaded at the bank barn." She strolled down the aisle, and I followed her outside.

"Night, Maddie."

She flipped a wave over her shoulder, and I got busy with my rounds.

The mare in the lot behind barn seven spooked when I stepped out of the storage area. She threw her head up and skittered across the frozen ground.

"Hey, girl. It's okay." I walked over to the fence. "It's okay, girl. Didn't mean to scare you."

She'd spun around to face me. Except for a vague outline, the only feature I could make out in the dark was a wide blaze that ran down the center of her face. It seemed to hang disembodied in the air. I looked up at the sky. The full moon that had kept me company Saturday was buried under a wall of cloud.

I reached into my jeans pocket and pulled out a roll of butter rum Lifesavers. She snorted when the wax paper crinkled. "Come on, girl. You like candy?" I chirped to her, and she tossed her head and took a step forward.

"Come on," I said softly. "It's okay."

I put one of the Lifesavers in my mouth and peeled off another strip of paper.

The mare approached the fence, and when she hung her head over the top board, I cupped my hand under her warm muzzle. Her strong lips probed my palm before she sucked the candy into her mouth.

"Somebody's spoiled you, haven't they?"

She stretched her neck, bringing her nose up to my face, and her soft nostrils fluttered as she smelled my breath. I leaned back and fed her another Lifesaver. "Yeah, you've been spoiled, all right."

She nudged my chest, and as I ran my hand down her sleek neck, I wondered what she thought of her life. *If* she thought. Like most racehorses, her life had been one long series of changes. She'd most likely entered this world on a breeding farm much like this one. Then, one day toward the end of summer, when the nights grew cool, she was taken from her mother's side. After she'd done a bit of growing and had filled out, she was introduced to a whole new world of demands and expectations and challenges at a training farm designed to prepare her for the track, where she'd undoubtedly changed hands dozens of times. And now, she was back where she'd started. And the cycle would begin again, with another life.

She lifted her head, and as she focused on something in the distance, a stray glimmer of light reflected off the curve of her wide liquid eye.

"You're safe here," I whispered, and she nodded her head at the sound of my voice. I fed her another Lifesaver; then I checked barn eight, made a pass through the training barns, and headed back to six.

◇◇◇

Despite Maddie's prediction, the Storm Bird mare didn't oblige and deliver her foal, and neither did the hundred and twelve other pregnant mares housed in barns one through six, so I managed to muck out ten stalls by morning. I was in the clinic, eating a peanut butter and jelly sandwich, when the aisle lights flicked off. I opened the door as Dr. Nash bent to the office door and fitted her key in the lock.

She looked over her shoulder as the key turned. "Oh, good. You're here. Please come into the office."

"Yes, ma'am."

Footsteps scuffed the asphalt down by the stallions' stalls as Jenny ran toward me.

She bounced to a stop at my side and looked up at me expectantly. "Did you have a foal?"

"'Fraid not."

"Oh, darn."

"Maybe tomorrow," I said as I crossed the aisle and followed Dr. Nash into the outer office.

She'd walked around Elaine's desk and was just stepping into the inner office when I reached the doorway. Dr. Deirdre, as Maddie liked to call her, slipped the leather duster off her shoulders and hung it on a coat tree just inside her office. Where Maddie filled out her clothes with sensual curves that any male with a pulse could lose himself in, Dr. Nash was all angles and taut lines and elegance. I hesitated, wondering if she'd intended for me to follow.

"Come in, Steve."

I detached myself from the mat in front of Elaine's desk and blinked when I stepped over the threshold and stood just inside my boss' office. I felt as if I'd been transported back in time and now stood in an eighteenth-century parlor outfitted with textured floral wallpaper and cascades of heavy velvet drapes that framed a bay window on my left. The delicate glass panes looked fragile, like thin sheets of ice rippled by a wind.

Beneath my feet, Elaine's vinyl floor had mutated into polished mahogany covered by scattered Persian rugs. A partner's desk anchored the far corner while a chintz sofa hugged the wall immediately to my right. Two deeply upholstered Louis XV wing back chairs were drawn close to the desk, and a magnificent floral display on the credenza behind Dr. Nash's chair caught the morning sunlight as it filtered through the window facing the parking lot.

Elaine should have felt cheated by the disparity. She had metal filing cabinets where Dr. Nash had a carved Provincial vitrine displaying leather-bound books and assorted trophies. The room had the same feel as my mother's library back home.

Dr. Nash settled into her chair. "Have a seat."

I looked down at my boots.

"Don't worry about it." She rooted through one of the desk drawers. "The carpet's treated."

Treated or not, it didn't take a genius to figure out what gunk was wedged between my boots' treads as I'd just spent the last six hours tromping through horse stalls.

Dr. Nash looked up as I stepped across the carpet and perched on the edge of a chair. A smile touched her lips. "I owe you an apology, Steve."

"Ma'am?"

She nodded and rolled her chair closer to the desk. "Thursday morning, I was so panicked when I saw that fire so close to the farm, I never once stopped to consider what it must have been like for you...or to thank you. So, I'm sorry, and thanks."

"You're welcome." I glanced at the sheet of stationery on her desk. "Have the police learned anything about the hit-and-run or the fires?"

"Nothing about the hit-and-run, but they've confirmed that the fire on Cannonball Gate was deliberate. Did you hear?"

I shook my head. She looked down at the blank sheet of paper centered on the blotter and reached for a pen. Her face was thin with a prominent nose and full lips that didn't quite go with her chiseled features, but her eyes were what grabbed you by the throat and didn't let go. Her light gray irises were flecked with darker specks, and her long pale eyelashes appeared translucent. The combination of coloring made you believe she could look straight into your soul.

She printed something on the stationery, lifted her eyes, and looked into mine. The overhead lights picked up red highlights in her hair as she held out the paper. I turned it upright. A list of names and phone numbers trailed down the left margin.

"Tuesday morning, Victor and I won't be here. We'll be gone for two nights. While you're making rounds, if you have any problems that require a vet, call Dr. Palansky. He's agreed to cover for me. After hours like this, you'll automatically be connected to his service. Leave a message, then page him. Frank's number's there, too, though you could just knock on his door if need be, and you have Maddie's number with you, correct?"

"Yes."

"Good." She rested her forearms on the desk. "So, how do you like the job so far?"

"It's fascinating."

She nodded. "Wasn't that foal you delivered the other night your first?"

"Yes, ma'am."

"It thrills me every time I see it." Her gaze shifted to the large window that faced Stone Manor Lane.

The sky had lightened to a thin yellow, and the clouds had broken up and were strung across the horizon like puffs of smoke belched from a steam locomotive. The lake had frozen over, the cold water trapped beneath a thin layer of ice that reflected the sky. The pearly light glinted off the barn roofs, and it was no longer possible to see that the aisle lights had been left on.

Dr. Nash pulled her gaze away from the window. "I've spent my whole life working with horses, and I can't imagine doing anything else."

"It gets in your blood."

"Yes, it does. I take it you didn't deliver any foals last night. Otherwise, Jenny would be pestering me by now."

"No, ma'am."

She nodded. "Well, Steve, thank you."

I tucked the paper in my back pocket. As I stepped around the chair, I checked the carpet and was relieved to see that I hadn't left any tracks on my way in.

When I left the office, Jenny was still down by the stallions' stalls, and since I didn't have anything to do until Frank organized the teams, I joined her.

"Who's this?" I said as I moved alongside her.

Jenny had her fingers hooked on the base of the grill that formed the upper portion of the first stall on the left. A big bay stallion towered over her with his forehead practically touching the bars so he could peer down at the little girl. "Order of Command, OC for short. He's my favorite."

She stretched her fingers between the bars as if she were trying to touch his nose, and I reflexively leaned toward her. "Be careful."

She looked up at me and frowned. "Of what?"

"He might bite."

She relaxed her fingers and let them drop back down on the ledge. "No, he won't. He's too sweet. Aren't you?"

OC lowered his head and snuffled, and one of his fuzzy ears tweaked between the bars.

"Maybe he thinks *you're* sweet," I said, "and he'll try to suck one of your fingers into his mouth."

Jenny giggled, and I wondered how I'd ever survive being a father.

"So why's he your favorite?"

"He's gentle when he's with a mare." She looked over her shoulder. "Not like nasty old Covey over there. Mom and Dad should get rid of him, but he belongs to Mr. Shane. His name's Covington Square, and he's mean. He lunges at them and almost pulls Mr. Frank off his feet."

"You've watched them…"

"Cover a mare?" Jenny finished the question for me.

I nodded. "Uh-huh."

"Yeah. Lots of times. They usually don't start breeding until right around three, when all the barn chores and palpations and teasings are done, so I get to watch because my bus gets here at three-ten. Then I do my homework in the office, and after Mom checks it, I can go ride if Dad's still in the training barns."

I pointed to a dark bay in the last stall on the right. "What's that one like?"

"I don't know much about him. Mom breeds him later in the afternoon, once everyone's gone home. He's shy and doesn't like a lot of people around, and he doesn't always want to do it. But he's Mom's favorite because he made a lot of money at the track, and his foals are doing better than he did." Jenny turned back to OC. "This one bites their necks, but he's real gentle about it."

Jenny rested her chin on her hands and gazed up at the big stallion, and I considered how unusual her life must be compared to most kids'.

"Jenny."

We both turned; then Jenny skipped down the aisle toward her mother, a worn copy of *Misty of Chincoteague* jouncing inside her backpack, the beaded animals flipping in a wide arc across the plastic.

When Jenny reached her mother, Dr. Nash bent down, gently touched her daughter's cheek, and said something I couldn't hear.

"Awh, Mom."

Dr. Nash stood and smiled softly as Jenny scuffed her shoes on her way into the office. My boss watched after her daughter for a brief moment, and the expression on her face was one I would have given anything to have seen in my own mother's eyes.

Dark shapes moved in the gap between the open barn doors. I shifted my gaze and Ronnie and Ben, the skinny blond kid, came into focus as they squeezed through the opening. I headed to the clinic, and we walked in together.

Ronnie wiped his nose on his sleeve while Ben dug around for his timecard. "Man," Ronnie said, "it's gotta be ten degrees out there. It's so cold, the snot froze in my nose." He looked at me and said, "I'm not bullshittin', either."

"Yeah, Ronnie. I know. I was out in it all night, remember?"

"Man, I'm glad I'm not on nights no more."

Ben punched his card and moved out of the way. "Yeah, Ronnie. We're all glad you're not on nights. It's been real quiet, now that we don't gotta listen to you whine."

Ronnie pulled a card out of the rack, peered at it, then shoved it back in. He pulled out another one and squinted at the name printed along the top. "Only thing good about nights was the company." He slid me a sideways glance. "Ain't that right, Steve?"

"Whew." Ben wrapped his arms around his chest. "Ain't that the truth."

Ronnie turned around. "So, how you like working with that girl?"

"She's fine."

Ronnie chuckled. "She fine, all right." He raised his hands. "Not that I know. Not with Mr. Lowbrow keeping tabs on her, I don't. I like my balls just they way they are, thank you very much."

"What about the guy before me?" I said. "Did he—"

"Screw around?" Ronnie realized he'd found his card and clocked in. "Might of. Him and Paul had a shoving match, but that's as far as it went, so I don't think so."

"Bruce and Paul? When?"

"Out in the parking lot, right before work."

Ben headed for the coffee machine. "They were lucky Dr. Nash didn't see them."

"Yeah," Ronnie said. "They would of kissed their jobs goodbye if she did."

"Did this shoving match happen just before Bruce quit? Was he fired?"

"Not right before, but not long ago, either." Ronnie sniffled. "As far as I know, Bruce quit. Just make sure you don't make the same mistake, least you get your face smashed in or get fired."

"Or both," Ben added.

Ronnie crossed the room and stuck his nose in front of the thermostat. "Don't say you wasn't warned."

The door opened behind me, and Ben suddenly became occupied with the intricate workings of the coffeepot lid.

I turned around as Paul looked at each of us in turn. There's nothing like walking into a room and having everyone clam up, and *Mr. Lowbrow* or not, Paul realized he'd been the topic of conversation. The awkward silence grew, and I was relieved when Frank stepped into the room.

Chapter 9

At noon, I slid into the Chevy's cab as the sun broke through the clouds. Its light bathed the barns in gold, and the ice on the lake glowed with a pearly luminescence, a stark contrast to the brown dormant fields.

I snagged Bruce's mail, let myself into his apartment, then cracked open a Miller Lite. The sooner he showed up, the better. Then Michael and Paul could indulge in their petty games and make asses of themselves all they wanted. I polished off half the beer as I separated out the bills and dumped the rest in the trash. One envelope in particular caught my attention. The return address featured Stone Manor's elegant logo. I tore the flap open and withdrew a paycheck.

By all accounts, Bruce was hard up for money, so why hadn't he come back for it?

I thudded the bottle onto the kitchen counter and flipped through the phone book until I found a listing for the Fauquier Adult Detention Center. Five minutes later, I ascertained that Bruce Claremont currently was not a guest at the Fauquier ADC.

A more extensive check of the state facilities could wait, especially since it would necessitate calling my buddy, Detective James Ralston. I drained the beer and smiled to myself.

Calling Ralston could definitely wait.

As usual, the apartment complex was as quiet as a tomb, and as usual the quiet was getting on my nerves. I switched on Bruce's stereo system. When I turned around, the folder of newspaper clippings lying on the coffee table caught my eye, and I remembered that I'd never gotten around to charting them on the calendar. I spread them on the dining room table and noted the date of the meth lab explosion, Sunday, February second. I printed METH in the block, then flipped to the next article. I'd already marked the first fire on February third, so I skipped to the account of the second fire. It had been set on Saturday, February eighth. I printed FIRE in that block, as well. I'd already marked *my* fire in Thursday's block. I added HIT AND RUN.

Then there was the question of someone besides Bruce dropping off his car. I backtracked two weeks from yesterday which took me back to the first weekend in February. I jotted CAR in the block for Saturday, February first; then I peeled January's page back over and wrote CAR on Friday the thirty-first. According to the old man, Bruce's car had been dropped off on a weekend night, but with everyone getting ready for work, a Sunday night would have felt like a weeknight not a weekend, so I left it blank.

I looked back at February first's block. Corey's birthday. I'd already determined that the first was his last day at work, but I hadn't marked it because Corey had become upset when she'd noticed Bruce's notation. I circled it now and thought over everything I'd heard at the farm and, just as importantly, what I hadn't. No one had mentioned anything about Bruce driving a different car to work or needing a ride, so I had to assume that his car had been left in the lot by someone who didn't work at Stone Manor. And if I remembered correctly, Paul had said Bruce went home early both Friday and Saturday morning. But when he left Saturday, how did he get home if someone else had dropped off his car around one-thirty that morning?

Later that Saturday, Frank Wissel had worked the six p.m. to midnight shift instead of Bruce. What the hell had happened at the farm early Saturday morning? If he'd been too sick to drive, someone would know about it.

If he was dead…

I rubbed my face. I had far too little information to entertain that thought.

◇◇◇

At six-twenty-five Tuesday evening, I drove through Foxdale Farm's wrought iron gates and pulled into the slot alongside Rachel's Camry. Light from a distant security light filtered into her car. It cast an orange tint across the hazy film that coated the inside of her windshield and highlighted a cluster of smudges in the window behind her head. She'd craned around the driver seat's headrest and was stretching to drop a bridle and plastic shopping bag onto the backseat. As she turned to face forward, she caught sight of my truck, and a brief flash of white teeth glimmered in the dark.

I slipped into her car and snicked the door shut.

"Hey," she whispered.

"Hey, yourself."

Rachel frowned as she leaned forward and tried to peer around my back. "What've you got there?"

The cellophane wrapper crinkled as I brought my hand around and angled the long-stemmed red roses from behind my back.

"Oh, Steve, they're gorgeous." She gathered them in her hands, and when she bent to smell them, her long black hair slipped forward and draped across the blossoms. "What's the occasion?"

"Seeing you."

She slowly lifted her eyes.

I leaned over the console and smoothed my hand beneath her jaw, felt her silky hair glide over my rough skin as I drew her close and kissed her mouth. A long kiss that tasted of peppermint. Her warmth and scent and nearness flowed over me, invading every pore until my skin tingled with the heat of wanting her. She broke off the kiss and sighed, and her breath swirled over my lips.

Rachel was wearing the purple satiny parka that she typically wore when she wasn't riding, and the little black dress beneath it barely cleared the coat's hem. She laid the roses on the dash, then twisted to face me. As she angled her slender legs beneath the steering wheel, the dress' hem rode up her thigh. I heard the soft rasp of her nylons, a brief swish of cloth, the sound of her breathing, and mine, and it seemed as if a barrier had floated down and settled over the Camry, separating us from the rest of the world. Traffic noises that had seemed so prominent a moment ago, the faint scraping of leaves as they skittered across the hood of the car, a distant voice, all dissolved into the dark night.

She inched toward me until her cheek cleared the curve of her headrest, then she relaxed against the backrest with her knees pressed between the console and gearshift. She lifted her chin and tilted her face toward mine.

"God, I missed you," I said, and my voice sounded raspy.

She smiled. "It's only been six days."

"Six days too many," I said as I bent to kiss her.

Rachel traced her fingers down my throat before she curled them around the collar of my leather jacket and slipped her fingertips beneath my shirt. When she parted her teeth and took my tongue into her mouth, her fingers brushed my collarbone as she withdrew her hand. She unzipped my jacket.

Her fingernails bumped over my belt buckle, and when she cupped her hand over my cock, my breath caught in my throat. "You *have* missed me," her lips twitched, "enormously, I'd say."

I moaned and said through my teeth, "More than you know."

She let her hand drop away as I gripped her coat's zipper pull, eased it down slowly, nudging the flaps apart with my knuckles.

I opened her coat and slid it off her left shoulder, smoothed my palm over her dress' thin strap and down her bare arm. When I cupped my hand over her breast and teased her nipple with my thumb, she shifted her legs so that her knees were jammed against the dash beneath the steering wheel. She inched her pelvis closer to the seat's edge.

The little black dress inched up her thighs.

As I wrenched off my jacket, I realized Rachel must have had the heat cranked up and the blowers on full blast before she'd switched off the engine, but I doubted the defrost had been on. Except for a hairline strip at the base of the windshield, the windows were coated with condensation. The dusk to dawn lamp on the indoor arena at the far end of the lot bathed the car in orange light that fractured in the film of moisture and scattered so that the glass looked frosted.

Rachel glanced around when she noticed me checking; then she wriggled both arms out of her parka. She flicked her tongue in my mouth when I kissed her, a brief tease that jacked up my blood pressure. I hooked my fingertips around the base of the thin little strap that slinked over her shoulder, then slipped my fingers beneath the fabric and stroked the curve of her breast.

After a moment, she lowered her seatback, and almost as an afterthought, hit the door lock. I followed her lead, then reached around and found the zipper at the back of her dress. I eased it down to her waist. I kissed her lips and chin and throat, then I drew the straps off her shoulders and lowered the material to her waist.

I moaned. "You are so beautiful."

Rachel latched her fingers in my hair and guided my mouth to her breast. I slid my hand up her thigh as I fluttered my tongue over her nipple, teasing it, drawing it up. I paused when my palm reached bare skin.

I slid her dress up to her hip and took in a deep breath. Her nylons were held in place by a lacy garter belt. "God, girl. You're killing me."

She chuckled. A deep throaty sound tinged with a hint of mischief. "Bring a girl flowers, you never know what'll happen."

"I think I'll become a florist."

Her response was cut short when she felt my fingers hook around the flimsy elastic straps that arched over her hips. I drew her panties down to her calves.

"Oh, God." She moaned and spread her knees.

I used my fingers and tongue, and when we were finished, she sagged against the seat as if she didn't have the energy to find those little spaghetti straps in the tangle of fabric twisted around her waist much less slip her arms into them.

I tucked my shirt in my pants and zipped up.

Something heavy jarred the back end of the Camry. The bumper sagged toward the ground, then sprung upward. The car rocked on its springs.

"What the hell?"

Rachel's eyes grew wide as she bolted upright and flipped her seatback up. I spun around but couldn't see a damned thing through the condensation.

Someone rapped on the window behind my head. "Hey, man. We don't allow no fornication 'round here."

I grinned, and Rachel blew out a breath. "Marty."

"Farm's got a reputation to uphold, you know?"

Rachel had managed to find the right armholes. After I reached around and zipped up her dress, she lifted her butt off the seat and straightened the fabric around her thighs.

"Come on, you two. Get your clothes on."

She switched on the ignition and powered down my window as I adjusted my seat.

Snowflakes swirled into the car as Marty grinned broadly at the two of us. He clasped my hand in both of his. "Great to see you, man." His gaze slid over Rachel. "Lookin' fine there, Rache."

"Marty."

He tore his gaze away from her with effort. As he rested his forearms on the hood of the car and ducked down so he could see us better, he noticed the roses on the dash. "Oh, man. I see our boy here's putting the move on you." Marty shook his head. "So, what's he done now?"

Rachel chuckled.

"A guy gives a girl roses, it means one of two things. Either he's making up for something he's done or something he's about to do."

I rolled my eyes.

"You can't tell me you're done in Virginia already. You found the wandering boy, then?"

"No. I wish. Speaking of wandering, what in the hell are you doing here this late?"

"Oh," he shrugged, "this and that."

Rachel leaned toward me and whispered in my ear. "There's a new boarder Marty's got his eye on."

"Ah." I rubbed my face and leaned against the headrest. "Thank God. For a second," I held up a finger, "just a second, it crossed my mind that you'd changed on me. You know? Become dedicated, professional, focused on your—"

"Boring," Marty added.

"—job." I grinned. "But I see your focus is where it's always been."

"As it should be." Marty straightened and backed up, gazed at Rachel one last time, then said, "Well, I'll let you two lovebirds go." He reached out and nudged my arm. "Come back soon."

I waved to him as Rachel jacked up the heat, then powered up my window. She canted her head and watched Marty through her side view mirror as he crossed over to his Firebird. After he slid behind the wheel and started her up, she rested her forehead on the steering wheel and giggled.

"What?"

"My panties are still around my ankles."

I peered into the foot well and smiled, reached down and slipped them up her sleek legs.

"You're going to get me in trouble one of these days," Rachel said as she pulled them on and adjusted her dress.

"Me? If I remember correctly, you were quite the willing accomplice in tonight's, uh…passion."

A smile crossed her lips. "True. But you've corrupted me."

I wedged my elbow against her headrest and leaned toward her, smoothed my fingertips through her hair. "You mind telling me how?"

"Your penchant for fooling around in unusual places, that's how. Like Greg's pool and your deck."

I smiled. "In the rain."

Rachel's lips twitched. "Exactly. I never would have considered this before I met you. So, yes, you're a bad influence, Steve Cline."

Several other settings had popped uninvited into my mind, like on a feed room's dusty floor or against some straw bales in a horse's stall, and I was thankful she couldn't see what I was thinking.

"Pretty soon, I'll forget what it feels like to make love in bed."

"Adds to the excitement." I grinned. "You should be grateful."

"I have enough excitement in my life. Dating you, for one." Rachel rested against her seat, slowly turned her head, and looked at me. "And your getting hurt all the time," she said so softly, I almost didn't hear her.

I smoothed my fingers through her hair and kissed her. "Not this time. I promise."

She sighed. "I've heard that before."

"You'll see."

Her gaze lingered over the roses; then she straightened in her seat. "Want me to drive?"

"You don't look like you have the energy," I said.

"You wore me out, but your truck's gotta be freezing by now. Why don't you drive my car?"

"Sure."

We switched seats, then decided on Clyde's as I drove into Columbia. Flurries swirled across the road. The flakes were so light, they funneled over the hood and swept across the windshield without touching the glass.

◇◇◇

I pushed my plate to the side and rested my forearms on the red-and-white checked tablecloth. Tilted the whiskey sour in my hand and watched the ice swirl round the glass as Rachel scooped a forkful of shrimp and sausage off her plate. Her paella was loaded with calamari, chicken, and vegetables, as well, and her meal had come garnished with mussels. She'd lined the shiny black shells in a neat row along the edge of her plate. I'd ordered a pasta dish stuffed with chunks of chicken, sausage disks, and vegetables drizzled with tomato-wine sauce, and now that I'd finished, my eyelids felt weighted.

I should have laid off the alcohol, but I suspected the fact that I'd only slept three and a half hours that afternoon probably had something to do with how I felt. That, and sex. Alcohol, food, and sex. There wasn't a combination better suited to put me under the table.

I tore off a chunk of bread and watched Rachel herd a couple of pieces of calamari into a pile. "You don't like squid?"

She looked up from her plate and curled her upper lip. "Is that what this is?"

"Uh-huh."

"Yuck. I thought calamari was an herb or something." She peered at her plate and nudged a piece of squid with her fork.

I chuckled.

"Uh." She looked like she wanted to spit as she gulped her iced tea. "Why don't they just say squid?"

I shrugged. "Maybe because it sounds disgusting."

She inspected the rest of her meal, and when she was satisfied that the squid chunks were properly segregated, she scooped up a forkful of shrimp and chicken and gestured to my plate. "Obviously you enjoyed yours?"

"Yeah. No squid," I stated, and Rachel rolled her eyes. "Plus, I was starving."

I signaled to our waiter to bring us more coffee, then relaxed against my chair. We were seated at a table for two along the windows that overlooked Lake Kittamaqundi, and we had the entire lower level to ourselves. Several parties on the upper level still lingered over coffee and dessert, their muffled voices occasionally drifting down to us, but most of the action was concentrated in the bar. Nine-fifteen on a snowy weeknight, I would have been surprised if the restaurant had been any busier.

Outside, it had begun to snow in earnest, and a powdery dusting coated the sidewalks. Streaks of light from distant buildings shot straight and true across the lake, sparkling on the choppy waves kicked up by a westerly breeze.

Rachel turned her head and followed my gaze. She looked absolutely stunning, a jumble of contrasts. The delicate silk straps cutting over the hard edge of her collarbone and her sculpted shoulders; her creamy pale skin and the taut line of her neck against her long black hair that draped over her shoulders like a shimmering curtain in the candlelight; her sultry dark eyes in shadow and a soft blush on her cheeks.

"I hope the snow doesn't amount to much," she said. "We're having a test prep tomorrow night."

"How's the class going?"

Rachel all but rolled her eyes. "It is *so* boring." She stabbed a sausage disk and piece of shrimp and popped them in her mouth. "The instructor's this shriveled old man who probably dreams in binary code. And…oh, God. He has this monotone voice that drones on and on. And some of the guys in the class who are right out of high school…tell me we were never that stupid." She chuckled.

"What?"

The waiter paused alongside our table, filled our coffee cups, and asked Rachel if she was finished with her plate.

"Yes."

He gathered our plates together. "Will you be having dessert this evening?"

"Yes," Rachel said, then asked me, "Want to share?"

"Sure."

"I was thinking about getting the Mochaccino Napoleon. That okay?"

I nodded, and after our waiter headed to the kitchen, I said, "You were saying?"

Rachel frowned at the tablecloth. "What was I saying? Oh, yeah." She chuckled. "Our instructor has this sinus condition. He's always sniffing. Wet, mucousy gunk that rattles in his nose." She paused. "It is rather disgusting listening to that all through class. Anyway, he's up at the overhead, going over code for our homework assignment, and he sniffs a little too energetically, and you can just tell that a big glob of something slipped into the back of his throat. His eyes get real big, and he excuses himself. Well, these two juvenile delinquents are just about rolling on the floor, they're laughing so hard. I don't know how the poor man had the guts to come back into the room."

I drained the last of my drink.

"One of the guys in particular is a real pain in the ass."

"How so?"

"He's obnoxious as hell. And conceited. Probably rich, too. He plays polo," she added as if that explained everything. "I don't even know why he's taking the class. He hardly ever shows up, and when he does, he doesn't do anything." She frowned. "Somehow, he figured out that I ride, and he thinks just because we have something in common, I ought to be falling all over myself to go out with him."

Suddenly, the meal I'd just eaten didn't sit so well in my stomach, and I could feel my jaw muscles tighten.

Rachel must have noticed. She arched her eyebrows. "You're jealous."

I shook my head. "Worried. He sounds like someone who doesn't handle rejection well."

"Probably not. But, like I said, he's hardly ever there."

I set my empty glass on the table. "He asked you out?"

She nodded.

"How do you think he found out you're involved with horses?"

"I have no idea."

I pictured the smudges on her driver's side window. Smudges that could have been made by someone cupping his hands to peer into her car. I touched her hand. "Be careful, will you?"

She smiled and took my hand in hers. "I'll be fine."

I smoothed my thumb over her knuckles. "How 'bout I come up tomorrow night? We can go out before your class."

She shook her head. "I have to study. Plus, that would be silly, driving all that way just to eat." I thought about what we'd done before our meal tonight, and she must have sensed some nonverbal message from me, a sudden stillness, or possibly an electrical impulse passing from my hand to hers, because she lifted her eyes, and her lips twitched when she noted my expression.

"What if I come up Thursday?"

"That'll work."

The waiter brought our dessert as I rooted in my jacket pocket for the little notebook and pencil I kept there. He placed the pastry in front of Rachel along with an extra plate and two forks before he headed back to his post. I jotted down Bruce's apartment number and the farm's cell phone number, tore out the sheet, and handed it to Rachel.

"I doubt you'll ever need to call the cell number, since I only have it with me during my shift, but just in case."

"Who has it the rest of the time?"

"When I get off at noon, it's kept in the office until the woman who trains me comes in. The day crew has to use walky-talkies. Apparently some crewmembers were using the phones for private calls."

"What's she like?"

"Who?"

"The woman who trains you."

"Oh. Dedicated. She knows the job backward and forward," I said, knowing full-well that wasn't what she had in mind.

Rachel frowned as she centered the dessert between us and handed me a fork. "How long do you think you'll be in Virginia?"

"Two weeks. Three at the most. If I haven't found him by then, I doubt I will."

She used her fork to slice through the thin pastry separated by layers of hazelnut, coffee, and mascarpone cream fillings. "Is it dangerous?" She slowly lifted her eyes.

"No. As far as anyone knows, I'm just doing my job. Nothing else."

She swallowed and wiped the corner of her mouth with her napkin. "I worry about you."

"I know," I said. "I'm sorry."

◇◇◇

During my last shift Tuesday morning, the Storm Bird mare had kept her eye on me, and I'd left work without delivering a foal. Wednesday morning was different.

"She'll go before daybreak," Maddie whispered in my ear as we stood in the middle of the aisle. She'd leaned in close, and her warm breath slid across my neck.

"Yesterday," I said, "it seemed like she was watching *me*."

Maddie chuckled softly, and as she turned to face the stall, her breast brushed my arm. "I swear some of the matron mares wait for me to get in the truck and head to another barn before they get down to business."

"Hmm."

She handed me the cell phone. "Well, good luck."

"Thanks."

"Oh, by the way. You've been mucking way too many stalls between rounds. They don't expect it."

She walked over to where her leather gloves lay on a straw bale and bent over to pick them up. Some other person did that, and I wouldn't even have noticed. Unless that some other person was Rachel. But Maddie had this way of translating every action into a movement that mirrored a sexual act and knocked my blood pressure off the chart.

She straightened and said over her shoulder, "Call me if you need me."

Her hips swayed as she strolled down the aisle, and just before she stepped through the doorway, she flipped her hair out from under her coat collar. God, that girl was hot. I swallowed and looked at the mare. She stood quietly at the back of her stall, but the patch of sweat that spread slowly outward from the spot where her hind leg blended into her belly, darkening her chestnut hair to black, betrayed her.

She was heating up. I grinned. Like me.

I slipped into the stall and flattened my palm on the mare's chest to evaluate just how hot she truly was. I kept my hand on her side as I moved back to her hindquarters and saw what

Maddie meant about the muscles relaxing. Her haunches and the muscles around her tail head seemed sunken and slack. I ran the rest of my check, noticing that Maddie had been nice enough to do up the mare's tail. And with a blue Vetrap, no less.

I flew through checking the rest of the barns, and when I returned to barn six, the mare was down. I sped back to the clinic, filled two buckets with hot water and was relieved to see her on her feet when I returned. Twenty minutes later, she delivered a chestnut filly into the world, and I'd helped her do it.

I went on another round, thinking Maddie didn't have to worry about me doing many stalls tonight. I stopped in front of Sumthingelse's stall when I noticed she wasn't squinting at the light like the rest of the mares. I went in and checked her. She had wax on her teats, but according to Maddie, they often waxed up a couple of weeks before they foaled. I stood by her shoulder, slipped my ice-cold fingers into the warm coat covering her muscular chest, and wondered if she was warmer than she should have been. But the air temperature was below freezing, and I'd been dunking my hands in and out of water for the past half an hour. Almost anything would have felt warm.

"So, why aren't you dozing?" I said aloud.

She swung her head around and touched my waist, pressed her muzzle into my coat like she was trying to tell me something.

"Go to sleep," I said as I left her stall.

No oxygen tank and breathing mask or container of special drugs sat in the aisle in preparation for a difficult delivery. When I glanced back into the stall, she'd turned her head and was staring at me with wide, brown eyes.

I returned to barn six and found that my new foal had kicked free of her umbilical cord, and the dam was up. I worked through the procedures, wishing I'd paid more attention to them instead of Maddie. When I finished, I realized I was ten minutes late for my five o'clock round, and I hadn't even begun to feed the barns.

Outside, a thick layer of frost coated the landscape, and the barns and fence boards and grass sparkled in the moonlight. I glanced at the sky before climbing into the Ford. The moon looked as if someone had taken a scythe to it and lopped off the right quarter. As I stood there, a plane passed silently beneath it.

I checked barn one, then froze when I hit the lights in two. A deep equine groan rumbled under the eaves. I sprinted to Sumthingelse's stall and threw open the door. It slid into the doorstop with a loud crack that startled her neighbor.

The mare was down and straining. When I crouched at her hindquarters, she rolled onto her sternum. She arched her neck and tried to lunge to her feet. A hind hoof dug through the straw and slipped on the wet asphalt, causing the mare to briefly lose her purchase before she scrambled to her feet. I cursed under my breath.

The straw was a sodden mess. An unpleasant smell hung in the air, and I realized that the floor was soaked because her water had broken.

I yanked the farm's cell phone out of my jacket and left my number with the vet's service; then I called his pager and keyed in my number. I called Maddie next, and as I listened to the phone ring, the mare lifted her tail, and a pearly white, translucent membrane glistened at the base of her vulva.

This was too damned fast. No wonder her placentas detached. Her uterine contractions must have been phenomenal, tearing the placenta from its anchor.

I hung up on the seventh ring and called Frank.

The mare sank to her knees, and when she collapsed to the ground, the impact forced a groan from her lungs.

I looked at the phone in disbelief when a busy signal shrilled through the earpiece. Who the hell was he talking to at five-twenty in the morning? I focused past the phone in my hand and watched the mare strain. According to Maddie, once a mare entered stage two, they often delivered their foals in less than fifteen minutes.

Okay. Don't fucking panic, Cline. Maddie said that if her placenta detached, I'd see a bright red velvety-looking membrane instead of the white sac…so, everything was proceeding normally. I hoped.

I punched in Maddie's number again. Where in the hell was she? On the sixth ring, I hung up and dialed Frank's number, and when the busy signal sounded, I flipped the phone closed and crouched in the straw. Something didn't look right. I swallowed. What was it? A bulge had formed below the mare's tail, and…Oh, no. My stomach twisted into a knot when I realized what was wrong.

They hadn't opened her up. Her Caslick sutures were still in place, and the foal's hoof was being forced against the vulvar tissue with nowhere to go.

I jumped up, pulled the door closed, and ran to the storage area at the back of the barn. I latched onto the foal kit and raced back to the stall, vaguely aware that all of the horses in the barn were tracking me as I ran back and forth.

The bulge had grown, and if I didn't take action soon, the mare would tear. I aligned the scissors with the puffy ridge of scar tissue left from repeated operations in her past and hoped Maddie was right, that I'd be able to tell when to stop cutting.

I swallowed, then drew in a shaky breath and gritted my teeth. I covered the bottom point of the scissors with my left index finger, so I wouldn't cut the foal by mistake; then I advanced the scissors and brought the handles together. The blades cut easily through the tissue. Blood welled around the incision and trickled toward the floor.

Okay. I breathed in. That wasn't so bad. I advanced the scissors again and repeated the process until the points connected with a wall of tissue they wouldn't cut through. I jammed the scissors in my back pocket, knelt in the straw, and caught my breath. A chill traveled up my back even though I was sweating.

Almost immediately, the foal's hoof slid into view. I tried all four numbers without luck, dumped my coat in the aisle, and rolled up my sleeves. The foal was coming whether I got hold of anyone or not, and it was coming now.

The foal's first leg was joined by the second, and when its muzzle was visible, resting on the legs just like it was supposed to, I heaved a sigh of relief.

The mare groaned, and in the next push, the head was delivered.

"God, girl, you gotta slow up."

I peeled the sac away from the foal's muzzle and kept light pressure on its forelegs, and two minutes later, the foal slid onto the wet straw. I pulled the sac off and rolled him onto his sternum. He jerked his head up and grunted.

"Good," I said relieved. "You protest. Let me know you don't like it."

I grabbed a towel out of the kit, cleared his nasal passages and rubbed him down, and he didn't like that, either.

As I straightened, the phone rang.

Now that the foal had been delivered and appeared healthy, Dr. Palansky tried to back out.

"Look, this is an Elusive Quality foal, and with the mare's history, Dr. Nash won't be impressed if you leave it 'til later."

He grumbled a bit, then said he'd be out by seven. Next, I called Frank, and this time, he picked up.

"Sumthingelse foaled—"

"Shit!"

"—and it's a boy."

Chapter 10

Frank's truck rumbled up to the barn doors at six-twenty, and I listened to his footsteps as he hustled down the aisle. He swung into the doorway, then paused and stared down at the colt. "I'll be damned."

I'd already completed most of the chores and was crouched in the straw, clamping a tail tag in the foal's hair. The colt thrust a hind leg out and smacked his dam's haunches. "He's full of himself."

"The good ones always are." Frank ran his fingers through his thinning hair. "Did she have any trouble?"

"No, but I had to open her."

Frank shook his head and sighed. "Her name's on the list, but Deirdre's trip put her behind schedule. How'd you know how to do that? I thought you said you hadn't foaled out before?"

"Maddie explained the procedure."

Frank nodded, then sidestepped the foal and lifted the mare's tail. "Nice job, Steve. Dr. Nash wouldn't have done any better."

"Thanks."

The mare reared her head back, then heaved to her feet. As she caught her balance, the afterbirth plopped into the bedding. She whinnied as she zeroed in on her foal; then she lowered her head and licked his neck. The colt jerked at her touch, a movement that was at once uncoordinated and highly reflexive. The other foals had done the same thing in the beginning. No doubt, being touched was an unusual tactile sensation after spending eleven months in his mother's womb.

When Frank dragged the afterbirth into the aisle, I commented on the fact that she'd shed it so quickly.

"Most take a couple hours, but I've seen them clean out right away, too. Did you call Dr. Palansky?"

"Yes. He said he'll be here by seven." I checked my watch. "I need to check on the Storm Bird foal, then I'll finish up here."

Frank raised his eyebrows. "You had a busy night, then."

"Yeah." I stepped out of the stall and latched the door. "Mr. Hadley wanted to be called when his mare foaled, but I didn't have time, and I thought it best not to call him anyway, since I was the only one here. Do you want me to call him now?"

Frank sucked on his lower lip. "I'll call him, and after you're finished in six," he gestured to Sumthingelse, "you'll need to wash her down where you cut her."

"Okay. Oh, and I haven't fed any of the barns."

"The crew will do it when they come in." Frank turned toward the exit, then, as an afterthought, he pivoted around and said, "You did good."

I smiled as I watched him head for his truck.

As promised, Dr. Palansky arrived at seven. He inoculated both foals and pronounced them healthy, and by nine o'clock, they'd worked out the mechanics of nursing.

Afterwards, I hooked up with the crew in barn one. As I stabbed the pitchfork into a clump of wet straw and flung it into the muck wagon, I appreciated Frank's management skills more than ever. He'd wisely avoided pairing me with Paul or Tiller. But I wondered how long that would last.

Dust and ammonia fumes clogged the air as Eminem blared from a boom box dangling from an electric conduit. Ronnie had brought it from home, and the volume was cranked so high, the cheap plastic housing vibrated against the stall's grillwork. But it beat the silence of an empty barn. I propped the fork against the wall and raked the rest of the soiled bedding into a pile. The sunlight streaked halfway down the barn aisle, raising the outside temperature above freezing. Even though the horses had gone out an hour earlier, the barn still held their warmth, and their smell.

Ronnie's walky-talky squawked, and after a moment, he poked his head in the doorway. "That was Elaine. They want you in two."

"Is something wrong?"

"Doesn't sound like it. The proud poppa's come to look at his new foal, is all."

I parked alongside the silver Viper and walked into the barn. Dawn, from barn five, and another girl, whose name I didn't know, stood side by side in the aisle with their heads bent together, whispering. Both girls clammed up as I skirted the muck wagon. Tiller looked up, but I didn't catch his expression. The other guy on the team was the only one working.

Shane Hadley turned at the sound of my approach. "Steve." He stepped forward and pumped my hand in his, and for a brief second, I thought he was going to hug me. Instead, he clamped his arm around my shoulders and propelled me toward the others. He said to Frank, "Deirdre needs to give this guy a raise or, at the very least, a bonus. After all, he practically had to perform surgery on my horse."

Frank nodded but was far more pragmatic about the whole thing now that the foal was safely on the ground.

Hadley let go of me, rubbed both hands over his face like he was still grappling with the idea that he had a live, healthy foal. His hands left his face, and he restlessly dragged his fingers through his hair. He kept it short and trim but long on top so he could spike it. He wore the same khaki jacket and immaculate jeans as the last time, only he'd exchanged the boots for loafers. He looked like he could have been modeling for the cover of *Details*, and Elaine's get-up didn't mesh with a barn environment, either.

Her black hair hung well past her shoulders. Every time I'd seen her, it had been straight, but she'd curled it this morning and had gathered it in a ribbon that matched her plaid skirt.

Her silky curls shimmered under the overhead lights as they cascaded over the collar of her nylon jacket.

Hadley exhaled and turned to look in the stall. "I still can't believe it. She lost two foals on me and two before I bought her. That's why I was able to get her so cheap."

The foal was on his feet. He curled his thin pink tongue around his upper lip and prodded his mother's flank, searching for breakfast. Hadley stepped into the stall and stretched out his hand. When his fingers touched the foal's back, the colt skittered around his mother, all long legs tangling in the straw and bumping into his mother's hocks. He almost toppled over before he made it to the other side.

Hadley stood there for a moment, staring after him; then he turned to us and said, "He's going to be something else." A smile lit up his face. "Just like his mother." His gaze slid right past Frank and me and locked on Elaine.

I glanced over my shoulder. It was difficult to judge her age, but based on the photograph of two young girls that she had propped on her desk, I guessed she was in her early thirties.

Hadley stepped out of the stall. "Frank, thanks for your help."

"No problem, Mr. Hadley." Frank had had enough standing around to suit him and took that as his cue to get going.

Elaine stepped over to the stall and peered through the bars. "What are you going to name him?"

Hadley gripped a bar in his hand. "I haven't given it a thought. To be honest, I didn't think I'd have to worry about it." He slipped a hand in his jacket pocket, turned around, and palmed a bill in my hand. "Here you go, Steve."

"Thank you, sir." I tucked the bill in my pocket.

"Hey, I'm having a party Friday night. Why don't you join us?"

"Uh." Movement to my left caught my eye. Tiller was standing near the front of the John Deere 5220, close enough to hear our conversation.

"Awh, come on. You'll have a great time. Bring a friend if you like." Hadley clapped his hand on my shoulder. "What do you say?"

"Thank you, sir." I glanced at Elaine and had a sneaky suspicion she wished she were the one receiving the invite.

"Shane. Call me Shane."

"Yes, s—" I grinned. "Thanks, Shane."

"Good." Hadley looked in on the foal one last time; then he and Elaine started down the aisle.

As they skirted the tractor, Tiller busied himself with checking the controls.

I could hear the foal's loud greedy slurps from where I stood. I went back in the stall and crouched down so I could watch him nurse. Milk droplets leaked from the corners of his mouth and trickled down his long whiskers. Apparently, whiskers were something a horse had to grow into because the colt's were as long as his mother's and lent him a comical look.

Something scuffed the asphalt outside the stall, and the sound raised the hair on the back of my neck. I turned around.

Tiller stood in the doorway with his hands jammed in his pockets. He'd lost his sunglasses, and he'd actually shaved for a change. "You brownnosing the owners, now?"

"Just doing my job. But then, I guess that's a novel concept for you."

He smirked. "You oughta skip that party, Cline. Fancy joint like that, you won't fit in."

"Hey, Tiller! Move the damn tractor!" one of the crew yelled.

He loosened his jaw, then stalked off.

Something touched the back of my thigh. I slowly pivoted to find the foal searching for a drink. "Sorry, kid. Wrong person, species, *and* sex."

I placed a hand on his chest and hooked my arm around his butt and inched him over to his mamma. He dug in and resisted every step of the way, but when I finally got him within striking distance, he forgot all about me, stretched his head under his mother's belly, and nuzzled her udder.

◇◇◇

When I pulled into Bruce's parking lot at twelve-twenty Wednesday afternoon, Fluffy dragged his master off the sidewalk.

I climbed out of the Chevy, and the old guy hobbled over and planted his hand on the bed's sidewall to catch his balance. I took the leash and felt like booting Fluffy but contented myself with tightening my hold on him, instead.

"Some weather we're having, ain't it? I'll be glad when it warms up some. Fluffy here don't like it none, either, but that don't stop him from wanting out ten times a day. His bladder ain't what it used to be, not that it was great in the first place." He wheezed and struggled to catch his breath. "Oh, I been thinking. That fella who dropped off the Firebird," he adjusted his grip on the Chevy's peeling paint, "I think he works construction."

"How do you mean?"

"He had dust down the front of his pants and on his coat sleeves."

"Great," I said although I didn't know what to make of it. "Thanks."

He nodded, still catching his breath. "I think of something else, I'll let you know."

I handed over Fluffy, then let myself into Bruce's apartment, took a shower, and decided that, whether I liked it or not, I'd have to break down and do the laundry. As I stuffed the clothes I'd been wearing into a plastic bag, I remembered the money Hadley had given me. I dug it out, unfolded the bill, and stared at it in disbelief. He hadn't slipped me a five or a ten, but a C-note.

After I started a load of laundry in the basement, I rooted through Bruce's medicine cabinet and pulled everything off the shelves in the linen closet before starting on the one in his bedroom. Wherever Bruce had gone, he hadn't felt compelled to leave any clues behind. His computer was a wasteland of games. His ISP had disconnected its service last September for nonpayment, and his phone contacts had led us absolutely nowhere.

I finished schlepping my way through the junk on the floor of the bedroom closet and had switched to searching pants pockets, when I noticed a brightly wrapped present on the top shelf. It sat behind the basketball that I'd tossed up there my first day in the apartment. I lifted it off the shelf. A card was tucked beneath an iridescent bow.

Corey's name was printed in Bruce's hand.

As I sat on the edge of the bed and fingered the bow, images from the past week slid behind my eyes. Corey curled up in the dining room chair, her head bowed as tears fell softly to her lap. The suds dripping off Maddie's arm. Paul's flushed face close to mine, tears brimming in his eyes as he stood in the barn aisle and pleaded with her. The moonlight glinting off a knowing equine eye. Storm Bird's foal taking its first breath.

My gaze drifted over the closet full of clothes and the duffle bags piled beneath them, then settled on the bunch of keys on his dresser. I couldn't think of one good reason that explained his buying Corey a gift, then not giving it to her. Or, at the very least, picking up the phone and calling her.

Not one damned reason except that he couldn't.

◇◇◇

Snow sliced sideways through the Chevy's headlights as I pulled into the clinic parking lot Thursday morning at three o'clock. Two inches covered the ground with another three expected by rush hour. When I pulled into a parking space, Maddie strode through the snow and reached the Chevy's door before I'd even climbed out.

"What's wrong?" I said as the door creaked open.

"Shit." She stomped in the snow and clamped her arms around her chest. "What the hell happened with Sumthingelse? Why didn't you call me?"

"I did." I pulled the brim of my ball cap farther down my forehead and stepped into the snow. "You didn't answer."

"When did you call?"

"Around five-fifteen, five-twenty."

"I didn't hear the phone," she said.

Something about her tone, and the fact that she couldn't bring herself to look me in the eye, led me to believe she was lying. I cut around the Chevy's hood and headed for the clinic. "Sure you didn't."

She stalked alongside me. "What the hell's that supposed to mean?"

I paused in the doorway. "Look, I'm sorry. I shouldn't have said that. I just thought you might be out…or something." Color tinged her cheeks, and I wasn't at all convinced that the weather was responsible.

"Where the hell would I have been at five-fifteen in the morning?"

Without intending to, my gaze raked over her body. "I don't know. You tell me." I headed for the clinic.

"Stop." Maddie grabbed my coat sleeve. "What did you tell Frank?"

"What do you mean?"

"About why I didn't show."

"It didn't come up."

"What do you mean, 'it didn't come up'?"

"Just that," I said. "Frank was too preoccupied calling Mr. Hadley and maybe wondering how he was going to explain his own absence."

"You foaled her out alone?"

"Yeah."

"Oh." Maddie caught up with me as I strode into the clinic and punched in. She moved closer and touched my arm. "Steve, I'm sorry. I didn't mean to be so bitchy, it's just that this job means a lot to me."

I sighed. "I know it does." I turned away from her and wedged a Coke and a Ziploc bag containing three pizza slices onto the top rack in the fridge. I straightened and closed the door. "Look. When Dr. Nash gets back, all she's going to focus on is that foal, and Frank's not going to bring up the fact that you weren't there. I have no reason to tell her, either, but Mr. Hadley's so excited about the delivery, it'll probably come up that I had to open the mare."

Maddie covered her mouth. "They didn't get to her."

"No, they didn't. Thank God you described the procedure. Anyway, if Dr. Nash asks why you weren't there to do it, I'll tell her everything happened so fast, I didn't have time to call you." I knocked the snow off my hat. "Which is just about the truth, anyway."

She tilted her head and looked into my face. This morning, her eye color fell somewhere between dark green and brown, and they were altogether way too sultry for her to be standing so close. Her red curls hung loose on her shoulders and had frizzed from the snow. She hadn't zipped her coat all the way, and the buttons of her flannel shirt were open, exposing a v-shaped slice of flesh.

She moved closer and flattened her hands on my jacket. "Thanks, Steve."

I swallowed. Every part of me ached to touch her, to feel her skin beneath my palms. Beneath my lips.

She reached up and traced the thin scar that tracked across my cheek with the tip of her finger. "How'd you get this?"

I clamped my fingers around her wrist and lowered her hand. "Where were you, Maddie?"

"What?"

"Yesterday morning. Were you with Paul?"

Her eyes blazed as she jerked her hand free. "That's none of your business." She spun around and headed for the door, then paused and said over her shoulder, "That gray mare in two foaled around seven. The foal's nursing well, so you probably won't have to do anything special except check the mare's teats every now and then to make sure he's still getting milk." She breathed in deeply. "Paul and I broke up, remember?"

"It doesn't seem to have registered."

"That's because he's stupid." She slammed the door on her way out.

I spent the next few hours mucking stalls and driving from barn to barn, rousting the mares from their sleep while the snow relentlessly blew across the landscape. It eddied through cracks beneath barn doors and swirled down the aisles and accumulated on fence boards and barn roofs and shrouded the parked trucks until they resembled inert lumps of rock embedded in the landscape. Except for an occasional snowplow scraping the roadway, the night was quiet. The snow sucked the sound from the air until it felt like the world had narrowed down to a tiny white cocoon.

When I finished feeding barn six, the sky had finally lightened in the east. Morning had come later than usual. I went outside, and as I slid the door shut, the muffled sound of a heavy diesel engine throbbed in the distance. I stepped away from the building and looked toward Bear Wallow. Unlike barns one through six, the hay barn was accessible from the main road. A compact pickup was parked near the corner of the building, and someone was backing a Massey Ferguson tractor, equipped with a blade, from beneath the roof overhang. I climbed into the Ford as the tractor swept past the lake and backed into the clinic parking lot. As I pulled down six's drive, I watched him back right up to the clinic door, lower the blade, and clear a path all the way to the road.

At first I'd assumed that Frank was the driver, but he owned a full-sized truck. Since it was already six-thirty, and none of the mares had been acting the least bit suspicious, I headed to the clinic as the driver backed toward the office door, preparing for another sweep through the lot. I paused on the road, at the mouth of the drive, as he chugged toward the exit, scraping a wall of snow toward the edge of the lot.

Michael Tiller stared through the cab's Plexiglas as he angled the tractor's nose toward the Ford's front quarter panel. His head bobbed in rhythm with the tractor's vibrations, and his dark sunglasses looked like an insect's eyes. Before I could slam the gearshift into reverse, he cut the wheel and grinned down at me as the large back tire swung perilously close to the front bumper.

"Asshole."

He pulled onto the road in front of me, and before he had a chance to shift gears, I spun the Ford down onto the lot and parked. The day went further downhill when Frank paired me with Paul. Ronnie and Ben rounded out the rest of our team.

I fingered the truck's keys as I considered my crew. The duct tape on Ronnie's parka had peeled away from an elbow, revealing a clump of matted filling that had once been white but now resembled tangled straw on a stall floor. The cold air had flushed Ben's pale skin, and his nose was red and pinched. He licked his lips, and they were so chapped and raw, a deep groove had split his lower lip.

"Because of the snow," I said, "I'll make two trips. Who wants to go first?"

"Me," Paul said as he slipped into his coat. "I'll pull the tractor out of the way so we can do turnouts."

Paul and I headed outside. Except for a ridge of snow surrounding the trucks that had sat in the lot all night, Tiller had cleaned the lot and moved on to barn one. Paul remained quiet until I backed the Ford out of its slot and shifted into drive.

He cleared this throat. "You and the guys can joke around behind my back all you want," he said, "but I love Maddie more than I've ever loved anyone in my life."

I glanced at him.

"I know what she's like." Paul shifted on the vinyl seat and planted his back against his door. "So I'm warning you. Stay away from her."

I turned onto Bear Wallow. "Like I told you before, I'm not interested." Well, most of me wasn't.

"The hell you aren't. Just stay away from her."

I switched on my left turn signal and applied the brake as a snowplow barreled toward us. The lake's dam was at eyelevel, and the snow stretched out flat and even and undisturbed to the far bank, where a clump of dead cattails poked through the snow in a ragged line.

"Like my predecessor stayed away from her?" I said and glanced at Paul. He clenched his jaw and squinted, boring his gaze into the side of my skull. I was suddenly reminded of Ronnie's unflattering moniker.

"You wanna stay healthy, you'll keep away from her."

The snowplow rumbled toward us, flinging a wall of snow twenty feet into the air. The spray splattered the berm and plastered a road sign that vibrated in the truck's wake.

"Did Bruce stay healthy?" I said in the sudden quiet.

"He ain't here no more, is he?" Paul said. His gaze swept across the frozen lake as he swiveled around to face forward, and a muscle at the base of his jaw twitched.

I accelerated and hung a left onto Stone Manor, wondering if I was sitting next to a murderer. Because of his obsession with Maddie, it didn't take much to imagine him resorting to violence, but murder? But his insinuating that he was responsible for Bruce's leaving could be nothing more than a macho ploy on his part.

I coasted to a stop and waited for Tiller to pull the big Massey Ferguson from the mouth of barn one's drive.

"Look at that asshole," Paul said. "He thinks he's a big shot 'cause he gets to spend the day plowing instead of mucking stalls."

"Was Maddie with you the night Sumthingelse foaled?" I said.

"Yeah, she was. Fucking my brains out, too."

I wordlessly dropped Paul off, swung around for the other two; then we got busy with turnouts. I latched my lead on the last mare in the barn, and when I slid the stall door open, she lunged through the doorway like it was a starting gate.

"Hey!" I yanked her head around. "Cool it."

She jogged down the aisle, curled around the hold I had on her halter. Her eyes grew wide as she noted that the dormant landscape she was accustomed to had been replaced with a blanket of white.

"Watch that mare," Ronnie yelled as he crossed the back lot with an empty lead dangling from his hand. "She's a screwball."

"No kidding."

Her neck tensed as three horses cantered past, a blur of brown against a field of white.

Ronnie changed directions, loped up alongside me, then forged ahead. "I'll get the gate."

"Thanks."

He swung it inward, and I led the mare through the opening and turned her to face me. She splayed her front legs and tensed every muscle in her body, waiting. Man, I hated it when they did that.

I reached up, and as I unclipped the lead, she wheeled around. The heavy bull snap at the end of the lead wrenched free of her halter and flipped toward my face. I stepped back and ducked as it sailed past my ear. The mare bunched her hindquarters and propelled herself away from us, stretching across the frozen ground at a dead run and flinging clumps of snow over the fence.

The horses galloped across the field, flowing over the gentle hills like a wave, a spray of snow rising in their wake. Most of them were no longer as fleet as they once were, burdened now with pendulous bellies that rocked between their legs, but they were graceful just the same. I pictured Corey galloping cross-country; then I wondered why her brother hadn't ridden and frowned when I realized I'd thought of him in past tense. Where the hell was he?

Chapter 11

Paul cranked the John Deere to life and pulled into the barn aisle as Ben joined us at the pasture fence. The herd swooped down to the far end of the field, but before long, one mare stopped to paw the snow, followed by another. In the next minute, the rest of the herd lost interest in their romp and joined in the search for blades of withered grass buried beneath the snow. The three of us kicked the snow off our boots as we trudged into the storage area. Paul was waiting for us in the barn aisle.

He stood by the first stall on the right, leaning on a pitchfork. "It's about time. This damned snow's gonna make us late unless we pick up the pace."

We cut over to the tool rack. Ben selected a pitchfork, and Ronnie argued that it was his favorite.

Ben rolled his eyes and held out the fork. "Here, have it. What do I care?" Ben lifted another pitchfork off the rack and hefted it, testing its balance. "Paul's right, you know? Last time it snowed like this, we was a hour late getting home, ain't that right, Ronnie?"

Ronnie nodded. "They yank Tiller off a crew to run the plow, what do you expect?"

"And Bruce didn't stay for the morning work, either," Ben said. "Remember?"

That caught my attention when I realized they were talking about the day before Bruce quit.

Ronnie grabbed the newest-looking rake before anyone else had a chance. "What was worse, it was a Friday."

"Yeah, well, it's not like you had a date or anything," Ben said, and Ronnie punched his shoulder. "Hey, cut it out." Ben chuckled and kneaded his arm. "Course, we would've been later if Dr. Nash had done her rounds like usual."

"Why didn't she?" I said, and Ben and Ronnie turned and looked at me. Maybe they were beginning to wonder why I asked so many questions, so I threw in another. "Does the snow alter her rounds, too?"

"Not usually," Ronnie said as Ben eyed the rake he'd selected. "I think she went up to the house."

I grabbed a rake with three missing tines. "Is that unusual?"

Ben and Ronnie looked at each other, and Ronnie raised his eyebrows. "Never known it to happen since I been here, and I been here a long time."

"Yeah. Dr. Nash is real efficient." Ben tested his rake in the dirt. "She never breaks her routine."

"Not 'nless she gone, like today," Ronnie said.

"Well, yeah. There's that." Ben hooted. "Hey, maybe we won't be late, after all."

Paul stepped around the corner and scowled at us. "You shits keep running your mouths, we're gonna be late, Dr. Nash or no Dr. Nash."

The three of us listened to him clomp down the aisle; then Ronnie mumbled under his breath, "Must have a hot date planned."

"Ronnie," I said quietly. "Do you think he ever did anything more than shove Bruce?"

"Why?" Ronnie whispered.

"I work with Maddie, remember? It would be nice to know what to expect."

Ronnie scratched his head, and the dreadlocks sticking between his fingers jerked around like bunches of dried corn-stalks. "Nah. He talks the talk but don't got the balls for the walk."

"I hope you're right."

A smile broke across Ronnie's face. "Just keep your distance from his girl, Steve."

"And what if Bruce didn't?"

Ronnie pondered that. "I don't know, Steve. I just don't know."

We got busy on the stalls. I was on my third one when Ronnie's walky-talky squawked, and Elaine's thin voice vibrated from the speaker.

"Ten-four," Ronnie said, and the talky squawked again as he poked his head in the doorway. "Head over to the clinic, okay?"

"All right."

"Find Elaine. She'll tell you what to do."

The cloudbank had fragmented in the east, and broad shafts of sunlight cut between purple-bottomed clouds and streaked toward the earth. The breeze had kicked up, and the air was filled with tiny specks of snow that glittered against the sky.

The farm's cell phone rang as I slipped behind the steering wheel. "Cline."

A female voice giggled. "You sound so serious," Rachel said.

I smiled. "Of course I do. What's up?"

"We got eight inches here. I don't think you should drive up tonight."

"No big deal," I said, then belatedly remembered the piece-of-shit tires I had on the truck. Adding weight to the bed only worked to a point.

"I know it isn't for you, but I'd spend half my evening worrying about you. Plus, I need to study. We have a test Monday."

"Did that guy bother you last night?"

"He wasn't there. Like I said, he hardly ever comes to class."

I started up the Ford and shifted into gear. "What about this weekend? You think you could come down? I work most of Saturday, but I get off at midnight. You could stay the night and Sunday day."

"I don't know. It depends on how I'm doing getting ready for this test." She hesitated. "Is Corey going to be there?"

"I expect so, but that doesn't matter."

"What do you two do?"

"Search Bruce's apartment, talk to people, spend a lot of time in the library combing through newspaper accounts."

"Sounds like fun." She paused. "Does Corey stay in the apartment…overnight?"

I smiled. "No. If she's here both days, she books a hotel room. It would be awkward, otherwise."

"Just wondered," Rachel said with a mixture of relief and embarrassment in her voice. "What if I come up next weekend, after I get this test behind me?"

"Great." I eased the truck onto Stone Manor. "I miss you."

"I miss you, too."

She said goodbye. I listened to the connection break, then slowly flipped the phone closed.

I found Elaine in the clinic, yanking our timecards out of the wall rack. She'd forgone nylons and a skirt in favor of a pair of black jeans and practical boots. She glanced over her shoulder when I opened the door.

Elaine shuddered. "Close that door. It's freezing."

I stepped in and clicked the door shut. "You need something?"

"Yeah. Give me a minute." She took another card out of the rack and carefully inserted it among the others.

Elaine grabbed another card, and apparently one was stuck to the back, because it floated to the ground. I picked it up. As I straightened, I noticed a card protruding from the bottom of the rack, wedged between the metal and drywall. I handed the card to Elaine, then crouched down and pried the other card free. I glanced at the name, and an icy tingle shot down my spine and coiled around my gut.

Claremont, Bruce was printed across the top edge.

I read through the dates and times of his last week at Stone Manor. Nothing looked out of the ordinary until the last day.

He'd punched out on Friday morning at six-fifty when he nor-mally wouldn't have left until noon. At least that concurred with everyone's account of his last weekend. He'd gone home early because he hadn't felt well.

He'd punched back in Friday night, January thirty-first, eleven-fifty-five p.m. Right on time to start his long day.

But he never punched out.

Elaine nudged my arm. "Didn't you hear me? What is it?" She stepped to my side and peered at the card.

I handed it over.

"Oh, I wondered where this got to. I had to cut him a check based on an estimation."

I pointed to the card. "He went home early Friday."

"Yeah, somebody complained about that." She tapped the card. "Oh yeah, that was the morning it snowed, and everybody was annoyed because of the plowing and extra work. Thank God I overheard them. If I'd paid him all the way to noon, I'm sure Dr. Nash would have objected."

"The snow caused the horse trailer to arrive late," I mumbled more to myself than to her.

"I'm not surprised. I barely made it to work, myself, my tires are in such rotten shape." She sighed. "I hate snow. To top it off, the kids had a two-hour delay. And that's always a pain in the rear since I have to leave them with my mother."

"He came back at eleven-fifty-five," I said. "Why didn't he punch out in the morning?"

Elaine raised her elegant eyebrows and shrugged. She'd twisted her hair into a complicated pattern at the back of her head, and loose wisps fell to her shoulders.

"Was he fired? If that's the case, maybe he didn't bother."

"No. Monday morning, Victor told me he quit."

"Well, why didn't he punch out?"

"You got me," she said. "Maybe he forgot, or maybe he couldn't find his card. If you haven't noticed, they get jammed in here ever which way."

I pictured Ronnie struggling to find his card every morning and figured his eyesight was partly to blame.

A cluster of thin gold bracelets jangled on Elaine's wrist as she sorted and alphabetized the rest of the cards. She wore a green sweater with gold threads embedded in the weave and gold hoop earrings. She didn't seem in any hurry to be rid of me, and to be honest, I wasn't exactly eager to join Paul and the rest of the guys.

I considered how closely she worked with Dr. Nash and the insider information she was privy to as a result. One of the guys had mentioned that she was divorced, but I checked her ring finger to be sure. "Hey, I'm going to that party at Mr. Hadley's house tomorrow evening, but I'd rather not go alone. Would you like to go?"

"Are you kidding? Of course I would. Have you seen his house?"

I shook my head.

"Oh, my God. It's incredible, and I've only driven past. I can't imagine what it's like inside."

"Good. Then we're set. Is seven-thirty okay?"

"Oh, yes. Wonderful." Elaine scribbled her phone number on the back of an intake form used for new arrivals at the farm. Then she drew a map so I could find her house, and I had an uncomfortable feeling that she would send out a posse to hunt me down if I didn't show.

After she explained that the sidewalks needed to be cleared and told me where to find a shovel, I left her standing in the clinic, smiling to herself.

At noon, I drove back to the apartment, took a shower, and fixed a bowl of cornflakes. I sat at the dining room table, spread out the calendar and newspaper photocopies, and read through everything again.

I looked at what I'd printed in the block for Friday, January thirty-first. I'd noted that someone other than Bruce had dropped off his car, but I'd already decided that that wasn't likely. I was fairly certain his car was dropped off early Saturday morning, so

I scratched out CAR and added LEFT WORK EARLY and SNOW. I flipped through the photocopies and verified that the accident on 95 happened early Friday morning. I printed I-95 in the block. Maddie told me that Bruce had been surprised when a van came in on his shift Friday morning, so I added VAN FROM FL to Friday's block, as well.

I dumped more cornflakes into the milk at the bottom of the bowl; then I read through the notations and tried to piece together Bruce's last weekend at Stone Manor.

It must have started snowing Thursday evening because the semi had jackknifed on the interstate around one in the morning. Bruce had reported to work around three, as usual. Then, he'd been surprised by the horse van from Florida, which I could only assume arrived late because of the tie-up on 95. And since the trailer originated from Florida, it offloaded at the bank barn. Bruce had left early Friday morning, supposedly because he hadn't felt well, and that had pissed everyone off since they expected to run late because of the snow. Then, for some reason unknown to the crew, Dr. Nash called off her barn rounds, an event unusual enough to catch Ronnie's attention. So, why the break from routine?

Saturday was Bruce's long day, and he'd returned to the farm Friday, just before midnight. And, as far as I was concerned, that's when it really got weird. Why did someone other than Bruce drop his vehicle in the apartment parking lot an hour and a half later?

That took me to Saturday morning. When the crew arrived at seven, Bruce wasn't in the clinic or on the farm as far as anyone could tell. But since he got off at seven, it didn't seem important. But why hadn't he punched out? And he certainly didn't come back Saturday evening because, according to Paul, Frank was working in Bruce's place when Maddie came in around midnight. And when, exactly, had Bruce told Mr. Nash he was quitting?

I drained the last of the milk from the cereal bowl and pondered a course of action. As far as leads went, I'd exhausted the apartment. That left trolling Sullivan's. I glanced at the photo-copies spread across the table. Or the library. The coverage on the fires had led me nowhere. Not in the present, anyway. But they did point to the past. To a twenty-year-old fire that had taken the life of Dr. Nash's fiancé.

I grabbed Bruce's Ravens windbreaker and drove to the library.

Bodell had mentioned that the fire had happened in the fall, so finding an account didn't take long once I selected the correct year.

Nineteen years ago, on October twenty-third, splashed across the front page of the *Fauquier Times-Democrat* were the following words:

FIRE TAKES LIFE OF WARRENTON MAN

A fatal fire that took the life of a Warrenton man Tuesday evening has been ruled accidental according to county fire officials.

Lloyd Strauss, 24, of Warrenton, Virginia was killed in a blaze that leveled a horse stable at 8303 Bear Wallow Road early Tuesday evening. Strauss, a recent graduate of the University of Virginia School of Law, and an avid foxhunter, had returned from an afternoon of foxhunting with the Farmington Hunt Club in Albemarle County and was tending his horses when the fire broke out.

Strauss had recently announced his engagement to Deirdre Thorndike, daughter of Dr. and Mrs. Philip Thorn-dike of Stone Manor Farm. Funeral services will be held at Moser Funeral Home, Warrenton, Saturday at 11 a.m.

County Fire Marshal Cornelius New-comb reported that the blaze appeared to have started in the haymow.

Seven horses also died in the fire.

I fed a quarter into the machine and printed the article. When I flipped forward in time, looking for his obituary, I blew right past it but found something much more interesting.

Five days after Strauss' death, a bank barn west of town went up in flames.

I advanced the knob slowly and felt a chill go down my spine when a grainy photograph of a huge barn engulfed in flames inched onto the screen. The headline read: EARLY MORNING FIRE RIPS THROUGH HUNDRED-YEAR-OLD BARN. Arson was the cause of a…

I didn't have to read further to know that the present was repeating the past.

But why?

All in all, I discovered write-ups covering two additional arsons in a ten-mile tract west of Warrenton. I backed up and scanned the months prior to the fatal Stone Manor fire and determined that the blaze that killed Strauss had been first in the series.

During my search, I also discovered a feature article, complete with an extensive photo spread, covering an extravagant engagement party thrown for the lucky couple at L'Auberge Chez François in Great Falls. By all accounts, the party had been a huge social event. The photos were grainy, but I spotted Dr. Nash and her betrothed easily enough. Actually, she'd been Deirdre Thorndike back then. In one photograph, they had their arms entwined as they prepared to sip from flutes filled with what I assumed was champagne. She'd tilted her head back, and as she gazed into Strauss' face, her expression was so intense and vibrant, I had an overpowering feeling that she'd been oblivious to everyone else in that room. Her long curls, entwined with ribbons and sequins and lace, tumbled onto her bare shoulders and complimented the simple evening gown she wore.

I read through the shorter engagement announcement, printed everything, then searched forward in time for coverage on Deirdre's engagement to Victor Nash. The microfiche tightened on the spool, and when I tried to advance the knob, the film broke.

"Shit." I glanced at my watch. I was ready to quit, anyway. I swung by Sullivan's for dinner and went to bed early.

◇◇◇

I polished off my second glass of Piper-Heidsieck Rare—try saying that three times when you've got a buzz going—and reminded myself I was there for a reason.

Unfortunately, Elaine had ditched me as soon as we'd crossed the threshold, effectively eighty-sixing my plan to question her. But I had to hand it to Hadley. He sure knew how to throw a party. Platters of food weighted down tables in a long dining hall that overlooked a formal garden with one of those vanishing edge pools that blends with the horizon. In this case, a lake that, at the moment, was locked under a layer of snow. The fact that the outdoor pool was closed for the season was of no consequence since an indoor pool, located behind a glass wall to my right, was in full swing. A steady stream of guests traipsed outside, braving the freezing temperature and a few stubborn flurries to sink into one of several spas that bubbled steam into the night air.

Fans turned lazily overhead, and a staircase behind where I stood accessed a balcony that overlooked both the dining area and pools. I'd spotted Elaine up there earlier, so I snagged another champagne and climbed the steps. For the occasion, I'd borrowed a pair of slacks and sport coat from Bruce's closet. I'd had to tighten my belt three notches to snug the pants, but I couldn't do anything about his loafers. They were a size too large and scuffed the carpeted steps on my way up.

Where the lower level consisted of bright lights and gleaming tile and glass and white wicker furniture, the lighting upstairs was subdued, and Sarah McLachlan sang broodingly from hidden speakers. Shag throw rugs bolstered the plush carpet underfoot, and piles of color-coordinated floor pillows lay scattered among groupings of sofas and mahogany coffee tables and chairs you'd need a crane to get out of. The jumbled sounds of voices and silverware and chairs scraping across the floor downstairs carried upward from the guests that mingled below, but the upper level carpet and furniture dampened the sounds.

Ripples of light moved languidly across the ceiling, reflected from the pool in the next room. I spotted Elaine in a far corner, gazing down at the crowd.

When I stepped to her side, she glanced over her shoulder and smiled. "This is wonderful, isn't it?"

"Yeah. It's something, all right."

She'd propped her forearms on the railing, and a mixed drink dangled from her hand. "You don't approve?" Her voice sounded raspy, and a slight lisp that hadn't been there before slurred her words.

"What's not to like? It's fantastic."

The back portion of the house was geared for pool parties and boat outings and casual gatherings. However, to reach it, we'd passed doorways that accessed a formal drawing room, a library, and a dining room that comfortably sat twelve. The rooms and halls were decorated with dark wallpaper and elegant wood molding, thick carpeting underfoot, and French Provincial furniture and gilded antiques that I strongly suspected were not reproductions.

"I didn't know Mr. Hadley kept horses here," I said, referring to an impressive stable visible on the drive in.

She nodded, and her drink tilted in her hand.

"Why don't we sit down?"

She looked around and selected a sofa that faced the indoor pool. A group of women were seated behind us, but their voices were soft murmurs. "Shane foxhunts most days of the week. He keeps his hunters here, where it's convenient, but of course, his breeding stock, he keeps with us."

"Of course." I swallowed some champagne, and the bubbles fizzed around my teeth. "I heard he owns Covington Square."

Elaine nodded. "This is the start of his fourth season with us."

"Who owns Order of Command?"

"Deirdre and Victor. They own Irish Dancer, too." Elaine settled into the cushions.

So, they owned the shy boy, as Jenny had described the stud that didn't like an audience and was bred in the late afternoon when the farm was quiet.

"You know," Elaine said, "we can go swimming if we want."

"I didn't bring—"

She flapped her hand. "They have everything you need down there."

"Are you going to?"

"I might. As much as I hate winter, it would be fun to get in one of those hot tubs with the snow piled all around."

"Yeah, it would." I had to figure a way to muscle the conversation around to the last big snow but didn't know how to do it without seeming obvious. I plunged in obliquely and hoped for the best. "Did you have any trouble driving home?"

"No. The roads were fairly decent."

"Not like the last big snow, huh?"

"You got that right," she said.

"I'm surprised they didn't cancel school that day. The roads were bad enough for it," I said like I knew what in the hell I was talking about.

"They should have."

"This morning, someone mentioned that Dr. Nash didn't do rounds that day. Was that because of the snow?"

"Oh, no." Elaine sipped her drink. "Well, maybe. Mr. Hadley came in right around nine and talked to Deirdre, then she hurried up to the house. Because of the two-hour delay, she still had to put Jenny on the bus, and to be honest, I think she lost track of the time. Anyway, Shane looked in on his stud like he always does. I thought he was waiting for Deirdre, but as soon as she came back, he left." Elaine swirled her drink and took another sip. "What happened next was weird, though."

I resisted an urge to lean toward her and lowered my voice, instead. "What?"

"He came back not more than five minutes later. Maybe I'm wrong, but he seemed agitated. I could hear their voices through the wall."

"What were they talking about?"

Elaine shrugged. "Something about the lock being broken on the trunk of his car. Well, what would Deirdre have to do with that? Unless something happened while it was parked in the lot, which I doubt. Anyway, they left."

I raised my eyebrows. "Together?"

She looked at me funny. "Why would they do that?"

I shrugged. "You don't know where Dr. Nash went, do you?" I said and was damned thankful she had a slight buzz going.

She shook her head. "So, there I was, running behind schedule and trying to get the employees' checks signed, which Deirdre has to do, by the way, and Victor comes in and pulls all the employee files and leaves. Well, you tell me. How was I supposed to get my work done?"

"Sounds tough. What do you suppose he needed them for?"

Elaine rolled her eyes. "Taxes." She crossed her legs and looked damned sexy in her black nylons and skimpy black dress that had slid halfway up her thigh. What was the thing with women and black dresses, anyway? "Of all the days to fool around with that, he picks a day I have to get the payroll out."

"What did you do?"

"Deirdre came back a little while later, but I'd already distributed the checks. Some of the employees cash them on their lunch break." She leaned closer and whispered in my ear. "Don't tell anyone, but I had to forge her name, and let me tell you, that was a first." Elaine straightened in her chair. "Well, I guess I won't be getting in the hot tub."

I followed her gaze. A young blond woman, who might have been eighteen, stood in the spa and jiggled her breasts. Under normal circumstances, that would have caught my attention pretty damned fast, but the fact that she was topless clinched it. She spun around and straddled some baldheaded guy for an up-close-and-personal, in-your-face lap dance.

"Where'd you say they kept the bathing suits?" I said.

Elaine giggled and smacked my leg, and her daiquiri sloshed onto the sofa cushion. "Ohmigosh."

I grabbed a napkin off the end table and blotted the liquid before it had a chance to soak into the pile.

"Here he is."

I stood as Shane Hadley and two other men stepped around in front of us. "Hello...Shane."

He pointed at me and grinned. "Almost caught you," he said, and it took me half a second to realize he was referring to the fact that I'd almost called him Mr. Hadley. He flipped on that high-wattage smile of his. "Ah, Elaine. You look lovely," he said before turning to his associates.

I glanced at Elaine and noticed she was blushing.

Hadley introduced us, then added, "This young man here just saved me a bundle, gentlemen."

The gentlemen murmured politely.

As Hadley recounted Sumthingelse's bloodlines and those of the stud, my gaze wandered back to the spa. It appeared that the lap dance had progressed to a very public grope and squeeze. As I watched, the amorous couple was joined by two young women clinging to a man wearing neon green trunks. Both girls had shed their tops, assuming they'd worn them in the first place.

"To be honest," Hadley continued, "I never thought I'd get a foal out of her, and now I have a colt by Elusive Quality."

A dark-skinned man, wearing khakis and a navy blazer, moved alongside the spa and raised a drink to his lips. Initially, he'd caught my attention because he was clothed, but something else about him sent a chill down my spine. There was something predatory in the way he moved into position, languid and loose-limbed, so he could leer at the blonde who had advanced to something more than a grope. She'd gripped the spa's rim with both hands and practically smothered the baldheaded guy with her breasts while the suds lapped at her waist.

I pried my gaze from her muscled back and firm round breasts and tried to focus on the guy in the blazer. Something else bothered me about him, besides his overt voyeurism. But what?

Hadley cleared his throat, then slowly turned his head and followed my gaze. He chuckled. "I see my guests are getting out of hand." He squeezed my shoulder. "Why don't you join them, Steve?"

"Uh…"

Elaine stood and looped her arm around mine. "Oh, that's all right. Steve's going to drive me home soon."

Hadley's eyes crinkled as he smiled broadly at Elaine; then his gaze shifted to me, and he winked. "Another time, perhaps."

I smiled. "Perhaps."

Chapter 12

Maddie sat sideways on a hay bale with her knees drawn up to her chest and her arms clamped around her shins. Her right shoulder and hip leaned into the stall front, and she'd rested her head on her knees. As I walked down barn three's aisle toward her, at five past midnight Saturday morning, I wondered if she had any idea just how titillating her pose was. To begin with, she wore jeans snug enough to cut off her circulation, but drawing her legs up as she'd done tightened the denim even more.

I sighed. Then again, maybe it was the mood I was in. I'd always found that lack of sleep triggered some primal need to copulate, and the party had completely messed up my schedule, not to mention the sensory input overload.

I smiled as I remembered Elaine's reaction to Hadley's invite and guessed she hadn't wanted to lose her ride to an orgy of sex and alcohol. She'd been anxious on the drive home, but I'd been thankful for her interjection and told her so. I liked my sex private.

Pulling my gaze away from Maddie, I glanced toward the dark storage area in the back and thought, as private as a horse barn, anyway. "What's going on?" I asked.

Maddie jerked her head toward the stall as I realized the mare wasn't standing in plain view. "I think she'll go tonight. She hasn't heated up yet, but I bet you'll have a foal before daybreak."

"Cool."

"Yeah, well it's not so cool for me if they're all gonna start waiting for your shift."

I grinned and stepped closer so I could see over the bottom half of the stall. As I looked over the edge, the bay mare rolled onto her sternum, touched her muzzle to her belly, and whinnied. "What's she doing?"

Maddie slipped off the hay bale and stood beside me, her right arm brushing mine. She whispered, "She's talking to her unborn foal."

"You're shitting me, right?"

"Uh-uh. She's had four or five foals already. She knows exactly what's going on, and she loves her babies. She's such a devoted mother, one of the best mares I've ever worked with. I've foaled her out two years in a row, now, and she's always talked to them."

I raised my eyebrows. "But before they're born?"

"Uh-huh." Maddie turned toward me and licked her lips. "And now, it looks like you're gonna have the honor."

"Hmm."

She slipped her hand under my coat and rested it on my waist. "Steve, don't you like me?"

"Well, yeah. Sure I do."

"So, aren't you attracted to me?" She moved closer, and her pelvic bone touched my thigh. "Just a little?"

I placed my hands on her shoulders and swallowed. "Yes, Maddie. Like you wouldn't believe." A soft smile touched her lips. "But, I have a girlfriend."

"Of course you do. You're too cute not to." She exhaled and slowly lowered her gaze to my chest. "If you ever need a…diversion, I've got nothing else to do at night."

I clamped my mouth shut as I pictured a little diversion in the haymow. Every guy's fantasy.

"Well," someone behind Maddie said, causing her eyes to widen, "ain't this touching?"

I jerked my head up as Maddie spun around and faced Paul.

"Thought you wasn't interested, Cline." He strolled down the aisle, and his face was like stone. "Ain't that what you told me just two days ago?"

He paused in front of Maddie and smoothed his fingers through her hair. "You still coming over tonight, darlin'?" he said as he fixed his gaze on me.

Maddie didn't answer.

Paul leaned closer, moved his mouth alongside her ear, and watched my expression as he reached around and cupped his hand over her ass. He slid his fingers into her crack, then inched them lower and wedged his hand between her legs. He fingered her crotch.

Maddie tried to wriggle away, but he grabbed her arm and kissed the side of her face. "You head on home," Paul said. "I'll be there shortly."

When she started down the aisle, it bothered me that I couldn't see her face. "Maddie!"

She turned around.

"Don't go unless you want to," I said.

She looked from me to Paul. "Oh, I'm going home, all right. But I'm going alone," she said to Paul before she turned and marched down the aisle.

Paul watched her leave, and his lack of emotion was more disturbing than an outburst would have been. He turned back to me when the farm truck cranked to life. "She'll change her mind. She always does. She thinks you're so sweet," he mocked, "covering for her when she didn't answer her phone the other night like she was supposed to. But you and I both know the real reason you kept her out of trouble, ain't that right?"

I crossed my arms but resisted the urge to roll my eyes.

"She thinks you're so special when all you wanna do is get in her pants."

Well, I guess he had me there.

"But she'll let me in." He smirked.

"Oh, wow, Paul. Clever play on words. Wish I could've thought of that."

Paul's face darkened. He stuck his finger under my nose. "Stay away from her, you hear?" When I didn't respond, he added, "'Cause I swear to God, I find out you touched her, I'll rip your fucking head off." He lowered his hand and glanced at the horses standing in their stalls behind me. "Working a job like this at night, by yourself, no telling what might happen. Shit. A horse could cave your head in with one swift kick, and nobody'd be the wiser 'til morning."

Even though I'd expected a threat of some sort, I seriously considered laying into him. But Paul had his own brand of punishment to endure, because any man who cared for Maddie was in deep shit.

Apparently, he didn't know how to take my lack of reaction, so he started backwards, mildly confused and greatly annoyed that I hadn't jumped all over him. When he was halfway to the door, he yelled a departing "I mean it."

I looked in on Maddie's mare. She'd risen to her feet and was nibbling her hay. "Humans," I said half under my breath.

Her chewing ceased as she turned her head toward me. When I didn't say anything else, she lowered her head and flapped her big old lips among the wisps of hay, searching for a choice timothy seed head or alfalfa sprig.

During my one o'clock round, I checked barns seven and eight and the training barns, then headed back to the main part of the farm. As I drove past the burnt down barn on Cannonball Gate, I glanced to my left and was surprised that I couldn't see the rows of light coming from the barn windows. Now that the aisle lights were kept on all night, I should have been able to see them. I put my foot down on the accelerator. The Ford's tires hummed on the roadway as I zipped past the mansion and cleared the high bank along the lake. From the entrance to Stone Manor, the dusk-to-dawn lights on each barn were visible, but all the aisle lights had been switched off.

"What the hell?"

I coasted the truck down barn one's drive, pulled all the way past the barn, and circled the back lot. It was empty, just as it should have been. I drove back to the barn's entrance, spun the Ford onto the grass, and centered the headlights on the wide barn doors. I'd left them open about two feet, and the high beams cut all the way down the aisle and puddled against the doors at the far end of the storage bay. I slipped my flashlight off the bench seat and eased out of the cab. One of the day crew had left a busted pitchfork handle in the Ford's bed. I picked it up and hefted it in my hand.

I spun around as I slipped through the gap between the doors and felt slightly foolish when no one was there. I hit all the light switches at once and peered down the aisle, listening. A hoof thumped against a stall wall as a horse clambered to her feet; otherwise, the barn was quiet. I paused when I reached the storage area, then flipped on the lights. Nothing. I crossed over to the back door and stepped outside, walked around the corner and stared down the lane that runs along the length of the barn and joins with the drive. Nothing. Not a goddamned thing.

I repeated the process in barns two through six. Someone had driven onto the farm, switched off all the lights, then left, and it didn't take a genius to guess who that someone was. Paul knew my routine as well as anyone, and he also knew it would freak me out, knowing that someone was sneaking around the farm. I rubbed my face.

Unless the arsonist had turned his attention to Stone Manor and was warming up to the job.

I drove over to barn three to check on Maddie's mare, carried the pitchfork handle into the barn just in case.

She was down, flat on her side. Patches of sweat had spread along her flank and neck. I checked that her water hadn't broken, then headed to the clinic. As I pulled into the drive, I realized the clinic lights were still on. If Paul was the culprit, it made sense, because he wouldn't have wanted Frank to catch him.

I was halfway down the lot when I realized something was seriously wrong with my old Chevy. I slammed on the farm truck's brakes and looked over my shoulder as I ratcheted the gearshift into reverse. I backed up and stared at my pickup in disbelief. The tires were flat. I jumped out and stalked around the truck. All four wheels sat on the rims.

"Fuck." I scanned the lot as I pulled the Ford down to the clinic doors. This was just great. There was no way I could afford new tires. Not four of them at once.

I decided to wait for morning before I called the cops because I sure as hell didn't have time to fool with a bunch of questions.

As I filled the buckets, I considered the possibility that the lights and my truck's tires weren't necessarily the work of the same person. I'd bet the cost of a new set of tires that Paul had slashed them to get back at me, but switching off the lights almost seemed too subtle.

If I wanted to play a mind game on Dr. Nash and knew her history, I'd do just what the arsonist was doing. I'd start out by setting a ring of fires that surrounded her farm. Then, when I planned to move in for the kill, what better way to set her on edge than to have her nightshift employees reporting that someone had been messing with the lights?

◇◇◇

I quit thinking about Paul or my truck or the arsonist when the mare bore down and delivered a beautiful colt onto the straw. I was crouched in the stall doorway, watching her lick his ears, when something fell in the back of the barn.

I slid her door closed, hefted the pitchfork handle in my hand, and approached the storage area. As I neared the end of the aisle, I pressed against the wall. I flipped on the lights. A pitchfork lay on the ground under the tool rack. I walked into the center of the open area and checked that no one was hiding behind the haymow, or on top of it, or around the grain chute, or behind the grain wheelbarrow or the stocks. I glanced at the back door. It was closed just as I'd left it. I hung the fork on the tool rack and got back to work.

At three o'clock, I stepped outside and stretched. Contrails crisscrossed the sky, illuminated by a half moon that had reached its zenith. Some nights, the jets' exhaust seemed to dissipate as soon as it hit the atmosphere, but on nights like tonight, they hung across the sky like strips of gauze.

I pivoted to see what the mountains looked like and realized the lights were on in the hay barn on Bear Wallow. And barns one and six, the barns at the mouth of Stone Manor, were dark.

I called the cops as I cleared barn six. Unlike Maddie, I hadn't seen one cruiser. The dispatcher told me they'd get out as soon as possible, and there was something about her tone that prompted me to ask how long she expected before they showed.

"I'm not certain, sir. We're short-staffed tonight, and there's an accident on I-66 that we're dealing with." She paused. "You're certain that the person has left the area?"

"As far as I can tell."

"A deputy will be out as soon as possible, but call back if you feel you're in danger."

"Yes, ma'am."

After she disconnected, I checked one, then drove over to the hay barn. The barn wasn't a barn, per se, but a three-sided storage shed that resembled Foxdale's implement building. It sheltered an assortment of farm equipment and a major supply of hay, and it would make one hell of a bonfire. I drove all the way around the building, spotlighting the interior with my flashlight and checking for vehicles that didn't belong. Once I'd ascertained that no one was hiding anywhere near the building, I climbed out of the Ford and checked the interior. Whoever had switched on the lights was long gone.

By six-thirty, I was dead on my feet. I gazed mournfully at my truck as I coasted down the lot, but when I nosed the Ford into a parking space, I saw I wasn't the only one up and about. Dr. Nash's Spyder was in the lot, and Jenny was standing in the narrow opening between the wide clinic doors, wearing a heavy-duty parka and riding breeches instead of her usual school clothes.

"Hey, kiddo," I said as I squeezed past her. "Why are you here so early on a Saturday morning?"

"You had a f-o-a-l?" she said in her high-pitched singsong voice.

"Yes, I did," and before she could ask, I added, "barn three."

"Are you going back over?"

"Maybe later. First, I've got to talk to your mom." When I put my hand on the office doorknob, I paused. "Jenny, why don't you see what the stallions are doing."

She frowned. "You want to talk in private?"

I smiled. "If you don't mind."

"Okay." She skipped down the aisle.

Dr. Nash looked up as I opened the door. She was perched in Elaine's chair, poring over a huge calendar and stacks of charts and lists spread across the desktop like an avalanche. Her eyebrows rose and disappeared beneath her bangs. "Is there a problem?"

"The horses are fine." I cleared my throat, and her face paled as I told her about the barn lights and my truck's tires.

"Did you call the police?"

"Yes. Around three-fifteen."

"You should have called me," she snapped. "Did they find anything?"

"Sorry, and no. They haven't been out."

"What?"

"They're shorthanded, and there's an accident on—"

Dr. Nash snapped up Elaine's phone and, from my end of the conversation, it sounded like she'd dialed Sergeant Bodell directly. "Dammit, Emmett, I want you handling it."

Bodell's voice wafted from the receiver.

She glanced at her watch. "Well, all right."

She slammed the phone into its cradle, and for Bodell's sake, I hoped he'd already switched off. "They'll be out soon." Dr. Nash rubbed her face, and when she smoothed her fingers through her bangs, a slight tremor shook her hand. "Since we returned from our trip, I haven't had a chance to talk to you about Sumthing-else." She sat up straighter and rested her forearms on the desk. "You did an extremely professional job, Steve."

"Thank you."

"I'm impressed. Not many experienced staff would have done as well." She rubbed her face again. "Have you called a service for your truck?"

"No, ma'am."

"Good. Emmett will want to look over everything before the tires are replaced. And we'll pay for them. You shouldn't have to suffer that expense."

"But—"

She waved her hand. "No arguments. As soon as Emmett gets here, I'll call my service."

"Thank you."

"Did Maddie have any trouble on her shift?"

"No, but she left at midnight."

"Oh, that's right."

"If that's all?" I said as I backed toward the door.

"Yes. Oh, wait a minute." She rubbed her left temple as she leafed through a stack of papers. "Four mares are coming down from Pennsylvania, maybe tonight. I want them stalled in eight."

"Yes, ma'am."

I hadn't taken a break at three, so I'd decided to take it then, even though I got off at seven. Not that I was going anywhere.

Jenny joined me in the aisle. "Can we go see the foal?"

"If your mom says it's okay, but if you don't mind, I need to eat first."

"Sure. Anyway, you wondered why we're here so early. It's because Mom has to catch up on work after being away."

"I get that, but why are *you* here?"

"I don't have anything better to do."

Jenny skipped alongside me, but when she seemed prepared to follow me into the clinic, I suggested she ask her mother first.

"But, why?"

"I think it would be a good idea, that's all."

She frowned. "All right." She popped into the clinic a minute later, after I'd snagged a Coke from the fridge and was unwrapping a peanut butter and jelly sandwich. "Mom says it's okay."

She described in great detail how she'd had to stay at her cousins' while her mom and dad were away, and I thought, if nothing else, she'd keep me awake.

"All they ever want to do is watch cartoons or play stupid computer games."

"Um-hum."

"I like riding."

"So I've noticed."

She grinned. "As soon as Dad gets a minute, he'll take me over to the training barns." She pushed a chair over to the sink and climbed onto the seat.

Jenny stretched over the faucet and planted her hands on the windowsill so she could peer through the glass. To the right of the stone mansion and bank barn, if you really craned your neck, you could see the roofs of the training barns, and I imagined that's what she was spying.

"I miss having my ponies in the bank barn because I could go see them whenever I wanted, but the training barn's fun, too, because I can gallop around the track every time I ride."

I wondered what the ponies thought of that.

"When they were in the bank barn, Mom or Dad had to get a horse and ride with me if I wanted to work on the track, because I had to ride on the roads to get there, so it was always a hassle. I told them, all they'd have to do was build some coop jumps between fields, then I could ride cross-country to get there."

"Hmm."

Jenny flopped into the chair and spun it around. "Did you know I might get a pony today?"

I shook my head. Okay, maybe she was going to put me to sleep, instead.

"Yep. It's a gray. A Welsh cob, I think. We're going to Culpeper as soon as Mom gets freed up. So, I might have a new pony tonight. I'm going to name it Peppermint after my first pony who died." She frowned. "I wish my ponies *were* in the bank barn, then I could go out and check on him right up 'til I go to bed and make sure he's happy in his new home. But, at least there's a wash rack in barn ten that I can use, with hot water and heat lamps and everything. And of course, that's really important when you have a gray horse. Now, I'll have two: Tinsel and Pepper. I thought Dad was going to build me a wash rack at the bank barn, but he moved my ponies, instead."

"When was that?"

"Umm…" She drew up her feet and gave the chair another twirl. "The Saturday right after we had that big snow. I was so mad because—"

The door opened, and Victor Nash stepped into the room. "What in God's name happened to your truck?"

"Uh…" I glanced at Jenny. "An unfortunate incident."

"Jenny, go into the office and wait for me."

"But, Dad—"

Nash placed his hand on his daughter's shoulder. "Go ahead. Tell Mom we'll be heading over to the track soon, okay?"

Jenny slid off the chair, and Nash ruffled her hair. When she put her hand on the doorknob, she said over her shoulder, "I told Mom something was wrong with one of the trucks, but she didn't pay any attention."

After she closed the door, I said, "Observant kid."

Nash looked at the door as if he could see right through it, see her crossing the aisle and going into the office. "She is that. And smart, just like her mother."

I repeated the story of our nocturnal visitor and told him the police would be out in case he wanted to talk to them.

"This is going to throw Deirdre. Does she know?"

"Yes."

"Damn." He fiddled with something in his coat pocket, and the sound of crinkling cellophane and paper triggered an image of Shane Hadley's manicured fingers gripping his pack of Marlboro 100's.

I'd never had much reason to talk to Victor Nash before. He came and went but spent most of his time supervising the training operation which, as far as I could tell, operated under a totally separate staff. None of the breeding farm employees had ever mentioned working in his barns. He seemed a good match for Deirdre, though. Nice-looking with wind-blown dirty blond hair and fair skin. He had unusually wide hands, worn rough and calloused from hard labor and the cold.

"Well…Steve, is it?"

"Yes, sir."

"We'll cover the cost of replacing your tires. There's no reason you should pay for them since it happened on our property."

"Thank you, sir. Dr. Nash said the same thing."

"Good." Nash backed toward the door. "Hey, do you need a ride home? I can drop you off and have someone pick you up when your truck's ready."

I pictured him leaving me at Bruce's apartment complex. "No, thank you. I'll wait."

"Well," he glanced at my half-eaten sandwich, "do you need something to eat? Some doughnuts or something?"

I smiled. "No, thanks."

◇◇◇

After Sergeant Bodell cruised over to the farm and did his thing, and the service switched out my old tires for Michelins that were worth more than the Chevy, I got exactly five hours sleep before I had to clock back in at six.

At a quarter to eleven, a horse van from Pennsylvania eased onto Stone Manor and idled down the road between the barns until he spotted my truck in front of barn two.

"Evenin'," he yelled when I pulled up alongside the cab. "Where's this lot going?"

"Barn eight. Do you know where that is?"

He pointed toward the northwest. "Round that way?"

I nodded, then headed over while he got turned around.

Dr. Nash had told me four mares were coming in, but when I walked down barn eight's aisle, I only counted three empty stalls. I grabbed a couple of flakes of hay and carried them to one of the lots behind the barn. As I pushed through the gate, headlights swept across the far end of the horse pasture as a vehicle on Cannonball entered a gentle curve in the road. I watched the beams sweep slowly across a distant knoll, thinking that the truck driver had turned around awfully fast. But when I didn't hear the rumble of a diesel engine, I studied the road. As the vehicle straightened out of the curve, I realized it wasn't the semi, after all. A car or compact pickup moved slowly past. I watched him until he'd driven well beyond the road that accessed the training barns.

The semi's driver showed up five minutes later and offloaded the mares. He did it himself, probably for insurance reasons, but I was thankful, just the same, as I had a thing about trailers ever since I'd been locked up in one.

I helped him put the last mare in the back lot. "While you were getting turned around, did you see a vehicle drive past kind of slow?"

"Yeah. He started to pull onto the farm road but backed up when he saw me."

"Did you notice the color or make?"

"An old car. Mid-sized. Other than that, I couldn't say."

"Two-door or four?"

"Oh." He paused and rubbed his jaw. "Four-door, I think. I wasn't really paying attention because one of the mares had started kicking her partition. Some of them get antsy after we've been on the highway for awhile, then stop."

"I wouldn't have thought you could hear them."

"Hey, we're high tech, now. I got a video feed in the cab."

"Cool." I gave him a hand lowering the ramp's sidewalls. "Do you deliver here much?"

"Fairly regular from now 'til June. Once a month, at least."

We each grabbed a corner of the ramp and slid it into a slot under the trailer floor. "Have you ever unloaded at the bank barn behind the stone mansion?"

He shook his head, then swung the door closed and pulled down the lever that locked it in place. "That's a mighty small driveway to be pulling into."

"Yeah, it is." A thump vibrated against the trailer's shell. "Where you headed next?"

"New York."

"I thought you came down from Pennsylvania."

"Nah." He hawked a wad of chewing tobacco halfway to the fence. "Came up from Florida."

"Shit. They're supposed to be in quarantine."

"Ain't nothing wrong with these mares or I'd've heard about it."

"You're sure?"

"Course I'm sure."

I followed him all the way around Bear Wallow. Light edged round the curtains in one of the mansion's rooms on the second floor, and a single light burned in the back of the house. I flipped open the farm's cell phone, called my boss, and asked if the horses should have been quarantined.

"No. Not those."

I pulled into the clinic parking lot. "Well, the driver said they came from Florida."

"Oh…they did. Just not from the area I'm concerned about." She disconnected.

But why had she said Pennsylvania?

I thought back to her explanation for the need to quarantine horses and couldn't remember if she'd ever named the virus she was guarding against. The more I thought about it, the less it made sense. In the first place, why house Jenny's ponies in a barn used as an isolation facility and risk exposing them to the virus she wanted to avoid? And what made even less sense was that they'd moved the ponies out of the bank barn the day after horses arrived from Florida. The same weekend Bruce disappeared.

At midnight, Maddie sauntered down the aisle as I deposited the last of the hay bales against a stall front so they would be easily at hand. "Hey, thanks for putting them out."

"No problem." I brushed off my jeans. "Maddie, Jenny's ponies were in the bank barn when horses came up from Florida, weren't they?"

She reached up and fingered the zipper pull on her jacket. "Yeah. So?"

"So, don't you think that's kind of strange?"

She shrugged, then sat on the hay bale I'd just shoved against the wall and crossed her legs. She flexed her foot, then bounced her leg with nervous energy as she watched me pick up my coat and slip it on. "Why aren't you driving a farm truck?"

As I told her, she quit bouncing her leg and became very still.

"So, be careful," I said. "If you see something out of the ordinary, lock yourself in the truck and call the cops."

She nodded.

I zipped up my coat and handed her the cell phone. "Did Paul stay with you last night?"

She focused her gaze on a spot across the aisle. "That's none of your business."

"It is if he slashed my tires. And it is if he's responsible for fooling with the lights. On the other hand, if he's the one who's been doing it, then I won't have to worry about you tonight."

She raised her eyes. Maddie had this way of looking through her lashes that was incredibly sexy. "That's sweet of you, Steve, but honest, I don't know. He could've been over here. He wasn't with me." She stood and stepped closer. "He's awfully jealous of you."

Like I couldn't figure that out. But the girl was wearing me down, so I got out of there before I did something I'd regret.

Chapter 13

Sunday morning, Corey showed up at the apartment earlier than I'd expected. I was sprawled on the bed, staring at the insides of my eyelids, when I heard her rap on the door, then jiggle the knob.

I smiled as I pushed off the bed and yanked on my jeans. The girl had way too much energy.

Her hair was the color of a field of wheat under a late summer sun, and her eyes were as clear and blue as a coldwater lake.

She rocked backwards on her heels and grinned. "Morning."

"It sure is."

She slipped past me. "Are you always this succinct?"

"Only before nine o'clock. After that, watch out."

She spun around and her gaze slipped over my rumpled T-shirt and bare feet. "Oh, God. Did I wake you?"

I reached out to take the grocery bag from her hands. "I don't think so."

She sidestepped me and rolled her eyes. "Well, I take it you haven't eaten, then?"

"Correct."

"Good. 'Cause I'm gonna whip us up a mess of bacon and eggs and sausage and biscuits."

"Uh-huh."

She added a shake of her head to go along with another roll of her eyes. "Succinct and silly. Maybe you oughta go back to bed."

The comeback that popped into my head wasn't entirely appropriate, so I kept my mouth shut as she turned into the kitchen. I watched her peer into the bag and lift out a roll of sausage. "Mind if I take a shower?"

"Uh-uh. Just don't be like my brother," she shot off, then became very still. She glanced at me, then bent to the bag. "And take forever," she said softly. She closed her eyes and took a few short breaths.

A tear slid off her lashes and tracked down the brown paper bag.

I stepped alongside her. When I touched her shoulder, she clenched her arms around my waist and buried her head against my chest.

I held her while she wept, her shoulders trembling as she took in long ragged breaths that caught in her throat, and the sound of her crying bore into my heart. I held her tighter, and she pressed against me as if she could lose herself in me and leave the pain behind.

"I'm so scared," she said in a thin shaky voice.

"I know." I smoothed my fingers through her hair. "I know."

I lifted my head and noticed the dark streak her tear had left down the front of the grocery bag, and it was unexpectedly sad and poignant. I thought of my own sister and imagined how I'd feel if she were in trouble. Or missing. I tried to push aside my growing conviction that Bruce would never come back. But, damn it. If he did, he'd better pray I wasn't the first person he ran into.

Eventually, her breathing slowed, and in a little while, her muscles relaxed. She said something, but her voice was muffled.

"What?"

"I need a tissue."

I hesitated. Her grip around my waist hadn't let up, so I wasn't sure what she wanted me to do.

"I need a tissue." Urgent this time.

"Okay." I moved sideways toward the sink, and she moved with me as if we were engaged in some sort of bizarre dance. I yanked a paper towel off the dispenser. "Here you go."

Corey waved her hand in the air, searching for the towel. I folded it into her palm, and she wedged it between us. Only after she'd covered her face did she relinquish her hold. She straightened and blew her nose. Her bangs were plastered in thick strands against her forehead, and her face was flushed and damp with perspiration. She'd yet to look me in the eye as she tilted her head and squinted at my chest.

"Oh." Her voice croaked. "You're all wet."

She allowed herself a brief glance at my face; then she snatched another towel off the roll and stepped closer. She dabbed my shirt. When I covered her hand with mine, she raised her big blue eyes, and the air suddenly felt very hot and dry and still around us.

Her mouth was inches from mine, and her breath trailed across my lips.

I bent her head and kissed her forehead, and when she straightened, a hint of a smile touched her lips. She cleared her throat. "I'm always crying in front of you, aren't I?"

"You have good reason to."

She stepped back, leaned against the counter, and rubbed her forehead with both hands. "Dad thinks I'm overreacting. And Mom…" Her voice trailed off and what she saw behind those pretty blue eyes of hers was not Bruce's tiny kitchen. She sighed as she slipped her vest off her shoulders. "I think I'm gonna need that shower."

"Be my guest."

Corey shook her head. "No. You go. I'll get started on breakfast."

"We could go out," I said.

"No. It'll be good for me to do something. Plus, I like cooking."

My gaze drifted over her slender build. Apparently, that didn't translate into eating.

◇◇◇

A trail of steam rushed over my shoulder as I opened the bathroom door, and my nose told me that Corey had been very busy, indeed.

I stepped into the kitchen doorway. A spatula dangled from her hand, poised above a frying pan full of scrambled eggs. She stared straight ahead, at nothing, and if she wasn't careful, we'd be eating little brown lumps of petrified egg.

I moved alongside her. "Need some help?"

"Actually, yes. Could you pour us some coffee and orange juice?" As I searched for mugs and halfway clean glasses, she said, "What are we doing today?"

"Another trip to the library. Revisit everything we've learned so far and go from there."

Corey was eager for me to fill her in on what I'd learned during the past week, but I steered the conversation back to Foxdale and horses and neutral territory until we finished eating. She barely ate as it was, and bringing what I considered disturbing news to her attention would kill her appetite for sure.

After we cleared the table and left the dishes to soak, she sat at the dining room table and propped her chin in her hand. "Okay, Steve," she said as I sat down. "Judging from your expression, and the fact that you've been skating around this moment, I have a feeling I'm not going to like what you have to tell me."

I couldn't argue with that. I scooped up the file folder and calendar and laid them out between us. "Several things are going on at Stone Manor. What's connected to Bruce and what isn't is difficult to say at this point."

I opened the folder and handed her the newspaper accounts of the fires, both present day and those that surrounded Lloyd Strauss' death. "I never really thought the fires were connected to Bruce, but I think they're somehow related to Stone Manor. For whatever reason, I believe someone is trying to intimidate my boss, and they're doing a damned good job of it." I told her about the nineteen-year-old fires, the first of which took Lloyd Strauss' life just weeks after he'd announced his engagement to Dr. Nash. "Maybe our present-day arsonist is copycatting the past, but it's also not inconceivable that the same person's responsible for them all."

"But why?"

I shrugged. "I don't know. Arson's apparently a common juvenile offense. If the same guy's responsible for both sets of fires, he'd be anywhere from his mid to late thirties, on up." I told her about the game with the lights and my tires.

"Oh, my God."

"There are two possibilities. Either the arsonist is trying to freak out my boss, or Paul's doing it to get back at me because he thinks there's something going on between me and his girl. I told you about him, right?"

"Yeah."

"If he truly loves Maddie, she's enough to drive any man crazy."

"Is he violent?"

"Yes, but enough to…uh, really hurt someone, I don't know. Bruce and Paul had a shoving match in the parking lot a couple weeks before your brother quit." I fingered the calendar.

If he quit, I thought.

"What? What are you thinking?"

I looked at her and hesitated. "Some unusual events happened at Stone Manor during Bruce's last weekend there."

I outlined everything I'd learned so far. How the accident on I-95 had caused the horse van from Florida to arrive later than usual. I told her about the quarantine procedure that didn't make sense, not with ponies housed in the same barn. I told her how Bruce had gone home earlier than usual Friday morning but had reported back to work Friday night, just before midnight. Then I watched her face blanch as I told her how a Hispanic-looking man had dropped Bruce's car off in the lot an hour and a half later.

"Oh." Her head drooped as she reached out and fingered the file folder.

God, I hated this. I breathed in deeply, then cleared my throat. "I'd like you to call the officer who took the missing person's report and see if he won't go over Bruce's car for fingerprints. Okay?"

She nodded and made the call right then and there. Came back from the kitchen with a slip of notebook paper in her hand.

"He'll be out early this week. He took your name and number and said he'll be in touch."

"Good. Something else happened on the farm this Friday—" I tapped the block for the thirty-first— "that altered Dr. Nash's routine. It might have been something as simple as the snow, but I don't think so. Whatever it was, she never did her morning rounds, palpations and ultrasound and stuff like that, and according to the crew, she's religious about sticking to her schedule."

"But what does that have to do with Bruce? You said he left early but came back to get ready to work his Saturday shift like usual."

"I don't know." I hesitated. "He never punched out on his last day."

She stared at me without blinking, then said, "Maybe he was mad when he left and didn't bother."

"Maybe. I hope."

"What about the other guy you told me about?"

"Tiller?"

She nodded.

"He's a bully, for sure, but I don't think he had anything to do with Bruce's leaving. He picks on everyone, but so far, I haven't heard anything to make me think he targeted Bruce in particular."

Corey glanced at her watch. "The library will be open soon. Why don't I finish up in the kitchen, then we can snoop around the records."

"Sounds good."

We cleaned up together, and afterwards, Corey went into the bedroom to change. I glanced at her breeches as she walked down the hall and wondered if she'd worked at the track. Her thighs were streaked with dried mud and speckled with horse hair. As I reached across the table to gather the photocopies together, someone knocked lightly on the door. My hand froze. I glanced at the closed bedroom door, then looked through the peephole. Whoever was standing on the other side had shifted so I could only see the back of his head.

I opened the door.

"Yo, Bruce," he said. "You fuckin' never home?"

I opened my mouth to correct him, but something about his manner kept me quiet. The guy was scared or nervous. Or both.

"Johnson sent me, man. Said you had some major blow I could score."

Oh, shit.

The guy thrummed his fingers on his thighs.

"Johnson who?" I said.

The guy shrugged. "Johnson. That's all I know." He stepped back and checked the stairs leading up to the third floor, and when he scanned the parking lot, the skin beneath his left eye twitched. "Look, man. You interested or not?"

"Maybe."

"Said you could do a whole kilo. That right?"

"Maybe."

"Look, man. What's with all the maybes? Either you got the shit or you don't." He glanced at me, narrowed his eyes, then went back to studying the parking lot. He didn't look like a drug dealer, but then, what did I know? He looked like a preppy ivy-leaguer masquerading as a drug dealer. Clean-shaven, short hair under a Bruins cap, designer jeans, smooth hands that hadn't seen work more strenuous than pushing a pencil. Maybe he was a cop. "I can do ten grand," he said.

My mouth fell open, and when I didn't respond, he tore his gaze away from the stairwell and noted my expression.

"All right. Fifteen. But that's all I can do. Swear to God."

I closed my mouth with a snap. Think, Cline. How could I make this work for me? This bozo didn't know Bruce, but Johnson did, whoever the hell he was. And he might even know what had happened to him. "I have a deal pending," I said. "If it falls through, I'll call you. Give me your number, and I'll get back to you."

"Fuck, man. I ain't giving you no number."

"All right. You got a memory?" I said. "I'll give you *my* number, and you can call me Wednesday at one in the afternoon. I should know by then."

"Yeah, well don't take too long, or I'll go somewhere else."

"Not at fifteen grand, you won't," I said and told him Bruce's number. "Think you can remember that?"

He slid me an annoyed glance, then jammed his hands in his pockets and sauntered down the steps.

I closed the door. If Bruce had been dealing, that changed everything.

Corey strolled down the hallway, wearing a snug pair of low-rise jeans and a fleece pullover that matched her eye color. She paused when she saw me at the door. "What? Was someone here?"

I told her who, and why, and not surprisingly, she didn't want to believe it.

She pressed her fingers against her temples. "He must have the wrong apartment."

"He asked for Bruce," I said softly.

She crossed her arms over her chest and turned away from me. "It has to be a mistake." She circled the living room, shaking her head. "No, he wouldn't do that."

I leaned against the door as she paced the room, running who knew what through her head. It's been my experience that people overreact when they know something to be true but don't want to face it. "Has he ever done drugs?"

Corey paused and looked at me. "Yes."

The word hung in the room between us.

She sat on the sofa, and after a moment, I crossed the room and sat beside her.

"He smoked a little grass, but his real Achilles' heel is alcohol." She swiveled around so she was facing me. "Bruce is scared to death he's going to become an alcoholic, if he isn't already. His way of managing it is to limit his drinking to social events. You know, nights out with the boys? Stuff like that." She picked at a thread on the afghan. "I knew he was slipping as soon as I saw the beer in the fridge."

"Did he ever do coke?"

She shook her head. "It must be a mistake. There's no other explanation. Look, let's go to the library. You had something in mind?"

In light of the current developments, looking into the old fires and my boss' past seemed a waste of time.

"Okay." I stood, and Corey untangled her legs and rose gracefully to her feet. "Like I said before, the more we learn about the people in Bruce's life, the better."

A warm front had blown across the mountains during the night, and the temperature had risen to a balmy forty-five degrees. I opened the Chevy's door, and Corey slid onto the bench seat and crossed her legs and arms to ward off the chill air.

"The truck's heater's not so good. Do you want to take your car?"

She smiled. "No, this is fine." When I climbed behind the wheel and backed out of the slot, she said, "How do you stand driving around all night in the cold?"

"It's not bad. I'm not in the truck much. As long as I keep busy, I stay warm."

She nodded. "You're right. I'm never cold when I ride. Only after."

"Tell me," I said. "Why's Bruce so worried about becoming an alcoholic?"

Corey looked out the side window. "Because our mother's one," she said quietly.

The new tires hummed on the asphalt while I tried to think of something to say.

"She's forty-eight but looks sixty-five. Bruce and I grew up watching our mother drink herself into a stupor most days of the week." She glanced at me, then stared out the windshield. "Suddenly, it was my job to manage the cooking and the cleaning and the laundry. Bruce mostly managed to be unavailable, and Dad…" She laughed. A sad, mirthless laugh. "Dad just pretended everything was normal, that his wife didn't really pass out on the sofa every night. To hear him talk, you'd think we were the Brady Bunch.

"Bruce was never much for academics. He'd hoped to ride a football scholarship through college. When he didn't make the cut, he just…gave up."

I glanced at her, but she was staring stonily through the windshield. Ugly ridges of blackened snow lined the streets, and when I pulled into the lot alongside the library, the gutter was submerged under a foot of swirling water from the snowmelt.

"As soon as I could swing it, I moved out. I scrimped and saved, worked two jobs. Schooled other people's horses in my free time, like I had much of that. But it paid off. Sweetwater was given to me, you know?"

I switched off the engine, and we sat there, listening to the ticks and pings as the engine cooled. My thoughts drifted to my own parents and their flaws. My mother had wanted kids but hadn't planned on the actual mothering involved. We were there in the background, ready to be pulled out like so many accessories to match her designer outfits when the need arose. And my father…God, my father. When he discovered that my mother had been unfaithful, and I was the result of her indiscretion, he'd dealt with his disappointment by distancing himself from all of us. I'd eventually convinced myself that he no longer loved me. And I'd held firmly to that belief until it was too late.

"I grew up fast," Corey said, and her voice and her closeness swept away the image of his casket. "I don't know if Bruce ever did." The vinyl creaked as she swiveled around to open the door.

"I'm sorry, Corey."

She sniffed. "I know."

An efficient librarian had had the microfiche patched, so I flipped through the year following Lloyd Strauss' death. On the social page, I found a notice announcing Deirdre Thorndike's engagement to Victor Nash and, a month later, a brief feature on their engagement party.

Corey had commandeered a nearby chair to read the photo-copies I'd made earlier on the Thorndike/Strauss engagement, and when she saw me making more copies, she peered over my shoulder.

"Your Victor got the short end of the stick, didn't he?" she said.

"There certainly is less coverage."

"Maybe it was a busy news week."

"I don't think so. The folks around here seem socially-minded," I glanced around the room, "to put it mildly."

"You mean class conscious, don't you?"

I grinned. "Yeah. There's quite the disparity between the haves and have nots, at least among the horsey set."

"Well, what's wrong with him? He's cute enough, but the poor guy barely ranked a paragraph."

"On speculation, I'd say it's because our Victor wasn't a UofV School of Law grad like Strauss. As a matter of fact, he doesn't seem to be a grad of anything."

Corey giggled. "He married well, though."

Three months into the future, I found a feature write-up on their wedding that had a bit more meat to it.

Corey breathed over my shoulder. "Wow, fancy spread."

"Yeah, but I have a feeling the news coverage was generated solely because of who Victor's in-laws were, don't you?"

"Um-hmm." Corey had leaned on the back of my chair, and her cheek practically touched mine. She reached over my shoulder and touched the screen, tapped her fingernail on a photograph of the wedding party. "Look. Pops doesn't look too pleased."

I chuckled. "What do you expect? Here's a nobody marrying his gorgeous daughter."

Corey frowned. "You think she's gorgeous?" She was so close, her hair touched the side of my face.

"More than he's cute."

She turned her head toward me, and we were so close, our noses practically touched. Heat flushed my face as I looked into her eyes.

She blinked, looked back at the screen, and frowned. "She's all right, I guess."

"No more all right than you," I said softly.

"Hmm. But you said she's gorgeous."

"I did, didn't I?"

It was Corey's turn to blush. She straightened, paused for a second, then crossed over to the table and gathered together the photocopies she'd been reading.

Before we left, I checked the snowfall record for the season. Outside of the most recent snow, the last Thursday and Friday of January were the only other days with measurable snowfall. I gathered together the papers for that weekend and flipped through them again. Along with Friday's startling photograph of the semi balanced precariously on the guardrail, in the next issue, I came across the usual shots of people shoveling sidewalks and one of a snowball fight among kids waiting for their school bus.

I wondered what Jenny had done with her extra two hours and figured she'd probably spent them with her ponies.

In the bank barn.

We stopped at Joe and Vinnie's for lunch, then headed back to the apartment. Corey spread the photocopies over the dining room table, and we read through them again.

While Corey focused on the various engagement and wedding articles, I picked up the photocopy of the meth lab explosion and read: A Warrenton man was killed in a meth lab explosion shortly after midnight Sunday. Andrew Johnson, 35, of 1379 Brittney Lane was pronounced dead at the scene....

Johnson? I glanced at Corey, then looked back at the paper in my hand. Andrew Johnson...A.J.

Shit.

I yanked Bruce's phone list out of the kitchen drawer and checked A.J.'s phone number; then I pulled out the LOUDON FAUQUIER phone book and flipped through the pages until I came to the J's. I ran my finger down the column: JOHNSON, Adam, Alan, Alexander S., Allison D., Andrew J.

Andrew J. Johnson.

I checked the numbers. They matched. Bruce's A.J. and the guy who'd blown himself up in the meth lab were one and the same.

Corey peered over my shoulder. "What's wrong?"

I told her and watched what little happiness she'd been able to build on since the morning dissolve like tears in the ocean.

Her face crumpled. I held her and rocked her and listened to her cry. When she finally caught her breath, she said, "Oh, God. He really must be dead."

"Come on. We don't know that."

"But his friend…" Her words were muffled against my shirt.

"Maybe he took off and is lying low. He could be in trouble, but we don't have any evidence that he's hurt."

Corey left around three.

I stood on the sidewalk and watched her pull away, looking tiny and deflated and alone as she sped down the road and made a left onto Van Roijen.

I took Bruce's photograph out of my pocket and wondered if the goalpost behind the high school was the one he'd leaned against when someone had taken his picture as he'd stared into the camera with a look of defeat in his eyes.

I scraped my thumbnail along the photo's edge. Bruce, what have you done?

Chapter 14

I should have gone to the cops, regarding my new-found drug dealer buddy slash possible undercover cop, but I was too damned tired. Besides, I wanted to talk to a detective, and if the Warrenton PD was anything like most mid-sized departments, all their detectives would be home, enjoying their Sunday afternoon basketball.

I did call Greg, an equine vet who just so happened to be my landlord.

"Hey, it's me."

"Where the hell've you been?"

I told him where and, briefly, why.

"Jesus. You haven't had enough excitement in your life, you gotta go out looking for it?"

"I'm just trying to help someone."

"Don't kid yourself. You could help someone by working at a food bank or the Salvation Army or Fidos for Freedom, but n-o-o, you go out and find something potentially dangerous."

"Fidos for what?"

Greg chuckled. "You know? Training companion dogs for the hearing impaired."

"Uh-huh. Right."

"Really. Their headquarters is in Laurel. So, what do you want to know?"

"Is there any reason a breeding farm should quarantine horses shipped in from certain areas in Florida?"

"Every breeding farm should quarantine new arrivals, but they never do. It's not cost effective."

"That aside, is there a reason to quarantine arrivals specifically from Florida?"

"Well, they've recently experienced outbreaks of EEE, along with Georgia and South Carolina, and—"

"Eastern equine encephalitis?"

"Yes, and West Nile, of course."

"What are the incubation periods?"

"Encephalitis is one to six days. West Nile, up to two weeks. But all their stock and arrivals should be vaccinated against both. Plus, it's pointless to quarantine animals in the middle of winter for either one. Even though we don't know much about the overwintering cycle, the mosquitoes are dormant, so there's little chance a horse would become infected. Then there's EVA, but Florida's guarding against that by restricting movement across her borders."

"EVA?"

"Equine viral arteritis. I'd say your farm's taking precautions against something they've been specifically warned about."

I sat on the bed. "What about this scenario? The breeding farm quarantines horses that come up from Florida, and a day or two later, they move some of their own stock out of the quarantine barn and into the general population."

"Well, that defeats the purpose, doesn't it?"

"That's what I thought."

"So, what are you really doing?" Greg said.

"Hell if I know."

I went to bed, thinking the quarantine story was just that. A story.

◇◇◇

Maddie was in the clinic, restocking a foal kit, when I reported to work Monday morning. She looked over her shoulder when I opened the door. "Hey."

"Hey, yourself." I punched my timecard then crossed the room and watched her fill an iodine bottle. "You had a foal?"

"Yeah, in one. They're doing good, so you probably won't have to worry about them."

"Any trouble with intruders?"

"Nope. Not last night, either."

"Good. Are any mares close?"

"No. You should have a quiet night." She wedged four Fleet enemas into the tote, then opened the cabinet under the sink. When she grabbed a handful of towels, she bumped the leather-covered cylinder, and it rolled halfway over.

"Hey, Maddie, what's that?"

"What's what?"

"That cylinder."

She draped the towels over the tote, bent down, and peered into the cabinet. "Oh." She giggled. "That." She closed the door and turned around. Her lips twitched into a mischievous grin. "Don't you recognize it, Steve?"

"Uh...no," I said, thinking she was having way too much fun at my expense.

Her smile never left her face as she slipped off her coat and dropped it on the counter. "It's an artificial vagina."

Oh, good. As she set the buckets in the sink and turned on the hot water, I caught her reflection in the window. She'd gripped her lower lip between her teeth and was trying hard not to laugh as she squirted disinfectant into the buckets.

She turned around and leaned against the counter as the buckets filled. Her skin was flushed and moist from the steam. She hooked her elbows on the counter's edge. "But that's weird."

I stepped alongside her. Damn, the girl looked good, even when she wasn't trying. "What?"

Maddie frowned. "Why would they have one here?"

"Seems kind of obvious," I said as the steam rolled out of the sink and rose toward the overhead lights.

She shot me a glance. "No, it isn't. Artificial insemination isn't allowed in thoroughbreds, although plenty of people would like to see that change."

"Why isn't it allowed?"

"Oh, I don't know. Something about overbreeding the outstanding stallions while the rest of the family lines become more and more obscure and die out altogether because nobody wants them."

"Well, wouldn't you have a better horse?"

"I guess, but part of the lure of thoroughbred racing is the star that comes out of nowhere. If everybody's breeding to the Secretariats or Alydars, we'll never have the surprise horse out of left field, like Lil E. Tee."

"And maybe we'd be plagued with problems because of inbreeding," I added.

"True."

I pictured Frank as he'd strode into the clinic ten days earlier, right after I'd discovered the cylinder and was actually holding it in my hands. He'd been gruff when I'd asked him about it, but at the time, I'd thought he was just distracted and concerned about my getting the foal I'd just delivered to nurse. Now, I had my doubts. If anyone knew Dr. Nash was breaking the rules, he would.

"What would happen if Dr. Nash had been using AI and was found out?"

Maddie gasped. "Don't even think that. Look," she waved her hand in the air, "maybe they used to have quarter horses."

"Would it ruin the farm?"

She nodded. "I'd think so."

I remembered what Jenny had said about the shy stallion and how he liked to breed when no one was around. Maybe the horse's preference had nothing to do with it, and I couldn't help but think that, where Dr. Nash and her husband might be willing to risk using artificial insemination, losing the farm might be an unacceptable risk.

Maddie rinsed the buckets and stowed them under the sink. "Well, I gotta go."

I did my three o'clock round like usual, but instead of starting in on mucking stalls, I drove back to the clinic and hit the Chevy's lights before I slid into a spot between two Stone Manor trucks. I checked that the penlight I'd slipped into my jeans pocket before leaving the apartment was still there, then I climbed out and clicked the door shut. A crescent moon hung low in the east. By tomorrow, it would be reduced to a wafer-thin sliver before it disappeared altogether.

I glanced at the office's outer door before I stepped into the aisle. I intended to go into the office, but standing under the dusk-to-dawn light, fiddling with the doorknob would not be my first choice. Instead, I quietly entered the restroom.

A nightlight, plugged into a socket over the sink, illuminated the dreary little room, so seeing wasn't a problem. A door to my left accessed Frank Wissel's living quarters. The one to my right opened into the outer office. As soon as I stepped through that doorway, I'd no longer have an easy explanation for being there.

When I'd hired on, Elaine had given me a key to the clinic that I hoped fit the office door. If not, I had no idea how I'd get in. I slipped it into the lock, held my breath, and felt the tumbler give.

I eased into the room and locked the door behind me. Two file cabinets sat in the corner behind Elaine's desk. I opened the first cabinet and flicked the penlight's beam across the folders. The generic labels covered topics consistent with any small business, from insurance to taxes to vendors. The second file cabinet focused on all aspects equine. Breeding records, client lists, feed dealers, stall floor mats. I doubled back and pulled out folders on all three studs.

I opened them on Elaine's desk and flipped through fertility reports on Covington Square, Irish Dancer, and Order of Command. The reports were organized chronologically, but Irish Dancer had had more testing than the other two. I left the most recent test results on each stud in place but withdrew a less current report and laid them on the desk. I replaced the folders and went back to the first file cabinet. Bruce's file was right where it should have been, in the Employees/Inactive section. Someone had written *resigned February first*, and as far as I could tell, his record had been closed out in a normal manner.

I stuck it back in the cabinet, and as I slid the drawer closed, a toilet flushed. I spun around. Bright light edged under the door to the bathroom.

I grabbed the fertility reports, squatted behind Elaine's desk, and thumbed off my penlight. The sound of running water filtered through the door.

Come on, Frank. Go back to bed.

When he twisted the faucet closed, the pipes rattled against a wall stud. He coughed and hawked and cleared his throat, and in a moment, his feet scuffed the floor. He paused near the door.

I held my breath and listened, hearing nothing.

He coughed again, then the light that streaked under the door switched off.

I stayed hidden behind Elaine's desk until my legs started to cramp. I'd planned on leaving via the bathroom but unlocked the aisle door instead.

It's funny what adrenaline will do to you. I'd managed to keep my nerves under control in the office, but after I climbed into the Chevy and was driving to barn one, my hands started shaking. I gripped the wheel tighter and tried to slow my breathing.

My four o'clock round confirmed Maddie's prediction of a quiet night. I checked the last barn, then sat on a hay bale alongside the tractor in three and read through the pages. The report for each horse included two ejaculate evaluations, the second having been conducted an hour after the first. I contemplated that for a moment. Not bad.

I refocused on Order of Command's report, skimmed over the general health evaluation, and concentrated on the semen quality parameters. The first thing I noted were the options allowed for collecting the sample: EE, AV, and Massage. Well, massage was self-explanatory, and I couldn't imagine doing *that* to a horse. AV obviously meant artificial vagina, and EE…well, I hadn't a clue what that stood for, but it didn't sound pleasant. In any case, it didn't matter. AV had been checked off on all three reports.

A good reason existed for Dr. Nash's having an artificial vagina in the clinic, after all. Apparently, in my search for wrongdoing, I'd jumped to a hasty and erroneous conclusion.

I read the rest of the report, anyway. The semen quality portion covered motility, both progressive and total, whatever that meant. Next on the list were color, volume, concentration, pH, and morphology, using both Eosin/Nigrosin smear and Diff Quick smear. Okay, whatever. The last values included total sperm produced, bacterial isolates, both pre and post ejaculatory, and total ejaculatory pulses. Ejaculatory pulses?

Okay. I focused on the total sperm produced. In all three stallions, the sperm produced in the first ejaculate was twice as high as the number produced in the second collection performed an hour later, and that made sense. And for whatever reason, the value for the second ejaculate seemed to have greater significance since it was boxed off to the side. But, as I compared the three stallions, it was obvious Irish Dancer's numbers were off. Where OC and Covey's sperm count numbers for the second ejaculate conducted in December read 1.1 and 1.2 billion respectively, his number was a paltry 350 million, and his motility ranged in the thirtieth to fortieth percentile, where the other two averaged eighty-five percent.

According to Jenny, Irish Dancer's career at the track had been excellent, and his progeny were outperforming him. But he was having trouble in the breeding shed. Had Dr. Nash resorted to artificial insemination so the stallion could breed more mares in one throw?

Had Bruce uncovered the truth and died for it?

I pushed that idea out of my mind as being ludicrous. His getting into trouble because of his drug involvement seemed a more likely scenario. I jammed the reports in my glove compartment and got back to work.

◇◇◇

Monday afternoon, I drove to the Warrenton PD and was referred to Detective Jim Brandon. His expression changed from one of incredulity to curiosity to interest as I described my activities during the last two weeks as they pertained to my search for Bruce Claremont. I didn't go into a lot of detail about Stone Manor, since all I had were vague speculations and not much else. I began with Corey asking for help and ended with the appearance of a drug dealer who'd been referred to Bruce through his association with the late A.J. Johnson.

Brandon took copious notes on a yellow legal pad in a hand so sloppy, he wouldn't need to worry about someone obtaining unauthorized information from his files. A gold wedding ring hung loosely on his ring finger, and his hands were unusually calloused and rough for someone who worked in an office. His face was tanned, as well, with a high forehead and receding hairline.

He tapped his pen on the pad. "Have you found any drugs in the apartment?"

"No, sir."

"And you have permission to be there?"

"Yes."

"From the sister?"

"That's right."

"But her name's not on the lease?"

I shook my head.

"Well," he sighed, "technically, you don't have legal grounds to be in his apartment, and neither do we."

"You're kidding."

Brandon shook his head. "But a drug connection changes everything, including our take on his disappearance."

"You mean, you think he's dead?"

"It's a possibility. But just as likely, he could be somewhere selling his stash." Brandon leaned back in his chair. "I'd like to show you some mug shots. See if we can identify this guy."

"Okay. Hey, if Bruce is in jail, would a missing person's report pick that up?"

"The family filed one?"

"Yeah."

He nodded. "He's not incarcerated, then. A standard missing person's would have caught that." Brandon jacked his chair away from the desk and told me he'd be back in a couple of minutes. He left the door open on the way out.

Unlike Brandon's sloppy handwriting, his office was compulsively neat and about as cheerful as a morgue. The notepad, pen, and complicated-looking phone were the only items placed on the blotter. No pictures or containers of pens and pencils, no paperclips or scraps of paper. I wondered if the lack of clutter was an outward sign of his need to control the flow of information. A computer sat in the far corner of his desk with squiggly lines silently twisting on a black background. No piped in music, just the muffled sound of a phone ringing in the next room and traffic noise that filtered through a high narrow window. A row of three filing cabinets took up wall space to the right of his chair. I glanced at the bare walls. Except for a row of matchbox police cruisers that lined the windowsill, the room was devoid of anything that could be construed as personal.

Detective Brandon returned and laid a computer-generated photo spread on the desk blotter. "Any of these guys fit?"

My first reaction was disappointment. The sheet contained only six photographs, but as Brandon slid it toward me, I spotted my visitor in the bottom row. I pointed to the guy in the middle. "That's him."

Brandon swiveled the paper around. "David Alexander Yates."

"How'd you narrow it down so quickly?" I said.

"Your description. We popped him awhile back for possession of less than one gram of marijuana. Guy paid a measly fine and was released."

"Looks like he's graduated."

"It sure does." Brandon leaned back in his chair. "I'll talk to my boss, tie up a few loose ends, and get back to you in twenty-four."

I stood up. "I'll need instructions by noon Wednesday, if you're going to do it."

Brandon nodded, then offered his hand.

He seemed overly reserved, but I guessed it went with the job. I shook his hand, then left.

I pulled out of the lot, then turned right on East Shirley. After work, I'd taken a shower but had skipped lunch, so I headed over to Sullivan's. The streets were clogged with traffic and it took me several turns around the block to find a parking spot.

I took a stool at the bar and was pleased to see that my barkeep was on duty.

He slid his bar towel down the countertop. "What'll it be?"

"Miller draft, a BLT, and fries."

"In a hurry, are ya?"

"No. Just starved."

He nodded. "I'll put a rush on it."

"Thanks."

He hobbled back toward the kitchen door, and the gleaming wood received another waxing. The barkeep returned a moment later, placed a cocktail napkin on the bar, and set down my beer precisely in the center. I watched him cross over to another customer; then I smoothed my fingertips down the cold glass and blotted them on the napkin. I thought about Rachel going to her Apps class tonight. Pictured that asshole looking in her car. I should have suggested she park at another entrance than the one she typically used. Walk out with a group of people if possible. Park under a pole lamp.

"Something wrong with your beer?"

I lifted my head as the barkeep rolled his toothpick from one corner of his mouth to the other. "Uh, no. It's fine. Hey, listen. Do you remember when I asked about a friend of mine, Bruce?"

"Yeah. You found him yet?"

I shook my head. "You told me he met some guy in the back booth one night." I slipped the photocopy of the meth lab explosion out of my back pocket and laid it on the bar. "Is this the guy?"

The barkeep squinted at the mug shot. "Crummy photo, but yeah, that could be him."

I turned the photograph around and studied it. The quality was poor, but I supposed he could have had his hair pulled back.

His bloated cheeks made it difficult to tell, and I'd just assumed it was cut short. "He had a ponytail?"

"Halfway down the middle of his back."

"Thanks."

So, what in the hell was Bruce doing, holed up with this guy on the weekend he quit Stone Manor, just days before Johnson blew himself up? If the sole purpose of the meet was to hook Bruce up with some coke, that would explain why he'd skipped out of his job, but it didn't explain his losing contact with his family.

◇◇◇

Victor and Jenny were standing in the doorway to the outer office when I walked into the clinic at six-thirty Tuesday morning after an uneventful shift.

Jenny practically hopped over to me. "Did you have a foal?"

"No. Sorry."

"Awh." She pursed her lips, and little frown lines crinkled the creamy skin between her pale eyebrows. Her mother had done up her hair in a loose ponytail adorned with pink ribbons, and wisps of curls had already worked free. They framed her face and trailed down her neck.

Victor stepped into the aisle with a steaming travel mug of coffee in one hand and two boxes balanced precariously on his right arm. "Now, Jenny. Don't pester Steve."

"Oh, he doesn't mind, do you?"

I grinned. "No, ma'am."

Jenny giggled.

"Here," I reached out to take the boxes, "let me help you."

"Thanks." Victor closed the door behind him. "They go in the clinic."

I glanced at the Fleet logo. "So I see."

Jenny and Victor followed me as I pushed the door open and placed the boxes on the countertop.

"After you've had your break," Victor said, "would you mind unpacking them into the cabinet over there?" He pointed toward the side of the room where most of the foaling supplies were stored.

"No problem."

"When are we going to ride tomorrow?" Jenny asked her father.

He collapsed into a chair and sighed. "Just as soon as I get free, honey." He looked at me. "The kids don't have school tomorrow, for some ungodly reason."

"Records day, remember?" She climbed into his lap, and the beaded animals swayed on the end of the zipper pull and clicked against the edge of the countertop before she settled down.

Victor swiveled the chair around so he could put his mug on the counter; then he smoothed his fingers along the side of her face. "Don't worry. We'll get to it."

I pulled a ham and Swiss sandwich out of the fridge and put it in the microwave.

"Too bad the snow's gone." A whine dragged out her words.

Victor looked at me over the top of her head. "We spent all day Saturday hill-topping with the Middlebrook Hunt, and Sunday with Glenmore, and I'm still recuperating."

"Oh, boy." Jenny swung her legs. "Wait 'til Mom lets me jump."

Victor tilted his head back and closed his eyes. "Mom can take you, then."

Jenny leaned against her father. "O-o-h, Dad. I'm a good enough rider to start jumping, now. By the time you let me hunt properly, I'll be old enough to ride with the field all by myself."

"That's not gonna happen."

"Hmm." Jenny smiled mischievously. "I'll probably be old enough to drive by the time you and Mom let me move up to first flight."

I cracked open my Coke. "First flight?"

"Uh-huh." Jenny swung her legs faster. "When you ride as close to the action as possible and jump all the jumps."

Victor sighed. "They grow up too fast. You'll see, when you have kids of your own." He rubbed his face as Jenny slid onto the floor. "I've been wanting to tell you," Victor said. "I looked in at

Sumthingelse's foal the other day. You did a great job. With her record, nobody thought she'd have a live one this year, either."

"Thank you."

Victor levered himself out of his chair and grimaced. He picked up his coffee mug. "Let's go see Mommy."

"Okay."

The microwave chirped as I watched Victor escort his daughter out of the room. He seemed like such a loving father and husband, I couldn't believe he was involved with Bruce's disappearance. So what the hell had gone on in the bank barn that weekend? And what about the fires? How did they fit? The idea that Victor had moved up to an entirely different social class after Lloyd Strauss' death had been niggling around the back of my mind, and I'd done my best to ignore it. But it was just too damned coincidental that two sets of fires surrounded the same woman. I was still staring at the door when it swung back in on its hinges.

Victor stuck his head into the room. "I almost forgot. When Elaine comes in at eight, stop in the office and see her. Deirdre said she has some forms for you to sign."

"Yes, sir."

He nodded, then quietly closed the door.

Chapter 15

At seven-ten, after the day crew had filed into the clinic, Frank finally put me on a detail that didn't involve mucking stalls.

When he noted my expression, he said, "You've been doing so many damned stalls at night, it hardly seems fair to stick you on stall duty during the day."

"Thanks."

I smiled when he dismissed my reply with a flap of his hand, but my amusement dissolved when my gaze slid over Frank's shoulder. Paul Genoa had been goofing around with Tiller a minute ago, but as he'd listened to Frank, his facial muscles had stiffened, and any hint of cheerfulness drained from his face. Tiller glanced from Paul to me. He nudged Paul's arm, leaned closer, and whispered something in Paul's ear, but Paul wasn't interested in Tiller's opinion. He shrugged a shoulder at Tiller, then slid farther down the counter. Both of them had been leaning against the countertop by the sink with the morning sunlight streaming through the window behind them, and the combination of backlighting and sunglasses made Tiller's expression difficult to read.

Frank ticked off names on his clipboard. "Paul, Mike, Ralph, Chuck. Barns one through three. Dawn…" Frank looked up and frowned as he waited for the girls to stop giggling. He cleared his throat, and the sudden stilling of movement in the room got the girls' attention. "Dawn, you Gina, Lisa, and Beth, muck out four through six."

Dawn glanced at me and smiled, and I wondered if she'd already figured out that I'd been working in six.

Frank started to assign barns seven and eight but was interrupted once again, when Tiller yanked Ben's ball cap off his head.

"Tiller!"

He froze. Ben snatched his hat out of Tiller's hand, then dumped two buckets in the sink and cranked on the hot water. Tiller had left his coat at home, switching it out for a lightweight jacket, as I'd done. The mercury hovered right around freezing but was expected to climb above fifty degrees, and the change in the weather had a noticeable effect on the crew. Generally, everyone trickled into the clinic half-asleep and borderline grumpy, but not this morning.

"Randy and Luke," Frank said. "You're with me."

The girls were the first to leave, as they'd been milling around by the door. Dawn strode into the aisle and looked over her shoulder, waiting for the rest of her group to catch up, when her gaze slid my way. One of the other girls latched onto her arm, and their laughter drifted into the room.

"Looks like you got an admirer," Ronnie whispered in my ear.

I slipped my hands into my jacket pockets.

"Man, guy like you got it made."

I glanced at Ronnie, then watched Tiller and his group mosey down the aisle. "What are we doing again?"

"Palpations, ultrasound, undoing Caslicks." Ronnie waved a sheet of paper under my nose.

Ben stepped in front of us, and I noticed he'd filled the buckets with the same strong-smelling disinfectant that Maddie and I used when foaling out. "Time to load up."

"Hold your horses," Ronnie said. "I'm filling Steve, here, in on the routine."

Ben rolled his eyes.

"Two of us get the mares on this list and bring 'em down to the stocks while one of us helps Dr. Nash. I figure that'd be you, since you don't know the horses yet."

"And what do I do?"

"Lock 'em into the stocks and hold their tails out of the way for whatever exam the boss gotta perform." Ronnie glanced at his list. "Looks like we're starting in two."

I backed the truck down to the clinic doors, and after Ronnie and Ben loaded the ultrasound machine and utility cart into the bed, we headed over to the barn.

Ronnie scanned the sheet. "This time of year, we got palpations and ultrasounds and Caslicks while Frank and his crew do the teasing to see which mares are heating up. Later in the season, after more of the mares have foaled, we'll be racing to get done, cause we gotta get at least two barns done before the stall crews finish mucking their first."

"Yeah," Ben said. "It's a race."

Ronnie said, "Once we clear out, the stall crews come behind us. If we get behind, they get behind."

I pulled into barn two's drive. "Seems like you must have a lot of free time when the breeding season comes to an end."

"Hell, no," Ben said. "Then we gotta knock down cobwebs and bird nests and fix fences."

"And weed whack," Ronnie added and held up the paper. "But this, I don't mind."

"Beats mucking stalls," Ben said.

We unloaded the equipment, then sat on the tailgate and waited for Dr. Nash.

"Here she comes." Ronnie sighed as the little Spyder zipped around the curve bordering the lake. "Man, what I wouldn't give for a car like that."

"What I wouldn't give for a woman like that," Ben said under his breath.

Ronnie and I turned to stare at him, and he actually blushed.

A smile touched my lips. "She's old enough to be your mother."

"She sure don't look it, though," Ben said as the tires skidded through the gravel when Dr. Nash applied the brakes. "Or drive like it."

The three of us slid off the tailgate and headed into the barn. I hovered near the stocks while Ben and Ronnie grabbed lead ropes and went in search of the first two mares on the list.

"Morning, Steve."

I nodded and backed out of her way as she reached for the cart.

She laid a plastic container full of syringes on the top shelf, then piled some surgical packs wrapped in blue paper off to the side. She moved alongside me as Ronnie led a dark bay mare down the aisle and into the stocks.

The mare stepped in placidly enough, and I took that as my cue and locked the back gate snug up against her hindquarters. She was now confined in a narrow chute constructed of heavy tubular steel. Dr. Nash pulled out a roll of gauze from a box on the bottom shelf and quickly wrapped the upper portion of the mare's tail.

She held out the free end of the gauze bandage. "Keep her tail pulled hard to the side."

"Yes, ma'am."

"We're performing some episiotomies this morning." She glanced at me. "But of course, you're already familiar with the procedure."

"I am?"

She smiled softly. "Yes, you are. I'm opening her up as I should have done with Sumthingelse."

"Oh."

Dr. Nash pulled on a pair of plastic gloves that reached her elbows, then carefully washed the mare in quick efficient strokes before drying her with handfuls of cotton. Her hair looked redder than usual under the barn's incandescent lights, and her lashes were almost as pale as her eyes. She exchanged the long gloves for sterile surgical gloves; then she picked up a syringe loaded with anesthetic.

"Ronnie, I'm ready for the twitch."

Ronnie slipped a chain around the mare's upper lip and tightened it just enough to keep her attention focused on him.

Dr. Nash injected the mare in tracks up one side of the vulva and down the other. A drop of blood formed each time she withdrew the needle.

"You know, if that mare had torn severely, her breeding career could have been jeopardized?"

"Hmm."

Dr. Nash glanced at me as she dropped the empty syringe in a trash bag that hung off the cart. A slightly lopsided smile, that I found incredibly charming, tugged at the corner of her mouth. "Jenny likes you, you know?"

"She's a good kid."

"She is that." Dr. Nash swabbed the mare with an antiseptic, then withdrew a pair of forceps and a scalpel from the blue wrapping. "Where'd you go to school?" she said as she started the incision.

"Uh…here and there."

"College?"

I nodded. "Two years."

"Go back," she said. "You're too smart to be doing this."

"I need to figure out what I want to do first."

"Maybe. But you might find the answer there, as well."

I wondered how she imagined I'd afford a nice little experiment like that.

Ronnie, Ben, and I followed Dr. Nash from barn to barn while she opened more mares or took cultures or palpated and occasionally used the ultrasound machine, then at eleven-fifty we headed back to the clinic. I'd forgotten all about Elaine and hoped she was still in the office.

As it was, I needn't have worried. She was eating a salad at her desk when I walked in. She looked up, questioning.

"Do you have something for me to sign?"

"Oh, yeah. A tax form." She frowned. "Now, where'd I put it?"

She wedged the salad container in one of the few clear spots on her desk and shifted an issue of *Cosmopolitan* out of the way. While she rifled through the mass of papers, I studied the photographs on the wall. Three were professionally composed conformation shots of each stallion. Others featured the local hunt meets. One was a photograph of Jenny on a gray pony. The reins draped from Deirdre's hand, and both of them had their arms wrapped in a bear hug around the pony's neck, their cheeks touching, their eyes sparkling as they laughed at a shared joke. It was a great photograph. Spontaneous and happy. Unguarded.

Only one photograph on the wall hadn't captured an equine behind the lens. Victor and Dr. Nash stood at the top of a curved flagstone staircase in a terraced garden. The sunlight had that orange quality it gets early in the morning or just before sunset, so I assumed we were talking early evening in spring, judging by the azaleas in bloom. Victor had slipped his tuxedoed arm around Dr. Nash's slender waist. She looked radiant in a full-length strapless gown. The breeze had caught the folds of silky material, and the hem flapped across Victor's calves as the two of them leaned into each other and smiled at the camera. Her hair normally had a bit of a wave to it, like Jenny's, but she'd curled it, lifting the bangs off her face and entwining them with sprigs of baby's breath. She wore a single pendant necklace and long silver earrings. I leaned forward and squinted at the photograph.

Elaine cleared her throat. "Steve…" I turned around, and she slid a paper toward the edge of the desk. "Here you go. I need your signature here," she flipped the page, "and here."

I took the pen from her hand. "Elaine, where was that picture taken?"

"Which one?"

"The one on the terrace, of the Nashes."

"I'm not sure, but I believe they're at this extremely posh restaurant in Great Falls." She smiled. "French, too. Not that I've ever eaten there."

"L'Auberge Chez François," I mumbled half under my breath. The same restaurant where Deirdre and Lloyd Strauss had celebrated their engagement.

"That's it," Elaine said.

I scribbled my name on the lines indicated. "They're dressed so formally. What was the occasion, do you know?"

"Um, Deirdre's parents' wedding anniversary. Their fortieth, I think." She sighed. "Hard to imagine being married that long, isn't it?"

"Yeah, it is."

"The sad thing is, that was their last."

"Don't tell me they got divorced?"

"No. They were killed," Elaine glanced at the door, "in a car accident."

"Oh, no."

"I know, that's horrible, isn't it?"

I nodded and felt Elaine's gaze on my back as I left the room.

◇◇◇

I took advantage of the McDonald's drive-thru on my way out of town and an hour and five minutes later drove past the guard shack at Washington Park. I pulled onto the grass strip alongside the perimeter fence and switched off the engine. The track was holding an abbreviated winter meet, and the first race had just gone off. A few indistinct shouts from the grandstand carried across the infield on the cold air, and even at that distance, I could hear the horses as they swept into the turn. But compared to my time spent here last summer, the backside seemed subdued somehow, as if the people, the horses, even the buildings had entered a stage of dormancy. The shriveled grass beneath my feet and the bare tree branches above my head looked as lifeless and drab as the deserted alleyways and dull whitewashed buildings.

On the drive in, I'd noticed that the barns most distant from the track were vacant. And even here, next to barn sixteen, Kessler's barn, activity appeared to have reached a low ebb. The Jamaicans who'd worked out of the barn across the way had packed up and headed elsewhere. Probably south. Even their roosters had flown the coop.

I jammed my hands in my pockets and strolled across the access road, stepped under barn sixteen's roof overhang and paused. Kessler braced his hand on a doorjamb midway down the shedrow and peered into a stall, said something I couldn't hear. Christopher J. Kessler, my father. I'd met him a little over seven months ago, almost by accident, after learning he was my biological father. He was a good, decent man, honest to a fault and hardworking. A loving father to his daughter. A fair man who treated his employees with respect. I'd come to like him a great deal, and most of the time when I thought of him, I was grateful for the chance I'd been given to get to know him. Other times, I had to clamp down the resentment I couldn't help feeling for what he'd done to my family. To the man who'd raised me. But, who was I to judge?

I'd made more than my share of mistakes in the past.

I noted the security cameras installed under the eaves as I started down the aisle.

Kessler glanced over his shoulder when I drew closer and did a double take. "Steve." He stepped forward and clasped my hand. "What brings you here?"

I usually didn't drop in unannounced and wondered if he hoped I was taking him up on his job offer. "I've been working on a breeding farm in Warrenton. Temporarily," I added quickly. "You got a minute?"

"Sure." Kessler told his groom, a man I didn't recognize, that the rundown bandages looked good and to be ready to go in fifteen minutes.

We headed to his office, and like so many times in the past, I sat in the hard plastic chair alongside his desk. I briefly explained what I was doing at Stone Manor and met a wall of silence.

"Why am I not surprised?" he finally said. "For Christ's sake, be careful."

"I will. No one has any idea what I'm up to."

"If I know you, that'll change. You dig around, you're bound to catch someone's attention."

"I've been careful. Listen." I leaned forward in my chair. "I know you're in a hurry. Is there any reason for a thoroughbred breeding farm to be using an artificial vagina?"

"No," he said automatically. "Ah…well, wait a minute. They use them when they evaluate a stallion's fertility for insurance purposes. And of course, a report would be required if they planned on selling one of the studs, but a vet would perform the exam, so I don't see why they'd have that equipment."

"The farm's owner's a vet."

"Well, then, maybe he would so he could run his own tests for comparison."

"He's a she." I handed Irish Dancer's fertility report to Kessler, and he frowned as he studied the figures.

"This horse is in trouble. At a bare minimum, you need five hundred million sperm per breeding, using AI, and that's with good motility and morphology." He tapped the page. "He doesn't have either. They'll be hard pressed getting his mares to stick because it's much more difficult with a natural cover."

"So artificial insemination would help?"

"You can't use that with thoroughbreds," Kessler said as he handed me the report.

"I know, but when a horse is having trouble like this one obviously is, would you have a better chance getting mares in foal?"

"It's illegal."

I ran my fingers through my hair. "I know, but would it help?"

"Yeah, sure. But with his numbers, it still won't be easy. They'd add antibiotics and semen extenders to the sample, which they'd deliver directly into the uterus with a pipette so there's no waste. But still…I wouldn't want to bet on the outcome."

"What would happen if the breeder was found out?"

"Christ. I'd hate to think. All the stud's foals would lose their Jockey Club registration, and if any have raced, or entered breeding themselves…" Kessler paused. "To be honest, I don't know what would happen, but I suspect the farm would be ruined."

"Hmm." I glanced around the little room as I folded the report and slipped it into my coat pocket. If anything, the office was more cluttered than the last time I'd been there. "How's Ruskie?"

"Pulling like a train." Kessler leaned back in his chair. "If all goes well, he'll run in the Blue Grass Stakes, and he's ready."

"And after that?" I asked, wondering if Kessler was considering the Derby.

"We'll see."

I smiled. It was almost as if he didn't want to acknowledge the fact that he was considering running Ruskie in the Kentucky Derby, as if the very mention of those two words would collapse the dream like a bubble bursting under the sun.

He filled me in on the rest of the stable as we strolled back into the aisle and stood in front of the great horse's stall.

Ruskie stepped toward the doorway as if he could walk straight through the nylon webbing that spanned the opening at waist height. He stuck his elegant head into the aisle, pricked his ears, and prodded Kessler's jacket with his nose.

"He's not spoiled, is he?" I said, and Kessler chuckled as he slipped several carrot chunks out of his pocket and cupped his hand under Ruskie's nose.

"You change your mind, Steve, and want to work here, you've got a job waiting for you."

"Thanks. How's Abby?"

Kessler sighed. "She's fine, and she won't care if you work for me. I even think she'd like having her brother around."

I grinned and patted Ruskie's neck.

We continued down the shedrow, looking in at each horse while Kessler told me that he expected to be traveling more in the coming year and that Ruskie's winning streak had brought him additional owners.

We stopped outside the bay gelding's stall as the horse's groom put on his bridle. "We've gotta head over now," Kessler said as the PA switched on, calling the horses for the second race. "You going to stay?"

I glanced at my watch. "Yeah. I've got time."

We walked down the track, and I stood with Kessler while he saddled his runner, then we went up to the third level and watched the race in quiet companionship. His runner, Jade's Risk, finished third, and Kessler seemed pleased with the result. We returned to the barn, and as I prepared to leave, he told me to be careful.

"I will."

I looked over my shoulder as I stepped into the alley and saw that Kessler was watching after me.

I stopped at the loft, switched out dirty clothes for clean, then called Detective Brandon. He picked up on the second ring.

"This is Steve Cline. What have you decided?"

"We'd like to proceed, if you're willing."

"Yeah, I am."

"Good. When do you get home tomorrow? We need time to brief you and rig Claremont's phone before he calls to set the deal."

"I get off at noon, and it'll take me ten minutes to get to the apartment."

"And he's calling at one?"

"Yeah."

"All right. One of my guys'll be waiting for you. Name's Tyler McPherson. Big guy. Looks like a goon with scraggly frizzy brown hair tied in a ponytail." Scuffling noises, followed by a squawk and laughter, sounded in the background, and I figured McPherson hadn't appreciated the description. "He'll meet you in the lot and get your phone set up for the call."

"Okay."

"And he'll accompany you when the buy goes down."

"What if Yates doesn't go for that?"

"He will. With that quantity, I doubt he'll be alone, either. If he objects, call it off, 'cause you aren't going to be by yourself."

I hung up and headed to Foxdale. Rachel typically arrived at three-thirty, and I wanted to surprise her. I waited in the pickup until four, then went into the office to use the phone. Mrs. Hill had already left for the day. The door to the lounge was locked and the room was dark. I left the lights off and dialed Rachel's number. Her mother told me that she'd gone out.

"Do you know if she intended to ride today?" I asked.

"I don't think so. She didn't take a change of clothes to work this morning."

"Thanks." I gave her the office number. "I'll be here until five. If she gets home before then, could you have her call me?"

She told me she'd relay the message. I said goodbye and looked through the Plexiglas window as I hung up. Karen's three-thirty class had finished their flatwork, and the riders had formed a disorganized line along the opposite wall as they waited for their turn to jump. A school pony headed toward a cross rail that was set so low, the gelding simply cantered over it while the little girl clung to his mane.

◇◇◇

Rachel never did show or call. I stopped at Sullivan's and got back to Bruce's apartment by seven-forty-five, dead on my feet and not in the best of moods. I opened the door to the sound of a ringing phone.

I snatched it up. "Rachel?"

"No," a gruff male voice said. "And if she's still with you, she deserves a medal."

I frowned, wondering how Detective James Ralston of the Maryland State Police had known how to get in touch with me.

"What the hell are you doing?" he said.

"What do you mean?"

"Don't play stupid with me. I just got off the phone with Brandon after spending ten minutes trying to persuade him to drop this bullshit controlled buy. You know how dangerous they are?"

"Controlled buy?"

"Controlled buy, drug sting. Whatever."

"His team will be careful."

"I don't give a shit how careful they are, it's still dangerous. Two months ago, one of our detectives had to shoot a suspect during a buy, and he was damned lucky *he* didn't get killed. The dealer was in the front passenger seat, and his buddy had slipped in behind them, and the guy up front tells our guy 'this is gonna be a holdup,' and they both pull guns on him. Well, Troy wrestled the gun out of the guy's hands and shoots the guy in the backseat. Killed him. The dealer in front takes off on foot and is shot by the cops monitoring the buy. And you know what?"

I didn't think I wanted to hear.

"Troy hasn't been back to work since. He'll probably retire. Do you know how fucking scared he must have been?"

"Yeah. I have a pretty good idea."

Ralston grew quiet, and for a moment, I was no longer standing in Bruce Claremont's kitchen. Instead, I was lying on a cold sidewalk in the rain with a gun in my hand, listening to windshield wipers slap across wet glass as my blood channeled down a crack in the concrete.

"Well…I guess you do," Ralston said and drew me out of the past.

"Listen, I'm in it now, so help me out."

"I know I'm not going to like this."

"Probably not, but would you run records' checks on some people down here? Knowing what I'm dealing with can only help."

"Help you get in deeper, I expect." He sighed. "What are their names and ages? Approximate will do if you don't know."

"Paul Genoa, 27, Michael Tiller, 24, Shane Hadley, 33, Victor Nash, 45." For the hell of it, I added Bruce Claremont, 26.

Papers rustled before he said, "Is there any way I can talk you out of this?"

"I don't think so."

"Do you know when the buy's going down?"

"Not yet." I gave him the farm's cell phone number in case I was at work.

"Be careful," Ralston said. "Just because you jumped into this with both feet doesn't mean you have to see it through."

◇◇◇

Maddie was uncharacteristically quiet at the three o'clock switch-over Wednesday morning.

"Do you expect any foals?" I said.

She shrugged as she punched out. "Just keep an eye on them."

"Maddie, what's wrong?"

"Nothing. I'm just tired." She left the clinic and closed the door behind her, and I had an uncomfortable suspicion that Paul had more to do with her mood than lack of sleep.

Out of curiosity, I opened the doors under the sink and checked the AV unit. As far as I could tell, it hadn't been disturbed. Maybe Dr. Nash only used it for fertility exams. I certainly had no proof that she was illegally using artificial insemination, but the fact that Irish Dancer only covered mares in the late afternoon bothered me. The day crew left at five, and Maddie didn't come in until six, so that gave them an hour's window of opportunity. And if they were using AI, Frank had to be involved because it took three people, one to hold the mare, one to hold the stallion, and one to collect the sample.

Had Bruce uncovered what they were doing, and had that knowledge become his death sentence? I couldn't believe the Nashes capable of that. However, I had no trouble picturing Paul becoming violent if he'd caught Bruce and Maddie engaged in a late-night romp in the hay. And violence could easily escalate to murder under the right circumstances.

An equally probable scenario was that Bruce had gotten in over his head with some drug dealers and had paid the price for his naiveté. If Corey was very lucky, Bruce was off somewhere, selling his stash. And just where had he gotten his hands on a kilo of coke, anyway? From his buddy, A.J.? And what if they weren't buddies as I'd assumed? A deal between the two could have gone sour, which could mean, at the very least, that Bruce had stolen the dope from A.J. At the very worst, Bruce might know more about the explosion than he'd ever want to admit.

I looked out the window toward the Nashes' home. Maybe the events revolving around the bank barn only appeared suspicious because of my attempt to twist them into something sinister. A simple fact that I had yet to uncover could easily drop all the pieces into place and provide a logical, innocent explanation.

I put my lunch in the fridge and locked the door on my way out. The temperature still hovered in the upper forties and felt incredibly mild after the bitter cold that had gripped the eastern seaboard for the last couple of weeks.

After I checked barns one through six, I climbed into the Chevy and headed over to seven and eight. As I sped down Bear Wallow, the headlights flashed across a clump of ornamental grass at the side of the road. No breeze rustled through the blades. Wind had a way of spooking horses, creaking the barn siding and snapping tree branches and swirling leaves across the ground, but sometimes, a lack of air movement could be equally unsettling. Tonight, the air was unnaturally still, as if the earth were holding its breath. And my moon was gone, swallowed in the expanse of black space.

As I'd learned from my sessions in the library, scouring the local papers, area residents fought suburban sprawl on a regular basis, but the terrain surrounding Stone Manor was relatively desolate. To the west, the Blue Ridge Mountains formed a starless black wall without depth as they rose and fell beneath a star-filled sky. In the foothills, a pattern of lights delineated the roads that crossed the valley. A few porch lights left on by mistake, scattered dusk-to-dawn lamps illuminating barn lots, an occasional pole lamp. Otherwise, wide expanses of black undefined ground spread out in all directions. Stone Manor itself took up hundreds of acres.

As I turned off Cannonball, my arm muscles tensed when I saw that barns seven and eight were dark. "Not again."

I angled the Chevy's headlights so that they cut through the gap between barn seven's open doors. I checked that my cell phone was in my jacket pocket as I slipped out of the cab. Turned toward the bed to grab the pitchfork handle before I remembered I didn't have it with me. It was in one of the farm trucks, if it hadn't been thrown away.

I shifted the Mag to my left hand and pulled out my pocketknife, unfolded the blade. I stepped around the front bumper and crossed over to the bank of light switches. I flipped them on. The mare in the first stall slowly turned her head and squinted at me. She was half-asleep and unconcerned. I blew out a breath, then checked the rest of the barn. Except for the relaxing sound of a mare contentedly chewing her hay, barn seven was quiet. No breeze eddied under the eaves of the run-in shed, and the band of mares must have been at the far end of the field.

I pulled up to eight. As the Chevy's door creaked open, a mare snorted an alarm, a sudden, high-pitched exhalation of breath that signaled danger. When I moved past the pickup's bumper, my shadow grew and spread across the barn doors. I spun around as I stepped through the opening and was relieved when no one was there. As I turned toward the bank of light switches, something in the aisle by the gate to the lot caught my attention. I couldn't tell what it was, but I had a gnawing feeling in my gut that I wasn't going to like what I found.

As I pointed the flashlight toward the switches, the mare in the first stall moved as the cone of light caught her eyes. They were wide and white-rimmed as she reared her head back in alarm. I angled my knife sideways and flicked the switches with my knuckles. I slowly turned my head to look at the object lying in the middle of the aisle.

I think I stopped breathing.

A foal's body sprawled across the hard asphalt in the very center of the barn, still and lifeless.

Chapter 16

I stayed put in the entryway and glanced nervously over my shoulder. The chilled air funneled over my neck as I listened for any noise that felt out of place. Any noise that was…human. As I started down the aisle, I kept my gaze focused on that foal. Although logic told me it was as dead as the hard ground it lay on, part of my mind expected it to move.

In barn eight, the run-in shed was to my right. Several mares cautiously entered the barn, but as others moved in behind them, they peeled around and ran back into the lot. One of the stalled mares snorted when I walked past, and the mare directly opposite the foal's body stared through her stall's grillwork, wide-eyed and alarmed.

I crouched down and studied the foal. He was smaller than most of the foals I'd delivered or had seen delivered but looked perfectly normal otherwise. Except that he was dead. Dead and lying in the center of the aisle. And the only way he could have gotten there was through human intervention.

His purple tongue lolled out of his mouth, but I was relieved to see that his eyes were closed. I reached out and touched him. Warmth still rose through his damp coat.

This kind of statement didn't gel with an arsonist's plan, but it smacked of Paul, and I was convinced more than ever that he was behind the lights. And it should have been obvious from the start. He hadn't pulled his tricks during Maddie's shift, only mine. I assumed he planned on spooking me out of the job, and tonight's effort was a damned good attempt.

The straw in the shed rustled as a mare approached the gate. When I stood, she spun away from me and kicked out at the heavy strands of afterbirth that slapped wetly against her hind legs. She lowered her head and humped her back, striking out at the unusual sensation as she cantered back outside.

I flipped open the farm's cell phone and keyed in Dr. Nash's number. She answered on the fourth ring.

"This is Steve. One of the mares in barn eight aborted."

"Oh, damn." Something rustled against the phone, and I pictured her sitting up in bed. "Is the mare in a stall or the lot?"

"She's turned out," I said.

"She and the foal need be separated from the rest of the mares."

"Well…uh, the foal's already separated."

"Oh, good. Where'd you put it?"

"I didn't put it anywhere. It's in the barn aisle."

Static hummed in the earpiece. After a time, she said, "What do you mean, 'it's in the aisle'?"

"Someone placed it in the middle of the aisle. And I assume that same someone also flipped off barn seven and eight's lights."

"One of us will be over," she said before her phone clattered into its cradle.

Five minutes later, headlights swept across the field out back as a vehicle turned off Cannonball and headed toward the barn. I returned to the entrance as Dr. Nash's Spyder slid to a stop alongside my Chevy.

Victor Nash unfolded himself from behind the wheel and glanced at my truck on the way in. His hair stuck out on one side, and he looked as if he'd hastily pulled on a pair of jeans and jammed his bare feet into some boat shoes. He stopped short as he stepped over the threshold and caught sight of the foal. It looked as disturbing and out of place in the glare of the incandescent lights as it had with my Chevy's headlights streaking down the aisle.

"God." Victor glanced at me, but his gaze was drawn back to the deflated little body. "This is how you found it?"

"Yep."

"Shit."

"That's what I thought."

He rubbed his face, then started down the aisle as slowly as I'd done. "Deirdre said the aisle lights were out like the other night. You have any idea who's doing this?"

When I didn't respond, he stopped and looked at me. "Well?" His eyelids were swollen, as if he'd been sleeping with his face jammed in a pillow.

"I have a couple ideas, but nothing to back them up."

He held out his arms. "Come on, Steve. We're not in a court of law, here. I don't give a shit about proof. I want your ideas."

"Speculation without fact to back it up. That's all I've got."

"Fine." Victor looked toward the run-in shed when the foal's dam approached the gate once more. "Oh, fuck. We can't leave her out there like that." He glanced at the mares in the stalls alongside us. "Look, I'll go down to the far end of the barn and see if I can't find a mare that's not as freaked as these. I'll put her in a lot out back while you see if you can catch her."

We both grabbed lead ropes, and I slipped into the run-in shed while Victor headed for the back of the barn. When I started toward the mare, she spun away. I stood there and waited, listening to a stall door scrape open farther down the aisle.

The mare hovered just outside the shed. The mercury vapor lamp shone down on her, illuminating the patchy sweat that coated her flanks and neck, and I realized she was trembling.

I walked through the deep straw bedding, not directly for her, but in her general direction. "Hey, girl. You're going to be all right. Just let me catch you," I said softly.

She raised her head and watched my approach with suspicion.

"I'll give you some nice alfalfa hay," I said. "I'll even shake out some fresh straw in your stall, and after awhile, you'll be able to relax." I calmly moved to her shoulder as if we did this every single night of the year.

Her head inched higher, and she rolled her eyes but held her ground.

"That's a good girl," I whispered. "Everything will be okay." I reached out and stroked her neck, then clipped my lead on her halter. I slowly exhaled a lungful of trapped air as I smoothed my palm down her neck. She lowered her head slightly, but it took a bit of coaxing before she would approach the gate.

We were about ten feet from the barrier fence when the mare slammed into my shoulder and knocked me to my knees. I kept hold of the lead, forcing her to spin around me. She began to canter backwards, tipping me forward, but somehow, I scrambled to my feet. I ran with her and wrestled her to a stop.

As I moved alongside her shoulder, I noticed Victor standing by the gate and realized she'd probably spooked when he'd first appeared at the far end of the aisle. This time, it took me twice as long to get her over to the gate. Victor swung it inward and stepped out of the way.

The mare curled her neck and skittered onto the asphalt.

"Let her go over to her foal if she wants to," Victor said as he latched the gate behind us.

I thought she was too freaked, but she walked right up to him and lowered her head. She licked his rump and sniffed his tail.

After a couple of minutes, when the sound of the mare's snuffling filled the quiet, Victor moved alongside me. "Put her in the stall, Steve. Hopefully she's figured out for herself that he's never going to get up."

"Shit."

"I know," he said and raised his tired eyes to look in my face. "It happens though. Usually something's wrong with the foal, and whatever it is triggers the abortion."

"But he looks fine."

Victor rested his hand on my shoulder. "Nature knows better than we do, Steve, believe me."

I put the mare in the second stall from the end, spread clean straw over the old, and gave her a flake of hay. Then Victor and I stood over the foal for a minute longer. When he reached down and grabbed the colt's forelegs, I gripped his rear cannon bones and was surprised by how cold they'd become. As we carried him down the aisle, his neck curved toward the ground, and his head brushed the asphalt.

We placed him gently on the ground, and his quiet body flattened against the cold earth.

I followed Victor back into the mare's stall. He peered at the brass nameplate on her halter. "All right, Steve. Who's been fucking with the lights," he gestured toward the dead foal, "and now this?" He paused. "And, I take it, your tires."

"I don't know."

"But you have an idea."

"And that's all it is. An idea." I stepped out of the stall, and Victor followed. When he reached up and rubbed his face, his jacket sleeves slid down his wrist, exposing an ugly paisley pattern on what could only be a pajama top.

"Well?" Victor prompted.

"At first, since the fires have been so localized, I thought it was the arsonist. But that didn't explain my truck's tires being slashed, and whoever's fooling with the lights hasn't done it during Maddie's shift." I paused. "This is just a guess, but Paul cares for Maddie a great deal—"

"Genoa?"

I nodded. "He's jealous of me. My guess is, he's trying to encourage me to quit."

"You're right. I can't take action based on that. If he comes back, whoever he is, try to get his license or vehicle description. Sometime tomorrow, check Genoa's car. If he's the one, you'll be able to spot it easier."

"I already have."

Victor looked in at the mare and sighed. "Tie up her afterbirth, and you'll need to come back and check on her during your rounds until she cleans out, okay?"

I nodded.

Victor left, and I followed him several minutes later. I'd expected him to go straight home, but as I passed the clinic, I saw the red flash of the Spyder's taillights beneath barn six's dusk-to-dawn light, and in that instant, I realized all the barns were dark. Except six.

It figured.

Victor and I checked the barns together; then he drove over to the training barns, and fifteen minutes later, I saw him pull slowly down the drive to the garage behind the stone mansion.

◇◇◇

Dr. Nash and Jenny didn't come into the clinic like usual Wednesday morning, which surprised me until I remembered Jenny had off from school. I ate my lunch, and at five after seven in the morning, when most of the crew had drifted in, Paul Genoa slouched in his chair and rested his chin on his chest. I was tempted to ask him why he looked so tired, but as I took a step toward him, the clinic door opened. Victor and Frank entered the room together, and the talking that had been going on petered out.

Victor cleared his throat. "It's come to my attention that the person who's been sneaking around the farm at night, vandalizing property and switching off lights we've left on for security reasons, may be a farm employee."

He let that hang in the air while most of the crew glanced at each other, and I noticed with satisfaction that Paul had centered his gaze on me.

"If this continues," Victor said, "have no doubt, I'll find out who's behind it, and that person will be fired immediately."

I dragged my gaze away from Paul and glanced around the room. Victor's comments had Tiller's attention, but not in a way that seemed suspicious.

"Sooner or later, most people who indulge in this type of juvenile activity brag about it," Victor continued. "If any of you learn who's behind this, I expect you to report it to me in private, because, if I find out you knew but remained quiet, you'll be fired, as well." Victor's gaze settled on Genoa for a second before he turned and left the room.

The crew was unusually subdued until Frank separated us into teams, and we headed to the parking lot. Thankfully, I was paired with Tiller, Ben, and Ronnie.

I smiled as I listened to their speculation.

"The boss don't know what he's talking about," Ronnie said as he opened the truck's door. "Ain't none of us would pull that shit."

Ben and Tiller agreed.

"Could be anybody," Tiller said as he climbed into the cab.

Ben scrambled into the bed. "Maybe gypsies are doing it."

That stopped me in my tracks, and Tiller and Ronnie swiveled around on the bench seat and stared at Ben through the glass.

"My grandma says they're around here. In the fall, they steal her grapes."

Ronnie shoved the cab's back window closed, and when he locked it, Tiller chuckled under his breath.

By the time we'd turned out the mares in barn six, and Ben and Ronnie had argued over who was going to use the best pitchfork, the general consensus reached was that the arsonist had been responsible for the lights.

By nine-forty, as we moved to barn five, Victor pulled alongside the farm truck in a beat-up Toyota pickup and caught my attention. "Steve, give the keys to Tiller. Sergeant Bodell's at the clinic, and he wants to talk to you."

I climbed out of the cab. "They're in the ignition."

Victor nodded and yelled to Tiller. "You've got the Ford. Steve and I are going over to the clinic."

I glanced at the Toyota's right front bumper before I climbed into the cab. It had a ding in it the size of a dinner plate. A large crater over the wheel well had been hammered out, and a deep gouge ran the length of the rear panel. Except for a swath of clear glass on the windshield, the entire vehicle was crusted over with a layer of hardened mud.

Victor shifted into reverse as I slid onto the seat and closed the door.

"Who's been driving your truck?"

Victor grinned. "I take it off road—"

"One would only hope."

His grin broadened. "There are some dirt tracks along the river that are a blast to plow through, especially when it's muddy. Unfortunately, an occasional tree or boulder gets in the way."

"No kidding. So, what does Bodell want?"

"Deirdre called him about last night." He rubbed his forehead. "Man, she's going nuts with this."

"Any news on why the mare aborted?"

"There was evidence of a bacterial infection. Deirdre's taken cultures from the mare and foal and will know in a couple days."

As Victor sped past the lake, a stiff breeze pushed ripples across the cold water and rattled the cattail stalks on the far bank. He slewed the little truck down off the road, and as we approached the clinic, Shane Hadley strolled out of the building and nodded to Bodell. Hadley paused alongside his silver Viper, turned his back to the wind, and bent to light a cigarette. He slid behind the wheel as Victor pulled up alongside Bodell's cruiser. Its sleek chocolate finish shimmered under the sun. Less could be said for the man himself. His overalls were embedded with grime, and I doubted his ball cap's frayed bill was a fashion statement. "Don't look too happy, does he?"

I chuckled.

Bodell had been scowling as he watched Hadley back out of his parking space and point the Viper toward the road, and I wondered if he resented Hadley's wealth or was jealous of him. Or both.

"Deirdre's got him wrapped around her finger," Victor said. "Not that I blame him. I swear, he'd stand on his head out here in the parking lot if she asked him to."

"Aren't they cousins?"

Victor grinned. "Distant cousins. Makes a difference."

Sergeant Bodell's old-boy charm was as polar opposite Deirdre's high-society as two people could get. As I climbed out of the Toyota, I thought back to his remark about Deirdre's being one classy lady. At the time, I'd thought what I'd heard in his voice was admiration, and maybe that's all it was.

Sergeant Bodell pushed off the cruiser's front quarter panel, yanked off his ball cap, and smoothed his palm over his balding head. "Hear you had a fun night."

"Yeah," I said. "Real fun."

Since daybreak, the sky had begun to cloud over, and a chilly breeze channeled down from the mountains so that the day felt colder than the preceding night. Bodell shivered under his lightweight jacket. When he suggested we use the clinic, the three of us went indoors.

After I'd repeated everything I could remember about last night and Saturday, when the guy had first started fooling with the lights, I was thankful when Victor was the one to put my theory about Paul into words. I was still uncomfortable naming him and was relieved when Bodell didn't seem overly impressed.

Bodell eyed one of the chairs, but chose to lean against the counter instead. He crossed his arms over his stomach and yawned. "I'll run a records check on Genoa and give his vehicle information to the watch commander. If any of us see him cruising around here after hours, we'll see what he's up to."

"You mean, pull him over?"

Bodell nodded.

"Don't you need probable cause?"

Bodell tilted his head back and closed his eyes. "Oh, yeah. I forgot. I'm dealing with Perry Mason, here." He opened his eyes and smiled as he lowered his gaze from the ceiling. "Why don't you become a real cop? Put your talents to good use. Course, if you decide to become a lawyer, I might have to shoot you."

I grinned and Victor chuckled as he reached into an upper cabinet and took down a batch of Styrofoam cups.

"Well, Steve," Bodell said, "I guarantee it. You follow somebody long enough, when you've got a lightbar on your roof, you're bound to find something to pull them over for."

"Legitimately?"

"Of course. You'd be surprised. Erratic or over cautious driving." He grinned. "Now, I admit, that might have something to do with the fact that we're tailing them. Going too fast or slow, not signaling properly, taillight out, license plate displayed incorrectly. I bet if I went out right now and looked over your truck, I'd find something I could get you for." Bodell switched his gaze to Victor and grinned. "Now, Victor's piece-a-shit truck's probably ripe for a dozen citations under all that mud."

Victor innocently spread his hands. "Hey, how'd this get around to me?"

Bodell's lips twitched as he straightened his spine. He slipped his wallet out of his back pocket and handed me a business card. "You see anything you don't like, call 911 first, then call my cell number. Now that I'm off third shift, I can get here in a minute or two since I live close. Just off Dunnottar."

Victor offered Bodell a cup of steaming coffee. "What shift they got you on now?"

Bodell accepted the coffee and grunted. "First, and it's just about killing me. The only thing good about it is that they got doughnuts at roll call."

I smothered a grin and shook my head when Victor held out a coffee and raised his eyebrows. In the two weeks that I'd worked the job, as far as I could tell, no one had thought to rinse out the filter basket, let alone wash it.

"Well, that's it, gents," Bodell said. "Unless you got something else I should know about."

"That's it." Victor pulled over a chair and sat down.

"I'll give you a call, then, after I check out Mr. Genoa."

Bodell placed his hand on the doorknob, but before he had a chance to turn it, the knob rotated beneath his fingers. The door swung inward on him, and Jenny bounded into the room. She paused in front of Bodell, and he tousled her hair.

"Hey, punkin," he said.

Jenny tilted her head back and peered into his face. "You catch any bad guys lately?"

"You bet." Bodell winked at her, and she giggled.

Jenny spun around and spied me. "No foals?"

"'Fraid not," I said as Bodell slipped out of the room.

Jenny's fine hair was plaited in one long braid down the center of her back, and she wore a pair of jodhpurs and boots. She nodded, then crossed over to her father. "Are you ready?"

"Oh, honey, not yet. I've gotta wait until that man from New York comes down and looks at those two yearlings."

"Awh, Dad, but you promised." She rested her hands on his knee.

"I'm sorry, honey."

Jenny hooked one foot behind her calf. "Well, can't I go by myself, or just ride on the track? I'm old enough to do that by myself."

I moved behind Jenny and waited for the opportune moment to interrupt them.

"You know you can't." Victor's gaze shifted from his daughter to me.

"Anything else, sir?" I said.

"You don't ride, do you, Steve?"

"Yes, sir. I do."

Jenny spun around, and her eyes widened in delight. "Can Steve take me on a trail ride? Please, Dad. I know the way. We won't get lost."

I glanced at Victor as a smile tugged the corner of his mouth. "Not a trail ride, honey. But maybe Steve can ride with you on the track." He looked at me. "Do you mind?"

"No, sir."

"I'm gonna go tell Mom." Jenny ran out of the room.

Victor sighed and slouched in his chair. "Thanks, Steve. I'll get you out of here by noon."

The three of us crammed into the Toyota, and Victor drove to the training facility. I checked the barns at night but had never gotten a good look at them in the daylight. Barns nine, ten, and eleven were laid out like racetrack barns but were far more elegant. Instead of the usual concrete block, a warm brown brick formed the exterior walls. The interior wooden walls were varnished and trimmed in black paint, and cupolas with antique weathervanes dotted the ridgelines. A half-mile training track, complete with furlong poles and an elaborate marker that simulated the finish line, sat on the opposite side of the access road. A lake filled the center of the track, and its gray surface mirrored the sky.

Victor left me to tack up Rocket, but before he'd gone three paces, he paused under the shedrow and backtracked. He stood in the doorway and grinned. "Oh, and Steve, don't let his name mislead you. This guy's as solid as they come. He raced for five years before we retired him to the farm. He's fifteen now, and he's seen and done more than most horses ever will. Deirdre hunted him for years after he came home, but now we mostly use him to pony the babies. He'll take good care of you."

I nodded.

Across the way, in barn nine, several employees milled around, scrubbing water buckets and cleaning tack. As far as I could tell, no one was working in ten. The stalls were cleaned and hay nets hung outside each stall, just like they did at the track. By my estimation, each barn had the potential to house eighteen horses, but barn eleven looked deserted.

Rocket turned his handsome head my way as I lowered the saddle onto his back and let it settle into position. He studied me with a kind, curious eye and stood stock still as I lifted the saddle pad's center seam off his withers so it wouldn't press on his thin skin. As I worked, I had an overwhelming impression that he was evaluating my level of expertise against the countless others who had come before me. I tightened his girth, then lifted the bridle off the stall guard. The bit jangled as I draped the reins over Rocket's neck and organized the straps. There was something wholly satisfying in the simple act of tacking up a horse. The smell of leather and horseflesh, the sound of creaking tack and jangling buckles. The anticipation of the ride. I picked out his feet, and as I led him into the shedrow, the farm's cell phone rang.

"Cline here."

"This is Ralston. Can you talk?"

I glanced toward the far end of the barn. Victor and Jenny stood next to a medium-sized gray pony. Its reins were looped over Victor's arm as he bent down to adjust Jenny's helmet. "Yes," I said. "For a minute or two."

"Bruce Claremont has one DUI and one minor possession charge for marijuana. He was fined for both instances."

"I'm not surprised."

"Fifteen months ago, Paul Genoa was arrested for simple assault. Because it was his first offense, he got off with six months' probation. Shane Hadley's gonna lose his license if he gets another point on his driving record. Victor Nash has two speeding violations and a couple parking tickets, and it took awhile to come by, but he has a juvenile record for setting fires in Prince George's County," Ralston added, and I think I stopped breathing. "He got a slap on the wrist and counseling. Michael Tiller's clean."

Victor was on one knee, now, struggling to tighten Jenny's chinstrap.

"Steve?"

"Huh?"

"Watch your back with Genoa."

"I will."

Ralston disconnected.

I folded the phone and dropped it into my jacket pocket as I stared down the shedrow at Victor. He couldn't be responsible for these fires. He just couldn't. I thought about Lloyd Strauss, burning to death in the old barn, and prayed to God he wasn't.

And if he had set those fires nineteen years ago, what did that mean for Bruce?

Victor hoisted Jenny into the saddle. He bent to check that her feet were properly positioned in the stirrups; then he lifted his head and smiled when he caught sight of me. "Come on, Steve. What're you waiting for?"

I led Rocket down the shedrow as Victor guided the pony into the weak sunlight. Once we cleared the roof overhang, I climbed into the saddle.

"Walk around the track once to warm them up," Victor said to me, "then do some trot work. After that, let Jenny canter as much as she wants, just make sure they cool down before you bring them back."

I nodded, and after I finished lengthening my stirrups, Victor sent us on our way. I glanced over my shoulder as we crossed the gravel road. His gaze was on his daughter, but when he noticed me looking, a lopsided smile lit up his face.

I had to be missing something. He couldn't be responsible.

Jenny led the way through the gate and onto the track; then she turned to the right. Even though she'd left a great deal of slack in the reins and didn't have hold of her pony's mouth, he arched his neck and lowered his head and marched purposefully forward as if he were pushing against an invisible wall. Rocket, on the other hand, ambled alongside the pony and spent his time taking in the scenery. In particular, a flock of geese bobbing around the lake held his interest.

"After we're done," Jenny said, "do you think you'll have time to ride with me when I take out my other ponies?"

"It depends. I have to leave right at noon today."

"Oh." Jenny looked over her shoulder. "Do you like Rocket?"

"Yeah. He's fine."

"He was a great field hunter. A bit wild, maybe, because he always wanted to be in front, like at the track. Mom said he used to pull so hard during his first season, she could barely lift her arms to take off his saddle at the end of the day. Then I guess he got the hang of it, because the hunt master wanted to buy him."

The cloudbank had thinned and given way to puffy, dark-bottomed clouds. In a few places, they'd separated, and shafts of sunlight slanted through the gaps and stretched down to the earth.

I pictured the heavy cord of smoke that had spread out from the fire on Cannonball Gate. It hadn't looked much different than the clouds drifting overhead.

"Mom doesn't hunt much, anymore. She's too busy, so Dad ends up taking me on the weekend. That's not so bad, though, because Mom's overprotective. She doesn't want me to gallop because she's afraid my pony will trip or step in a ground hog hole."

As I listened to her, I wondered if she was ever lonely, growing up as an only child; then I pictured Dr. Nash's tender expression that day in the clinic and had no doubt that she loved her daughter very much. And what about Victor?

Jenny pivoted around in her saddle and frowned. "You're not listening."

"Huh?"

"Have you ever hunted?"

"No." Before she could start up again, I said, "Jenny, remember the day your dad moved your ponies?"

"Uh-huh."

I squeezed my calves and moved Rocket up so I could see her expression. "Did anything else out of the ordinary happen that day?"

Jenny frowned and stared off into the distance as she pondered my question. "Like what?"

"Oh, I don't know. Did anyone else go to the bank barn that day? You know, people who normally don't go back there?"

She shook her head. "I went up there right after breakfast with a bag of carrots. Mom had saved some apple slices from when she made pies, so I took them, too. I could hardly wait to ride in the snow, but Dad ruined it because Mom was going out, and he had a meeting to go to, so—"

"What kind of meeting?"

Jenny shrugged. "I had to go to my cousins' for the day. I hate going there. Caleb is always whining about something and knocking people's toys down. As soon as Lexi gets the last block balanced on a pyramid, Caleb kicks it over. He does that all the time, and it gets annoying. And he does this." Jenny turned to face me, shoved her lower lip out, and squinted. "And his face turns red."

"Hmm."

She settled back in the saddle. "He's a brat."

"Sounds like it."

"Mommy says he can't help it, but everybody can help what they do, can't they?" Jenny tilted her head up and peered at me from under the brim of her riding helmet. The cold breeze had brought color to her cheeks, and she looked so sweet and innocent, it hurt.

"I don't know, Jenny. They should." I glanced down the track and realized it wouldn't be long before she'd want to trot, and I expected our conversation would come to an end at that point. "And your ponies were moved by the time you got back?"

"Uh-huh. I was pretty mad because I'd missed riding in the snow, and I wouldn't be able to go out and see my ponies whenever I wanted to anymore. But it's not so bad having them here. I can gallop them a lot, and that's important if I'm going to be a jockey."

"A jockey, huh?"

"Yeah. I'm gonna be the best girl jockey that ever lived."

I smiled. "How about the best jockey, period."

Jenny raised her eyebrows. "Maybe."

"Were the other horses still in the barn when they took your ponies out?"

She nodded.

"Jenny, you said that Bruce checked the bank barn at night. When was the last time you saw him do that?"

"The night it snowed."

"Was anyone else with him?"

"Uh-uh."

"What time was it, do you know?"

"It was real late, but I don't remember what my clock said. I just know it was late because I kept waking up to check the snow. I was sure we were going to have the whole day off, but all we got was a measly two-hour delay."

"Was that the same night the horse trailer went to the bank barn?"

"Yep. The truck woke me up, and I couldn't go back to sleep. The light from the barn comes through my window, and I'd left my blinds open so I could watch the snowflakes swirl past my window. Sometimes the flakes were real big, and sometimes they looked like they were going up instead of down. And if I squinted my eyes just so, they looked like streaks of light."

"Did Bruce go into the barn when the trailer was there?"

"No. After."

"Well, do you know how long he was in the barn? How long were the lights on?"

"I didn't mean the inside lights. I meant the light on the side of the barn, up by the corner. That's what shined in my window."

"Okay, but how long were the barn lights on when Bruce went in?"

"He never turned them on," Jenny said, and the first stirrings of dread fluttered in my chest. "He went inside, and a couple minutes later, he came out."

"Where'd he park?"

Jenny shrugged. We were nearing the gate, and she had started to gather up her reins. "I didn't see the farm truck."

"What about a car?"

Jenny squeezed her legs, and the gray broke into a trot. "He didn't have a car, either."

Rocket, not to be outdone by a pony, flipped his head in annoyance, then slipped into a collected canter of his own accord. "Jenny, this is important," I said as I shortened the reins. "Can you remember anything else?"

"No."

Chapter 17

I got off the farm as soon as possible, punching out at eleven-thirty and not giving a shit whether anyone would question it tomorrow. I didn't know what to think, but I no longer wanted to entertain the idea of Jenny's father being responsible for Bruce's disappearance. There had to be a perfectly logical explanation for the activities taking place at the bank barn during Bruce's last weekend on the farm. There just had to be. If not, then the answer would most likely destroy Jenny's life, and I didn't want to be a part of that.

I headed straight home. Home? What the hell was I thinking?

In exactly an hour and a half, I had a phone appointment with David Alexander Yates, drug dealer/undercover cop look-alike, and I didn't want to mess it up. More than ever, I just wanted Bruce to be off somewhere, screwing up his life but alive. What the hell? If he'd been hanging out with some unscrupulous druggies, then maybe, just maybe, he'd get out of it unscathed.

If Victor or Paul Genoa had had anything to do with Bruce's disappearance, then I doubted Corey was ever going to see her brother again.

I skipped lunch and pulled into the parking lot in front of the apartment complex. I hated to admit it, but finding the dead foal, along with the pending drug sting or controlled buy as Ralston had called it, and my growing certainty that Bruce had met a bad end, had combined to leave me rattled. I parked in front of unit six-forty-one, and as I switched off the engine, a light green Sebring four-door sedan glided into the spot next to my Chevy. The driver clicked open his door and climbed out. He wore a scruffy-looking denim jacket, jeans, and sneakers, and judging by his build and frizzy hair held back with a rubber band, I figured he was Detective Tyler McPherson.

McPherson nodded at me before he leaned back into the car and withdrew a Giant grocery bag with a bright orange package of Spicy Doritos sticking out the top.

I stepped around the Sebring's hood. "McPherson?"

"Cline?" McPherson's eyes sparkled with amusement; otherwise, his face was without expression. He swept his gaze across the lot as he turned to follow me up the steps. "You catch the game last night?"

"Nope." I flipped through my keys. "I'm usually sleeping then, because of my shift."

"That's gotta stink. I think we would've beat the Celtics if Stackhouse hadn't been nursing that knee of his."

"Maybe." I glanced over my shoulder as we stepped into the foyer and noticed a Toyota pickup pull into the lot.

"I thought our defense was good," McPherson said as he followed my gaze, "and we rebounded well. We just gave up too many points in the fourth quarter."

I slid the key into 2D's mailbox. "So I heard." Turned the key, glanced back into the sunlight. David Alexander Yates climbed out from behind the Toyota's wheel and took his time scanning the lot. The passenger's door opened. He had company. A dark-skinned guy with a shaved head and manicured goatee. Probably Hispanic, but not the guy Fluffy's owner had noticed driving Bruce's car. Not unless he'd grown a goatee and added five inches to his height.

"We got company," I whispered as I gathered the envelopes in my hand and shut the door. "Yates and a friend."

McPherson pivoted toward the entry and slipped his hand under his denim jacket at the small of his back.

"What'll we do?"

"Just go with it," McPherson said quietly as they approached the steps.

"Uh-huh." Sure. We were just going to go with it. Nice. "Eddie Jordan's got his work cut out for him," I said, referring to the Wizards' coach.

"Yeah." McPherson watched them climb the steps. "Arenas had a great game, but when he missed that free throw with seven seconds left in regulation, that clinched it."

"Yeah. It sure did."

Yates eyed McPherson as he paused in the entryway; then he looked at me while the Hispanic guy settled into a wide-legged stance and clasped his hands behind his back. "Talk to you alone?" Yates said.

I jerked my head toward McPherson. "He's with me."

Yates glanced over his shoulder. "Well, let's go up. Talk some business."

I thought about that for a second and didn't see any reason to go upstairs, where we wouldn't have backup or a way out if they decided to pull something. If all he intended was to set up the exchange, it could be done right in the foyer. "I don't think so. Come back when you've got the money."

"I got the money now."

My gaze flicked over both of them. Neither had a package, and I didn't think fifteen grand would be easy to hide. Unless he'd left it in the truck, he was lying. "Bullshit. Anyway, I won't have the blow 'til tomorrow. You want it, come back then."

"When?"

McPherson shifted beside me. "Three o'clock."

Yates narrowed his eyes. "I ain't meeting here."

"You were ready to a minute ago," I said.

"Well, let's just say, I changed my mind." He glanced at the bag McPherson had shifted to his left arm when I'd first mentioned that they were in the lot. "Meet me behind the Giant."

Since I had no idea what controls the police needed in place, I waited for McPherson to say something.

"Sounds good," he said. "Three o'clock. And show up in the Toyota, or we just might not stick around."

"And what will you be driving, Mr....?"

"Derek," McPherson said. "You won't have any trouble spotting us, but we'll be in a green Sebring."

"Fifteen grand," I said to Yates, "or you won't even see the shit."

They glanced at each other. Yates shrugged; then they turned and headed for the parking lot.

When they reached the sidewalk, McPherson backed toward the steps, and when I joined him, he handed me the bag and said, "Upstairs."

I dumped Bruce's mail in the bag as McPherson yanked a cell phone out of his pocket and keyed a number. He headed up the steps. "Did you pick them up?" McPherson said. "A blue on blue late-nineties Toyota pickup?" He paused on the first floor landing, and we watched the Toyota pull out of the lot. "Heading west toward Van Roijen," he said, then spun around the banister and headed up the second flight. "Good." He paused, then said, "I'll call him in a minute."

I sorted through my keys one-handed, and after we entered the apartment, I locked it behind us and ignored a slight tremor that shook the key in my fingers.

McPherson crossed over to the sliders and looked down Waterloo. He keyed in another number, and from his end of the conversation, I guessed he was speaking with Detective Brandon as he explained that we'd made contact earlier than expected.

I set the grocery bag on the coffee table, lifted out the Doritos, and gathered up the mail. Two plastic-wrapped sandwiches, two Cokes, and a bag of Chex Mix sat on top of a black plastic case.

He described the Hispanic guy, told Brandon the exchange had been set to go down behind the Giant, then listened for a couple of minutes without speaking. "Great." He nodded. "We'll go over it when I get back. It's not as ideal as the apartment, but it's got a lot going for it."

He fiddled with the cord that opened and closed the drapes. "A box compactor, a bunch of carts, and they've always got trailers parked back there. Yeah, it'll work real well, and we can park our truck there, and they won't give it a second thought."

McPherson glanced in my direction. "Yeah, he did good." He turned back to the window and listened for another minute or two. "Okay. Later."

McPherson closed his cell phone and crossed over to the sofa. A broad grin lit up his face as he held out his hand. "Name's Tyler."

We shook. "Steve."

McPherson rubbed his hands together. "Well, Steve. You did good. Better than a lot of guys who've done this kind of thing before."

"Thanks."

He rummaged in the bag. "You want something to eat?"

"Sure."

He handed me a ham and cheese on kaiser, then pulled out a Coke and sandwich for himself. Ever since Yates had driven off, I'd sensed McPherson's energy level building. A kind of nervous energy that fizzed around him like static electricity.

"So, what's tomorrow gonna be like?"

McPherson perched on the edge of the sofa's armrest. "Brandon tell you anything?"

I shook my head as I bit into my sandwich.

"We'll set up behind the Giant well ahead of schedule, especially since they didn't stick to the game plan today. Backup'll already be in place in several locations, behind the compactor or one of the trailers and in a beat-up delivery truck we got. Looks like a piece of shit, but runs good and has plenty of room for our tactical team and all their gear. We'll be in the Sebring with the dope. Yates will probably be the one with the cash, and no doubt he'll bring his goon. I'll try to get them in the car with us, so the guys don't get in a chase." McPherson took a bite of his sandwich, then wiped his mouth with the back of his hand. "After the transaction, as soon as they get out, we'll pull away, and the guys'll grab 'em before they have a chance to get in the truck."

I swallowed some Coke. "What if they try to rip us off?"

"Backup will be all over them. We'll be fine."

"I had a feeling they would have ripped us off today," I said, "if they thought they could get their hands on the dope."

McPherson stopped chewing. "Hard to say."

"'Hard to say'? You thought so, too."

"Look, Steve. They're paranoid. Difficult to judge at the best of times. We'll be okay. You'll see." He looked around the room. "This isn't your place, right?"

"Right."

"After the bust, you're gonna want to clear out. They'll both be in the joint until they make bail, but you never know who they might call. You don't want to worry about them sending someone over here…"

He didn't finish his sentence, as it wasn't necessary. I swallowed some more soda. "If you get a lead on Bruce Claremont, I won't need to stay here any longer."

McPherson nodded. "Ain't no guarantee they know what happened to him, and if they do, ain't no guarantee they'll talk."

"I know."

He grinned. "Then again, they might get the misimpression it'll help their case if they tell us what they know."

"Sounds good to me."

McPherson shifted onto a seat cushion and slouched against the backrest. "So, what got you into this? Looking for Claremont?"

I shrugged. "A friend asked me. His sister. Since there weren't any signs of foul play, the cops wouldn't look into his disappearance, but it needed looking into."

He nodded. "Besides the drug connection, you have any other ideas on his whereabouts?"

I glanced at my half-eaten sandwich and drained the rest of the Coke. "None that I'm ready to talk about."

"Fair enough."

McPherson finished his sandwich. "Can you get over to the station by one tomorrow?"

"I'll be there."

McPherson folded the bag, bundling the rest of the contents into a wad.

"What else you got there?" I said.

"Gear for recording the phone call."

"And the reason for the food?"

"Props," he said. "Plus, I knew I'd be hungry and didn't think you would have had a chance for lunch, either."

"Thanks."

He shrugged. "Thanks for helping us."

Before he left, I unlocked Bruce's car, and McPherson slid behind the wheel and dusted surfaces likely to yield prints. He paid particular attention to the back of the rearview mirror and the door handles. After he took off, I switched to a Miller Lite and sank into the cushions. In the past two weeks, I'd gathered a lot of facts about the people who worked at Stone Manor. The problem was, I had way too many theories. Assuming Yates knew what he was talking about, I liked to think that Bruce had sold his dope and had gone to Florida or Vegas. In that case, he wouldn't have taken his car since it was likely to break down. He would have hopped a plane or bus. But why not call his sister? Was he that irresponsible?

I didn't have anything on the agenda for the rest of the day. Rachel had her Applications class, and if I sat around Bruce's apartment any longer, I'd end up worrying about the pending *controlled* buy—why in the hell did they call it that, anyway?—so I took a shower and drove to the library.

It took me an hour to find an article on the accident that killed Deirdre's parents. Seven years earlier, Philip and Frances Thorndike left their home on Bear Wallow Road to attend a Christmas party in Loudon County when Dr. Thorndike lost control of his car. The vehicle careened off the pavement and crashed into a rock outcropping that jutted from a streambed.

Although the temperature had been below freezing, the roads were dry.

A nighttime grainy photograph, thankfully lacking in detail, showed the tail end of the sedan's undercarriage. Apparently, the vehicle had slipped behind a guardrail and traveled parallel to it for sixty feet before plummeting down an embankment where it had impacted a boulder the size of a dump truck. Although the reporter didn't come out and say it, it appeared speed had contributed to the accident.

I printed the article, then twisted the knob, skimming the days that followed, looking for coverage on the funeral arrangements. When a blurry photograph slid onto the screen, my fingers tightened on the knob.

The hulk of a burnt down house loomed against a cloudless sky.

An early morning fire Thursday tore through a newly constructed two-story house southeast of Warrenton, leaving nothing but a brick shell and fireplace standing....

I scrolled through the weeks that followed and discovered two more fires at regular intervals before they stopped altogether. I printed the articles, but whether or not they were connected to *my* fires remained to be seen. Each one had involved a house under construction, not vacant buildings or barns. Technically, they didn't fit the profile, but they were close enough. Close enough that I couldn't stop the one question I would have preferred left unasked from squirreling its way into my mind. Had Victor set them?

When I pulled into the apartment complex at a quarter to five, most of Bruce's neighbors were still at work. The temperature had taken a nosedive as the sun sank toward the mountains, painting the ridge gold and deepening the eastern face to purple in the failing light. Long shadows stretched halfway across the high school's grounds, yet I could swear the grass had begun to green after a few days' warmth.

I took the steps two at a time, and as I rounded the banister on the first landing, I stopped short. A guy I didn't recognize stepped off the landing midway between the first and second level. He gripped the railing with a meaty hand, and the smooth metal squeaked under his palm as he hustled down the steps toward me. I backed out of his way and didn't start breathing until he circled around the banister and continued down the stairwell.

I stood still and listened to the whine of tires on the street below, to the sound of a trash truck in the Food Lion's back lot lowering a Dumpster to the asphalt with a shuddering crash, to the hum of traffic on 211. The noise pushed against the apartment building and eddied around the corners and filtered into the foyer. I listened for any noise, a scrape of a shoe, the clearing of a throat, anything that indicated that someone was in the stairwell above me.

When I heard nothing out of the ordinary, I continued up the steps. The second floor landing was empty. I glanced in the stairwell leading to the third before I crossed over to Bruce's door. I let myself into his apartment and locked the door, feeling slightly foolish that I'd let myself get so spooked.

I got a Miller Lite out of the fridge; then I organized all the articles I'd collected over the last two weeks into chronological order. I spread them across the living room carpet before rooting through the kitchen cabinet for my marked-up calendar and a notepad. I scribbled *Victor/arson/juvenile record/age sixteen* across the top line and added *30 years ago*. I knelt on the floor at the beginning of the row of printouts. The next event occurred ten years later: Deirdre's engagement to Lloyd Strauss followed almost immediately by his death in a barn fire. That event had been the catalyst for three more fires. A year later, Deirdre and Victor married, catapulting Victor into a social bracket he would have been unlikely to achieve on his own. I listed the events along with their dates.

Three years after they married, Deirdre graduated from the University of Pennsylvania with a degree in veterinary medicine, and ten years later, Jenny was born. As she neared her first birthday, Deirdre's parents were killed, and their deaths were followed by another series of fires. What I found increasingly disturbing was the fact that Victor had benefited hugely from both events. First, he marries into money. Then, since Deirdre had been an only child, one would assume she'd inherited the farm and accumulated wealth after her parents' death. Victor and Deirdre had certainly made the most of it, transforming what had been essentially a gentleman's farm into a hugely successful breeding operation. And they were still expanding. The training barns were so new, the paint had barely had a chance to dry.

I didn't know much about the psychology of arson but supposed stress could be a natural trigger. The fact that Lloyd Strauss' death and the automobile accident were both followed by fires did not bode well for Bruce.

I moved back to the beginning of my row of papers, spaced over the floor like so many playing cards, and started through them, again. The afternoon sun slanted through the sliders, casting long bars of shadow across the carpet and warming my shoulders. When I finished reading the article about Deirdre's engagement to Strauss, I was once again struck by the difference between the expense lavished on their party versus Victor's. As I studied the photograph of Deirdre and Strauss, I wondered how she could have moved on so quickly. If I'd loved someone enough to marry them, I doubted I would have recovered as fast. Before I turned toward the next article, a figure in the far corner of the photograph caught my eye. I squinted and, for the first time, noticed a young Victor standing on the fringe of the party.

I went to bed around seven, tired but restless as I waited for sleep that wouldn't come. But sometime after ten, when the dark had deepened to a blackness achieved only in the dead of night, I slipped into a restless sleep. Disjointed images paraded behind my eyelids: Jenny tilting her head back to look in my face, a smudge of chocolate on her upper lip; Dr. Nash narrowing her eyes and telling me something I couldn't hear; Victor standing in the cold sunlight outside barn ten, his face lit with a broad smile; the hem of Elaine's dress slipping up her thigh as she crossed her legs; an unshed tear caught in Corey's long blond lashes; a thin brown streak tracking down a grocery bag.

A metal door swung open, and barn eight's aisle stretched before me. The dead foal was back where I'd found him, a silvery lump spotlighted under a cone of white light. A cold breeze curled under the eaves and stirred the dust particles that hung in the air. They swirled beneath the harsh light like a sudden exhalation of breath. I had no intention of walking down there. Yet, while I had the distinct impression that I was anchored in place, the row of stalls at my side and the roof above my head and the asphalt beneath my feet began a slow crawl to a point somewhere behind me, and I was propelled deeper into the barn.

Something large and heavy and primal rustled through the straw to my right as the foal's inert body drew closer. I slowly turned my head. A muscular stallion leaned into the stall front. His wild eyes caught and held the light as he stared down the aisle. He turned to circle his stall once more, and I noticed his massive erection and felt the wave of intensity that emanated from his sweat-soaked skin in a wall of heat that burned my face.

His stall continued its slow slide past me, along with the rest of the barn, and a feeling of dread welled up in my stomach and tightened around my lungs. The foal was moving closer. I wanted to turn and run. To get out of that barn. To stand under the stars and breathe in the clean night air. I forced myself to look down the aisle and watched in horror as the dead foal lifted his head off the ground. He splayed his front legs and lurched to his feet; then he swiveled his neck around and looked at me with milky, lifeless eyes.

A child's laughter sliced through the cold air like the tinkling of glass bells, and Jenny stepped into the barn aisle directly in front of the foal. She wore a ruffled pink dress and white tights and shiny patent leather shoes. Her hair was lifted off her neck with curled ribbons, and she looked like she should have been blowing out birthday candles instead of standing in a dark barn in the middle of the night. She stretched out her arms and spread her fingers toward the foal's face, and I wanted to yell at her, to warn her. I opened my mouth as a film of red moved across the foal's milky eyes.

Although no sound came from my throat, Jenny turned her head as if she'd heard my cry. Her gaze was drawn to something above my head as the foal reared onto its hind legs and clawed the air. Her mouth gaped open as she stared at whatever horror rose behind me and breathed its hot foul breath on the back of my neck.

I tried to warn her, to tell her to run as the heat intensified and seared my back. I jerked my eyes open and stared at the bedroom ceiling. I was out of breath, as if I'd been running, and a film of perspiration coated my skin. I shifted on the damp sheets and squinted across the room at the red glow from Bruce's alarm clock. Two-thirty. Time to get up.

◇◇◇

Maddie was in barn two, foaling out the mare in the stall next to Sumthingelse. She was crouched at the mare's hindquarters with her hands gripping the foal's slippery cannon bones. The head and neck had been delivered, and the mare was bearing down in an effort to push the shoulders through.

"You want me to take over, Maddie?"

She shook her head. "Not until I get him out, then you can finish."

I smiled. Maddie would want to mark this one down as her own, and rightly so, even though the follow-up chores would be left to me. Rubbing the foal dry, clipping on the tail tag, medicating the navel…I'd learned that she kept a record of every foal she'd ever delivered, the date and time, all the details of the birth, the foal's pedigree.

I scanned the aisle. Maddie had assembled everything I could possibly need. Her people skills had something to be desired, but she sure knew her job.

The mare groaned and, with a final gritty effort, delivered the foal into the straw. Maddie peeled the amniotic sac down to the foal's hips and cleared his nostrils before she slipped out of the stall.

"We got a filly or colt?" I said.

"Colt." She pulled a pen out of her back pocket as she moved around me, and there was something odd in the way she hunched her shoulders forward and canted her head, and I suddenly realized she hadn't once looked at my face. She crouched down in front of the door and jotted the time of delivery on the index card that stuck from behind the stall's name plaque.

"Maddie," I said softly. "What's wrong?"

The tip of her pen froze above her initials.

I put my hand on her shoulder. "What's happened?"

"Nothing," she whispered.

She stood and stared into the stall. As I pivoted her around, she lowered her head and turned away from me. Her thick curls fell forward across her cheek.

I placed my fingertips under her chin and turned her to face me.

An ugly bruise darkened the skin around her right eye. The swelling forced her eyelids closed. She bit her lip and looked back in the stall.

"Bastard." I gritted my teeth. "Where does he live, Maddie? Tell me."

She shook her head. "I'm going home," she whispered. "You've gotta stay here and take care of the horses."

"Maddie, are you hurt anywhere else?"

"No. He didn't mean to do it," she said. "It just happened."

"The hell it did."

"He loves me more than anyone ever has, it's just that…" She shrugged and exhaled a shaky breath. "It's nice to be loved, I just don't love him back."

I smoothed her hair off her forehead. "This isn't love, Maddie."

"My whole life," she swallowed and looked me straight in the eye, "all I've ever wanted was for someone to love me." She pulled away and headed for the exit.

"Maddie?"

She kept walking, and in a moment, I heard the farm truck start up and churn through the gravel.

Chapter 18

I mucked out the newborn's stall, then ran through the motions of my first barn check. Afterwards, I could only be certain that none of the mares were in labor. The other details I usually paid attention to were lost to a haze of jumbled thoughts and the anger that thrummed through my veins.

I left barn six, paused at the mouth of Stone Manor, and cut the engine. The Chevy's hinges creaked as I climbed out and eased the door back until it settled against the frame. Behind me, barns one through six stretched down both sides of the private road, evenly spaced long bands of white where the aisle lights shone through the stall windows. Dusk-to-dawn lights cast circular pools of light on the ground in front of each barn, outlining a fence in one place, an expanse of frost-coated grass in another. Beyond their reach, the terrain slipped into a darkness so black and deep you couldn't see where ground ended and sky began.

Most nights, once my eyes adjusted to the dark, the sky held more light than I would have thought, but tonight, a heavy blanket of cloud blotted out the stars. It absorbed the night sounds, except for the rush of a raw wind that funneled down the eastern slope of the mountains. Even the sporadic traffic that normally punctuated the night had dropped off.

I looked past the lake and the clinic and studied the Nashes' house. The windows were dark. An orange light burned in the bank barn's forebay, and a dusk-to-dawn light in the barn's peak bathed the back of the house in a soft glow.

The night's overriding darkness was at once a blessing and a hindrance. Normally, a casual glance out a window would not likely spot me, but tonight, I'd be forced to rely on a flashlight to see where I was going. I checked my watch. Four-thirty-five. That gave me twenty-five minutes to work with. With luck, the Nashes were asleep, and I'd have nothing to worry about. I considered approaching the house on foot, but that would take too long.

I rolled down the windows and pulled onto Bear Wallow. Once I'd driven past the clinic, I cut the headlights and throttled the truck down to a crawl. Couldn't see a damn thing. Couldn't see the edge of the road or the curve that loomed ahead. I flicked on the parking lights, and that worked. When I eased onto the gravel drive, stones popped under the tires, sounding like artillery fire in the night. I cringed. Logic told me that the mansion's foot-thick stone walls would block out the noise, but the adrenaline humming through my veins tightened my fingers on the steering wheel and clenched the muscles in my jaw.

Okay, Cline. Take it easy. I had an easy out if caught. But if I found something in the bank barn that no one wanted uncovered, something Bruce had seen, then all bets were off.

I stopped before I reached the end of the hedge that lined the drive and shut off the engine. The wind rustled the bare branches and whistled through the boughs in a stand of pine trees to my right. I inched the door open, and the hinges creaked and groaned.

The cold air tore the heat away from my body, but my skin felt clammy beneath my jacket. I cut around the Chevy's hood and kept to the grass. When I'd walked far enough, I glanced at the back of the house and was relieved to see that all the rooms that faced the barn were dark. One of those windows opened into Jenny's bedroom, and I hoped she was sleeping soundly, dreaming of her ponies or whatever eight-year-old girls dreamt about.

I clamped my hand over the flashlight's lens, switched it on, and spread my fingers. A narrow beam stretched into the darkness. I skirted around the parking lot that served the four-car garage. Then I continued past the bank barn, keeping beyond the range of the light that shone from the forebay where the bulk of the barn's massive second level extended well past the foundation wall. It formed a substantial overhang and protected the wide opening that accessed the lower level where Jenny's ponies would have been stalled. The doorway loomed like the entrance to a bottomless cave.

I planned on checking the lower level but had no intention of crossing the lot where the horse trailer had sat the last time I'd been there. Instead, I continued straight back, got my bearings, and doubled back, approaching the barn from the rear.

An earthen ramp led up to the wide wagon door on the barn's second level. Since I was out of sight of the house, I slipped my fingers off the front of the flashlight and raised the lens until the light centered on the heavy wooden door. As I walked up the ramp, adrenaline coiled through my muscles until they felt like springs that had been wound too tight.

The flashlight's beam stretched toward the barn's peak, bringing the weather-roughened planks into sharp relief as I tugged on the metal handle. The wheels squealed in the rusty track above my head. I shoved the door open and squeezed inside.

When I pointed the Mag toward the rafters, the darkness swallowed the cone of light before it reached the ridge beam. The barn reminded me of a cathedral with its high walls and gracefully arched roof. I moved deeper into the barn as a gust of wind pressed against the west wall. A sudden shower of dust and flecks of old hay drifted through the shaft of light. Straw and grit crunched under my boots as I crossed over to a haymow. Approximately four hundred bales had been stacked to the left of the wagon door, although I imagined the barn could hold twenty thousand more. A new lawn tractor and assorted junk cluttered the open space in the middle of the barn. Parts to an old swing set, a push lawnmower, a stepladder, wooden wine barrels, a tin wash tub. As I turned to leave, the light glinted off something shiny nestled among a stack of paper bags. I refocused the light and realized what they'd once held.

Concrete.

One of the bag's plastic inner liners had been exposed, and I realized that that's what had caught my attention. I counted sixteen bags. Not enough for a big job...like Jenny's wash rack, but a helluva lot of concrete, nonetheless.

I started toward the door and stopped suddenly. Flailed my arms to keep my balance. A trapdoor gaped open at my feet. I backed up, squatted at the edge, and peered down into an empty stall. I raised the light and saw what I'd missed earlier. An entire stretch of floor, running perpendicular to the central axis of the barn, contained trap doors that lined up with stalls on the ground level. Another line of doors ran along the length of the west wall.

I stepped back outside, scrambled off the edge of the earthen ramp, and rounded the corner of the barn. I walked straight into the forebay like I had every right to be there and entered the lower level with apprehension raising the hairs on the back of my neck. I'd never liked bank barns. Their design was more suited for cattle than horses, and they were too dark and airless for my taste. The concrete floor and stone walls were cold and damp, and as I stood under the low ceiling, I had a sense of the weight of the upper barn pushing down on the joists above my head.

The wide doorway accessed a large common area. To my left, a couple tons of straw bales were stacked on wood pallets. I stepped deeper into the barn. The stalls to my right stretched down to the far corner then continued along the west wall, forming an L-shaped area. There were eleven stalls in all. I crossed over and stood in the open doorway of the last stall. The floor was bare concrete, covered with thick rubber mats, and the rough fieldstone wall along the back was laced with cobwebs. The stall partitions were constructed with ancient two-inch-thick oak boards that ended a foot short of the joists. Instead of the usual metal grillwork, chain link fence enclosed the upper portion of the stall fronts. The setup was serviceable but not ideal. For one thing, if a horse reared, he'd knock himself out on the low ceiling.

An open space to the left of the stalls served as a grooming area. Empty bridle hooks and blanket bars and saddle racks lined the back wall. A tack trunk sat beneath them, and everything was covered with a layer of dust. Everything but the trunk.

When I crossed over to open the lid, my boot knocked into something hard and metallic. I lowered the light and centered the beam on an old combination lock. I picked it up. The dial was busted. I laid it back on the floor and peered in the trunk. Other than a rusted hoof pick, the trunk was empty.

A narrow wooden door was set into the stone wall at the end of the row of stalls. I pressed down on a lever that ran through a hole in the door, and the latch rattled as it slipped out of its catch. The door swung outward. I slipped outside and stood in a grassy area on the western side of the barn. Except for blinking red lights on the radio towers that crossed the mountains, the horizon was without definition.

I shone the light at the ground. The wind rustled the coarse dried grass, and it crackled under my feet as I crossed over to a low wall on my right. It rose to waist height and formed a cylinder approximately four feet in diameter. As I rested my hand on the edge and peered inside, I realized it was an old-fashioned cistern. The walls were six inches thick and rough like sandpaper. I raised my flashlight, and the light pooled on the well's floor two and a half feet below the rim. The concrete was new, as white as bone and impossibly smooth. Smooth except for some letters scrawled in the center.

Someone had scratched TINSLE in crude block letters in the center of the cistern with a stick that lay half-frozen in a paper-thin layer of ice that remained at the base of the wall.

Tinsle? She'd spelled it wrong, but one of Jenny's ponies was named Tinsel. An image of her, doubled over the wall with a tree branch gripped in her fingers, filled my mind. She'd written her pony's name in the fresh concrete. I pictured the empty bags lying on the barn floor, and as I considered the timing, a dread as cold and gripping as the wind channeling down the mountains froze in my lungs and pushed against my chest.

I prayed to God I was wrong.

The barn seemed darker than before, more threatening, when I went back inside. The latch rattled into place, and I headed to the exit with a fresh burst of adrenaline squeezing my heart. There had to be a simple, harmless explanation. Maybe they'd decided to raise the floor of the cistern in case Jenny fell in. At a depth of less than three feet, she could easily climb out. But, damn it. Sixteen bags? How much difference would they have made compared to the original height? Not much, I suspected, but sixteen bags would have been enough to cover something. Like a body.

I clamped my fingers over the Mag's lens as I stepped into the forebay.

A shaft of light streaked in front of my face. "What are you doing?"

I spun to my right, brought up my hands, and centered my light on Victor's face. "Jesus. You scared the shit out of me."

Victor grinned as I lowered the Mag. "So I see."

I sucked in a lungful of air. "I thought I saw movement back here. A light where there normally isn't one, but it looks like I was wrong."

He crossed his arms over his chest, and the beam from his flashlight shot into the night sky. He wore thin plaid pajamas and a velvet robe with satin trim, and he'd stuck his bare feet into a pair of slippers. "Should we look around together?"

"No. I already did, and everything's quiet."

Victor nodded. He turned toward the house, then glanced over his shoulder, waiting for me to follow. "A trailer's coming up from Florida Saturday, so if you see activity around here, it's probably them."

"Okay."

He gestured to my truck. "Why'd you park down the drive?"

He'd said it casually, and I wondered if I'd just imagined the hint of suspicion that seemed to strain his vocal cords. "I didn't want to wake you," I said as we entered the parking area adjacent to the garage.

He paused at the sidewalk that led to the back door. "Have any foals tonight?"

"Maddie did."

"Which mare?"

"A gray in barn two, next to Sumthingelse. I don't remember her name."

He nodded, said goodnight, then crossed over to the back porch. As the screen door creaked shut, I figured my reasoning had gone off course somewhere, and the combination of a dark night and unsettled dreams and an overactive imagination had undermined my ability to think.

◇◇◇

Jenny and Dr. Nash arrived at the clinic promptly at six-thirty Thursday morning. I'd been watching for them, but when they both went directly into the office, I settled back into my chair and opened a can of Coke. I ate a slice of cold pizza and felt tired to the bone. The morning had lightened to a dreary gray, and as I sat there, wondering how the day would play out, it began to rain. A few scattered drops spit against the glass. At noon, I would head over to the police department, and not knowing what to expect had me edgy.

I wheeled the chair I was sitting in across the floor until I could see the office door; then I opened a pack of butterscotch Tastykakes. I'd finished one when Jenny be-bopped out of the office and headed for the clinic. She peered through the Plexiglas and signaled that I should join her.

I stepped into the aisle.

Jenny flapped her hand toward the door. "Mom says I can't go inside when the crew starts coming in, and since one of them is sitting outside, I thought I'd better stay out here," she said as she eyed the last Tastykake.

I looked down the aisle and saw Paul's car parked out front. He sat behind the wheel like a lump of stone with his head turned so he could stare into the barn.

Jenny started toward the stallions' stalls. "You have a foal last night?"

"No," I said as I walked alongside her, "but Maddie did."

Jenny squinched her nose at the mention of Maddie's name. "Are you done with them?"

"Yeah. The colt's nursed, and they're both doing well."

She paused in front of Order of Command's stall. "Darn."

I frowned. "What's wrong?"

"Mom said I can't keep dragging you all over the place to see the foals every morning, unless you still had work to do."

I smiled.

She pointed at the butterscotch Krimpet. "Can I have one?"

"Sure, if you think it'll be okay with your mom."

"She won't care." Jenny licked her lips then carefully peeled the cellophane off the cake's icing. "These are my favorite."

"Mine, too."

The stud's ears flicked at the sound of the crinkling plastic. He neighed and stepped forward, canted his head for a better look between the bars.

Jenny's eyes sparkled as she bit into the Krimpet with the concentration of a connoisseur. She chewed and swallowed and examined the cake before she took another bite.

"Jenny, when did you write Tinsel's name in the concrete in the cistern?"

"Cistern?" she mumbled around a mouthful of cake.

"The well behind the bank barn."

"Oh." She curled her finger around a film of icing, scooped it out of the corner of the wrapper, and popped it in her mouth. "Right after they moved my ponies."

I looked up when someone entered the barn. Victor Nash watched us as he strolled toward the clinic door.

"Remember, Steve?" she said as I glanced at her father. "I thought Dad was going to build me a wash rack but he filled in the well, instead."

Victor paused at the clinic door, fifteen feet farther down the aisle. Her back was to him, and I hoped like hell he hadn't heard what she'd said. He frowned at his daughter. "Jenny, what are you doing?"

She spun around and held up the wrapper. "Steve let me have a Tastykake."

He looked past his daughter, and his gaze locked on my face. "Go into the office, Jenny." His gaze lowered to his daughter when she didn't move. "Go ahead."

"Awh, Dad." The books and pencil case jiggled in her backpack as she strode down the aisle.

I opened my mouth to apologize, but Victor was already slipping into the clinic.

As the door clicked shut, Paul Genoa strolled into the barn with his fists jammed in his pockets. He took his time, scuffing his feet on the asphalt. His shoulders were hunched forward under his parka, and he never once looked in my direction. He followed Victor into the clinic.

I sat on a hay bale and drank my Coke and didn't go inside because I didn't trust myself in the same room with the asshole.

By six-fifty, most of the personnel had straggled in from the parking lot. Frank Wissel stepped out of his cramped room and yawned before taking his time feeding the studs. When he headed for the clinic, I stood and followed him. The door swung open as we reached it, and Victor indicated that I should follow him as he stepped into the aisle. He walked toward the parking lot and paused alongside the open area where they bred the horses.

"Look, Steve, it's not that I don't trust you, but Deirdre would flip if she knew Jenny had accepted food from one of the crew."

"I'm sorry about that, sir."

Victor grinned. "She has a way of getting what she wants. Takes after her mother." He shook his head. "Women. They have a talent for convincing us that we're the ones in charge, and all the while, they're pulling invisible strings that we're oblivious to."

I smiled.

"Ah, but you're too young." His eyes sparkled. "You get to be my age, especially if you have a daughter, you'll see what I mean." Victor glanced over my shoulder when the clinic door opened, and the crew spilled out into the aisle. "Next time, just tell her no."

"Yes, sir."

He nodded, then wound his way through the stream of employees as he approached the office.

Frank Wissel paused alongside me. "Cline, you're with Paul, Ronnie, and Ben. The four of you will be working with Dr. Nash."

I nodded and caught Genoa's smirk as he hovered behind Wissel.

Frank's gaze flicked over Ronnie's dreadlocks as he handed him a list. "Dr. Nash is getting an early start this morning, so get going."

As Frank headed for the office, I pulled the farm truck's keys out of my pocket and handed them to Ronnie. "You can drive. I have to leave on time today, so I'm taking my truck."

Paul stirred behind Ronnie. "Got a date, Cline?"

"No. But you might."

"Huh?" He narrowed his eyes. "What the hell's that supposed to mean?"

I didn't want to get into it with him, not then. But I'd been thinking about Maddie's swollen, bloody eye all morning long, and the temptation was just too much. "You might want to check with your health care provider, schedule an appointment for yourself, because I have a feeling you're gonna need it."

Both Ronnie and Ben followed the exchange with their heads swiveling back and forth like they were watching a tennis match. Ronnie's mouth hung open, and his eyes widened when Paul stepped toward me. He moved like a bull with his head jutted forward on his thick neck and his beefy shoulders hunched aggressively under the parka. His arms swayed away from his body as he clenched his hands into fists.

He got in my face. "Is that a threat, Cline?"

"Sounds like one to me."

The office door creaked open as Paul raised his hands. Dr. Nash's voice drifted into the aisle. "No, Jenny. You stay with Daddy."

I shifted my gaze past Genoa. Jenny must have been standing behind Elaine's desk as her mother blew her a kiss.

Genoa whispered "prick" half under his breath and moved away as Dr. Nash stepped into the aisle and frowned. "Something wrong, gentlemen?"

No one answered. Ronnie scuffed his feet as Ben studied his shoes. Dr. Nash scrunched her eyebrows together and pursed her lips as her gaze lighted on my face. "Steve, come with me."

"Yes, ma'am." I started after her and caught sight of Paul in my peripheral vision, mimicking me as he mouthed *yes, ma'am.*

While Ronnie and Ben prepared to cover the ultrasound machine with plastic, I followed Dr. Nash into the clinic and helped load the cart with speculums and gauze rolls and boxes of gloves and liters of sterile saline solution.

"So," Dr. Nash said. "What's going on?"

I hesitated. I supposed she'd find out about Paul soon enough, but before she did, I wanted the opportunity to get back at him. "A misunderstanding," I said and left it at that.

She looked past me and stretched her arm toward the counter on my right. "Hand me that box, will you, Steve?"

I pivoted and spied a clear plastic box lined with compartments containing needles and syringes and drug vials. I held the box out to her as the heater above our heads vibrated to life.

A few strands of her fine brown hair swept across her forehead. She brushed them from her eyes with long slender fingers. Her pale skin was flawless. She wore no makeup or jewelry, except for a pair of thin gold hoop earrings; yet, even dressed in navy coveralls and leather boots, she looked elegant and incredibly sexy. And each day, when I punched out at noon, she somehow managed to emerge from a morning of palpations and minor surgeries and ultrasound scans looking as neat as when she'd set out.

Dr. Nash squatted and arranged balloon catheters and several packets of surgical tools that had been run through the autoclave on the lower shelf. When someone tapped lightly on the door, she smiled softly. "That would be Jenny."

Jenny hung onto the doorknob as the door swung inward. Her fingernails were done in a pink polish that matched the ribbon woven down the seam of her jeans. She wore a yellow rain slicker and pink and purple tennis shoes. "Mom?"

"Uh-huh?"

Amusement lit up Victor's eyes as he stepped silently behind his daughter.

"Can I go with you this morning? Please? If you start in two, I'll be able to see the newborn."

Dr. Nash didn't rise to her feet but twisted at the waist and watched her daughter step closer. She rested one knee on the floor, and as Jenny stood in front of her, their heights matched. With their fine silky hair, straight eyebrows, and light complexions, mother and daughter looked very much alike.

She smoothed Jenny's bangs off her forehead. "I'm scheduled to start in one today. You know that."

"Can't Steve take me?" Jenny said.

Dr. Nash glanced at me, then looked at her watch. "No. I need him with me. Besides, you only have twenty minutes."

"So?" Her voice was a soft whine.

Dr. Nash smiled. "If you want, you can come with us, but you'll have to wait until after school to see the foal."

"See what I mean?" Victor said to me from the doorway. "They're born knowing how to get what they want."

"Can't I just stay home today?" Jenny ignored her dad, but Deirdre raised her eyebrows and looked at both of us before she rose to her feet.

She moved like a dancer, fluid and lithe, and I wondered what she was like in bed. One thought led to another, and I pictured her in bed with me. She sighed, and I took it that she'd heard Jenny's request more times than she cared to admit. She turned her gaze my way, and I was thankful she couldn't read my mind.

"Take the cart out, and we'll meet you in one."

"Yes, ma'am."

Ronnie and Ben were set up, and I'd just offloaded the cart and wheeled it into position alongside the stocks when they arrived. On the drive over, sleet had begun to mix with the rain, and it clattered on the metal roof above our heads as Jenny drifted down the aisle. She paused at each stall door and rose on tiptoe so she could peer through the grill.

Paul led the first mare into the stocks. I latched the gate, but when I reached over to lift the mare's tail out of the way, Dr. Nash touched my arm, and the sensation sizzled in my blood.

"Wrap the tail head, Steve. She's getting a uterine lavage, and I don't want any stray hairs getting in the way."

"A what?"

"A lavage. I have to flush her uterus with sterile saline solution."

I ripped open a packet of gauze and wrapped the mare's tail while Dr. Nash gloved up and prepared the tubing she'd be using. Jenny wandered back down the barn and stood next to me, and after Paul applied a twitch to the mare's nose, Dr. Nash inserted the tube and flushed the mare's uterus with copious amounts of fluid. She went through two liters and was twisting the cap off the third when she glanced at her watch.

"Oh, Jenny. You're going to miss your bus. Ronnie, switch places with Steve." She looked at me. "Would you mind driving her back to the clinic?"

"No, ma'am."

Ronnie slipped behind me and grabbed the mare's tail, but as Jenny and I reached the doorway, the school bus sped past the clinic driveway with the strobe light on its roof slicing through the icy rain. It slowed as it entered the curve in front of the

Nashes' house, then picked up speed and headed west on Bear Wallow.

"Oh, oh," Jenny whispered.

We turned around as Dr. Nash looked over her shoulder. "Don't tell me?"

"Sorry, Mom."

"Uh." She spun around and bent to her work. The liquid that squirted down the mare's legs had changed from amber to clear.

Jenny glanced at me before approaching her mother.

"Can I stay home now?"

I grinned, and Dr. Nash shot me an annoyed glance. "No. I'll take you as soon as I finish this mare. The four of you," she said to Paul and me, "grab some tools and go help the crew in two muck out until I get back." She tore off her gloves, and when she heard Ben leading a mare down the aisle, she yelled to him to put her back.

Jenny tugged at her mother's overalls. "But, Mom. I'll be early."

Dr. Nash glanced at her watch. "Not by much, and you can use the extra time going over your spelling." She ticked off a notation on her list and smiled softly when Jenny sighed in disgust.

I unwound the gauze as they headed for the exit. Beyond the doorway, the little Spyder glistened under a layer of rainwater that had beaded on the sleek finish.

As I walked toward the storage area at the back of the barn, Paul and the mare cut into the aisle behind me. Her unshod hooves sounded hollow on the asphalt, and the sound had been something I'd had to adapt to. In the past, the horses I'd worked with had been shod, and although I hadn't been consciously aware of it, I'd grown into the habit of evaluating whether their shoes were snug or loose or under-run based solely on the sound they made striking the asphalt.

I'd almost reached the end of the aisle when the mare's pace quickened. A sharp crack sounded, followed by a yell. The mare's hooves scrabbled across the ground.

Before I could turn, she careened into my back.

The collision lifted me off my feet. I slammed against a post. The hard edge caught my shoulder, and the impact rattled my teeth.

I bounced off the wood and bounced again when I hit the asphalt.

Paul was still yelling, and as I lifted my chin off the ground, the mare's tail swooshed in front of my face. She skittered around, and her hind hoof came down on my back, then slipped down my ribcage and wedged between my side and arm before she snatched it up. She lunged forward and caught the back of my thigh with a shuddering blow.

Her hooves clattered across the ground as Paul yelled at her to quit. She strained at the end of her lead, and when I saw she was coming around again, I covered my head with my arms.

She knew exactly where I was this time and scrambled in an effort to avoid me. Her hooves scraped past, then clattered to the ground, and I realized she'd jumped right over me.

I lunged forward, or tried to. My left arm had gone numb, and it wasn't until that moment that I heard Ronnie and Ben screaming at Genoa to stop.

Chapter 19

"Are you crazy?" Ronnie screamed.

I blocked out the sound of his voice and listened for the clatter of hooves on asphalt.

The mare was still, but I heard her drawing in shallow, rapid breaths. Or was that my own breathing?

I lifted my head.

She'd splayed her hind legs and had plastered herself against the far wall. Her head was raised against the tug of the lead, and white shone round her eyes. The flesh along her flank quivered beneath taut skin.

Paul dragged the mare around and led her into an empty stall.

Ronnie and Ben inched closer, and by the time Paul had exited the stall, I'd managed to make it to my knees. I cradled my left arm against my side as he strolled toward me. My ribs hurt like hell, and the inside of my arm burned.

I'd landed close to the end of the aisle, at the entrance to the storage area, where the asphalt gave way to dirt. I kept my gaze focused on the ground in front of me and tried to control my breathing. Paul's legs shifted into view.

"Sorry about that, Cline," he said. "I don't know what spooked her, but that's the thing with horses, isn't it?"

I clenched my left hand, then tried to flex the muscles in my arm.

Paul hooked his thumbs in his belt loops. "You can never predict what they'll do next. But speaking of predictions. Looks like you'll be the one needing that doctor's appointment."

He chuckled softly, then turned toward the storage area. As he took a step, I lunged forward and latched my right arm around his trailing leg. He went down and grunted as he hit the ground.

Dirt billowed off the floor around him.

When I tried to lift my left arm, the muscles seized, and a stab of pain radiated from my shoulder. I yanked my right arm free and gripped his waistband, then scrambled onto his back. He yelled when I latched my fingers in his hair and jerked his head.

I slammed his face against the ground and managed to drag my left arm into a position where it could be of use, but when I put weight on the elbow, my shoulder gave out.

Genoa heaved upward, and I lost my grip. I rolled off and landed on my back.

He rose to his knees. Powdery dirt coated his skin, transforming his face into a surreal mask as he raised his fist.

I slammed my legs into him, and as he toppled over, I flipped onto my stomach and planted my hands in the dirt. Before I could get to my feet, he crashed into my back. His wiry fingers latched onto my hair, and he shoved my face against the ground. A bony knee dug into the small of my back as he shifted his weight and drove my nose deeper into the loose soil.

Dirt clogged my nose and mouth, and I couldn't breathe. When I coughed, my next inhalation dragged another lungful of dirt into my throat, and Sergeant Bodell's opinion of drowning ran uninvited through my mind.

Lack of oxygen is a powerful motivator. I pushed with my right arm, but Genoa must have picked up on the fact that my left side was more or less out of action. He'd anticipated my move by bracing his leg.

Genoa suddenly rose off my back. He clawed at my shirt, then clamped his forearm around my neck.

As he moved back, I was lifted off the ground. I became aware of raised voices, then—Ben and Ronnie's—and realized that they'd been yelling all along. The two of them yanked Paul backwards.

His arm tightened around my throat.

I dragged my heel down his shin and stomped the top of his foot.

He cried out, and as he released his hold, I spun around, dropped my shoulder, and slammed my fist into his gut.

His breath wheezed past my ear.

"Jesus Christ!" Frank Wissel practically hopped into view alongside Ronnie and Ben. "Stop it! Let him go!"

Ronnie and Ben looked at each other over Paul's head. He'd doubled over and was sucking in a lungful of air. I pictured the scene Frank must have walked in on, both of them restraining Genoa while I laid into him.

As soon as they released their hold, Paul braced his hands on his thighs.

Frank moved next to me, and his voice shook when he spoke. "Cline, you're fired!"

I spun around, and as I opened my mouth to speak, movement flashed in the corner of my eye. I jerked my head back as Paul sucker-punched me. His knuckles grazed my cheek and specks of white light darted behind my eye.

"Cut it out!" Frank yelled as I caught my balance.

Ronnie and Ben latched onto Paul again, and he kicked out.

"Genoa!" Frank screamed. "You're fired, too! You make another move, I'll call the cops and have you arrested."

That caught him up, but I was still thankful that Ronnie and Ben were reluctant to turn him loose.

"Paul tried to make Lotsamagic run over Steve," Ben said.

Genoa yanked his arm free and glared at Ben. "What the fuck?"

Ronnie cautiously released his hold on Genoa and turned to Frank. "It's true. She trampled him, and Paul made her do it."

"I did not!" Paul screamed. "She just freaked."

Ronnie backed up a step and flailed his arms. "She freaked 'cause you made her." Ronnie waved his arm at Genoa as he turned back to Frank. "He spooked her on purpose so she'd knock into Steve, then he kept running her round in a circle so she'd step on him."

"I didn't!" Paul screamed. "She spooked."

Ronnie glared at Genoa. "Bullshit."

"Both of you weren't even looking when she started."

"Yeah," Ben said, "but you were chasing her."

"Was not! I was trying to get her under control."

They went back and forth for a minute or two while I cradled my left arm. My breathing had dropped down to something bordering normal, but a shitload of adrenaline still buzzed through my muscles. Despite its numbing effect, a deep ache had begun to build in my shoulder, and my skin felt damp where the mare's hoof had sliced over my ribs and the inside of my arm.

"It just looked like I was chasing her," Paul yelled.

Frank Wissel turned to me. "And what do you have to say for yourself, Cline?"

I straightened, looked Frank in the eye, and stated matter-of-factly, "Genoa attacked me because I threatened him in the clinic this morning."

Frank's eyebrows crept up his forehead, and the folds of puffy skin that normally hung below them, like a second pair of lids, flattened out. "You threatened him?"

"Yes, sir," I said.

Wissel waited for me to continue. But timing is everything, so I remained silent until he asked me why.

"I was angry, sir," I said flatly. I turned to face Paul. "I was angry because you beat Maddie."

"Did not!" Genoa searched our faces and saw that no one believed him. "I didn't," he repeated but the conviction had drained from his voice.

"She had a black eye this morning," I said, "because of you."

"Genoa, clear out," Frank said. "If I catch you on the property, I'll have you arrested for trespassing."

Genoa's face had turned red under the layer of powdery dirt. He waved his arm in my direction. "What about him?"

"Clear out, Paul. I'm not kidding."

Genoa started to back up, and as he shifted his gaze in my direction, his scowl dissolved into a smirk. "Watch your back, Cline," he said; then he turned and strode into the aisle. His gait looked choppy, a jumble of nerves and anger.

When he was out of hearing range, Ronnie said, "You oughta go to the police, Steve."

I shook my head as Frank said, "From what I saw, both of you have a case for assault."

"But he started it," Ben said.

I crossed over to the haymow, lifted a towel out of the foal kit, and wiped the dirt off my face. "Doesn't matter. I went after him when he was walking away, and what he did with the horse is way too open to interpretation for my liking. Plus, I did threaten him."

Frank shook his head. "How bad are you hurt?"

I shrugged.

"The mare was all over him," Ben was saying, but my attention was elsewhere, focused on the powder coating the towel in my hand.

The guy who'd dropped Bruce's car in the lot the weekend he disappeared, his coat front and sleeves had been covered with dirt. Fluffy's owner had thought the guy worked construction, but you didn't wear a coat when you hung drywall. But you sure as hell would wear one if you were outside in the middle of winter, restraining someone in the back of a dusty barn. Or mixing concrete.

Frank narrowed his eyes at me.

"What's going on?" a female voice demanded.

Ben and Ronnie flicked me alarmed glances as Dr. Nash stepped into the storage area.

"Where's Paul going?"

Frank cleared his throat, and if I wasn't mistaken, even our stud manager was a bit rattled at the prospect of relaying what had just transpired.

Feeling a bit conspicuous, I quit supporting my arm and hooked my left thumb on my jeans pocket, instead.

To give him his due, Frank explained the sequence of events clearly and fairly, and I was once again impressed with his intelligence. Outwardly, the guy looked haggard and shriveled, like a raisin that had been left baking in the sun, but he was sharp-witted and observant, and I couldn't help but like him.

For some reason, I was more nervous standing under Dr. Nash's scrutiny than I'd been facing down Genoa's rage. I consciously kept my shoulders back, head up, and focused on keeping my expression calm and confident, but when I glanced past her and noticed Ben and Ronnie drifting backwards toward the barn aisle, a smile twitched my lips.

Dr. Nash snapped at them, and they froze. "If I have any questions, I want you right here, understand?"

They nodded, and I thought Ben's head was going to shear off his neck.

Dr. Nash's gray eyes blazed with anger when Frank told her about Maddie. She peered at me. "You saw her this morning, with a black eye?"

"Yes, ma'am."

"And she told you Paul did it?"

I hesitated, then sighed. "She said he didn't mean to."

That got Dr. Nash going. She threw up her arms and paced around me. "Why? Why do women put up with that kind of crap? 'He didn't mean to'! I can't believe it."

I thought about the load of shit Maddie put him through and wondered if she felt she'd deserved it.

Dr. Nash paused in front of me. "And what about you?" she demanded.

"I'd never hit—"

She waved her hand and cut me off. "Your injuries. How bad are they?"

"Oh." I exhaled. "I'm fine."

Ben started telling her how the mare had trampled me, and I shot him a look that shut him up.

"Okay, Steve. Frank can take you to the hospital so you can get checked out."

"But I'm—"

"Fine?" Dr. Nash raised her elegant eyebrows. "I don't think so."

"Really. I am."

"Prove it, then."

I opened my mouth.

She raised her hands and wiggled her fingers, impatiently indicating that I should get on with it. "Come on. Take off your jacket."

"I'm fine."

"Let's see. I have workman's comp and liabilities to consider."

I almost smiled. And here I'd thought she cared about me.

I managed to raise both hands and undid the buttons. Let the denim jacket slip down my arms. Dr. Nash caught it and handed it back to Ben. All three of the guys stood in a semicircle, waiting to see the damage. That was bad enough, but under Dr. Nash's cool eyes, heat crept up my neck and flushed my face. I undid the flannel shirt and shifted it off my shoulders.

"I need your T-shirt off to examine your shoulder properly."

I crossed my arms and hooked my fingers under the hem, but as I raised my arms, pain stabbed my shoulder like someone had driven a knife into the joint and twisted the hilt. I froze. So, maybe I wasn't okay.

Dr. Nash stepped closer. She reached behind me, and I felt her cool fingers on my skin. I looked down into her face as she lifted the shirt up my back. Some of her professionalism seemed to have drained from her features. Her movements grew awkward as the mechanics of removing my shirt drew her closer.

The fabric had stuck to my ribs and the inside of my arm, and when it peeled off the scrapes left behind from the mare's hoof, the cold air burned like acid. I flinched and pulled away from her as the T-shirt slipped over my head.

I sucked in a lungful of air and jerked my eyes open. Dr. Nash had become very still.

She slowly lifted her gaze to mine, and an emotion I couldn't identify clouded her gray eyes. "I can't believe you're standing there like nothing's wrong. You need to have that treated. An abrasion this severe is exactly like a burn. It needs to be dressed, and you'll need to be put on antibiotics, and if your tetanus isn't up to date, tell them."

Her gaze flicked over my chest before settling on my shoulder. She stepped to my side and lightly touched my upper arm, then smoothed her fingertips along my clavicle. She palpated the joint and muscles with an efficient but gentle touch. "You have a nasty hematoma and probably some crushing of the deltoid muscle and possibly axillary nerve damage. You need to be evaluated. Frank, drive him over to the hospital."

"I'll drive myself," I said. "I need to be somewhere at noon."

She frowned at me and pursed her lips. "Well, we certainly can't abduct you, now, can we?"

I grinned.

"Our insurance company will need you to address this right now and get the paperwork started." She turned to Frank. "Follow him," she looked back at me, "and make sure he doesn't get lost."

I slipped the flannel shirt and jacket back on and carried my T-shirt as I headed for the Chevy. I paused outside Lotsamagic's stall.

Frank stopped alongside me. "What're you doing?"

I nodded my head toward the big bay mare. "I want to check something."

She stared warily through the grillwork as I slid the door open. I stepped toward her. "That's okay, girl. Nobody wants to hurt you."

She was standing on the far side of her stall, and as I approached, she raised her head.

I murmured softly as I reached out and touched her shoulder. Her muscles flinched under my palm, but as I stroked her coat, she relaxed slightly, and after a moment, she curled her neck around and looked at me.

"Yeah, that's right. You're okay." I scratched her withers as I moved toward her barrel. "Hey, Frank," I said over my shoulder. "You got any idea why you'd have to smack a horse when you're trying to calm her down?"

"Don't reckon I do."

"Well, she's got a welt on her stifle. Looks like Paul smacked her a good one with the leather shank he was using."

Frank moved quietly to my side. "Well, I'll be damned."

The hospital was right off East Shirley Avenue, a short jog from the apartment. I parked and switched off the wipers and sat there, listening to the sleet clatter on the Chevy's roof. Just what I needed. Another hospital visit and a new set of bills. Despite Dr. Nash's assumption that workman's comp would cover the expense, I suspected they'd contest it. They had at Foxdale. The only thing that had saved me there was the owner's generosity because he'd picked up my bills when they'd come to his attention.

I was thinking that there had to be something seriously wrong with me when Frank stepped up to the driver's side window and peered through the glass. I rousted myself, grabbed a ball cap off the dash, and climbed out.

I lowered the brim on my forehead. At least Frank had had the good sense to wear a rain poncho. "This is stupid," I said, "going to an emergency room for this."

"You got a doctor? We can go there."

"No, I don't." I stomped toward the double doors as an ambulance glided silently under the portico with lights flashing. Frank dutifully followed me into the lobby and hung around after I checked in with the intake nurse.

"You don't have to wait," I said after I'd completed the requisite paperwork.

"Ah, but I do. You skip out, and Dr. Nash'll have my hide."

I smiled as I carefully lowered my butt into an upholstered chair. The ache that radiated outward from my shoulder had somehow managed to converge with the throbbing sting on the other side of my body and the ache in my thigh until I had to concentrate to find a square inch that didn't ache or burn or throb. "How long have you worked for her?"

Frank perched on an armrest. "For Deirdre, about sixteen years, now. Soon as she graduated vet school, she and Victor started the farm. The ten years before that, I worked for her parents."

"Wow. I thought tuition bills did everyone in for at least a couple years," I said, hoping to keep him talking.

"Usually, but not Deirdre. Her parents owned the house and more than five hundred acres and did anything they could to help her succeed."

"I guess they were glad when she married someone who was in the business."

Frank snorted. "Not hardly. I got the impression Victor wasn't exactly who they'd envisioned for a son-in-law. As for him being in the business, if you'd told him a horse had thrush around its frog, he would've either been looking for a brown songbird or something green and slimy that goes *ribbit*."

I chuckled. "Well, it looks like he learned quick."

"Yeah, he's a fast learner, all right." Frank clamped his mouth shut like it occurred to him that he'd been talking too much, and when a nurse called my name, he shifted off the armrest. "Call me if you decide not to come in at three."

"Yes, sir."

"Of course you won't be doing stalls, and I'll have the day crew feed when they come in."

I nodded, then watched him stroll toward the exit. If only I could think of a way to get him talking. With his history, I was certain he knew a great deal. But he was obviously loyal to Deirdre and would only share information if convinced he was helping her. And if she'd been using artificial insemination to breed Irish Dancer, he knew about it because she could trust him to keep quiet.

The examining doctor's diagnosis proved that my boss knew her stuff, despite the fact that she specialized in another species. A nurse cleaned the abrasions, an experience I'd just as soon never repeat; then she applied thick dressings over the wounds. She finished by taping the bandages in place with athletic tape wound snugly around my chest and upper arm. I was contemplating their removal when she told me that the get-up needed to be left in place for five days.

"Five days?" I said, incredulous.

She nodded and smiled just a shade too happily. She was a big woman, taller than me with broad shoulders and a thick neck.

"What about showers?"

"No showers. Sponge baths."

I made a face and thought I heard her chuckle as she bustled out of the room.

No showers presented a problem, and foaling out would be a pain in the ass. My clothes often got soaked with blood and who knew what, all of it raunchy and foul smelling. I left the building with my arm in a sling and two prescriptions in my pocket. The sleet had switched back to a cold, miserable rain. Traffic in Warrenton was light, all things considered. Ugly dark clouds hung low in the sky as rainwater channeled down the gutters and glistened on sidewalks, and the sound of the wipers grated on my nerves.

I felt strung up and exhausted all at once and didn't know if the tension that gripped my spine and knotted the muscles in my neck was an aftereffect of the attack or nervousness about the afternoon's agenda or a combination of both. I didn't like the notion that my fate and safety would be left in someone else's hands. But they knew what they were doing. They were professionals, and based on my track record, I'd probably be a lot safer under their control.

After I got the scripts filled, I went back to the apartment and changed clothes. I had time to eat, but my appetite had gone south with the weather. At twelve-fifty, I ditched the sling and headed out the door. On the drive to the police department, I considered ending my search for Bruce. I could go home and lounge around for the five days it would take until I got the damn bandages off. Then I thought of Corey and the fear that haunted her nights and shadowed her waking hours and knew I wouldn't quit until I found him.

The woman at Warrenton PD's front desk unlocked a side door and directed me down a narrow corridor to the last room on the right. As I reached it, the door swung inward on its hinges, and a cop stepped out of the room. He stared openly at me before he turned and headed in the opposite direction. Not hostile but not friendly, either. Cops are rather interesting in that they view civilians as outsiders, and for good reason, considering they're lied to most days of the week. A healthy dose of skepticism colors their worldview, and generally speaking, they trust no one.

Detective Tyler McPherson, a.k.a. Derek to the druggies, Detective Brandon, and another man I didn't know had gathered in a conference room. The walls were painted institutional gray to waist height, white above, and the carpet underfoot was an equally dismal blue/gray blend. An audiovisual stand occupied the center of the room and rows of cheap plastic chairs with fold-down desktops stretched to the back wall. Someone had sketched a crude diagram on the blackboard that covered the wall at the head of the room.

Brandon gestured to a black man with a wiry build. "My partner, Dan Sweeney."

I nodded. "Detective."

Sweeney grinned. "Call me Dan. Everybody else does."

Detective Sweeney was exceptionally dark-skinned. His lean musculature, closely cropped hair, and coloring were dramatically opposite McPherson's bulk and unkempt hair.

McPherson waved me to a chair. He'd been cracking a wad of gum between his molars, but as I walked into the room, his gaze locked on the bruise on my face. He narrowed his eyes as I eased onto one of the hard plastic seats. "What happened to you?"

"I had an accident at work this morning."

"You going to be okay going through with this?"

"If all I've gotta do is sit in a car, I'll be fine. Anything other than that would be dicey."

McPherson popped his gum. "You'll be all right, then."

"Yeah," Brandon said. "We got it all worked out." He stood and crossed over to the blackboard.

I glanced at McPherson, who'd settled his bulk on the edge of a conference table shoved against the side wall, and seriously doubted his ability to fit in one of the desk-chairs. He bounced his right leg on the edge of the table, and his nervous energy reminded me of the buzz I'd sensed after Yates had driven off the day before.

Brandon picked up a pointer and indicated a long rectangle drawn across the lower portion of the backboard. "This is the back of the Giant. There's a door right here," he tapped the board, "with a compactor here." Brandon pointed to a squiggly box. "We've parked our step van directly east of the compactor, and there's a trailer perpendicular to the compactor here. McPherson will back his car between the two."

Detective Brandon paused and turned toward McPherson, who'd been cracking his gum and was presently in the middle of blowing a huge bubble. The bubble froze. When McPherson sucked it back into his mouth and grinned, Brandon turned back to the board. "One of our reserve officers will be behind the door so none of the employees walk outside at an inopportune moment. Backup will be in the van and between the compactor and trailer, so when the deal goes down, they'll grab the guys before they can get to their car."

"Pickup, you mean," McPherson said and popped a bubble. He slipped off the table and crossed to the front of the room. "Fauquier County SO will have unmarked cars embedded in the general parking lot out front, at both ends of the complex, and they'll ease toward the back corners after they get word that Yates and his man have arrived."

The sheriff's office? Just wonderful. If Deputy Bodell was among them, my cover at Stone Manor would be blown.

"The Toyota's going nowhere once it enters the back lot," Brandon added.

"What happens if they try to rip us off?"

McPherson and Brandon glanced at each other, then Sweeney spoke up. "We'll move in and deal with it. We're trained to handle these things."

Well, that made me feel a whole lot better.

Brandon asked me to sign a cooperating citizen's agreement that informed me of my limitations while working with the police. I couldn't discuss my activities concerning my involvement with anyone. I couldn't break any laws while working with the police. I paused over that one. I had to follow the law in gaining evidence. Farther down the page, there was a brief paragraph about my holding the department harmless. I didn't bother reading beyond that point but figured the words injury and death were somewhere in the fine print.

Before we headed out, we detoured to a locker room, and McPherson and Brandon fitted me with a Kevlar vest, and the funny thing was, that didn't make me feel any better, either. The four of us left the building by a back door. The rain had slackened to a fine mist that drifted on the breeze and clung to our clothes and hair. After McPherson keyed the Sebring's lock, I slipped onto the bucket seat, and the movement jarred my shoulder. Pain shot across my clavicle and snatched the breath from my lungs.

Brandon bent forward between the open door and the sedan's frame. "You okay?"

I nodded as McPherson removed a packet wrapped in duct tape from a brown paper bag, slipped it into the console, then tossed the empty bag to Brandon. When McPherson caught me watching, he said, "The coke."

"The real thing?"

"Yep. They'll want to test it before they hand over the cash."

Ten minutes later, McPherson backed the Sebring into position between the compactor and step van, and even though I knew the cops were there, I didn't see them. Not the unmarked cars out front or anyone loitering behind the building. The metal door at the back of the Giant looked solidly locked.

"You sure backup's here?" I said, and McPherson grinned.

"Yep." He popped a bubble as he jerked his head to the right. "Two guys are in the van. Two are holed up between the compactor and trailer to your left, behind that stack of pallets and the refrigerator carton."

"You're kidding."

"Nope."

"Uh-huh. And who said cop work was glamorous?"

"Somebody who's never done it." He cracked the gum between his teeth. "By the way, the only prints I got off the Firebird were yours and Claremont's."

I nodded.

"You up to driving?"

"Yeah, why?"

"Let's switch seats, then. I need to be able to move around, just in case."

I rolled my eyes, and McPherson grinned.

"Great," I said.

After we'd settled into our new positions, I clicked my door shut and frowned. Because of the injury to my shoulder, handling the door was a bit of a problem, and between the shoulder and ribs and the ache where the mare had stomped my thigh muscle, I'd stiffened up. And I felt claustrophobic. Trapped behind the wheel.

I wasn't going anywhere if something went wrong.

McPherson checked his watch. "One of our uniforms is positioned across the street. He's dealt with Yates before, so when he sees him pull into the lot, he'll signal backup."

"Hmm."

McPherson glanced at me. "You nervous?"

"A little."

"It'll go down smooth. Remember, we don't show them the dope until they flash the cash."

I nodded. "Does backup have any audio on us?"

McPherson nodded. "They've got visual on us, too, and they'll record everything that goes down. Don't worry. The guys in the van will be all over them when the time comes."

It began to rain, again. Big, fat drops that beaded up on the hood and splattered the windshield. The heavier ones rolled over and collided with smaller ones before joining together in channels that snaked across the glass like liquid tree branches. Even though the defrost was on, condensation inched up the inside of the glass, tinted green by a trick of light.

I tried to relax into my seat as the breeze kicked up. It buffeted the car and plastered sodden newspapers in the shrubs growing on the steep slope that rose from the edge of the lot. A paper cup from a fast food joint blasted past us, bouncing across the asphalt until it disappeared from sight. The rain suddenly increased to a downpour as cleanly as if someone had flipped a switch.

"Oh, this is just peachy." The words hadn't left McPherson's mouth before Yates' pickup glided around the corner.

Chapter 20

McPherson straightened in his seat as Yates' truck slid to a stop in front of us. He cracked open his door, hawked the wad of gum onto the pavement, then clicked the door shut. "Fuckers are early."

Yates had pulled across the Sebring's nose. I glanced at McPherson and wondered how I was going to drive off as soon as the deal went down. Yates and the Hispanic guy jumped out and raced across the narrow gap between the vehicles.

Cold, moisture-laden air and the sound of the rain pounding the asphalt funneled into the car when they yanked the back doors open. Yates slid onto the seat behind McPherson, and the sedan's frame rocked when the Hispanic guy thumped onto the seat behind mine and slammed the door. He'd had something tucked under his jacket, but I couldn't tell what.

Yates closed his door, and the sudden decrease in noise was unsettling. For a brief moment, no one spoke as the rain pummeled the roof over our heads. And in that moment, I realized I was out of breath. My heart pounded against my ribs, and my head buzzed.

As I recounted my instructions, I noted that McPherson had casually shifted in his seat so that he was facing the back. I glanced at Yates over my right shoulder. He'd leaned toward the gap between the bucket seats, and a water droplet slid off the tip of his nose and landed on the console. Miniature globes of rainwater clung to his buzz cut as another drop tracked down the side of his face.

Between their sodden clothes and our breathing, the windows were fogging up fast, and in another minute, backup wouldn't be able to see inside the car. I considered kicking up the blowers a notch as Yates clamped his right hand around McPherson's headrest.

"Let's see what you got," he said.

I glanced over my shoulder. "Let's see the cash first."

"What, you don't trust me?" When I said nothing, Yates smirked and straightened in his seat. "Show 'em the cash," he said to his partner.

I looked in the rearview mirror as the Hispanic guy shifted in his seat. His nylon jacket rustled, and in my peripheral vision, I saw Detective McPherson draw his gun.

"Police!" He lunged toward the gap between the bucket seats in the same instant that the Hispanic guy latched his fingers in my hair.

He yanked my head back as Yates' demand for the coke was cut short. McPherson slammed his left hand into Yates' chest and screamed at the Hispanic guy to drop his gun. The muzzle dug into my skull above my right ear. I felt around for the door handle as they screamed at each other, the Hispanic guy repeatedly yelling, "*¡Lo mataré! ¡Lo mataré!*" And if I remembered my Spanish correctly, I was in deep shit.

He increased his leverage to the point that breathing became difficult.

McPherson scrambled to his knees and jammed his right sneaker between the transmission hump and firewall, his voice growing hoarse with screaming.

I jerked my gaze back to the rearview mirror as my fingers slipped around the handle. McPherson's Glock was practically jammed in the guy's cheekbone, but as I watched, McPherson swung his gun toward Yates, instead.

I jerked on the handle and lunged to the left at the same time.

A spider web splintered across the windshield as my knees hit the asphalt. The side of my face bumped against the door-frame.

Glass shattered somewhere behind me as the Sebring's rear door swung open. My left foot had snagged between the seat's frame and running board, and the asshole still hadn't let go of my hair.

When a red-faced cop screamed instructions in Spanish, the Hispanic guy suddenly let go. I flopped to the ground.

As combat boots scrambled through a puddle in front of my face, I drew my arms toward my head. They dragged the Hispanic guy out of the car and slammed him to the ground, then cuffed him.

A cop helped me to my feet. When I turned and looked in the car, I wished I hadn't.

They wouldn't be cuffing David Alexander Yates.

He was just sitting there, legs spread, feet splayed in the narrow foot well, head lolled to the side with his chin resting on his right shoulder as if he were taking a nap or peering at the curtain of rain gusting through the open door. His left shoulder and arm twitched as the arc of blood that had been spraying from his throat dropped down in jolts like someone had just turned off the pressure in a hose. A glob of blood and tissue matter plastered the seat cushion behind his head, and the rest of the car's interior looked like several gallons of red paint had been flung into the vehicle as it spun on a turntable.

Apparently, a Glock 9mm is capable of significant damage at close range, and I'd just chalked up another horrific image that would no doubt haunt my dreams.

Yates' forearms dangled across his thighs, and as I backed up, I noticed a snub-nosed revolver still clutched in his left hand.

As I stared across the Sebring's roof, it dawned on me that the only sounds I heard were the raindrops pinging off the roof and splattering the film of water that clogged the lot and the distant flap of the Toyota's wipers. The shouting had stopped, and in fact, no one was speaking.

I focused on McPherson. He'd moved several paces away from the open passenger's door. As I watched, he bent forward and planted his palms on his knees. One of the other cops huddled over him and said something while he rested his hand on McPherson's back.

The sound of tires sluicing through water drew my attention to a sheriff's car and Warrenton PD car as they approached from the east. An unmarked car glided to a stop from the opposite direction, and Detectives Brandon and Sweeney climbed out and slammed their doors. Brandon took in the scene with an irritated glance before his gaze lingered on McPherson. He looked back at the Sebring and seemed to notice me for the first time. He snatched at his poncho's hood as he strode across the lot.

Detective Brandon paused alongside me and narrowed his eyes. "You hurt?"

When I shook my head, water flipped off the ends of my hair and the tip of my nose. The rain had plastered my bangs to my forehead, and rainwater streamed down the back of my neck and soaked into my sweatshirt. I realized I should have been freezing. Although I could feel the rain and the driving wind and hear the raindrops drumming on the Sebring's roof and the voices that had started up around me, I felt curiously disconnected, as if a current of energy buzzed around me and dampened my senses. Now that I was no longer in mortal danger, I felt rooted to the spot, unable to move or speak.

I slowly turned my head and realized that Brandon had been speaking.

"…get you out of the rain," he was saying. He signaled to one of the sheriff's deputies, then took hold of my arm.

I walked along with him, feeling as if I were dragging my feet through sludge.

Brandon asked the deputy for a blanket when we joined him at his car; then the two of them draped it over my shoulders and hustled me into the cruiser.

◇◇◇

I'd been staring through the windshield for half an hour when I began to shake. It started innocently enough, a slight tremor that vibrated at the base of my spine and spasms that clenched my jaw, but before long, the vibrations traveled up my back and intensified until my arms and legs shook uncontrollably. My teeth began to chatter until I was certain I could no longer open my mouth. I clamped my arms around my waist and told myself I had the shakes because my clothes were soaking wet and it was fucking cold.

And I almost believed it.

Tightening the blanket around my neck, I leaned forward, closed my eyes, and tried to slow my breathing. I'd seen another man, once, who'd bled to death from a neck wound. Physically, the only difference lay in the fact that he'd been knifed, not shot. But unlike Yates, he'd been an innocent bystander. Someone who'd gotten in the way of evil.

For whatever reason, I thought of my father. The man who'd raised me. Maybe because he'd died a grisly, horrible death in a car, alone and terrified. He'd drawn his last breath as a tractor-trailer crumpled his Mercedes into a heap of twisted scrap metal.

I drew in a ragged breath. He'd been dead eight months and two days, and there wasn't a day that went by that I didn't regret how I'd treated him. Our relationship had been strained to the point that he'd kicked me out of the house at the end of my sophomore year at college, and we'd rarely spoken afterwards. When he'd attempted to reconcile, I'd been too headstrong and stubborn…and hurt…to let him in. I swallowed. God, how I wished I'd handled things differently. Every time I thought of him dying, convinced that I hated him, a little part of me died, too.

God, I was such a fuck-up. Rachel was right. I was an immature, thrill-seeking adrenaline junkie who couldn't mind my own business. She'd sworn that I was obsessed with proving myself when I had nothing to prove. And maybe I was obsessed, just a little. But I couldn't stand by and do nothing when I saw a need to act.

No one else was ever going to look into Bruce's disappearance unless I uncovered evidence strong enough to justify an investigation. Even the drug bust didn't guarantee extensive police involvement. And now that A.J. and Yates were dead, who knew what information had died with them.

I turned sideways in the seat, tightened the blanket, and rested the side of my face against the headrest. The shakes had subsided to a few spasmodic trembles that shot up my spine without warning. The pain medication was holding its own, but exhaustion had seeped into my limbs and weighted my eyelids. I thought of the prospect of returning to work in approximately twelve hours and flipped open the farm's cell phone.

"I'm not coming in," I told Frank when he picked up.

"I didn't think so. What about Saturday? Think you'll be up to doing rounds?"

Saturday was my long day. Midnight to seven, then six p.m. 'til midnight. Maddie would shit if I didn't come in. "I'll be there."

Frank exhaled, and his breath buffeted the phone's mouthpiece. "Thanks."

"You're welcome."

Next, I called Corey and told her to avoid the apartment.

"But why?"

"We busted the guys who thought they were buying drugs from your brother. Just in case…" Well, I couldn't say *they*, anymore. Could I? "Uh, anyway, there's always the chance someone will want to retaliate, so we have to stay away from the apartment for the time being."

"You sound strange," she said, and fear tightened her vocal cords. "Are you hurt?"

I didn't feel like explaining what had happened, so I said, "I'm just tired. Didn't sleep well last night." At least that was true.

"What happened with the drug thing? Did you learn anything about Bruce?"

"Not yet. There's a lot of work to be done at this point. The cops haven't even interviewed the guy yet." Like they were going to. I thought about the form I'd signed at the police department and said, "I'll fill you in this weekend, after I've had a chance to find out what I'm allowed to talk about."

"Are you sure you're okay? There's this edge to your voice…"

"Yeah. I'm fine," I lied.

"Where are you going to stay if you can't use the apartment?"

"In a motel. Probably the one across from the Frost Diner. I'll call when I know where. Just don't go to the apartment."

"I won't." She paused. "Listen, Steve. No one's ever helped me like this before, and I just want you to know…it means a lot to me."

"I know."

I thought about calling Rachel but decided, if Corey could tell something was wrong, Rachel definitely would. I glanced at my watch and realized she was most likely wrapping up her workday. And since she hadn't gone to Foxdale Tuesday, she would no doubt ride today. I decided to hold off calling her.

◇◇◇

Since the drug sting had escalated to an officer-involved shooting, the state police took over the investigation. Eventually, they transferred me to a state cruiser and drove me to their facility on East Shirley Avenue where my ensuing interview and statement were videotaped. Afterwards, they gave me a ride back to my truck, and it was after nine before I cleared my gear out of Bruce's apartment and found a hotel room that wouldn't obliterate half a week's pay. I swallowed the maximum amount of painkiller allowed and spent all of Thursday night and most of the following day in bed.

When I eventually rolled onto my back and opened my eyes, it took me a second to remember where I was, and when I did, the memory of the drug bust and an image of David Yates jarred me fully awake.

I scrunched the wafer-thin pillow into some semblance of a shape, tucked it under my head, and stared at the ceiling. On the wall to my right, the smoke detector's red light winked into the darkened room. A brown stain had seeped into the plasterboard from a leak on the floor above, and a seam in the wallpaper had pulled away. The paper curled and caught the red light like a cupped hand.

The clock radio read five-thirty. I double-checked that the a.m. indicator was off; then I squinted at the heavy drapes that covered the window. A hairline thread of sunlight edged into the room where they met. Okay, it was definitely the afternoon—Friday—which gave me six and a half hours before I had to clock in at Stone Manor.

My stomach growled as I kicked off the bedspread and lowered my feet to the dingy carpet. I rubbed my face. Thanks to the combination of rest and pain medication, the burning sting over my ribs had cooled to a dull ache and throbbed only when I moved wrong. Twisting was definitely out of the question. The knot on the back of my thigh no longer cramped my muscle like a vice, and my headache had disappeared without my noticing. My shoulder was the most troublesome injury, and though I didn't care for the sling's restriction, I decided that it would be best if I wore it to work.

I shaved, then bent over the sink and carefully washed my hair. Afterwards, I ran the hot water until the mirror fogged over, soaped up a washcloth, and bathed without the luxury of a shower. The bandage couldn't come off soon enough. I managed to pull on a pair of jeans and clean socks one-handed, jammed my feet into my workboots but left the laces undone for the time being. I squatted and was rooting through my duffle bag when someone rapped on the door.

My hand flinched.

I straightened and stared at the door.

Another knock. Lighter this time.

I cut across the room diagonally, pressed the side of my face against the wall, and eased the edge of the curtain a fraction of an inch away from the window frame.

Rachel stood on the sidewalk, huddled in her coat. As I extended my hand toward the doorknob, I caught sight of the strapping around my chest. I snatched a T-shirt out of my bag and wriggled into it.

"Just a minute," I yelled as I latched onto a flannel shirt that had become entwined with the rest of the clothes jammed into the duffle. I slipped it on and felt my smile falter when I opened the door. "You okay?"

"No." Her voice was tight.

I moved aside and opened the door wider.

Rachel crossed the threshold and took in the dreary little room as she turned to face me. Her gaze lingered on the bruising on my face before she said, "Corey told me where you were, and she also told me you were involved in a drug sting yesterday."

"True." I took a step toward her and lightly gripped her arms, felt her muscles locked with tension. She'd squared her shoulders, and her neck was stretched taut, her head held high. I smoothed her bangs off her forehead and touched her cheek. "I've been trying to reach you. I should have called last night. I'm sorry."

She turned her back to me, glanced at the unmade bed and the only chair in the room with its grimy seat cushion and faded upholstery. She remained standing. "You've been saying that a lot, lately."

I moved closer but said nothing.

"I understand you were hanging around Foxdale Tuesday afternoon."

I cleared my throat. "I wanted to surprise you."

She nodded, and strands of her silky black hair caught in the tufts of fake fur that trimmed her hood. "I feel like I'm the only one in this relationship bending to the other, giving in to your wants and needs while ignoring my own. You know how I feel about these investigations you seem so compelled to involve yourself with. Potentially dangerous investigations. And even knowing how I feel, that I'll worry, you still go off and do what you want. Even when you know it hurts me. And I thought, how could you do that if you loved me?" She drew in a shaky breath. "How could you?"

She'd said it so softly, I almost didn't hear.

"Last Tuesday was so nice and normal. The way a relationship should be." Her voice wavered. She brushed her cheeks with her fingers. "But then, you're off again, on your crusade, just like I knew you'd be. And I'd reached a point where I needed to make a decision. To accept you as you are…or get out."

I swallowed and dragged in a ragged breath.

"I talked to Corey last night. I saw her come in when I was riding, but all through my ride and cooling out and putting my gear away, I didn't see her again. It was like she'd walked into the barn and stepped off the face of the earth. You know how she is. A quick groom, then she hits the trails or schools over fences. Well, I'd walked past her horse's stall a couple times and never saw her. I couldn't figure it out. So, before I left, I walked right up to the stall, thinking maybe she was doing up leg wraps or something like that." She paused for so long, I wondered if she was going to continue. "But you know what she was doing?"

I shook my head, but of course, she couldn't see since she'd yet to face me. "No," I whispered.

"Crying."

A television talk show switched on in the room next door.

"She was on the floor in her horse's stall, pulled into a tight little ball with her arms clamped around her legs, and she was crying."

Rachel cleared her throat. "We all go to the barn to get away from our troubles, to have fun. And there she was, in a place where she should have been happy, and she's sobbing so hard, she couldn't catch her breath. I didn't know what to do. I didn't want to embarrass her, but at the same time, doing nothing didn't feel right, either. I was trying to make up my mind when her horse shifted his weight and moved toward me, and she realized that I'd seen her."

Rachel turned to face me, and her dark eyes glistened with tears. "You see? That's the difference between you and me. I was tempted to sneak away and not get involved because doing so would have been…uncomfortable. As a matter of fact, I'd made up my mind. That's exactly what I was going to do before her horse drew attention to me. And that would have been the cowardly thing to do. The easy thing." She swallowed. "You never do that."

I placed my hands lightly on her shoulders.

"That's when she told me how you'd discovered that her brother was involved with drugs, and that you'd helped the police catch some guys who thought they were buying from him.

"Last night, I saw how important it is that she find out what's happened to him, because...until she does...her life will be a living hell."

She slipped her arms around my waist. "I still don't like it, but I think I understand why you do what you do, even if you don't."

I cleared my throat. "Meaning?" I nodded, swallowed. Cleared my throat again because I didn't trust my voice. "Oh, I get it. The 'proving myself to my father' thing that you're convinced is behind all this."

Her lips twitched. "Yeah, that 'thing.'"

I bent down and kissed her softly on the lips.

"But you have to promise me one thing," Rachel said, and her chin trembled.

"What's that?"

"That you'll do your best to stay safe."

"Always."

She laughed, a short nervous laugh that was more a release of tension than anything. "Well, that doesn't make me feel any better."

I kissed her again and barely noticed the abrasion on my side when she tightened her arms around my waist.

◇◇◇

When I stepped into the clinic, Maddie glanced over her shoulder, and the tentative smile that had risen to her lips vanished when she focused on the sling and the bruises on my face. She looked down at the can of Diet Pepsi balanced in her lap. The little black-and-white television that typically sat wedged in the corner next to the autoclave was pulled out and switched on.

Canned laughter from an old sit-com vibrated from the cheap speakers.

I punched my timecard, then crossed the room. "It's all quiet?"

Maddie nodded as she leaned forward and switched off the T.V. "Since yesterday, four of them have waxed up." She listed their names and barn assignments. "You know who they all are?"

"Yep."

She swiveled around and looked at me. "You have a good memory, Steve, and you catch on quick. Lots of people that I've trained couldn't tell one mare from the next."

I leaned against the counter. "When I worked at a show barn that housed, oh…about two hundred horses, this reporter once asked me how come we didn't get them mixed up. Of course, new employees messed up sometimes, but most of us could identify them fairly well. To her, they were just horses. But, I can't imagine not being able to tell them apart. They have different expressions and personalities and mannerisms, and their conformations are vastly different. I guess it all boils down to familiarity."

"And being observant," Maddie said as she unfolded her legs and stood. "What was the reporter writing about?"

I shrugged. "Some Lifestyle article on a summer kids' camp we did."

"Hmm." She stepped closer. "How'd you end up working here?"

"Fate, I suppose."

Maddie nodded and kept her gaze focused on my chest. "Look, Steve. I've been wanting to apologize for what Paul did."

I sighed. "It's not your place to apologize for him."

"I know, but now that he's gone, I feel so much better. I wanted to thank you for that."

Something about the tone of her voice, a casual callousness, caught my attention. "Maddie," I said slowly, "what did you tell him about us?"

She glanced up at me, then looked away. "What do you mean?"

"Come off it. You know perfectly well what I mean. You used me to set him up, didn't you?"

"I don't have any control over him," she said, and as I listened to her words, I realized she'd effectively manipulated both of us. Maddie flipped her hair off her shoulder. "And I certainly didn't make him attack you."

"But you led him to believe that there was more between us than there really was, didn't you?"

"No," she said, but a slight vibration in her vocal cords told me she was lying. "Besides, I know you're attracted to me."

"Maddie, look at me." I lifted her chin with my finger. "This is important. Did you do the same thing with the guy who worked my shift before I started here?"

"Huh?"

"Claremont. Did Paul believe you had a thing going with him, too?"

She jerked her head away from my hand and stepped backwards. "What the hell's wrong with you?"

"When you broke up with Paul on New Year's Eve, did he think you and Claremont were involved?"

"What's it to you?"

I grabbed her arms. "He's been missing since he left here, Maddie," I gritted my teeth, "and no one's seen or heard from him since."

She frowned. "He's missing? How do you know?"

"I'm a friend of his sister's, and she's worried about him."

"Paul wouldn't do that."

"Do what?"

"Well…you know? Kill someone because of me."

"Goddamnit. He didn't mind running me over with a horse. What makes you think he'd stop at that?" I gestured to her face. "Look what he did to you."

"He was just mad."

"You're a stupid girl, Maddie. He's not going to get out of your life just because he isn't working here anymore. If you really want him to leave you alone, you need to start acting like it, instead of stringing him along."

Maddie grabbed her coat off the back of a chair. "I'm going home."

"Were you having sex with Claremont?"

She paused on her way to the door and spun around. "You'd be hard pressed to find a woman Bruce *didn't* sleep with."

Maddie strode out of the room, and I guessed that was answer enough. The door rattled against the jamb when she pulled it closed. As I exited the building, she sped down the lot and gunned her little car onto Bear Wallow without slowing down. Her brake lights flashed once as she entered the curve in front of the stone mansion; then her taillights disappeared around the bend. I listened for the sound of an engine turning over or a vehicle accelerating from a standstill, but no traffic sounds disturbed the night. If Paul planned on intercepting her, as he had so many Saturday nights in the past, he hadn't hung around here to do it.

I frowned as I headed to my truck. She lived in Warrenton, which raised the question: why had she driven off in the opposite direction? I didn't know where Paul lived, but I wouldn't have been surprised to find that she'd headed to his place.

The girl didn't know what she wanted. And if she repeated what I'd just said, I'd find out soon enough.

I paused in the lot, beyond the reach of the dusk-to-dawn light. Thursday's driving rain had preceded a cold Canadian front, and its passing had scrubbed the grime from the air so that the stars glittered like Christmas lights above my head. I wondered if Bruce had ever looked at the stars on a night like this. I wondered if he was looking at them now.

None of the horses were doing anything more exciting than dozing. I couldn't muck stalls, so I returned to the clinic and filled two buckets with enemas and cotton rolls and Vetrap and a bottle of iodine, so I could replenish the foaling kits on my next round; then I sat in the chair Maddie had occupied earlier. There was something to be said for hard work and staying busy. I'd only been on for one hour and was already bored. I stared at the silent television screen and couldn't be bothered with switching it on.

Between Thursday night and Friday day, even with a follow-up interview at the police station, I'd slept more hours than I typically slept in three days. Yet I felt drained. As I propped my head in my hand, a light reflected on the window's smooth glass. Someone had switched on the lights in the bank barn's lower level.

Shit. Victor had told me a shipment was coming up from Florida, and I'd completely forgotten about it. If I had any hope of discovering what went on in the bank barn, I'd have to get over there, but that meant leaving the mares unattended. I decided to risk it. If my excursion took too long, I'd think of something.

I switched off the clinic light, drove to barn one, and switched on all the lights. If anyone wondered where I was, they'd think I was working or delivering a foal.

I left my Chevy parked by the barn door, so that the aisle light shone across the hood; then I cut across the field that stretched toward the clinic. When I reached the back fence line, I no longer had the luxury of slipping through a gate. I'd have to climb the fence, and doing it one-handed would not be easy. I grabbed the top board with my right hand, hitched myself over, and dropped clumsily to the ground. My left shoulder was holding up just fine, as long as I didn't use it, but the burn across my ribs began to ache. As I reached the outermost stallion paddock, the distant sound of a diesel engine broke the silence. I looked over my shoulder when headlights crested a small knoll. The engine's pitch changed as the driver slowed. He passed the clinic, then turned into the driveway that cut past the Nashes' house and ended at the bank barn.

I broke into a cautious jog through the coarse grass. An occasional depression or clod of earth tripped me up as I circled farther to the north so I could approach the barn from the back.

I'd brought my flashlight, but using it was out of the question. The twang of springs and clank of metal against metal sounded in the still air as the driver lowered the trailer's ramp into position. I slowed to a walk as I neared the barn. The pasture fence loomed in front of me, strips of charcoal gray backlit by the barn lights. I paused and caught my breath. Sweat dampened my skin and tingled under the strapping around my chest. The abrasion across my ribs had stoked up to a burning sting, like raw skin beneath a blister exposed to air.

A man's voice carried across the darkness. Victor, giving instructions to the driver. I considered what I was about to do and decided there were two possible outcomes. Either I'd discover that the activities in the bank barn were inconsequential, more than likely mundane and totally unrelated to Bruce's disappearance.

Or they were the reason for it.

In either case, this time, I didn't have a ready excuse to explain away my presence.

I clamped my hand on the fence, planted my boot on the second board, and sprang off the ground.

The board cracked and sounded like a gunshot tearing a hole in the night.

I slipped back to the ground, crouched behind the fencepost, and stared at the corner of the barn. The light fixture that hung in the forebay bathed the ragged edge of the stone foundation in a soft yellow light. As I watched, no one hustled around the corner. No one shouted. No lights switched on to illuminate my hiding place.

I couldn't see the truck from my position, but the driver had done what they all do, he'd left the big engine idling. Maybe they hadn't heard the noise over the diesel's rumble.

I moved to another fence section and tested the board before putting my full weight on it. I hustled across the lawn and climbed the earthen ramp to the big wagon door. The yellow light that shot straight and true beyond the corner of the barn had the dual effect of lighting the side yard while pitching the area behind the barn into a darkness deeper than the pervading night. I could barely discern my feet on the ground.

Smoothing my palm across the splintery, weather-roughened wood, I located the door handle, but as I slipped my fingers around the cold metal, the rust-pitted surface beneath my fingertips reminded me of my previous visit. The wheeled brackets that hung the heavy door from the tracks above my head were equally neglected, and they'd made a hell of a noise the last time I'd snuck into the barn. Victor and the driver would not miss the high-pitched sound of metal screeching against metal. Sweat prickled the back of my neck and itched under the strapping as I viewed what I knew of the barn's layout. I could recall only three entrances, the wide livestock entrance under the forebay, the small entry door by the cistern, and the huge wagon door directly in front of me.

No breath of air curled around the barn's western corner or creaked against the plank siding or rustled the tall grass that grew on the steep sides of the ramp. A strong breeze would have worked to my advantage. Now, every sound carried on the still air. I considered my options. The barn's second story was optimal as far as spying went. With the trap doors, I most certainly would find a good line of sight. So I'd have to wait. Wait until the semi's driver dropped the big old diesel into reverse.

A thin bead of light flashed in a gap between the barn's fieldstone foundation and the sill plate. A heavy thud, much like the sound of a stall door closing, vibrated through the wood siding, followed by an urgent whinny. I knelt and peered through the crack, but the only thing I could see was the thick header that formed part of the stall front. I rocked back to my feet as the diesel revved to life. It was now or never. I shoved the door open, and the wheels screeched in the track above my head. I squeezed through the opening and stepped to the side, pressed my back against the wall and listened.

I waited for a full minute, and in that minute, I doubted I would have heard an approaching herd of elephants for all the pounding and swooshing and racket my pulse made against my eardrums. I breathed through my mouth while a surge of blood slammed through my arteries and throbbed along my spine.

Apparently, they hadn't heard.

Stretched out before me, pencil-thin lines of light squeezed through gaps between the floorboards like a massive grid. Five trapdoors ran in a straight line, parallel to and approximately ten feet distant from the wall I had my back to. Off to the right, six more ran along the west wall. And from each square, a column of dust-laden light pointed toward the rafters. The light shining through the trapdoors to my right appeared weaker compared to the ones spread out in front of my current position, which indicated that most of the activity would take place directly beneath my feet. I stepped toward the square of light to my left, placing my foot on the wooden planks as if I were walking on eggs.

I was standing over a stall, and as I stepped closer, the chain link fence that formed the stall front came into view, framed by the trapdoor. Another step brought the stall floor into range. A chestnut mare circled below me, and a bay foal skittered alongside her as if an invisible band held them together. Looking down into a stall wasn't exactly what I'd had in mind. I carefully knelt on the floor, braced my right hand on the worn plank, and lay on my stomach.

The mare grunted and leapt forward, and her baby emitted a shrill whinny. Her elegant chestnut neck tensed, and her ears periscoped around, searching out danger. Although she couldn't see me, she knew someone was moving above her, and she didn't like it. Thousands of years of being preyed upon by saber-toothed tigers and leopards had ingrained a healthy fear of movement overhead that domestication had been unable to erase. I lowered my chin to the floor and peered over the stall header. The semi's airbrakes hissed when the driver reached the road.

I checked that my knife was in my pocket, and when I patted down my coat, I closed my eyes and gritted my teeth. Maddie hadn't given me the farm's cell phone before she left, and I'd forgotten all about it.

Damn.

Someone entered the barn. A man. From my vantage point, I could see a pair of scuffed cowboy boots and worn jeans. If I moved now, he might hear me.

I turned my head to the side and rested my cheek on the dusty floor. He fiddled with a cigarette in his left hand, a cord of blue smoke drifting toward the ceiling before he lifted it to his lips. His attention seemed focused on the mare below me. He strode across the open area, and I held my breath as he stepped into the space directly in front of the stall. Victor Nash.

He inhaled deeply on the cigarette clamped between his lips and squinted as he studied the mare. I guessed his wife's peace of mind didn't mean as much as he claimed, after all.

"Settle down, girl." He'd said it softly, but his voice scraped across my nerves like the edge of a knife.

Victor glanced at his watch, took another drag, then dropped the cigarette to the floor. He ground it out with the heel of his boot, and as he nudged it into the gap under the stall door, the sound of an approaching vehicle echoed under the forebay's roof and channeled through the doorway. Victor turned to watch the vehicle pass before it accelerated into the back lot and swept up the ramp.

Every muscle in my body seized when the headlights pierced the gap beside the wagon door.

Chapter 21

Because of the ramp's steep incline, the light slanted toward the rafters. A swirl of dust and engine exhaust drifted through the open door and rose toward the ceiling.

I believed I wasn't in the driver's line of sight, but I didn't dare turn my head to check. Any movement at all would catch his attention. The lights switched off when he cut the engine, and a metal hinge creaked as a car door opened. I listened to one set of footsteps tromp through the tall grass, then crunch over the loose gravel in the forebay.

He paused in the doorway just as Victor had done. Unlike Victor, he wore sharply creased twill pants and tasseled loafers. He thumbed the underside of a gold ring on his right hand. "Where is she?"

"Hold your horses. She'll be down in a minute. She wanted to make sure Jenny was asleep."

Oh, no. Not her. Not Dr. Nash.

I held my breath as the guy stepped forward, but he stopped almost as soon as he'd started so that the bottom edge of his jacket came into view. "This time of night?" he said, and the annoyance I thought I'd only imagined deepened his voice and cast an edge to his words.

"Sure. You never know with kids."

"Well, she better get her ass down here. I don't have all night."

Victor stirred below me. "Shut up," he said. "You don't even have to be here."

"And take a chance like before? I don't think so. The shit goes with me as soon as Deirdre fishes it out." The guy strolled back to the entryway, and I heard him light up a cigarette. "Who's on tonight?"

"Cline."

"Looks like he's in barn one. How long's he been over there?"

Victor shrugged.

"I don't like it. He's too sharp. Ever notice that he takes everything in?"

"No."

The other guy scoffed, and I wished he would move closer, but I had a feeling I wouldn't be surprised when I saw his face. "I want you to fire him."

"I'm not going to fire a good employee just because you say so. You've got us jumping through too many hoops as it is. Deirdre's a bitch to be around every time she has to do this shit. She hates it, and so do I. And you said we'd only have to do it once."

The guy stepped closer and no matter how I positioned my head, I couldn't see his face. "Things change. Too bad your lovely wife couldn't resist breaking the rules."

"She didn't do it for the money," Victor said.

"I don't give a fuck why she did it. The news gets out, you'll both be ruined." He paused. "Then, there's that other issue *you* need to keep in mind."

"You mean Claremont?"

"What else?" He snapped. "The two of you will help me for as long as I want."

"That wasn't supposed to happen," Victor said, "and you know it."

Handsome rich playboy Shane Hadley stepped into view and raised his eyebrows.

"There were other options," Victor said.

"I don't think so." Hadley took another drag on his cigarette. "You'll do exactly as I say, including firing Cline, because I'm sure you wouldn't want your lovely wife to find out what you did."

A boot scraped the floor by the entrance, and half a second later, Dr. Nash stepped into the work area, carrying a clear plastic case in her left hand.

"'Bout time," Hadley said.

Dr. Nash tilted her head back, and a section of her reddish brown hair caught on her eyelashes. She jabbed at it with her fingers and looked into Shane's face with pale bloodshot eyes. "This is the last time, Shane." Weariness dampened her vocal cords, a tonal vibration that softened her normally resolute voice. Or was it fear?

Victor stepped behind her and placed his hands on her shoulders.

"Report me if you want," she continued, "but I'm not doing it again, and the only reason I'm doing it tonight is because they're here, with your poison in their bodies."

Shane chuckled softly as he exhaled a stream of blue-gray smoke that drifted past my face.

"And get rid of that," she said.

The coals flared red as he took another drag. He flicked the cigarette to the floor and ground it out with the sole of his shoe.

"Don't ship another group up here," she said, "because if you do, I'll call the police the moment they arrive."

Shane's facial muscles stilled into a hard flat mask devoid of emotion. The amusement that typically sparkled in his eyes vaporized, and something dark and empty and evil took its place. I'd seen an expression much like it before, and the recognition of the mercilessness it signified clamped a vise around my gut and trapped the air in my lungs.

"Oh, my dear Deirdre, I think you'll change your mind." He looked past her and said to Victor, "Isn't that right?"

Victor pulled her close.

"It's gone way beyond a little rule breaking with the Jockey Club, my dear doctor," Shane continued. "The police won't

care one little bit that you're using artificial insemination now
and again, although the perceived fraud element will no doubt
come back to bite you. But my darling Deirdre, they will most
certainly care very deeply about your husband's recent involvement in a little matter of inconvenience."

"What inconvenience?"

"Oh, I'm sure he'll tell you all about it, but right now, we
have work to do. You don't want one of the kilos to rupture,
do you?"

Dr. Nash spun around and glared at her husband. "Damn
it, Vic. What have you done?"

When he didn't answer, she slammed the plastic case on a
hay bale that fronted the stall. As she unclipped the latch and
flipped the lid open, Victor hurried off, then returned a moment
later, carrying a lead rope and a long-handled twitch. She glared
at him as she pulled on a pair of plastic gloves.

From my position above the first stall, I heard her snip a
few stitches somewhere in the proximity of the mare's vulva.
She slipped the scissors into a pocket, then carefully withdrew
a flexible clear tube. The sensation caused the mare to flag her
tail as a thick sausage-shaped bundle slipped from her body. I
expected that Dr. Nash had completed the procedure but saw
that the tube had not come to an end. She continued to exert
pressure. The stall's overhead light glinted off her forehead, which
had become damp with perspiration in the cold air. Another
bundle slipped from the mare, followed by another, until four
bundles, each individually wrapped and encased in the tube,
cleared the mare's vulva. They must have snaked deeply into her
uterus, and with disgust, I realized that each bundle probably
contained a kilo of cocaine.

Deirdre blotted her forehead with her sleeve. "Jesus Christ,
Shane! Four bundles!"

"Come on, Deirdre. There's more room in a mare that's
recently foaled," Hadley said.

"I can't believe you. You're going to kill one of them."

I recalled the shipment that had arrived with a sick mare onboard the weekend before Bruce disappeared and wondered if one of the kilos had leaked. The mare had died almost as she stepped off the van.

Hadley peered into the stall. "Did any of them rupture?"

"No."

"Well, then. Everything's all right."

"Everything is not all right! This is dangerous."

"Calm down and finish up. Then you can go back to sleep between your silk sheets in your warm bed in your lovely aristocratic home. And by tomorrow morning, you'll have convinced yourself what a fine upstanding member of society you are, and you can go to church on Sundays and to Jenny's parent/teacher conferences, and all will be right in your little world."

When Deirdre banged the door against the frame and moved on to the next stall, Shane drifted over to the exit. "Cline's still in one. What the hell do you think he's doing?"

"Delivering a foal or mucking out," Victor said. "Frank usually has him work in one or six between rounds."

"So, why doesn't he ever leave?"

"He probably just got back. Quit worrying."

"He's not mucking out," Deirdre said to her husband. "He got hurt, remember?"

I closed my eyes. Deirdre, be quiet.

"Well, what the hell's he doing?" Shane asked.

"Maybe he's just hanging around," Victor said, and Shane drifted back over to the door.

I considered leaving, but if a board creaked beneath my weight, they'd hear it. So I stayed where I was and hoped like hell Hadley wouldn't get any ideas.

After Deirdre finished working on the next mare, Shane scooped up the kilos she'd cut out of the tubes, eight in all, and left the barn. I listened to his footsteps as he walked around back and opened the trunk of his car. I don't think I breathed until I heard him return. Four mares had been offloaded, and it took Deirdre ten minutes to finish up. Although I couldn't see her, I heard a stall door close and the metal latch clink shut as Shane gathered the last bundles together.

"See. That wasn't so bad," he said cheerfully.

His words met a wall of silence, and the level of unease in the room below seemed to seep through the floorboards beneath my chest.

As soon as Shane left the barn, Deirdre spoke. "What was he talking about, Vic?"

"Nothing, honey. He's just blowing smoke. I'll make him understand we have to stop. You'll see."

I flattened my right palm on the worn plank under my chest and carefully shifted an inch to my left, then slowly settled back against the wood. I wanted to see what they were doing, but they stood just beyond my line of sight. I moved again. When I exhaled, my breath flowed across the floor and pushed a clump of chaff over the edge. The flakes showered down to the stall floor. I held my breath and was relieved when their conversation continued uninterrupted.

"You better," Deirdre said, "because it's driving me nuts. I didn't become a vet to do this crap. It's vile."

"I know," Victor said softly. "I know."

Deirdre sighed. "I'm sorry I got us in this mess."

Shane's trunk squeaked open, then shut.

"We're both to blame," Victor said, and I wished they'd move closer. "But don't you worry. We'll get out of it. I've figured a way to make Shane leave us alone."

"How?"

I rested my cheek on the cool wood. Yeah, how?

Grit pressed into a floorboard beyond my boots, and as I scrambled to my feet, the lights high up in the rafters switched on.

Shane Hadley shook his head like a schoolteacher who'd just caught someone cheating. "You shouldn't have come over here, Steve," he said, and his words were so soft, I barely heard them over the rush of blood churning behind my eardrums.

I lowered my gaze. Shane gripped a revolver firmly in his right hand with its muzzle aimed at my chest.

"Victor," he shouted, and his voice carried easily through the hay drop. "Send your lovely wife to bed. We need to talk."

The sound of footsteps scuffing the concrete below floated past my ears, and we both heard Deirdre's protest as they tromped through last summer's dried grass at the edge of the ramp. Shane moved sideways, away from the door before either one of them had a chance to enter the barn.

Victor paused in the threshold when he saw me. "Oh, fuck." He spun around and spread his arms in an attempt to stop his wife, but he'd hesitated too long.

Deirdre stood frozen like a statue in the entryway and stared at me as if I were the Easter Bunny and had just beamed down from Mars. "Oh, no."

Victor gripped her shoulders and tried to turn her around. "Go back home. Check on Jenny."

"No." She broke his hold and pushed past her husband. Stopped dead when she saw the gun in Hadley's hand. "Shane?"

He waved her toward the center of the barn. "Stand over there."

She stumbled backwards with her gaze fixed on the revolver. "What are you going to do?"

"What do you think?"

I felt totally helpless…and stupid, standing flatfooted with my left arm immobilized in a goddamn sling. I'd worn it as a reminder, a self-imposed restriction so I wouldn't move wrong and risk making a sound in reaction to an unexpected jolt of pain. But it had been a mistake. Possibly fatal. I glanced at the hay drop.

"Uh-uh. Don't move," Shane said. "Vic, close that trap."

"Shane." Deirdre's thin voice sounded like it had come from a million miles away. "You can't do this. Vic," she pleaded. "Don't let him do this."

Victor warily stepped past me and flipped the trapdoor closed with his foot. "We don't have a choice. Do you want to go to jail?" He moved alongside Deirdre and reached out to touch her.

When she jerked away, Victor turned and faced Hadley. "Isn't there something else we can do? There's got to be another way."

"None that I can see. Go downstairs and chase the mares out of the barn."

"Why?"

"Just do it!" Hadley's rumbling voice raised the hair on the back of my neck.

Victor looked solemnly at me then at Deirdre before he turned for the door. Deirdre called out to him, and he paused.

Come on, Victor, I thought. Stand up to him.

Without turning around, he strode down the ramp. I wondered if he was prepared to kill again and hoped against reason that he'd change his mind and pick up a phone, but when the first door jarred open, sending a wave of concussion through the wood beneath my feet, I had my answer.

He whooped at the mare, and when he scraped something along the chain link fence, hooves skittered across the slippery concrete. A bead of sweat trickled down my back.

Dr. Nash stirred beside me. "Shane, you can't do this." Her voice sounded breathless. "We won't say anything."

"Darling Deirdre, you are so superbly naïve, but even in your naïveté, you won't breathe a word of what's about to take place here tonight. Not to anyone. Because my dear Deirdre, if you do, you will most certainly condemn your precious daughter to a life without a father and, quite possibly, a mother."

Another stall door slid open.

"How devastated she'd be if the two of you were rotting in prison while she set off on her first date or took her first driving lesson." Shane chuckled.

It was a damned smart tactic. Deirdre loved her daughter more than anything in this world, which gave Shane a great deal of control and put me in a very dangerous position.

The third stall door crashed open and hooves clattered across the ground.

"And what about that long walk down the aisle?" Shane continued. "Who will give her away if not her own father? Hell, Vic could even get the death sentence for what he did."

Deirdre's chin trembled. "What did you make him do?"

"Oh, Deirdre. Everyone makes their own choices, and Vic made his." He waved the gun. "And so did you when you decided to use AI with Irish Dancer. True, it's a crime to watch his spectacular qualities dry up along with his testicles, but that's life. You chose to alter it."

The last stall door rattled open. In a minute, Victor would return, and that knowledge, along with Hadley's speech, sent a chill up my spine. I feared his words were effectively sealing my fate. Somehow, I had to convince Deirdre that helping me would protect her *and* her daughter.

"You can still get out," I said to Deirdre. "Prove you were coerced. They know what kind of person Shane is," I lied.

Shane raised the gun. "Shut up, Cline!" He glanced over his shoulder when Victor strode up the ramp. "Good. How much gasoline do you have for that mower?"

Victor stared at him openmouthed. "What?"

"Don't be stupid. The old well was perfect for Claremont—"

"Shut up!" Victor screeched and flicked a sidelong glance at his wife.

Shane's gaze slipped over Deirdre like oil on water. "Ah," he smiled, "secrets. Don't you just love 'em?"

"Vic, what's going on?"

"Nothing, hon."

"They killed Bruce—" I said.

"Shut the fuck up!" Victor screamed and both men stepped toward me.

"—and put him in the cistern because he stole some coke."

Victor pointed at me and practically jumped up and down. "Shoot him, Shane, for Christ's sake. Kill him."

"Stop it!" Deirdre screamed. She raised a trembling hand and covered her mouth. She looked like she was about to vomit. "Oh, God, n-o-o."

Shane shoved Victor out of his way. "How do you know that?"

I kept my mouth shut as Victor strode over to Deirdre, grabbed her arms, and yanked her to him. "Get control of yourself!" he screamed. "Think of Jenny."

Her shoulders drooped as she tilted her head back and looked in her husband's face, and for a moment, she looked like she was going to pass out. "Oh, God," she cried. "What have you done?"

Victor pulled her closer. "He'll kill us both," he whispered in his wife's ear, "if you don't pull yourself together."

"Stop it!" Shane stepped closer, annoyed that he hadn't heard what was said.

It dawned on me that he was reluctant to use the gun. A bullet in my body would not be easily explained away. And it worried me that he'd been so careful to stay by the doorway. Did he plan to kill us all?

"Drench the haymow," he said to Victor, "then light it up."

Deirdre lifted her eyes. "No, Vic. Don't do it."

"I'm sorry," Victor said as he let her go. "Shane's right. There's no other way."

She watched her husband obediently carry three five-gallon cans over to the mow. "Vic?"

He turned away from her and set to work, saturating the hay with gallons of gasoline. The tangy odor hung in the still air and coated the back of my throat.

"Deirdre," I said and was surprised I could speak at all. "Your husband killed Lloyd Strauss," I blurted. "He helped kill Bruce, and he might have engineered your parents' acci—"

Something heavy slammed into my back and sent me sprawling across the floor.

The wooden planks creaked as Victor stepped closer. His boot bumped into my foot. "Shut up! Shut up! Shut up!"

Deirdre sank to her knees in front of me. "Oh, my God," she wailed. "How could you?"

"He's lying!" Victor screamed. "He's just saying that to confuse you."

"Fires followed each event. Fires set by your husband," I said to Deirdre. "He's done it since he was sixteen."

"Shut the fuck up!" Victor kicked me in the ribs, a vicious blow that shot the air out of my lungs.

Shane latched onto Victor's jacket and pushed him away. "Shut up, all of you!" He turned to Victor. "Dump the rest of the gas and hurry up."

When Deirdre tore her gaze away from her husband and looked down at me, I realized I was groaning. I gritted my teeth and clamped my mouth shut. Her eyes were wild with fear and shimmered with unshed tears. Fine beads of sweat glistened on her forehead, and her skin had blanched to a sickly grayish white.

I shifted and got as far as my knees before Shane planted his foot on my shoulder and shoved me onto my side. "How do you know so much?"

I looked past my feet and watched Victor splatter the mow. Gas gurgled through the nozzle and sloshed inside the metal can, and the sounds tightened my muscles and squeezed my chest.

Shane kicked my thigh. "Answer me!"

A jolt ran up my spine as the metal can clattered to the floor.

"Goddamnit!" Shane circled back toward the door.

Victor picked up the last can. He unscrewed the nozzle, then flipped the can upside down, allowing the gasoline to soak into the century-old wooden planks as he walked toward us.

I got to my knees. "Victor, don't be stupid. Shane intends to kill us all."

Victor hesitated as Shane stepped forward and pointed the gun at my head.

"No!" Deirdre bounded to her feet and grabbed his wrist. He shook her off, then brought his right hand around in an arc and slammed the gun against her skull.

Victor screamed her name as she crumpled to the floor. His face contorted into a mask of rage as he charged Shane.

Shane dragged his gaze from Deirdre's inert body and slowly turned his head toward Victor as he lunged across the plank floor. Gasoline sloshed out of the opening where the nozzle should have been, soaking Victor's jeans as his leg swung forward. When his boot jarred the floor, a rope of gasoline rose from the opening and seemed suspended in midair.

The gun's muzzle tracked past me as Shane spun to meet Victor's advance.

I scrambled to my feet, feeling as if I were moving through quicksand.

Shane's knuckle bulged, and he squeezed the trigger.

I yelled but couldn't hear my voice as the barrel jerked upward. Flames spat out of the muzzle.

The gasoline fumes ignited with a whoosh. Victor's eyes widened, and his mouth opened as a curtain of fire draped over the right side of his body and streaked like an arrow toward the haymow.

He kept coming, stumbling now, raising his arms as he charged Hadley. A horrific scream vented from his lungs. The sound rattled in my skull, and if I lived, I didn't think I'd ever close my eyes at night without hearing it.

The gas can in Victor's hand rose higher as his momentum carried him forward, and the remaining gasoline arced toward Shane.

He should have run. Instead, he panicked and pulled the trigger in the same instant that the metal handle slipped from Victor's fingers. The red can rotated through the air in slow motion while the fabric on Victor's jacket jumped as a bullet tore into his chest. A spray of gasoline hit Shane in the face and splashed onto his shoulders and chest and flared up a millisecond later.

The metal can tumbled to the floor. It rolled to a stop alongside Deirdre, pulling a wall of flame with it.

Victor's head cannoned into Shane's stomach as I shoved my left arm out of the sling. They crashed backwards onto the wooden planks, locked together in a writhing cocoon of flame, smoldering cloth, and burning flesh. I latched my fingers around Deirdre's wrist and jerked her away from them.

Victor lay motionless across Shane's legs.

I bent to scoop Deirdre into my arms as a high-pitched wail forced its way past Shane's lips. He turned his head, searching for me. Searching for someone to help him. Flames rolled off his clothes, his hair, his skin. His blue eyes swiveled around amid the blackened, raw flesh of a face that no longer looked human. His gaze slid past me, returned with a jerk, and he stared at me, begging, as that wail rose into a howl that pierced my eardrums and fizzed through my blood.

He lifted his right arm and stretched trembling fingers toward me. The fire's light glinted off his gold ring.

I slung Deirdre over my right shoulder and averted my eyes as I straightened, caught my balance. I did not want to see what another second of inferno could do to a man.

Flames lapped at the plank floor in a ragged line that paralleled the north wall and terminated in a colossal bonfire that had once been the haymow. Black smoke mushroomed toward the barn's peak and rolled over in a crashing wave, carrying a shower of sparks that floated to the floor like spent fireworks. The wall of heat and sound pressed against my face and pushed me deeper into the barn.

I spun around and confirmed what I already knew. There was no way out.

Chapter 22

Panic welled in my chest and squeezed a fist around my heart. An image of Shane flooded my mind, and I realized I no longer heard his cry over the roar of the fire.

There had to be a way out, but if there was, I couldn't see it. Oily smoke curled down from the ceiling and seared my throat with each breath. Tears streamed from my eyes, and the overhead lights had been reduced to dim yellow smudges. I could barely see my feet as I stumbled toward the junk pile in the middle of the barn. You were supposed to crawl, get down low where the air was cleaner, but I couldn't crawl and carry Deirdre at the same time. When I bumped into something metallic, her arms knocked against the backs of my thighs. A dented water trough stood in my way. As I skirted around the hulk of rusted metal, I thought of the cistern beyond the west wall.

The west wall…

Stalls lined the west wall, and they'd each been fitted with a hay drop. I broke into a stumbling run. The fire hadn't spread that far.

A dim square of light filtered upward through a narrow layer of clear air that undulated over the plank flooring. Deirdre moaned when I knelt and eased her forward off my shoulder. She slid down my thigh and sagged onto the floor like a rag doll. Despite my best efforts, her head tipped back and knocked against the wood. Her eyes fluttered open.

"Deirdre."

Her lids drifted shut.

I unceremoniously flipped her onto her stomach and shoved her over to the opening so that her feet dangled in space above the stall floor. I latched onto her overalls and shoved her farther, until her legs pointed straight toward the straw bedding. I didn't trust my left shoulder to hold up under strain, so I gripped her wrist with my right hand and let her weight pull her deeper into the hay drop. Her pelvis scraped over the edge, then her stomach. Her breasts caught momentarily, then gravity did its job, and she plummeted through the opening. Deirdre's face bumped against the wooden lip, and her weight pitched me over.

I swung my right leg forward and almost fell headfirst through the hay drop, but my boot caught the far side of the frame.

She swung like a pendulum beneath me, her head resting on her shoulder, her feet dangling above the straw. She jerked her head up, and the sudden movement threatened to break my hold.

"Deirdre!" I yelled. "Try to land on your feet!"

She tilted her head and looked up at me as her wrist slipped between my fingers. "Look at the ground!" I screamed.

Deirdre scissor kicked, and the sudden movement broke my grip. She knocked against the stall front before collapsing in the straw with her right leg doubled beneath her. I swung my feet into the opening as she flopped onto her stomach and tried to draw her knees under her. When I scooted my butt closer to the edge, wood splintered behind my back. I looked over my shoulder as a section of roof caved in above the haymow. The sudden inrush of air blasted a solid wall of heat and smoke and flames toward me.

I glanced between my feet and pushed off the edge like a diver slipping into water.

I hit the ground and rolled as a shower of sparks tapped against the hay drop's wooden frame, sounding like sleet hitting glass. The burning embers sifted through the opening and drifted down to the straw.

Deirdre moaned softly as she swayed on her hands and knees. I scrambled to my feet, slipped my arm around her waist, and yanked her upright. She sagged against me.

"Come on, Deirdre. Help me out, here."

When the straw bedding directly beneath the hay drop ignited, I thanked God that someone had left the stall door open. We lurched through the doorway and paused. If there was hell on earth, this was it. Sparks rained into the stalls along the north wall as heavy black smoke oozed downward through the hay drops and coiled back up to the ceiling like tentacles. Flames rose from the straw bedding, and the roar above our heads shook the walls.

I spun Deirdre around. Her right leg buckled beneath her as I propelled her toward the little door that cut through the west wall's foundation. My foot kicked something metallic, and when it slid across the floor and clunked into the tack trunk, a piece of the puzzle fell into place. For whatever reason, they must have stored the coke there. When Elaine had overheard Hadley complaining about a broken lock on a trunk, she'd naturally assumed he was talking about his car.

We reached the door, and I jiggled the antique latch. It wouldn't open. I swallowed my panic and forced myself to slow down, carefully pressed the lever, and the outside bar flipped out of its slot. The door swung outward. We staggered into the tall grass and collapsed. The coarse blades felt blessedly cold against my face. I closed my eyes and gulped a lungful of air. A spasm squeezed my chest. I coughed and wheezed and retched, and when the heaving subsided, I rocked to my knees and wiped my eyes.

Deirdre was kneeling in the grass beside me. "Where's Vic?" Her voice was a whisper on the night air.

I turned my head and watched a tear track through the soot that coated her face. "He's dead."

She hung her head and cried.

After a moment or two, she pressed her sleeve under her nose. "You said Vic killed Lloyd. How do you know?"

"I was hired to look for Bruce and learned of the fires that followed your fiancé's death and your parents'." I looked past her, and my gaze fell upon the old cistern's roughened concrete. "And Bruce's disappearance."

"Is he really dead?"

"Yes. He's in the cistern."

Deirdre scooted away from the curved wall like it would reach out and suck her into the ground. "Vic said he ran away after he stole some of Shane's drugs." She rested her hands on her thighs. "And I believed him."

"He didn't run far."

A beam creaked high above our heads. "We'd better move." I stood and pulled Deirdre to her feet.

"Oh, God." She raised her hands to her mouth. "Jenny." She started to sprint toward the house, but her right knee buckled, and she went down.

I helped her up, and we hustled past the garage and cut through the lot. Deirdre limped up the steps to the back porch, and as we passed through the mudroom and stepped into the kitchen, I was stunned to find the room so peaceful and quiet. And normal.

"I have to check on her," Deirdre whispered.

She hobbled into the hallway and climbed the steps.

I was wondering if I'd been wise to let her go when I heard her soft tread on the stairs. When she rounded the corner, she was crying.

She slumped into a chair. "What am I going to do?" Her voice was thin and high and sounded like a child's. "They'll take her away from me."

I thought of my own miserable childhood. I knew firsthand what it was like not to be wanted. For years, I'd believed with all my heart that the man I knew to be my father hated me. I'd kept to myself, hid my pain away until I was no longer certain I could love or be loved in return. Not in any way that truly mattered.

Not being loved, or wanted. That's what I feared more than anything in this world.

Who would give Jenny the love she needed to grow up whole and healthy if not her own mother?

"Maybe," I said and hesitated. "Maybe you can convince the police that you weren't involved."

She slowly lifted her eyes.

"Is there anything in the house that might link you to the drugs?"

Deirdre shook her head.

"Convince them you had no knowledge of your husband's dealings with Shane, and you might be okay." I paused. "Jenny might be okay."

She rose shakily to her feet. "You won't tell?"

"Promise never to do anything like this again," I said, and the words sounded childish.

"I promise," she breathed. "You've got to believe me."

"I do." I stepped toward the table. The adrenaline rush was wearing off. "How did Shane know you were using AI?"

"He heard Vic…" She swallowed and gulped as a spasm constricted her throat. "We were arguing about it, and he heard. No one else knows. I swear to God."

"Except Frank."

She nodded. "He won't tell."

"You'll have to sell Irish Dancer."

She nodded vigorously, then her eyes widened, and she covered her mouth with a trembling hand. "Oh, no."

"What?"

"They'll interview the drivers. They'll find out I was at the barn at night."

"Tell them you started checking shipments after that one mare offloaded sick. The one you had to put down. Tell them Victor tried to talk you out of it, but you insisted."

She nodded. "What about the quarantine story?"

"It's plausible, isn't it?"

"Well, not really."

"Maybe they won't suspect anything, and if they do, tell them Victor convinced you that precautions were prudent, or you were just placating him because he was obsessive about it. And the bruising on your face," I said, and she touched her temple, "tell them I alerted you to the fire, and when we ran into the barn to get the horses out, one of them swung her head around and smacked into you. And your knee. You stumbled and fell backward."

I considered every possible line of questioning that would come up and thought of one I couldn't prepare for. "Deirdre?" I said, and she lifted her head. Her eyes had gone glassy, and I figured she was probably going into shock. "Do the people at the other end know about you? Do they know a vet's taking the drugs out?"

"I don't know. I assume a vet's putting them in. That procedure's much more difficult than removing them. Anyone could do that."

"Okay. If they say a vet had to take them out, just tell them what you told me. Anyone could have done the procedure. Victor could have done it with ease."

She nodded and looked toward the kitchen window. An eerie orange glow tinted the glass. "How will we explain…"

"We don't know anything," I said. "We don't know where Victor is, although we fear for him because he's missing. We don't know how the fire started. We never heard gunshots. We didn't know a car was parked behind the barn, but when you see it, you'll recognize it as belonging to Shane Hadley. That is, if you do. It didn't sound like the Viper."

"He uses a plain car when he transports drugs because the cops are less likely to pull him over."

"Okay. You didn't know it was parked there in the middle of the night, and neither one of us knows where Shane is. I was working in barn one and saw the fire. I came over here and banged on the door."

"Why didn't you call the fire department?"

"I forgot to get the farm's cell phone from Maddie. And my first thought was to get the horses out before it was too late," I said, and Deirdre nodded. "When you got out of bed, Victor wasn't in the house. We ran into the barn and chased the horses out."

"What about your truck?" she said. "It should be over here."

"Damn. I'll go get it."

"Hurry."

As I pivoted toward the door, a small voice cried out.

"Mommy?"

Deirdre spun around and covered her mouth with her hands; then she scooped her daughter into her arms.

"What's happening?" Jenny whined. "Where's Daddy?"

Deirdre speechlessly pressed her daughter to her chest and rocked her. Jenny's tiny bare legs dangled from beneath her nightgown, and the sight of bunny slippers on her feet twisted a knot in my gut.

"Call 911," I said. The screen door creaked when I stepped onto the back porch. No sirens wailed in the distance, but I didn't have much time.

I raced across the fields and thought I'd throw up by the time I reached the Chevy. I sped back to the mansion and slammed the truck into park in the lot behind the house. As I walked toward the barn, feeling the heat on my face, the remaining portion of roof creaked and groaned as it caved into the shell of the building. Burning embers floated across the lawn and filtered through nearby trees, and the first siren sounded on the cold air.

I turned back as an emergency vehicle rounded the bend on Bear Wallow. As I crossed the lot, a vehicle slewed around the corner. The driver slammed on the brakes, and Paul Genoa unfolded himself from behind the wheel. He gawked at the fire as he stepped around the hood.

Oh, God. Not now. I bent forward and braced my hands on my knees. Tried to catch my breath. "What you want, Genoa?"

"Where are the Nashes? Is everybody okay?"

"Dr. Nash is in the house with Jenny. I don't know where Victor is." I leaned harder on my hands and dragged in a lungful of air. "Why are you here?"

"I came here to bash your teeth in…" he said, and I lifted my eyes and watched his gaze track back to the inferno. "But it looks like my timing's off. What do you need help with?"

"Get Frank. Tell him I sent you." A wet cough rattled my lungs. "Tell him about the fire and that we've got four mares and their babies running around here somewhere, and they need to be found."

"Gotcha."

"And Paul." I swallowed as he paused and faced me. "You deserve better than Maddie."

He stood still for a second, then got back in his car. I sank slowly to my knees and watched him drive off. I was still there when the first tanker pulled down the lane.

◇◇◇

Some dates are embedded forever in my memory. Traditional events like birthdays and anniversaries and others because of the joy they signify. Like the day I met a man who means so much to me now. Still others will stay with me forever because of the sorrow they represent. The day I buried the man who'd raised me, for one. And the day they dug Bruce Claremont out of the well behind the Nashes' barn.

A month has gone by since that day.

◇◇◇

I stood on the backside at Washington Park with my elbows resting on the rail and my ball cap pulled low on my forehead. Corey checked the buckle on her helmet's chinstrap as the bright chestnut colt she was riding strode eagerly through the gap in the fence. She bit her lower lip and furrowed her brow as she guided him to the left where he did not want to go. Going left meant walking, and maybe a brisk jog, when all he wanted to do was run. As they passed by, he swished his tail and threw in a cow hop for good measure, but she managed to coax him into a relaxed walk.

She didn't look my way as she eased the reins through her fingers because I hadn't told her I was coming. I'd seen her last at her brother's funeral and had no idea if she could stand the thought of seeing me. Her hips swayed in rhythm with his stride as the warm spring sunlight bathed them in a golden wash that reflected off her helmet and rippled across the colt's gleaming hindquarters like molten copper.

In Warrenton, both drug investigations had reached satisfying conclusions. Detective Tyler McPherson phoned me two days earlier to thank me for my testimony. He'd been exonerated and had returned to work almost immediately but didn't sound keen on pursuing undercover work in the near future.

The sheriff's department concluded that a drug smuggling operation conducted by Shane Hadley and Victor Nash had gone horribly wrong, and ballistics evidence conclusively linked Hadley to the murder of Bruce Claremont. As for Deirdre, it was clear that the detectives investigating the case wondered about her from the outset, but they never discovered evidence that implicated her in any wrongdoing. I smiled as I recalled the image of Sergeant Bodell climbing the steps to her back porch with a grocery bag in his arm. He'd been spotted hanging around the Nash household on numerous occasions thereafter.

Corey and her charge had reached the 7/8 pole, and as I watched, she guided him in a wide turn that took them to the center of the track. She rose in the stirrups as the chestnut automatically broke into a collected canter.

The investigation into the fire that killed Andrew J. Johnson had been reopened. The general consensus was that Bruce had gone to A.J. for help selling the stolen coke, and Hadley had caught up with him as he covered his bases. Whether the investigators would find evidence to support that theory remained to be seen.

Even though it was not quite seven in the morning, the temperature had already hit sixty degrees. Corey had long since exchanged her fleece vest for a lime green windbreaker, and I expected she'd shed that in the next hour.

It looked like we were in for another hot summer.

Besides Deirdre and Corey, I never did tell anyone about the arsons that followed Victor through his adolescent years to his death. As for the hit-and-run at barn seven my second night on the job, I was fairly certain that, buried beneath the layer of mud crusted over Victor's Toyota, the cops would find paint that matched the barn and farm truck. But no one had even considered Victor. In my mind, the fires signified a very sick psyche, and I had no doubt that he'd been responsible for Lloyd Strauss' death. Dredging that up would help no one.

It wouldn't bring Bruce back, but it would most certainly hurt Jenny. And she'd gone through enough.

The chestnut colt cantered toward me in a rolling, collected frame, fluid and strong, obedient even in his desire to go faster. Corey's weight sunk into her heels with each stride, and the leather fringe on her half-chaps flapped against her calves. She'd bridged the reins above the colt's arched neck and glided past as if she were water skiing. A slight smile tugged the corner of her mouth as she lost herself to the exhilarating centuries-old partnership of man and horse.

I watched them until her tiny form was reduced to a neon speck at the far end of the track. Directly in front of me, a trio breezed past, bunched together along the rail, their riders crouched low in the irons. The rhythmic sound of the horses' breathing combined with the thud of hooves on the ground as the impact forced the air from their lungs. A voice called out when someone whistled. Behind me, a horse whinnied. I thought of Kessler, gearing up for another long day on the backside with no break in sight.

Corey's charge looked content now that he'd expended some energy. His head nodded in rhythm with his steps, and his back swung freely, relaxed and supple. Corey had let the reins out so that her left hand gripped the buckle, but as she approached the gap, she gathered them together. When she lifted her head and caught sight of me as I stood by the opening in the fence, a smile lit up her face and sparkled in her blue eyes. But in the next second, her smile faltered, and I knew she'd thought of her brother.

She rode through the gap, and I followed alongside her until we'd moved far enough to the side to be out of the way.

I took off my ball cap and pushed my bangs off my forehead. "What barn's he from?" I said, knowing she wouldn't dismount until she'd reached the shedrow.

Corey gestured to the barn directly in front of us. "Right here." She dropped her stirrups and slid lightly to the ground. A groom approached as she slipped the reins over the horse's head and removed her saddle.

I gripped my hat in both hands and cleared my throat. "I hear you've started galloping for Kessler."

She nodded and smoothed her hand down the colt's muscled neck. "When I can. Is that why you're here, to see him?"

"Yes." I watched the groom lead the horse toward the barn. "Right." I cleared my throat. "And I wanted to see how you're doing."

She changed her hold on the saddle, rested it on her hip, and squinted toward the track. "Okay," she said softly. "As well as expected, I suppose."

I stood there quietly, not knowing what to say as her eyes filled with tears. She brushed them away with the back of her hand.

"It's so sad." Her voice broke. "But you know?" She turned to face me, took my hand in hers as the early morning sunlight glinted off the moisture that clung to her pale lashes. "As sad as it is, not knowing would have been unbearable."

She stretched up on tiptoe and kissed me; then she turned and headed for the barn.

Author's Note

I hope you've enjoyed this glimpse into the world of a large-scale breeding farm. Foaling out mares on the night shift was one of the most enjoyable, rewarding jobs I've had the pleasure of doing, and I owe that experience and my thanks to Nelson Wert, DVM.

When an author describes a world that's at least partially unfamiliar to the reader, questions arise, and one of the questions that came to me early on, from a knowledgeable horseperson, was: "Don't the farm employees practice foal imprinting?" Foal imprinting is the process of desensitizing foals to the many stimuli they'll have to tolerate as they mature and live in our world, such as inserting a nasogastric tube or rectal thermometer, clipping the coat, handling the head, or trimming the feet. But for financial reasons, big operations like Stone Manor often do not practice foal imprinting because it's a rather lengthy procedure that should be repeated at least once, and it just takes too much time, i.e. money.

Another question that came my way was: "Would the mares really spend so much time on the breeding farm where the board has got to be expensive?" Well, the truth is, the length of time a horse stays at a particular breeding farm varies wildly and depends on many factors too complicated and individual to go into story-wise.

Many mares stay at a particular farm year after year, no matter the cost. Many come and go at a moment's notice. Others arrive a month or so before they foal, have their babies, and stay until they're determined to be in foal; then they go somewhere cheaper until their delivery date approaches. Then, they're shipped to whatever farm stands the stud the owner wants the mare bred to next. But in February, all the breeding farms fill up since the season for breeding thoroughbreds runs from January to June. And with valuable horses, owners want them boarded where the help is experienced, the fencing safe, and where their animals can be turned out with other pregnant mares and foals. Also, many ex-racehorses are syndicated, and the syndicate may opt to keep their stock on a breeding farm all year long. What might seem exorbitant to me or you may be practical to someone else.

So, the answer, like life, is all over the board.

To receive a free catalog of Poisoned Pen Press titles, please contact us in one of the following ways:

Phone: 1-800-421-3976
Facsimile: 1-480-949-1707
Email: info@poisonedpenpress.com
Website: www.poisonedpenpress.com

Poisoned Pen Press
6962 E. First Ave. Ste. 103
Scottsdale, AZ 85251